Rescued

by Felice Stevens

Rescued
Revised Edition: September 2016

Copyright © 2016 by Felice Stevens
Print Edition

Cover Art by Reese Dante
www.reesedante.com
Licensed material is being used for illustrative purposes only and any
person depicted in the licensed material is a model

Edited by: Flat Earth Editing
www.flatearthediting.com

Published in the United States of America

This is a work of fiction. Any resemblance to persons living or dead is
entirely coincidental.

Ryder Daniels is all too familiar with rejection. His parents cut off contact because he's gay and his boyfriend left him, choosing drugs over love. Aside from his rescued pit bull, his only joy is hanging out with his younger brother. Then his mother does the unthinkable and forbids them to see each other, leaving Ryder devastated and alone. His friends urge him to date, but Ryder would rather throw himself into working at the dog rescue and figuring out a way to see his brother again.

When Jason Mallory's girlfriend gives him an ultimatum to get married, he shocks everyone by breaking up with her instead. He believes he's too busy for a relationship now that the construction company he started with his brother is taking off. When he discovers a group of abandoned pit bulls and calls the local dog rescue group to pick them up, an uncomfortable encounter with Ryder causes Jason to question feelings he's hidden deep inside for years.

Jason and Ryder build a friendship, until an unexpected kiss sparks the attraction they've been fighting. Jason gives Ryder unconditional love and helps him reconnect with his brother while Ryder shows Jason the passion he's always missed in relationships. Together they must battle through their family differences and ugly prejudices. Only then can they prove that once you find the right person to love, there's no turning back.

Dedication

To my husband and children. The reality has been so much better than any dream.

For my parents, I wish you were both here to share the joy. Thank you for always letting me read under the covers after it was bedtime and even giving me the flashlight. I miss you both every single day.

And to all the fur babies in rescues and shelters…hang on. Your forever home is out there!

Acknowledgments

To Pamela Fradkin and her rescued pit bull, Pearl. It was Pam's idea for me to take the plunge and write a romance. Pam, you are an inspiration as a person, and I love you. This book also would never have have been possible without my two friends Sandy and Lindsey.

To Hope and Jessica from Flat Earth Editing, thank you for helping me take Ryder and Jason's story to another level. No chicken salad in this book.

For everyone who loved Ryder and Jason's original book, I hope their re-edited and expanded story gives you as much joy to read as it gave me to write.

To Riley Hart and Kade Boehme, thank you for being there whenever I need you and being my friend.

To Cardeno C, thank you for your wonderful books which always inspire me. But most of all thank you for your friendship, which means the world to me.

For up to date news on new releases, exclusive content, sneak peeks at what I'm working on, join my mailing list! No spam ever, and you might even win one of the contests I run every month!

Newsletter: bit.ly/FelicesNewsletter

Chapter One

THERE WAS NOTHING like waking up from a deep sleep to a warm, wet tongue licking your neck. Mmmm, that was one talented mouth. Ryder Daniels stretched in sleepy abandon, luxuriating under the cocoon of covers on his bed. Still in that half-asleep place where Ryder didn't know if he was awake or dreaming, he moaned as that tongue continued its delicious torture. God, it had been so long since he'd shared his bed with anyone. His cock jerked and swelled.

As he struggled to pull himself up out of the depths of slumber, anxious to taste his lover's tongue, lust spiked through him sharp and deep. He missed the smooth slide of a foot on his calf and the scrape of an early-morning beard on his back. It had been way too long since he'd held a hard body next to his. The friction of the sheets against his dick sent torturous desire rippling through him. Rolling onto his side, he reached to pull his man closer, desperate for the contact he remembered only his mouth could give.

A cold nose found its way to his ear.

"What the fuck?" Wide-awake now, he flipped over, squinted an eye open, and groaned. "Shit."

Stretched out next to him was his recently rescued pit bull, Pearl. Tongue lolling out of her mouth, hopeful brown eyes shining and tail wagging furiously, she huffed out a growly bark.

Almost a year without sex would make anyone desperate and horny as fuck. Scrubbing his face with his hands, he drew in a shaky breath. Arousal still hummed through him thanks to the total mindfuck his body had played on him. Damn, he was in worse shape than he thought if he'd become so turned on by his dog licking him. He groaned again, this time in pure frustration.

At least his dog truly loved him. "Come here, girl." He patted the place next to him, and Pearl whined with happiness as she wriggled across the bed. Smoothing her short white fur, he crooned to her. "That's my sweetheart. Let me get up, and I'll take you for a walk."

As if she understood, she yelped in response, jumping down to the floor, her nails scrabbling on the exposed floorboards. She raced out of the room, only to return a few moments later holding a leash in her wide mouth.

He laughed. "Okay, okay, let me brush my teeth and put on some clothes first." Raking back the tangled hair from his face, he glanced down and took in the state of his aching cock. Though he knew he was better off alone than with his son-of-a-bitch ex-lover, neither his mind nor his body got that message. Both his heart and his dick still missed Matt.

Screw it.

He threw off the down comforter and placed his feet with care on the cold wood floor. Even though it was Thanksgiving Day, he still was unprepared for the chill on his bare feet. Shivering, he pulled on the jeans that lay crumpled next to the bed and found a clean sweatshirt on the pile of laundry he had yet to put away. Ryder shoved his feet into his sneakers and laced them up.

He quickly brushed his teeth, bundled up in his fleece and left the apartment, Pearl jumping around his feet. Outside his breath blew out in cold white puffs and neither he nor Pearl had any desire to remain outdoors any longer than necessary. In less than ten minutes, they were back inside the warm apartment and Ryder fed Pearl.

After he took a shower where a swift, mind-numbing jerk off brought a temporary physical release to his body, he re-dressed and had just finished lacing up his sneakers when the phone rang. He checked the number on the caller ID and his heart dropped, while hope flared in his chest.

Mom and Dad. He stared at the screen as the phone rang a second time.

What could they want? Maybe he'd have someplace to go for Thanksgiving after all. He snatched up the receiver, gulping down a nervous breath.

"Hello?"

"Ryder, is that you?" A cautious bubble of joy rose in him at the measured, elegant sound of his mother's voice. It had been three long months since they'd spoken. Perhaps his parents were at last coming around to welcoming him back home.

"Hello, Mom. Happy Thanksgiving."

"Yes, well, about that." Her voice grew strident and he winced, the cautious hope in his heart snuffed out with those few words. "Your father and I want you to join us tonight. This foolishness has gone on long enough. You need to give up this lifestyle experiment and take your place back in this family."

And a happy fucking Thanksgiving to you, too. Was she serious? Any positive thoughts he might have had for this conversation flew straight to hell, where all good intentions ended up.

He fought to keep his voice cool and calm. "Mom, nothing's different since the last time we spoke."

"Don't be ridiculous." Her voice snapped at him, all pretense of a warm family chat gone.

Ahh, now that was the mother he remembered. God forbid you disagree with her or get in the way of her plans. She was a cement steamroller in the guise of a five-foot-tall ice-for-blood society matron.

"We've given you ample opportunity to find yourself, experiment with your sexuality—whatever you want to call it. Now that you've had your little fling, you need to come home, join the firm, and find a nice woman to marry. I've already made some inquiries. Remember that sweet Olivia Martinson? She's back in town after finishing a year at the Sorbonne and—"

"Mother." The control he fought so hard to maintain whenever he spoke to her reached its limit and broke. She'd never tried to understand him, and she never would. It wasn't in her makeup to bend to other people's wills. They learned to bow to her or get out of the way. "I'm not experimenting with anything. I'm gay, goddamn it, and you need to accept it."

She blithely carried on speaking as if he hadn't interrupted her. "Now, tomorrow night at the Yale Club, there's a get-together. Helen, Olivia's mother, has assured me they will all be there. I told her you'd be there as well."

Ryder couldn't help but laugh. "Are you serious? Have you listened at all to what I'm saying now and have said for the past, I don't know how long? I'm not going to marry *any* woman. I love men. I kiss and have sex with men." Stalking around the room, he gave the football that rested on the floor in his path a vicious kick. Pearl took off, chasing it down the hallway.

He didn't give a damn anymore if he hurt or shocked his mother. He'd been cut off from his family as if he'd died for simply loving the wrong gender. "The sooner you understand and accept me, the sooner we can try to work out becoming a family again. I'm trying to keep it civil, but you're making it impossible for me." He fell back on the bed and closed his eyes against the hot prickle of unshed tears. Damn it, he wouldn't let her get to him again.

He pictured her now, those red glossy lips pressed thin and tight, her pale blue eyes narrowed as she lectured him over the phone. "Why do you always have to be different? And you're aware, it doesn't only affect your father and me." His stomach clenched, because he knew what was coming.

"Mother, stop."

"What of Landon? He worships you and doesn't understand why you haven't seen him."

An involuntary groan escaped at the thought of his younger brother, the brother he loved with all his heart but wasn't allowed to see as long as Ryder refused to follow his parents' wishes. "Mom," he begged, hugging his pillow to his chest. "Please, don't do this." He swiped at the wetness falling down his cheeks, hurt by her refusal to love him unconditionally. His voice broke even as he struggled to maintain his composure. "Why can't you accept who I am? For Christ's sake, you're my damn mother. You're supposed to love me no matter what." Pearl whined and jumped on the bed.

Shit. He couldn't believe she'd reduced him to begging for her love, crying like a little kid, yet he couldn't give up on trying to make her understand. "I miss you and Dad and Landon. I want to come home."

"It's time you stop trying to be different." Her familiar exasperated tone cut through him sharper than any cold wind ever could. Since childhood, she'd never

understood him, never tried. She had some precon-
ceived notion of how her life should turn out, and
having a gay son did not fit her plan. "Even as a child
you were always rebellious, but now your actions don't
only impact your life, they affect all of us. Know your
choices have consequences, though."

"What kind of consequences? What does this have
to do with Landon?" Ryder thought back to two months
or so ago—the last time he'd seen his brother. Ten years
younger than him and a high school junior, Landon was
good-looking, popular, and definitely straight. "Landon
knows I'm gay. It doesn't matter to him in the least.
He's my brother and says he loves me no matter what."

Like you're supposed to.

"This has nothing to do with love. You're our child;
nothing can change that." The obvious distaste in her
voice lent credence to the fact that she wished she could
change that fact and have him be anyone else's child but
hers. From his earliest memory their family's social
standing meant everything to her. He watched as her
quest for perfection took precedence over everyone else's
needs, even if it meant him living a lie. She'd set an
impossible standard for him to live up to and deviation
from the norm—her version of normal—in any way was
not accepted.

"Your decision to live an openly gay lifestyle affects
everyone in the family. No matter how enlightened you
think people are, your father would be horribly
embarrassed at the firm having to explain not only to

the partners that you're gay but to his clients as well. You may think everyone is so accepting these days, but Daniels and Montague has some very important conservative clients that wouldn't appreciate a homosexual attorney. They could take their business elsewhere."

"I wanted to make it on my own, though. That's why I chose a different route and decided not to work at the firm. Dad supported me; he told me so."

"Your father is a foolish, weak man, but let me tell you something. It broke his heart when you joined West and Hamilton. How do you think he felt, having his son turn down a position in his firm? Daniels and Montague has passed down from father to son for almost one hundred years." Ryder squeezed his eyes shut as he listened to his mother prattle on about how his behavior affected her and her social standing amongst her peers. In the life of Astrid Daniels, the sun and moon revolved around her; she sat at the center of her own private universe.

"We know about your little fling with that other attorney in the firm. Do you know how much money it cost us to pay off that man? I live in constant fear he'll break his confidentiality agreement and spread some vile gossip about us. Could you imagine the scandal?"

At the mere mention of his failed relationship with Josh, Ryder trembled and bile rose in his throat. "What are you talking about?" White-knuckled, his grip on the cordless phone tightened until his fingers turned numb.

His mother chattered along, as if it were a story in a magazine she was gossiping about, not her son's personal heartbreak. "No, you wouldn't know, but that man—Joshua was his name, I believe, approached your father, claiming he needed money for his wedding, and if we didn't want a story spread about your deviant behavior, we'd pay him before he left. A considerable sum I might add. So don't say that we don't care about you. We protected you from his blackmail attempt."

Deviant behavior? That little piece of shit. Right after he started working at West & Hamilton, he'd met Josh, and they clicked. For six months they dated and Ryder thought he might be in love with the sweet, slightly geeky young man with the wicked sense of humor and an obsession for coffee. The night he told Josh he loved him, Josh laughed at first, but when Ryder, numb with hurt and shock, said nothing, Josh grabbed his coat, pulling it back on in a hurry. *"You can't be serious. Shit, man. It was all fun and games, you know. I wanted to see what it would be like to have someone else besides my girlfriend suck my dick. Hell, you were great, but I'm getting married soon. No hard feelings, huh?"*

And Ryder, brokenhearted and shaking, feeling as if his heart had been ripped out and stomped on, merely smiled. *"No, no hard feelings."* He had no feelings at all as Josh shut the door behind him, walking out of his life as easily as he'd walked into it.

I can't handle this shit anymore. Obviously his emotional stability, his *life* meant less to his family than the balance sheet for the law firm. Because everything always revolved around money for his father. If the firm's clients' conservative viewpoints didn't match Ryder's lifestyle, better to walk away from his son than a multi-million-dollar payday. Nothing could be permitted to interfere with the carefully cultivated existence Ryder's mother crafted for herself, including her son's happiness.

Inhaling deeply, he congratulated himself on remaining calm and controlled. "Look, this obviously isn't going to work. I'm warning you, though. I won't let you shut me out of Landon's life. You and Dad may not want to see me anymore, but that's your choice. I will see Landon and there's nothing you can do to stop me. Oh, and Happy Thanksgiving."

He cut the phone off and, as if trying to prove a point, immediately dialed Landon's cell phone number. He and his brother had managed to keep in touch by texting and calling each other. A strange beeping occurred, then he heard the message: "*Welcome to Verizon Wireless. The number you were trying to reach has calling restrictions that have prevented the completion of your call.*" He pulled out his cell phone and tried texting, only to get the same message, citing restrictions on texting.

"Son of a bitch!" He threw the phone on the bed. Even before they'd spoken she'd put her plan into action. She must have checked Landon's cell phone logs and blocked him. The only way he'd managed to keep his sanity these past months was by speaking with his brother. Now she'd found the ultimate weapon to break his spirit and his heart. He grabbed his coat from the closet and tried to snap on Pearl's leash but missed the clasp because of his shaking hands. Closing his eyes, he employed the yoga breathing techniques his friend Emily taught him to deal with stress.

Namaste, Namaste.

Nope, not helping. He still wanted to punch a wall. After a moment he tried again, this time with moderate success.

He'd figure out another way to see and talk to Landon. First he had to take care of Pearl, then go to the soup kitchen over on the Bowery to serve dinner for the homeless. Thanksgiving dinner for him tonight would be a takeout meal shared with his dog.

After walking Pearl, he began the trek from his apartment in the Village to the Bowery mission. A half hour later—fingers and toes numb—he reached the shelter. Waving hello to Meredith, the director of the shelter, he took his place in line next to his best friend, Emily.

"Hey, baby, how are you?" He kissed her soft cheek. She smelled like clean soap and fruity shampoo. "Happy Thanksgiving. Where's your lesser half?"

"Hey, bro, keep your lips to yourself." Emily's husband, Connor, pretend growled at him as they bumped fists and exchanged a hug. "Happy Thanksgiving." His sharp green gaze raked over Ryder. "What's up? You look like crap."

As they put on their aprons and plastic gloves and began serving the turkey-and-all-the-trimmings dinner, Ryder briefly filled his friends in on the conversation with his mother. Their matching horrified expressions actually had him laughing.

Outraged, Emily placed her hand on his arm. "I'm sorry, sweetie. Your mother sounds like the biggest bitch." Her clear blue eyes shone with sympathy. "What are you doing after we finish here? Please come home with us for dinner, right, Con?" She nudged her husband.

"Yeah, definitely. We'll put the game on, eat pie, and get drunk." A smile flirted on Connor's lips. "Emily promised I could if you came over." He blinked, pouting at his wife, who rolled her eyes at him.

"Idiot," she muttered, her eyes softening. But she kissed his mouth and whispered something in his ear and Connor's eyes glazed over for a moment.

Ryder wished he could find a relationship like they had, built on unshakable trust, friendship and love. Emily and Connor supported each other and were the living example of true soulmates.

"I don't know, you guys." Ryder placed some turkey on a toothless old man's plate and gave him an extra helping of mashed sweet potatoes. "You don't need me moping around being a third wheel."

Emily poked him with a spatula. "Don't be a jerk. You can't be alone on Thanksgiving." She smiled at a young woman holding the hand of a little boy. She gave them both extra meat and the kid some extra marshmallow topping on his sweet potatoes. She was such a softy. "It's, like, against the law or something."

Chuckling, he continued to serve the long line of people who had no other place to go for the holiday meal. He should be grateful for what he had: a roof over his head and enough money to pursue his passion. Guilty from his pity party, Ryder vowed to stop thinking about himself so much and volunteer here more often. These people had real problems with no solutions in sight.

He felt a squeeze at his elbow. "Don't let her do this to you, sweetie. Come over tonight. Bring Pearl, and tomorrow night we'll go out dancing at that new club, Tops and Bottoms." Emily's smile lit up her pretty face. "You know we love going to the clubs with you. Maybe you'll finally find a nice guy."

"Not likely at a club. If I want a quick blowjob in the bathroom, well, that's a different story."

"Blowjobs? Did I hear someone mention blowjobs?" Connor waggled his brows.

"Oh, you're such an idiot." She glared at her husband.

Ryder pulled Emily into his arms. "But he's your idiot."

She giggled into his chest. "Yeah. I think I'll keep him. He's good for…stuff."

God, he loved these two. He'd met Emily after he

left West and Hamilton, and introduced her to his best friend, Connor. They'd married not long after that. Unwilling to stay at his firm after the humiliation of Josh, and needing a fresh start, he decided to work full-time at Rescue Me, the pit bull rescue organization she and Connor had started. He and Connor handled all the legal work the business required, and went out on rescues, but Emily was the heart and soul of the place. Nobody loved those misunderstood dogs as much as she did. Woe be to anyone who took her petite frame, sweet face, and pale blonde looks for weakness. She held a black belt in karate and never went anywhere without her two muscular pit bulls, Laurel and Hardy. No one could get near Emily as long as her faithful bodyguards were with her.

Connor, a legal aid attorney who worked in downtown Brooklyn, specialized in helping LGBT teens and young adults discriminated against in housing and/or the workplace. His casual joking manner hid a rapier-sharp intelligence and lightning-quick wit. With his ever-present grin, perfect smile, and cascade of dark curls, men and women alike fell for his charm. His shrewd yet mischievous green eyes never failed to see through anyone's bullshit, including Ryder's. They'd met the first day of law school and had become study partners and best friends.

Connor and Emily were passionate about dogs, gay rights, food, and each other. They were the best friends he'd ever had, and he loved them to death. He had a standing invitation for Sunday brunch every weekend. They got him drunk when his parents rejected him, and told him what a piece of shit his lover had been to dump him. Emily even went so far as to tell him that the next time a man broke his heart, he'd have to deal with Laurel and Hardy.

"You haven't hooked up with anyone in forever, my man. Tomorrow night we're gonna take you out and get you laid." Connor hooked his arms around Emily's waist and, humming Dylan's "Lay Lady Lay," danced her around the tables holding the food trays.

Emily swatted her husband. "Stop it. Ryder doesn't need that. He needs to find someone who'll love him and care about him." She laid her head on her husband's chest. "I know the right man is out there for you, sweetie."

Ryder smiled and shook his head as he watched them dance. "Em's right. You really are an idiot. But as for the other, I'm not interested."

He was the real idiot to think he'd ever fall in love again. Love for a gay man or at least for him, brought nothing but heartache. All he needed were his dog and his friends. Once he found a way to get his brother back in his life, he'd find some quick anonymous fuck somewhere. But until then, he had no intention of risking his heart and falling in love.

Chapter Two

"CHLOE. WHERE THE hell are you? I told the guys we'd be there at eight, and it's already eight thirty." Night after night Jason Mallory wasted hours waiting for his girlfriend to fix her damn hair and makeup and it pissed him off. No matter what they had planned, even if it was to hang out at their local bar, Drummers, she thought she was making an appearance at the damn Oscars.

"Oh, chill, Jase. I'm coming." She stopped halfway down the stairs, waiting with an expectant look on her face.

"Finally." He huffed and motioned her to hurry down the rest of the steps, rolling his eyes, knowing she wanted him to compliment her on how good she looked. The guys in the neighborhood all thought she was hot with her curly black hair, big brown eyes and large boobs, but after dating her for three years he was pretty immune to it all.

Yeah, she was cute and fun, but that was about it. At twenty-four she had no desire to move ahead, learn new things, or even get a job. She'd never gone to college, and bragged that the only degree she wanted was an MRS. When she wasn't shopping, thanks to Daddy's credit cards, she filled her days with hair, nail, and tanning-salon appointments.

Sometimes he thought about suggesting they see other people, but he worked so hard at his job and she seemed so content with their relationship, he figured, why bother? Hopefully once he and his brother got their construction business up to full speed, he'd be able to make more time for the two of them, maybe go away to the Caribbean. Even the idea of an exotic vacation with her, though, didn't excite him like it should. At twenty-seven, he already felt like he was in a rut.

If he had to admit it to himself, he had little desire to keep the relationship moving forward. When they'd first started dating he found Chloe to be light, easy, and fun, but now as they grew older and he'd begun to take on more responsibility in his life, he had less and less time for her frivolous, childish behavior. It saddened him, as they had known each other for so many years, but at this point, he had no idea who she was. Their relationship became a force of habit—something you did because it was readily available.

He felt like a shit, but she never complained, aside from wanting to get married. The fault for their mutual boredom and half-hearted sex life lay as much or perhaps even greater with him than with her and Jason didn't blame her for any of it. Late at night after he'd

FELICE STEVENS

taken her home, Jason would sit up wondering when he'd lost his passion. Or was sex supposed to be so mechanical, with no heart and soul behind the act?

Lately, and with a disturbingly greater frequency, the memory of a long-buried night occupied his thoughts, and while that one encounter never failed to arouse him, Jason refused to question why, and what those feelings meant. It might be the explanation behind his lack of passion for Chloe and almost every woman he'd ever dated, but Jason, who preferred as little conflict in his life as possible, chose to be an ostrich and stick his head in the sand, rather than delve too deeply into his own psyche.

Not going there. No way.

When he bent to kiss her, she offered her cheek instead of her glossy lips. "Don't mess the makeup, hon." Her heavily mascaraed eyelashes batted at him. "I hate smudged lipstick."

Hmph. Must be the reason why he couldn't re-member the last time he'd had a blowjob from her. And wasn't that pretty damn pathetic? Placing his hand at the small of her back, he steered her out the door of her modest two-family house in Bensonhurst, Brooklyn. He idly admired her toned thighs as she slipped into the front seat of his truck and crossed her ankles in her strappy heels.

After he started the engine and she picked the radio station, Chloe pulled down the visor to check her makeup. "Did I tell you that Joey and Brianna got engaged?"

Whoa. That was a shocker. "Nope. When did that happen? The two of them haven't known each other that long, have they?" His surprised gaze flickered over and he saw the red nails digging into the palms of her hands. Uh-oh. "What's the matter?" As if he didn't know.

"That's the point. They haven't known each other that long. When she showed me the ring today at the nail salon, everyone was so surprised. That bitch Deena even said to me, *'We all thought it would be you and Jason since you've been dating so long.'* What was I supposed to say to them?"

Yep. Exactly what he thought. *Here we go again.* The nightly harangue about getting married. He found himself gripping the steering wheel, palms dampened with sweat. Not even together fifteen minutes and already getting bitched at about marriage. "We've had this conversation before. Mallory Brothers is starting to get some good clients. I can't afford to get married yet." His mouth tightened into a thin line of aggravation. "Jesus, I'm twenty-seven, and you're only twenty-four. What's the rush?"

"It's been three years since we started dating, and you haven't even said we're gonna get married. I don't have a ring or nothing." Her voice started to take on that screechy, nail-through-his-head tone.

"What the hell? Why are you attacking me?" He pulled into a parking space half a block away from the bar and shut off the engine, but made no move to get out. Maybe the time had come to have that talk after all. As he stared at her taut, angry face, it occurred to him he hadn't been happy in a very long time.

"Talk to me." He reached over to touch her arm, but she pulled away, folding her arms across her breasts. "You're angry because your friend got engaged before you."

"Well, yeah. They've only dated for six months, and I've known you since I was thirteen." She twirled an ebony curl around her index finger. "You spend all your time at work and never want to do anything fun. Like, guys are always telling me I don't need someone who'd rather leave me alone than take me out and show me a good time."

How nice. His girlfriend thought he was a bore. Amused, he settled back in his seat and shot her a look. "Go on, sweetheart. Tell me how you really feel."

Totally clueless as to how shallow she sounded, Chloe bumbled forward. "I mean plenty of guys have asked me out, and I've been tempted, for sure. Why wouldn't I be, when someone like Jimmy Goretski tells me I'm hot?" She examined her nails. "He bought a new Mercedes and asked me to go to Atlantic City with him this coming weekend. He has a suite at the Borgata."

Jason growled. "That fucker. He knows we're together."

Chloe shrugged. "He said we weren't engaged after all these years, and I looked like my man wasn't paying enough attention to me." She stared at him, a challenge obvious in her eyes. "He told me he could make me happy. I haven't given him an answer yet, 'cause I wanted to talk to you first."

That little pink tongue of hers licked her lips. It all seemed so calculated now. At least his parents would be happy if he and Chloe broke up. They'd never liked her, nor did his sisters. They called her a big *Glamour* Magazine *Don't*, which he really didn't understand but wisely didn't question. He had no idea what his brothers thought.

Memories washed over him—the times they'd spent together at the beach or hanging out at Coney Island. Their first kiss and the hot, desperate nights of making love. It was a sweet ache of loss, for what might have been and what was gone. It may not have been love, but there were years together. That had to count for something.

He knew this was it, the end of their relationship, and that after tonight, he and Chloe would never be together again.

Triumph flared in her eyes when he put his hand to her cheek. She thought she had him. "Hey, Chloe?" He unclipped his seat belt and unlocked the doors.

"Yeah, honey?"

"Go be happy. Have a great weekend in Atlantic City with Jimmy. I wish you both the best." He stepped out of the truck and slammed the door shut. Through the windshield he could see the shocked look on her face. Her mouth formed a perfect O of confusion and outrage. After struggling with her seat belt, she scrambled out of the truck in full panic mode.

The beep of the vehicle's remote signaled the doors were locked, and he waited for her, flipping the key chain in his hand. "Come on. I told the guys I'd watch the game with them."

"How can you talk sports at a time like this? We're having a crisis in our relationship, and all you can do is think of your friends?"

And right on cue, the tears began to fall. Well, that might work for dear old Daddy, but not him. "No, we aren't. There's no crisis."

"Oh honey, I knew you were kidding me." She took his arm. "You'd be stupid to let me go. I mean, no offense, but it's not like you're gonna do better than me." Miraculously, the tears dried up. She giggled and snuggled next to him.

Once they reached Drummers, Jason pulled her into a corner before he joined his friends. "When I said there was no crisis, I meant that I'm fine with you and Jimmy being together. Go to AC with him and have fun. You haven't been satisfied for a long time; I can tell."

Not wishing to be hurtful, he didn't say he felt the same way, but it was true. No spark of attraction existed between them; he had no aching desire to see her after a long day at work. Jason was hard-pressed to remember ever wanting to share a triumphant moment, like when he was awarded the winning bid on a big construction project or the times when he woke up in a cold sweat, terrified that he'd made the wrong decision striking out on his own with his brother. Shouldn't he have wanted her comfort and strength to lean on? Only once had he mentioned it to her, and she'd tossed it off, telling him, *"Do whatever makes you the most money."*

Three years together and she had no clue what made him tick, what his hopes and dreams were, nor did she care. They'd become familiar strangers sharing a bed and their bodies but not their lives or their hearts. Neither one was willing to be the first to admit the relationship had run its course, or that they no longer satisfied each other. Fear of failure and being alone made for sad bedfellows. With work consuming him so much lately and stalking his every thought, rather than shake up the status quo and say good-bye, it had been easier to stay the course.

"You don't mean that." Wild-eyed, her mouth hanging open, Chloe grabbed his arm. "You love me. I know you do."

For the first time, Jason felt sorry for her. He patted her hand. "Don't worry, babe. You can tell everyone you broke up with me, if that makes you feel better." With something akin to regret, he leaned over and kissed her cheek. "Bye."

Then he turned and walked away to join his brothers and friends at the bar.

"What was that all about?" His older brother, Liam, passed him a beer. "You and Chloe looked like you had some serious shit going down."

Jason downed half the bottle in one gulp, the coolness spreading through his chest as he swallowed, relieving some of his tension. "I broke it off with her." His body hummed as he bounced on the balls of his feet. Lighthearted for the first time in months—maybe years—Jason breathed deeply, shocked at how that simple act swept away the grayness and malaise he'd been living under. The declaration to his brother and friends revealed the sad truth of his relationship, forcing him to see everything he'd been hiding behind. He swung the neck of the bottle between his two fingers and grinned at their shocked faces.

Mouths open, they stared at him, and Jason couldn't help but laugh. "You all look like a bunch of fish." He took another swig of his beer. "She wants to get married, and I don't. Plus, Goretski is dangling his bank account, and I'm not into throwing dollar bills at her."

His little brother, Mark, grunted. "Surprised it took you that long to dump her. She always was a bitch."

Jason eyed Mark. Only twenty-one, his youngest brother had the keenest insight into people. Maybe that was why he excelled at Brooklyn College as a psych major.

"What do you mean? I thought you liked her." Jason raised a brow.

"Oh man, she had you by the balls. You were always too nice a guy to see her for what she was. A total bitch." Mark spat out his words like nails.

Jason and Liam gaped at their younger brother. He wasn't one to use language like that about a woman. A creeping suspicion wormed its way into Jason's mind. "Mark, tell me. Do you know something I don't but should?"

Mark eyed him with sympathy. "I never thought it meant anything, but I saw the two of them, her and Jimmy, hanging out a few weeks ago at some bar in downtown Brooklyn. I shoulda said something, but I didn't suspect she was cheating on you." With his hand balled into a fist, Mark gestured over to the couple at the opposite end of the bar. "I'm sorry. I could beat the crap out of him if you want." The hopeful tone in his voice had them all laughing and earned him another beer.

Jason shrugged, and while disappointed, the reality of Chloe's betrayal didn't hurt him as badly as it once might have. Probably because he didn't care enough about her. "Nah." Their sex life might have been infrequent but he hoped she hadn't been screwing both of them at the same time. He shot a look over at the opposite corner of the bar and saw Chloe tucked into Jimmy's side, his hand clamped on her skinny-jeaned ass, their mouths and hips fused together in a very public display of affection.

Guess that answered his question.

After three years together, he thought he'd be angry or at the minimum upset, watching his girlfriend tongue-fuck another guy in public. Oh, right, ex-girlfriend now. Nope, it didn't matter in the least.

"Don't worry about it." He grabbed a chicken wing off the platter on the bar and gnawed on the meaty drumette. "It's been a long time coming. I didn't realize it."

His friend and the bar's owner, John, who normally kept his opinions to himself, swallowed a slider in two bites, belched, then offered his opinion. "That bastard Goretski better not think I'm gonna keep his tab running forever." He slid another beer across the bar to Jason. "On the house, dude."

Jason tipped the bottle in a salute of thanks. "I thought it would bother me more than it really does. I don't like seeing her making out with him in front of me, but I don't care all that much and can't really blame her." He stole a glance at them. They'd broken their lip-lock, and now Chloe was sitting on Goretski's lap, having her cleavage manually inspected by his lips. "I honestly wish her well."

Liam swallowed his beer. "Well, there are plenty more fish in the sea. I say you jump right back and show her you can get any woman you want."

The thought hadn't even crossed his mind, but really, what was the point? Jason studied his brothers as they discussed whom they thought he should ask out. Why start a new relationship when he'd only be accused of the same thing—being uncaring, unaffectionate, and not romantic enough? His gaze slid over the various women nearby, but none caught his interest. He sighed and drank his beer. "I dunno."

"Maybe Jase needs to take a break from dating women for a while." John met his gaze with a neutral expression, yet Jason sensed there was something he wasn't saying. Or John knew something Jason wasn't ready to discuss. Nervous, Jason broke eye contact, his stomach churning as he took another hasty gulp of beer. Perhaps he'd been mistaken, though, for when he glanced over again at John, he'd moved to the opposite side of the bar to take a call from his cell phone, paying no attention to him.

"I don't have time for a new relationship now. We need to make sure we get our business in order, Liam. Now that the housing market has come back and people are renovating again, we have to strike while the iron is hot. There's a lot of money to be made."

"It's gonna be a long, cold winter, though, dude." Liam's speculative gaze held his. His dark eyes were sympathetic and understanding. "You're used to having someone around to talk to, and especially to keep you warm at night."

"We didn't have much to talk about. And, ah, the nights were nothing special, if you get what I mean." His face heated as he started in on the plate of nachos John placed on the bar. "Damn, these are spicy." The cold beer he gulped down doused the burning hot sauce. He fanned his mouth with his hand, hoping to end the conversation.

Mark huffed a laugh. "I'm not surprised she was a bore in the sack. Probably didn't want to get her hair messed up."

Jason hoped the dim lighting in the bar hid his burning face. Mark's comment hit a little too close to home. "Yeah, well, it doesn't matter anymore. Liam and I are busy now, and Mallory Bros. Construction will be taking up all my free time."

Nope, he was finished with relationships and women for the present. If he wanted companionship, maybe he'd get a dog.

Chapter Three

THE PULSE OF the music pounded into Ryder's brain. Why he allowed Connor and Emily to drag him here, he couldn't say. They meant well, but he had no desire to chat up some random guy, or to have hurried sex in a bathroom stall or a dark hallway.

"Come on, let's get some drinks. This place looks like it could be fun." Connor pushed him toward the large glittering bar, waving at the shirtless bartender to get his attention. "Two Sam Adams, my man, with lime, and one Sea Breeze." He grinned, and Ryder saw the bartender wink and smile at his friend.

"Another conquest, Con." Poor guy would be sad to know Connor was straight, here with his wife and not into threesomes. Ryder accepted the mixed drink from his friend and passed it to Emily. She stood, facing the dance floor, enthralled by the men dancing, the light show, or both. "Em, here, take your drink."

"Thanks." She reached out to take her drink, but her gaze remained fixed on two men out on the floor. Their bodies moved in sync, arms sinuously entwined, lips pressed together. To Ryder, they looked hot, wild, and sexy as fuck.

"They're so free and beautiful, aren't they?" He had to bend down to hear her. "I can't see how anyone could think this is wrong."

A tight little grin thinned his lips. "Well, obviously my parents do, since they have no desire to ever see me again unless I become '*normal.*' Their definition of course." He gulped half his beer without tasting it.

Connor draped an arm over his shoulders. "Screw 'em, I say. You're doing nothing wrong. Live your life and find some happiness. We'll always be here for you. You know that, right?" Ryder bit his lip and shrugged in answer to Connor's question.

"They'll come around one day, Ryder. You have to believe that. In the meantime, find someone to share your dreams with." Ryder watched his friend's gaze flicker over to Emily, who returned his look with her sweet smile. "It's no good to be alone, man. It sucks the soul out of you." Connor took his wife's half-empty glass and placed it on a mirrored shelf cluttered with glasses next to where they were standing. "Now I'm going to dance with my wife, and I want you to find someone to dance with." He took Emily's hand and pulled her onto the floor.

Ryder chuckled and took another swallow of his beer. When he finished, he looked for a place to put his bottle down, but instead caught the eye of a man who stood at the edge of the dance floor, watching him. He recognized that look. It spelled heat, desire, and the need to get down and dirty as fast as possible. His dick responded, but he ignored the man and instead returned to the bar to get another beer.

It took a while to make his way to the front of the bar, but he finally caught the bartender's attention and ordered a drink. As he stood waiting for his beer, a large palm pressed against the small of his back. "Why did you turn away from me?" A slightly accented voice murmured in his ear, sending tingles up his spine while a hard body pressed him into the wooden railing of the bar. An impressive erection nestled into the crease of his ass and heat poured off the man's body, enveloping him.

Ryder froze. He took his change from the bartender, then spoke through gritted teeth. "You need to take your hands off me."

"Come on, I only wanted to talk and maybe get to know you better." The man moved even closer, rubbing himself up against Ryder's ass. In another minute the guy would be humping him in public.

That did it. Snarling, Ryder whipped around to face him. "I said back the fuck up, man."

The stranger was extremely handsome. European, Ryder surmised, with a pale complexion, dark hair and eyes and a full, sexy mouth that hinted at all things wicked. His six-foot-plus frame was clothed in an expensive suit, which did little to hide his broad shoulders and narrow waist. The thin shirt he wore pulled against the muscles of his chest, and Ryder could see the hard nipples poking through the silky fabric. A smoldering fire blazed in his glittering black eyes.

"I noticed you as soon as you walked in, so beautiful with your golden hair and skin and those bright blue eyes like a summer sky." He licked his lips, drawing Ryder's attention once more to their fullness. "I like your mouth too. I watched you drink your beer and wished your lips were wrapped around my cock instead of that bottle. Imagine, a grown man being jealous of a bottle."

Ryder sucked in his breath. He'd never been so blatantly seduced. In his mind he pictured this man stripped bare, pale body, glowing damp with perspiration, draped over Ryder's own naked flesh. If he wanted, he knew he could take him, lead him to the back, and have him on his knees within minutes. Ryder imagined sliding his zipper down, pulling out his dick, and stuffing the man's sexy, full mouth.

Sex with a stranger, in a club. How predictable and fucking depressing.

Finishing as much as he wanted of his second beer, Ryder reined in his temper. "I don't like people touching me unless I give them permission first." He leaned closer, catching a whiff of the man's cologne, mixed with the faint aroma of tequila and sweat. "And I didn't give *you*"—Ryder jabbed at the man's well-muscled chest with his fingertip—"permission to touch *me*."

The man closed his eyes, his mouth opening in

anticipation of what, Ryder neither knew nor cared to discover. He took the opportunity to escape and join his friends on the dance floor. Emily slipped her arm around his waist. "What was that all about, sweetie? That guy looked hot and totally into you."

Ryder shrugged and swayed his body to the music as he danced with his friends. "Nothing and nobody. Someone looking for a fuck buddy for the night." The music changed, and he made a face. "I hate this song. Come on, let's get another drink." He grabbed her hand, pushing his way off the dance floor, Connor trailing behind them, grumbling about rude friends.

"I've got this round. What'll it be?" It was so tight by the bar they overlapped shoulders. Connor, touchy-feely bastard that he was, clasped the back of Ryder's neck, resting his hand there.

"Get me another beer and Em another Sea Breeze."

He'd given the bartender his order when he came face-to-face with the man he'd left before. Only this time the sexy mouth was sneering, and his handsome face twisted in an ugly grimace.

"So you let this pretty boy touch you, but you disappear on me?" His anger forced Ryder to take a step back, causing Connor's grasp around the nape of his neck to tighten. The man's eyes flashed. "He came with a woman. I saw. You like it three-way, maybe? I can arrange for that." He stepped in closer, and disgusted, Ryder lost the little desire he had to remain at the club and turned away.

"I'm out." He spoke over his shoulder to Connor. "See you tomorrow." Ryder pushed past the crowd and hustled out of the club. A cold wind bit through his shirt. Shit, he forgot his jacket inside. He texted Connor to get it for him from the coat check and take it with him when he left. No way in hell would he go back in there. Hailing a cab was simple, and within minutes he was hurtling down Broadway back home. Another disaster. Letting his head fall back on the headrest, he closed his eyes, and as always when he was alone and depressed, his thoughts turned to his former lover, Matt.

Was the man even alive, or had the path he'd chosen—drugs over love—sent him to an early grave? What a waste of life. Matt had been so vibrant and healthy when they'd first met at the gym. But his easygoing, California-surfer-dude mentality hid a dark side. Drugs had always been prevalent in the music industry, but Matt wasn't into weed. He liked the hard stuff—heroin. Ryder begged him to get help, to go to rehab, but Matt insisted he didn't have a problem.

The last ugly episode, when Ryder came home to find Matt passed out on the floor, a syringe by his side would remain forever scalded in his brain. Never in his life had he been as scared as he was at that moment.

"Matt, Matt." His earsplitting screams had no effect on his unconscious lover. Ryder thought he'd go mad, waiting for the ambulance to arrive. He tried slapping Matt, pushing him, anything to rouse him out of his stupor. But Matt remained unmoving.

Three days later in the hospital, still looking like shit, Matt tried to joke it off. "Come on, dude, it wasn't so bad. I promise I'll cut back." He grinned the wide-open smile that before had always melted Ryder's heart.

Not this time.

"I can't do it anymore. You have to make the choice."

Matt's grin faded. "I don't know, man. It makes me feel good. And life is all about feeling good, you know?"

No, Ryder didn't know. He hadn't felt good in a very long time. "I'm sorry, but no. I don't want any part of it." He stared at the man he thought he loved. Did he even exist anymore, or had the drugs leeched into him too deep to break free of their grasp? Was he wrong, forcing Matt to choose? "Aren't I enough to make you feel good?"

"If you loved me, you wouldn't make me choose." Matt's face tightened in anger, and his brown eyes darkened. "But it's no problem, dude. I'll pick up my stuff and head over to Troy's. He's cool with me."

Pain sliced through Ryder's chest and he gasped. "Have you been sleeping with him?" Though they always practiced safe sex, he didn't want to know his lover had cheated on him.

A sigh of relief escaped him when Matt shook his head. "Nah, man. Troy's not gay. We're friends." His face softened. "I'm sorry, Ry. We had fun, though, right?"

Fun. That was all their year together meant to the man? So Matt didn't love him, never had. Ryder turned on his heel and left Matt's room and the hospital.

He never saw Matt again.

The gruff voice of the cabbie interrupted his thoughts. "Hey, buddy. We're here."

He swiped the credit card, tipped the driver, then took his receipt. Anxious to get inside and out of the cold night air, he scrambled out of the cab. In the short time period it took for him to get home, the temperature must've dropped below freezing. By the time he made it to the entrance, his face and hands ached from the cold. Clarence, the doorman, pulled open the door.

"Mr. Daniels, where is your coat? It's freezing tonight, sir."

Ryder chuckled. "Clarence, you're like a mother hen. Connor has it, and I'll pick it up tomorrow. I trust you had a nice holiday?" His numb fingers fumbled a bit as he dug for his keys in his pants pocket.

The elderly, gray-haired doorman smiled. "Yes, all the grandchildren were there, and they kept my lap busy. I trust you had a nice holiday, sir?"

Ryder nodded and knew his strained smile didn't fool the man. "Well, good night, Clarence."

"Shane wanted me to tell you he walked Pearl and fed her tonight. He even stayed and played with her a bit. Good night, sir."

"When you see him, tell him how much I appreciate it, please." Ryder took the elevator to the sixteenth floor and when he opened the apartment door found a whining Pearl waiting for him. She hated being left alone. Ryder gave her some treats, drank two glasses of water, and after shedding his clothes, fell into bed.

Within moments he'd fallen asleep, his arm around his dog.

§ § § § §

At eleven o'clock Monday morning, Ryder, manning the phones at Rescue Me, fielded an emergency call.

"Tell me the address, please." He jotted down an address in Red Hook, Brooklyn—an area well-known to harbor dogfighting rings. "Okay, we'll be there within half an hour at the latest. Don't touch the dogs, and give them plenty of space." He hung up the phone. While he'd been taking down the information, Emily had begun preparations for the rescue, taking out muzzles, large blankets, and some food and bowls.

"I'm ready, Ry. You can fill me in on the way there." She, along with Laurel and Hardy, jumped in their van. Crates secured to brackets on the floor took up the entire space in the rear. Ryder slammed the van door shut, and they started out on the drive to the construction site.

"Apparently it's a large construction site with abandoned buildings going through some renovations." Ryder took the turn at the corner at a steady rate of speed. "The foreman came upon some dogs he suspects are pit bulls and doesn't know how to handle them. Naturally he's afraid of getting bitten, so he called us."

"I hope we can help." Emily stroked Laurel's massive head. "I'd hate to find they've been too abused to rescue and foster out. The shelters are overwhelmed as it is."

As if she understood their conversation, Laurel heaved a great sigh.

Not twenty minutes later, they bounced along the cobblestone and broken-up streets of one of Brooklyn's strangest areas. One block might see some of the toughest housing projects in the city, but on the next were gentrified townhomes, and expensive, charming restaurants. They pulled into a double-wide parking area, their van squeezing past a truck with *Mallory Bros. Construction* emblazoned on the side.

From the driver's seat, he spotted a crowd of men standing around, some in hard hats, along with curious onlookers. Two men stood apart; one with curly brown hair, broad and beefy in his shirtsleeves, talked into a phone, gesturing wildly. The other man caught Ryder's attention.

Several inches over six feet, the man's dark hair fell in loose waves to curl at the nape of his neck. Ryder couldn't help but notice how his thin, button-down shirt strained across his muscled chest. As cool as it had been on Thanksgiving, the temperature had risen to an almost balmy fifty degrees today and he'd rolled his shirtsleeves up to his elbows, showcasing his powerful arms.

"Wow, that is one cute guy." Emily nudged him. "I see you staring at him. Make sure you go over and speak to him."

Ryder scowled at her. "I'm here to work, not make a date."

Emily squeezed his thigh and poked him. "Maybe you can do both." She winked and gave him her saucy smile.

He kissed her cheek. "Now I see why you and Connor are perfect together. You're both annoying."

Her eyes sparkled as she kissed him back. "You love it. Come on, let's go." She opened the door to the van and hopped out.

When Ryder looked out the van's window, he locked eyes with the dark-haired man's intense stare. Inexplicably nervous, he licked his lips and saw the man's eyes widen in response, before he flushed and looked away.

What the hell was that about?

All thoughts fled as he saw a group of men approach the row of houses and start up the stairs. They held bats in their hands, and one clutched a chain. Adrenaline kicked in and in a flash he jumped down from the van and raced toward the group of men.

"What the fuck do you think you're doing?"

Chapter Four

J ASON PACED UP and down the paved area of the driveway. Time equaled money, and these people from the pit-bull-rescue place Liam had called better get here soon. The crew was plain lucky the dogs were tied up or in no condition to hurt anyone when they found them. Still, he knew they couldn't handle them, and since one of the crew knew about this place, they'd made the call.

Now all they had to do was wait for these people to show up.

Finally, he watched a van pull up and park near his truck. The passenger, a cute blonde, didn't look a hundred pounds soaking wet and couldn't possibly do much, but the guy next to her looked big enough to handle the job. Jason watched as they talked for a few seconds, and she kissed the guy's cheek. Either boyfriend or husband. Jason didn't care which; he wanted the job done.

The blonde hopped out of the van and though she possessed a smoking hot body and pretty face, he felt zero physical attraction to her. He met her boyfriend's gaze through the windshield and a funny feeling pinged through his gut. The guy stared at him with eyes that screamed sex on the brain. Then he licked his lips.

To Jason's shock, his dick hardened and his jeans grew uncomfortably tight. He shivered, breaking out in a cold sweat.

What the fuck?

Jason bit back a curse and stalked over to the blonde. "Uh, hi. I'm Jason Mallory. We found these dogs in one of our buildings that we're preparing for rehabbing. Some are tied up, some aren't, but they all look in pretty bad shape, so we've stayed clear of them."

She nodded with approval. "That's smart. Ryder and I will take over from here. Make sure your men stand back—"

A loud commotion came from the front of one of the buildings, and a shout rang out, presumably from the man racing like a fifty-yard Olympic sprinter toward the house.

"Oh shit, what now?" Jason took off after the rescue guy. "What the hell's going on?" His shout came in a panting breath as he caught up with the crazy man.

Then he spotted the bats. "Who the hell are you, and what the fuck are you guys doing here?" These weren't his workers but rather random guys from the neighborhood who must've heard about the dogs they found.

One of the men leaned on his bat and glared at him.

"I'll take the dogs and sell them. I can get good money for them. Gimme me a few minutes to get them outta there."

With a snarl, the guy from the pit bull rescue pushed his way to the front of the building and blocked the entrance. "No fucking way. We're taking them." He widened his stance and crossed his arms, his eyes ablaze, a murderous snarl twisting his lips.

Jason admired the guy's balls to stare down these thugs.

They laughed at him, though, unconcerned. "Listen, you pussy. Move the fuck out of the way. Go back to Williamsburg or wherever your skinny hipster white ass came from. The dogs are ours." As if to prove his point, he swung the bat a few times.

Liam came up behind Jason. "Should we call the cops? This could get ugly real fast."

As Jason was about to agree, a piercing whistle split the air, and blurred, growling figures shot past him, coming to rest beside the rescue guy. Two huge black pit bulls sat panting at his feet, their tongues lolling out and those oh-so-sharp teeth making an appearance.

Three of the men took a few steps back, but the one with the big mouth decided to challenge both the man and the dogs and took a few steps closer.

Wrong move.

Jason winced as the dogs jumped up on all fours and began barking. Like a shot, all the men dropped their bats and chains and took off running. After they had disappeared from sight, the dogs sat back down, mouths open and tongues hanging out. If Jason had to admit it, they looked like they were smiling. Even more shocking, the guy and his wife—he saw her wedding band and engagement ring—were petting the two beasts like they were sweet little puppies. And the dogs loved it.

"Son of a bitch, that almost gave me a heart attack," Liam whispered in Jason's ear. "I thought pretty boy was gonna get his ass kicked."

Jason nodded, taking another look at the man. With his shiny, golden hair, bright blue eyes, and long, loose-limbed body, he looked like he belonged on a California beach rather than the hard-scrabbled streets of one of NYC's roughest neighborhoods. Guess he should go over and thank him.

"Hey, that was pretty damn amazing." He stuck out his hand. "I'm Jason Mallory, and that chickenshit over there is my brother Liam." Liam waved but stayed away and off to the side. "Thanks for running interference with those thugs. That was pretty intense. Do you run into these kinds of problems all the time?"

The guy stopped petting his dog and stood to shake his hand. "Name's Ryder. Ryder Daniels. Yeah, we run into this kind of shit all the time. It's why we bring the pups with us." He glanced down at the two massive dogs with a smile.

"Pups?" Jason choked out a laugh. "Man, these dogs are huge." One of them gave his pant leg a sniff, and nervous, he stepped back.

"Don't you like dogs, Jason?" The blonde frowned at him.

"Yeah, absolutely. I don't want him to like me for dinner, that's all." He huffed out a nervous laugh as the second beast joined his friend in an exploration of his leg.

Both the blonde and Ryder laughed. They made a cute couple, although he noticed that Ryder didn't wear his wedding band.

She smiled. "Oh, don't let them fool you. Laurel and Hardy are really pussycats. Aren't you, my big babies?" She knelt on the ground, and the two dogs licked her face, their long tails wagging furiously.

Amazed and still a little freaked out, Jason snorted. "Jesus Christ, that's crazy. They could rip her face off if they wanted to."

Ryder chuckled. "They're Em's bodyguards. She's walked through the most dangerous neighborhoods, and no one would think of touching her as long as those two are by her side. Better than any weapon." He leaned up against the door, squinting in the sunlight. "What are you guys doing with this property, anyway?"

"We're gutting the houses and upgrading. Putting in all new wiring, roofs, and bringing everything up to code. There are a total of fifteen homes here, and the developer has another ten a few blocks away we hope to win the bid on if he's satisfied with this work." Jason was proud of what they'd accomplished, even though to an outsider, it must appear like one big mess.

Ryder surprised him, however. "It looks like you've done a solid job. Did you have a lot of trouble getting permits from the city for the C of O? This area isn't landmarked like the Heights and Park Slope, is it?"

Jason stared at him. "How do you know about all that stuff?"

The woman piped in. "Ryder used to work in real estate. He was a lawyer at one of the top firms in the city, specializing in real estate development, right, sweetie?"

An uncomfortable-looking Ryder kept is head down and refused to meet his eyes. Hard grooves deepened by his mouth as he frowned. "Yeah." He kicked the ground with his sneaker. "Em, let's get the dogs, okay?"

"But Ry—"

"Emily, please."

Jason watched the interchange with avid curiosity. No matter what his wife said, it was blatantly obvious the guy didn't want to talk about his old job, and Jason wondered why she pushed him. Remembering how Chloe used to nag at him, Jason empathized with Ryder.

"Hey, man. I know how it is to be bullied by a girlfriend, so I can only imagine it must be harder when your wife is doing it."

Emily burst out laughing, and even Ryder cracked a smile.

"Did I miss a joke or something?" Jason looked from one to the other.

Emily continued to laugh, as Ryder clued him in.

"Em and I aren't married. We're friends, best friends. She, her husband Connor, and I all work at the rescue. He's a legal aid attorney."

After they all finished laughing, Emily took the dogs back to the truck, and Jason led the way to the part of the house where the dogs had been discovered. He continued to talk over his shoulder to Ryder. "I didn't take an accurate count, but there are at least three dogs, maybe four. One is a puppy and didn't look in great shape, poor thing."

Ryder's lips thinned in disgust. "I fucking hate this shit. They use these dogs for bait, if they can't use them as fighters."

"You're really dedicated to this, aren't you?" Jason asked in a low voice. He was curious about a man who'd give up such a lucrative career to help unwanted dogs.

"I am. I love these dogs. They're so misunderstood, and society would rather throw them away than take care of them. I can relate." Ryder's blue eyes shuttered.

Jason articulated an inconsequential noise of understanding, even though he had no clue what Ryder meant. Obviously Ryder had some personal issues, and giving up a career in the fast lane was a form of self-punishment. Since everyone knew high-priced real-estate lawyers earned megabucks in the city, it must've been some heavy shit that forced him walk away from that life.

As they started down the dim, narrow hallway, the piles of construction debris forced them to pick their way carefully. Jason called out a warning to Ryder. "Be careful here. There's tons of crap all over the place."

Behind him he heard the man swear, then yelp in pain. "Ow, shit, damn."

Jason spun around to help, but Ryder's falling body slammed him into the wall. Before he had a chance to take a breath, Ryder lay flat up against him, his long, lean torso pressing him into the crumbling plaster wall. They stood roughly the same height, with Ryder maybe having an inch on him. Ryder's head missed crashing into the wall, and instead his cheek took the brunt of the hit. He grunted in pain when his face made contact with the rough plaster.

The two of them stood in the hallway, their bodies frozen in place. The comforting heat from Ryder's body seeped into his own, and Jason caught the faint scent of Ryder's cologne, as well as the warm smell of his skin. Ryder's breath puffed across his cheek, and Jason felt the push-pull of his chest as it rose and fell against the other man. His own breathing slowed, and—holy shit, this was not happening—once again as it did earlier when he first spotted Ryder, Jason's dick hardened, only this time, with Ryder pressed firmly up against him, Jason couldn't hide it and run away.

Son of a bitch.

Ryder pulled back to stare him in the face and Jason saw no embarrassment or shame, as he knew his own eyes portrayed. No, this man's eyes blazed with defiance and pride.

Oh fuck, the guy is gay and here I am with a raging hard-on...

In a flash, Jason realized why the guy must've left his cushy job to work with the rescue group. He could only imagine those snooty white-bread law firms might not want someone so open and proudly gay. No matter that New York had made same-sex marriage legal, the stigma remained.

None of that meant jack shit to Jason, whose body ached at the feel of Ryder, firm up against him. Heat washed over him and Jason burned from a combination of embarrassment and fear—what if Ryder thought he was making a pass at him? What if he kissed him? A little voice whispered, *Maybe you'd like it.* A dark thrill shot through Jason for a second then he bit back a curse and took a deep breath.

"Um, Ryder, are you hurt? Or dead? 'Cause if not, can I ask you to move off me?" Jason bit his lip.

Ryder glared at him, those blue eyes no longer bright, but dark as midnight. "Don't worry, Jason. I'm not contagious. You can't catch gay." The sarcasm in his voice pinched Jason's heart with shame. But Ryder moved away, then bent down to rub his ankle.

Should Jason be concerned about Ryder's ankle or pissed off about his attitude? Health concerns first. "Uh, how's the ankle?"

Ryder barely gave him a glance. "It's fine. I'll live."

"Oh, good. I'd hate for you to die of a twisted ankle. It would fuck up my insurance rates for the job."

Jason caught the curl of a small smile tugging at the man's lips. "So, about the other thing. I hope you don't think I was making a pass at you. I, uh, I'm not, like, gay or anything."

Ryder merely raised a brow, then glanced at the obvious bulge in Jason's pants.

Jason huffed out a nervous laugh. "Yeah, well, about that. I broke up with my girlfriend, and our sex life had been dead for a long time, so I guess… Shit. I don't know." What the hell was he telling a total stranger this for? Jason knew he sounded like a bumbling asshole.

"So I'm any dick in the storm," Ryder drawled in what could possibly be the most sarcastic voice Jason had ever heard.

"No. I don't know what it was. Don't go all right-eous on me. I'm not homophobic because I said I wasn't gay." He struggled to explain himself. "I don't even know you at all. You're here to do your job, and I have my own to finish, so if you're okay, can you get those dogs, please?"

In an instant, Jason regretted his speech. He knew he came off sounding like an absolute douche. "I didn't mean it that way…" His voice trailed off, weak and halfhearted.

A cold smile twisted Ryder's lips. "Hey. No problem. Like you said. I'm here to do a job. I don't fuck where I eat, so don't worry about it." He tucked his hair behind his ears and bent down to rub his ankle again.

Jason did feel bad the guy hurt himself. "If you need

the ankle wrapped, we have a first-aid kit in the trailer."

Ryder shrugged. "It's fine. Can I see the dogs now? Emily will be in soon with the equipment." His voice was cool and distant, his eyes flat.

Jason breathed out. "Sure. Let's go. They're right through this door." He led Ryder into a corner room and moved aside so he could enter. Ryder passed through the doorway, surveyed the scene, and walked up to the first dog, tied to one of the iron rings bolted into the wall. He immediately sank to his knees. Jason watched with increasing admiration as Ryder soothed the suspicious dog. He sat on the floor, talking nonsense to the animal in a quiet singsong manner. In his hand appeared what Jason surmised must be dog treats. After several minutes, the growling stopped, replaced by whines and snuffles.

Damn, this guy was good. The dog, a brown-and-white mix that hadn't stopped giving Jason the stink eye when he stumbled into the room earlier today, now had his head in Ryder's lap, eating out of his hand. After finishing the last treat, the dog heaved a shuddering sigh and closed his eyes.

"He's really good, isn't he?" Jason started and looked down at Emily who'd noiselessly appeared at his side. Her eyes were fixed on Ryder as she spoke. "I think because he has so much feeling inside him. It's like he takes on their pain, you know?" She stared at him, unflinching. "He knows what it's like to be used and discarded. But like these dogs, any man who ends up with Ryder in his life is the lucky one."

Shit, had she seen what went down between him and Ryder? Well, screw it. He didn't owe her any explanations. "I'll leave you two to do this. If you need anything, let me know." He turned on his heel, beating a hasty retreat down the hallway. Not quick enough though, to escape the uncomfortable feeling of Emily glaring at his back, wishing him evil. Once outside in the bright sunlight, Jason paused to catch his breath, and calm the alarming reactions Ryder caused in his brain.

One hour later, Ryder came out with the dog Jason had last seen with its head on his lap. He was in a crate, which Ryder had no trouble carrying, despite the fact that it must weigh well over fifty pounds. Jason remembered the hard-muscled body pressed up against him. His blood sizzled, and he squeezed his eyes shut, willing his mind away from those all-too-disturbing thoughts.

Emily had moved the van closer to the site and Ryder placed the crate with the dog inside, swapped it for an empty crate, returned to the house, and within fifteen minutes came out with another dog in that crate. This dog sounded less friendly than the first, and Jason winced as he heard low growls coming from the crate. From a quick look inside, Jason saw that dog had a muzzle over its powerful jaws.

"Isn't it dangerous for them?" Liam came up behind him. "I'd be afraid they'd bite the shit out of me. That guy's got balls."

Yes, he does. Two large ones and a pretty hefty dick as well, from what I can tell.

He was going out of his mind. Emily came out with a bundle in her arms, cooing and making kissing noises into the blanket. Curious, Jason left the steps of the trailer to join her. Smiling at her antics, he pointed at the dog in her arms. "What do we have here?"

She bit her lip, and he could tell she was struggling not to smile. She really was sweet, the way she defended her friend against him. "He's still a puppy, undernourished and undersized. He may have something wrong with his paw. I'll have to have him checked out by our vet."

Jason watched as the little nose of the puppy poked out from the blanket to take an inquisitive sniff. "May I touch him?" He didn't want to do anything wrong that might hurt the little guy.

"Sure, but not on the face. Try behind the ears, gently, with no jarring movement." She showed him where to place his fingers.

The puppy's head felt silky smooth, and when Jason rubbed behind his ears, he whined and looked up into Jason's eyes. Such trust and affection from a creature who'd known nothing but pain and fear in its short, miserable life rattled him.

"He likes you. This one's a sweetie pie."

Jason agreed. "He's a trouper, that's for sure."

Emily took his hand in hers. "Here, let him smell you."

She put his hand in front of the puppy. The little guy sniffed his fingers, then licked them. His tiny, raspy tongue tickled. Soon, the puppy had washed Jason's entire hand.

A shadow fell over them. Jason looked up. Ryder stood over them, unsmiling. "Ready, Em?"

"Sure, sweetie." She smiled at him. "This little guy likes Jason here."

"That's nice." He took the bundled puppy from her. "I'll put him in the van." He walked away without a good-bye.

Jason motioned Emily into the trailer. "Come, I'll write you a check. A donation for the rescue."

"Cool, thanks. We appreciate it." She followed him inside, leaning her hip on his desk as he wrote out the check. "So, Jason, are you married?"

"Nope. Single."

When she opened her mouth, he cut her off before she could say anything. "My girlfriend and I broke up after dating for three years." Was that a flash of disappointment he saw cross her face? "Here you go." He held out the check, and she took it, folding it in half and slipping it into her back jeans pocket.

"Well, see ya around, Jason. Nice doing business with you, and please recommend us to all your friends." She waved farewell and left the trailer.

Within moments he watched the van pull out and disappear down the street. "She was cute."

He jumped out of his seat. "Jesus Christ, Liam, you scared the shit outta me. What are you sneaking up on me for?"

"Making an observation, is all. Why didn't you ask her out?"

"Because, asshole, she's married."

"To that guy?" His brother snorted. "I don't think so."

Jason cocked his head. "No, not him, but why are you so sure?"

"It's the vibe I get. He's gay, I'll bet."

"Does that matter to you, if a guy is gay?" Funny they'd never discussed this before.

"Nah, I don't really care where a guy sticks it, I don't want to have it shoved in my face, though ya know?" Liam laughed. "Figure of speech."

Jason winced. "You're a pig, dude. Yeah. Well, now that the dogs are gone, let's get a move on the rest of the removal. We have a lot to do."

"That was a cute puppy. What are they gonna do with it?"

Jason shrugged. "Not sure. It has something wrong with its paw, so they need to call the vet."

"I hope it can be fixed. Otherwise they'll probably have to kill it." Liam opened the door. "I'm heading out. Gonna check the delivery on the other site, 'kay?"

Jason nodded, his mind back on the puppy.

"No fucking way are they gonna kill that dog."

He picked up the business card on the table and slipped it into his back pocket.

Chapter Five

RYDER DRUMMED HIS fingertips on the desk, staring at the last text from Landon on his cell phone. Seeing his brother forced to use a classmate's phone was the final straw. To hell with their mother and her precious social standing; he was going to see his brother.

He left Rescue Me and took the train into the city. Landon's private school was on the Upper East Side, and according to a copy of his schedule, which Ryder had downloaded months ago, his last class finished at two o'clock. As usual, the subway crawled its way uptown, and Ryder wove his way around people trudging up the stairs and out into the street, hurrying so as not to be late and miss Landon.

As he stood on the corner, waiting for the light to change, he spotted his brother exiting through the doors of Hawthorne Academy, the private school he attended. It had only been two months since he'd last seen him, yet Landon had changed so much. Almost as tall as him now, Landon shared the same lean body and coloring. Unlike the other kids who celebrated the end of the school day, a subdued Landon walked down the block with a group of kids. Emotion choked Ryder as tears threatened, then receded. The light changed, and he hurried across the street, plastering a grin on his face.

Any doubts as to how Landon felt were blown away by the huge grin that split his face when he spied Ryder. Landon waved good-bye to the group of boys and ran over to greet him. Conscious of putting on an overly emotional public scene, Ryder fist-bumped him, giving him a grin. "Hey, dude. How's it going?"

Landon's smile said it all. "I'm great now. Shit, Ry, I missed you so damn much."

There went those tears again. Blinking fast, he slung an arm around Landon's shoulders. "Let's go. I thought if you wanted to, we'd hop a cab down to my apartment, order some Indian, and hang out for a while. It's better than sitting around a coffee place or restaurant, in case Mom has her little spies out."

Landon shifted his backpack. "Cool. Sounds excellent. I want to see Pearl, anyway. I'll tell Mom I have an SAT study group after school until after dinner. That'll give us plenty of time to catch up." He pulled out his phone and texted a message. "Done. Now she won't bother me. If she thinks it's for school, she leaves me alone."

Guilt swamped Ryder. "Hey, I don't want you to have to lie to her to see me. We can figure out some other way." He stopped on the corner and searched his brother's face, inwardly cursing. No seventeen-year-old kid should have the strain on his face that Landon had. But then again, no seventeen-year-old should have to lie to see his older brother. Damn his parents for putting them in this untenable position.

Angry blue eyes, so like his own, held his gaze. "Do you know why she said you weren't home on Thanksgiving?" The midafternoon crush on Second Avenue was dense with shoppers out for the after-Thanksgiving Day sales, so Ryder had to lean close to hear.

"I have a feeling I'm not going to want to hear this."

"When we sat down to dinner, I asked where you were. She said, *'I spoke with your brother.'* She doesn't ever call you by your name anymore; it's always 'your brother.' Anyway"—Landon gave a kick to an empty coffee cup that rolled to his feet—"she said, *'I personally invited him, but he had other plans, probably with a man, and wouldn't be able to join us, no matter how hard I begged. Obviously, he chose a stranger over his own flesh and blood.'"*

It broke his heart to hear his brother in so much pain. Ryder prided himself that under the circumstances, the fact that he hadn't lost it and gone bat-shit crazy was pretty damn amazing. Without answering, he hailed a cab and waited until the two of them got comfortable to speak.

"Look at me, Landon."

His brother faced him, the evidence of his inner torment apparent by the hurt in his eyes and the trembling of his lips as he tried not to cry. Ryder knew those emotions oh, so well. He'd lived with disappointment his entire life; his teen-aged years had been filled with tearful self-recrimination and hiding his sexuality from his parents, friends and teachers. Once again Ryder wanted to punch something. His brother shouldn't have to deal with anything other than his next trig test and how to sneak beer into the school dance.

"I'm only going to say this once. I would never turn down dinner at home. Yes, I spoke to her, and yes, she invited me, but only if I promised her to give up my *lifestyle* and start dating the women she wants me to."

The look on Landon's face was priceless. "She thinks you can give up being gay? Like cigarettes or too many shopping trips to Bloomingdales?" He gave a crooked grin. "That's pretty fuckin' stupid even for her."

God, he loved his brother. Landon *got* it. "Yeah. She even had my future wife all picked out for me." He burst into laughter at Landon's boggled eyes. "Don't worry, not happening."

Landon moaned. "Maybe I'll apply to the University of Tibet or something so she won't be able to bother me."

They shared a laugh all the way downtown and were still laughing as Ryder opened the door to his apartment. Pearl came loping down the hall, barking like crazy when she saw Landon. She and Landon loved each other, but his mother would never let Ryder bring his dog over to their apartment on Park Avenue, for fear she'd rip the throats out of her tiny teacup dogs.

Landon dropped his backpack and rubbed Pearl's belly. "She looks great, Ry. I'm so glad you took her in."

"Me too. She's been a great friend and keeps me company."

They took her out for a walk, then let her loose in the dog run for an hour. On the way home, Ryder stopped by the local grocery store and, leaving Landon outside with Pearl, grabbed some snacks, soda, and more beer for himself. They came home, and Pearl went right for her water bowl, slurping noisily. He brought over a soda for his brother and a beer for himself and threw several bags of chips and pretzels on the coffee table. Watching Landon eye his drink, he pinned him down with a stern glare. "Don't even think of asking, buddy. Just 'cause I'm your cool, gay older brother doesn't mean I'm gonna let you drink when we hang out."

"Not like I haven't had it before." Landon rolled his eyes and grumbled as he popped the top of the soda can.

"Don't be a schmuck. That's all I need, for you to go home with beer on your breath. Mom will find out, and then when will we ever see each other?" Ryder took a swallow of his beer. "Are you all going skiing as usual during Christmas?" Every year, they'd always gone to Jackson Hole for two weeks of skiing and snowboarding.

Uncomfortable, Landon nodded. "Yeah. I guess you weren't asked to come."

"Nope, and I didn't think I would be." Ryder

switched on the TV and handed Landon the Xbox controller. "Come on, I haven't tried out the new *Call of Duty* game."

Nearly choking on his drink, Landon grabbed the controller out of his hand. "Dude, how did you score this? It's sold out everywhere." He turned the Xbox on and immediately started playing. "This is so awesome. Wait till the guys find out."

"Remember Matt, the guy I used to go out with? He had a contact, and even though we aren't together anymore, the guy always sends me the newest games before they hit the stores."

Landon shot him a look before training his eyes back on the TV screen. "Yeah, I remember him. You really liked him. Whatever happened between the two of you?"

With the innate sense that dogs have to pick up when their owners always need comforting, Pearl came to him and put her head on his knee, looking for a scratch. "It's been a long time. We wanted different things."

Landon stopped playing. Whoa. That meant something serious was about to go down.

"I'm your brother, Ry. I may only be seventeen, but you can tell me. I mean I know you're gay. So what? I know you loved him. Did he cheat on you, the fucker?"

Ryder was touched to see how much his brother truly cared for him. Maybe he was wrong not to push his mother and demand he be allowed to see him in the open, instead of going behind her back. But then remembering how she blocked Landon's phone service, Ryder knew meeting Landon on the sly was the best he could hope for right now.

"No, he didn't. It's that he loved his drugs more than he loved me, and I wasn't willing to be second place." He petted Pearl's soft, silky ears. He wondered if he was ever really in love with Matt, or if he was in love with the idea of being in love.

"So is there anyone new, anyone you're interested in?" Landon's voice was crunchy with chips.

Unbidden, an image of Jason Mallory, with his curling black hair and dark blue eyes, came to mind. Since their first meeting, Ryder had woken up many nights, gasping for breath, sweat-dampened sheets twisted around his ankles, his hand wrapped around his hard and aching dick, in the throes of a spectacular orgasm. And each and every time, his dream had been of Jason Mallory, on his knees, taking him deep into that sexy, full mouth of his, or deep inside him, sliding in and out, over and over, harder and harder, until the friction and the burn, the thrust and the glide became so intense Ryder came, spurting endlessly into his sheets, the walls of his empty apartment echoing with his shouts.

Fuck me now.

"There is, isn't there?" Landon's eyes danced, his face bright with excitement. Thank God Pearl's head had moved to Ryder's lap and hid the bulge in his jeans he'd gotten from remembering his decidedly erotic and nasty wet dreams of Jason.

"No. There isn't."

"Bullshit. You can't hide from me. You were thinking of someone." Landon went to the kitchen to get another soda. Even with Landon's head in the fridge, Ryder heard the laughter in his voice. "Besides, you have a boner the size of a salami, so don't tell me there's no one."

Fuck my life.

"Forget about it. I'm not discussing my sex life with my seventeen-year-old brother."

Landon stood before him, challenging him. "Why not? If you were straight, I bet you would. Is it 'cause I haven't been with a girl yet? That doesn't mean I can't listen to you or help you out."

Agitated, Ryder jumped off the couch. "Let's order dinner. It's already five o'clock."

"Wouldn't you want me to talk to you about having sex for the first time, or if I had a serious girlfriend? Don't you know I'm there for you, and you don't have to be embarrassed to tell me because you're gay?" To his surprise, Landon grabbed him around the shoulders. "Don't shut me out. You have no idea how awful it is at home. Mom's constantly criticizing everything I do, and Dad's hardly there, always working."

Parenting needed to come with a manual. Either that, or some people should never have children. Being straight didn't mean you'd make a good parent. That should be obvious to everyone, with all the abused and neglected children in the world. Yet somehow he was the pariah, unfit to be a parent and, according to his mother, unfit to be her son.

"It isn't that." He pulled Landon down on the sofa next to him. "I'm not embarrassed. And yes, I hope you will come to me so I can teach you about safe sex."

Another eye roll. "I know all about it."

"Knowing it is one thing. Practicing it in the heat of the moment is another thing." Ryder knew he sounded like an old fart, but safe sex was too important to joke about.

"Have you ever, you know"—Landon's face flushed bright red—"not used a condom?"

"No, not ever."

Landon exhaled loudly. "Good." He punched Ryder in the shoulder and shot him an evil grin. "Now tell me about the guy."

Ryder shrugged. "Nothing to tell. He's straight, recently broke up with his girlfriend, and not into guys. End of story." He breathed out. Not so bad, finally saying it in the light of day. "I'm not interested in a relationship anyway. Too hard on the heart. Best to keep everything light and easy, you know?"

Landon's smile was sympathetic. "You can say it, but I know you. You're too caring. I know you'll find someone who's right for you. He smiled. "I'm starving. Let's order dinner. I want tandoori chicken and garlic naan."

"When did you get to be so smart about love, my man?" Ryder snickered. "Are you sure there's no girlfriend?" He placed the order and tossed the phone on the sofa.

Landon turned red. "Nah. No one. Let's play this game. I wanna beat your ass tonight, before I have to go home."

They played until the food came, and after they ate, Landon reluctantly agreed to leave.

Ryder hailed Landon a cab but held on to him before he got inside. "I promise I won't let her keep us apart. Let's make it a set time that you come here every Wednesday for a brothers' night."

Landon's face lit up with happiness. "Cool, definitely."

Ryder gave him twenty dollars and watched the cab's taillights disappear down Broadway, then headed back inside to his apartment. He heard the phone ringing as he opened the door and, thinking Landon had forgotten something, dove headfirst onto the couch where he'd left the handset.

"Landon?"

"Um, is this Ryder, Ryder Daniels?" The deep voice sounded somewhat familiar and he searched his memory to place it, as he caught his breath.

"Yeah, who's this?" With the phone wedged between his ear and shoulder, Ryder threw the takeout containers in the garbage and the cans in the recycling bin.

"Hey, it's Jason. Jason Mallory, from the construction site a few days ago. Remember me?"

Ryder almost dropped the phone. *Holy shit.* "Hey, yeah, sure, I remember you. What's up?" He sank into a kitchen chair. "Wait a minute. How did you get my home number?"

He'd bet his left nut it was Emily.

"I called the office, and Emily gave me your number."

Of course. Emily Halstead, matchmaker extraordinaire.

"Okay, so what can I help you with, Jason?" The guy's nervousness intrigued him.

"Well, I know this is gonna sound lame, but you did such a great job with the dogs, and I wanted to say thanks."

Yeah, it did sound lame, but what the hell. "Okay. You're welcome. Anything else?"

Ryder knew he sounded like a prick, but he wasn't in the mood.

"Uh, yeah. I spoke to Emily, but she said to talk to you about it. I'd really like to adopt that puppy if it's possible."

Ryder couldn't help but smile. He'd seen the interest Jason showed in the puppy and hoped he'd want to adopt him, but as the days dragged on, Ryder figured the guy had forgotten about it.

"That'd be great. His paw is healing nicely, too. He responded really well to the antibiotics for the bites, and the vet said other than that, he's clean."

"Wow, that's great." There was true happiness in Jason's voice. "I really fell for the little guy. Um, there's one more thing."

Ryder braced himself. "Yeah?"

"I'd like to invite you and your friends over to my friend's bar tonight to watch the game if you're not busy. You do like the Nets, right? Tell me you're not a Knicks fan, 'cause I may have to take back the invite." He laughed.

Ryder liked the teasing in his voice. This was good. He, Connor, and Emily could all hang out with Jason and his friends, no big deal. "Sure, that sounds great. Give me the where and when."

"Well, the game starts at eight, so anytime after that works. When I told Emily, she said to tell you Connor wants you to find your own way there and back. I could hear him laughing in the background, so I presume you understand why that's funny?"

"It's Connor being a douche." Oh, he knew why. Connor wanted Ryder to go home with Jason. God, the two of them needed to stop trying to set him up with every unattached guy they met.

The object of his current nighttime fantasy sounded confused. "Well, all right. So I hope to see you. The place is called Drummers, and it's in Bensonhurst, off of 18th Avenue…a neighborhood place."

"Sounds cool. Thanks. See you then." He ended the conversation and looked at the clock. It was six thirty.

He had time for a quick run and a shower before hanging out with the first man to interest him in almost a year.

Gorgeous, nice, and 100 percent straight. A sure recipe for disaster.

Chapter Six

"SO WHO ARE these people, Jason? You've never invited anyone over to hang out with us before." Mark dug into the platter of nachos as John set up the glasses on the bar. "Is the girl cute at least?"

"Her name is Emily, and she isn't a girl, you Neanderthal. She's a woman, and she's married." Jason finished his beer. "Her husband's name is Connor, and he seems really cool, but I doubt he'd appreciate you talking trash about his wife."

John slid another beer across the bar to him. "There's another guy coming, you said?"

Liam joined them. "Yeah, some surfer-looking dude named Ryder. No competition, though, for us with the chicks, 'cause the guy's gay."

John raised a brow. "You sound like you got a problem with that."

Jason couldn't believe it. "Are you serious, man? Liam doesn't give a shit, do you?" Aside from that one stupid comment the day the dogs were rescued, Liam had never made any negative remarks about gay people before.

His brother grunted, took a plate, and started loading up on wings and sliders. "As long as he doesn't make a pass at me, I'm fine." He gulped down his beer and, waving a chicken wing in the air, declared, "I'm strictly a ladies' man. I don't want anyone's dick in my ass."

Jason winced at his brother's crudeness. As he reached across the bar to pick up a plate, he froze at the sound of the voice that, for some reason, he couldn't get out of his mind.

"Oh, good. I'll make sure to keep it in my pants instead of hanging out in the open, looking for any ass in the storm like I usually do."

Fan-fuckin-tastic. Jason's heart sank as he heard Ryder's icy-calm voice.

"Shit, man, this is really fucked-up," John muttered. "I'm guessing this is the other guy, Jase."

"Ryder, hey, glad you came." At the guy's sardonic raised eyebrow, Jason grabbed him by the arm. "C'mere." He pulled the guy over to an empty table. "Let's sit for a few."

"I'd rather stand, thanks. If I'm going to get my ass beat or listen to any more bullshit, I'd rather be able to leave in a hurry." But he joined Jason in sitting down at the table.

This was not how the night was supposed to turn out. He thought he'd invite Ryder, Emily, and her husband over and get to know them since he wanted to adopt the puppy from them. Emily told him Ryder always did the family evaluations to make sure dog and potential owner were a good match. But inviting them here to hang out with his friends was about more than adopting the puppy. He kept thinking of that confrontation with Ryder in the hallway of the town house but instead of it ending in anger, wishing they came out as friends.

When he thought how dedicated Ryder was to the animals, his admiration grew ten-fold for the guy and he wanted to become his friend. It didn't matter to Jason if Ryder was gay, like he didn't care that the other two were married. It was none of anyone's business who slept with whom. Hell, if he wanted to sleep with a guy, he'd probably want to sleep with Ryder; he was beautiful to look at. Plenty of women in the bar gave him the once-over when he walked by, but of course he was oblivious.

"Have you always known you were gay?" Jason couldn't believe he'd blurted that out. From the speakers hanging above the bar, Michael Stipe of REM crooned about losing his religion. Jason was fast losing his equilibrium and his mind.

Ryder seemed to take it in stride, shrugging. "I knew something was different. I mean in high school, I went out with a few girls and tried to kiss them, but it did nothing for me. Then one day, I was in the locker room, changing after track and the football team was finishing up. I thought the room was empty, when one of the guys came over to me, slammed me into the wall, and started kissing me." Ryder's eyes took on a distant look, as though he were sixteen again and back in that locker room as he told the story.

"Ahh, that sounds like it might've hurt." Could Jason sound any stupider? He downed another gulp of beer.

Ryder's lips curved up in a sweet smile. "You would think, but I was so turned on I thought I'd explode. As it was, it took him three simple strokes to get me off." He blinked, as if realizing what he'd said out loud. He blushed a fiery red. "Crap, I'm sorry if I embarrassed you."

Jason couldn't tear his eyes away from Ryder. For some inexplicable reason, his body responded to Ryder's story. Maybe Liam was right and he did need to get laid. "Don't be stupid. Look who I'm dealing with, if you want to know embarrassing." He pointed to his brothers, then slid a sideways glance to Ryder.

What was happening here? Lately, no matter how hard he tried to think of something else, the memory of his one crazy night years ago in college with another guy wouldn't leave him. But in his dreams it was Ryder he was kissing, not the friend whose name and face he struggled to remember. He sat hunched over his beer bottle while his mind spun out of control. Picturing a young, semi-naked Ryder, kissed into oblivion, all that silky golden hair spread behind him, lips probably wet and bruised from hard and rough kissing had his dick aching and his blood pounding. How could Jason still believe he was straight, yet confess that the story Ryder told him turned him on in a way he'd never thought possible?

"Damn." He swore into his bottle, downing the rest of the beer.

"Hey, what's the matter? You don't look too good." Ryder leaned across the table, his concerned face disturbingly near, and Jason caught a whiff of his scent again. His cheek was close enough so Jason could see the golden stubble on his jaw.

This is too fucking weird. He stood up so abruptly the stool almost toppled over. "Wait right here a sec."

Before the night turned into a complete disaster, Jason dragged his brother back over to where Ryder was sitting. "Okay. Liam is going to apologize for his dumbass remark, right?"

Liam had the grace to turn red. "Yeah. I'm sorry, man. I didn't mean it the way it sounded. I guess I meant to say I'm not into guys."

"And you don't want them in you," Ryder shot back.

Jason cracked up. "Good one, Ryder."

Liam's lips twitched. "Am I allowed to laugh? 'Cause that was pretty fucking funny."

Ryder snickered. "Yup."

After staring at him hard, as if he was taking his measure, Liam smiled. "I like you, Ryder. Let's get a beer."

Crisis averted, Liam pulled Ryder over to the bar,

with Mark in tow. Jason breathed a sigh of relief. He spotted Emily entering the bar with a dark haired man Jason presumed was her husband and waved them over. "Hey, guys, come on over. Ryder's already here."

Emily introduced them to Connor, who draped his arm over her shoulders in the universal symbol of possessiveness. Couldn't blame the guy. If Jason had a woman like her, he'd want everyone to know it too. Gorgeous, nice, and smart—a killer combo.

"Hey, Jason." Emily kissed his cheek, while Connor slapped his back, eyes on the bar and the platters of food.

"Oh man, are those nachos and tacos I spy with my little eye?" The man sounded like he might cry from happiness. "And there's fresh guac. I'm in heaven. I'll send your drink over, Em." He kissed his wife and headed over to the food, giving Ryder a fist bump as he passed.

Emily's met Jason's amused gaze and groaned with mock despair. "He can't help himself. His stomach is like the black void." She waved to Ryder, who winked at her but continued talking to Liam and Mark.

"Who are those guys Ryder's talking to? One of them looks familiar." She accepted a Sea Breeze from the bartender with a wide smile. John blinked slowly as he fell under her spell, returning her smile with one of his rarely given grins. Emily was like that, Jason noticed, one of those exceptional people whose presence brought out the best in others around her.

"The tall one with the blue sweater is my brother Liam. He was at the construction site. Next to him is my brother Mark. He's the youngest. Our friend John behind the bar, he owns the place."

She looked over her shoulder at John and waved. Startled, he gave her a hesitant smile back. Jason had never seen John react to any woman before. Perhaps she could bring him out of his self-imposed shell. Connor, holding a full plate and munching on a taco, joined Jason's brothers and Ryder and as they all laughed at some joke Liam told, Jason was happy to see the earlier fiasco hadn't spiraled out of control. As to how he'd physically reacted to Ryder before, he chalked it up to mere curiosity. Perfectly normal.

"Do you have any other family, Jason?" Emily sipped her drink and nibbled on a slider. "Oh, these are very good. You may never get rid of Connor."

"John's a great cook. He'll make a good husband one day. And to answer your question, yes, I have two sisters, Nicole and Jessica."

"And none of you are married. How about girl-friends?" She looked up at him. "You said you broke up with someone recently, but are you dating or involved with anyone yet?"

"You're full of questions, aren't you?" Jason huffed out a laugh. Why did he feel as though she was interviewing him for a position?

She smirked. "One of the benefits, or downsides depending on the way you look at it, of being married to a lawyer. Take your pick." She narrowed those pretty but sharp blue eyes at him. "You still didn't answer my question, though."

He nudged her arm. "Nope. Not involved with anyone. I'm not really looking."

"Probably 'cause no one would want you anyways." A sneering voice interrupted him.

Spinning around, he came face-to-face with Chloe. He hadn't seen her in the weeks since they'd broken up, and he hadn't missed her at all. "Hello, Chloe."

She stood before him in her barhopping uniform, now that he recognized it—black skinny jeans, tight tank top to emphasize her breasts, and killer heels. Dark curls bounced over her shoulders, and the eye makeup rivaled Lady Gaga's on a rough night. "Who's this, Jase, my replacement? I didn't think you were into skinny blondes."

God, how could he have gone out with her as long as he had? It was almost embarrassing to have to introduce her to his new friends.

"Hello, my name's Emily. Are you Jason's exgirlfriend?" Class act, that Emily, Jason noted.

Chloe's dismissive gaze flicked over Emily, up and down. "I broke up with him a few weeks ago, honey. Don't bother, though. He's not interested in getting married."

Jason was about to open his mouth when Connor came over and slipped his arm around Emily. "Who's this, sweetheart?"

FELICE STEVENS

With reluctance, Jason introduced Connor and Ryder. Chloe dismissed Emily with a sniff. "Huh. I figured you couldn't be his girlfriend. Jase is too boring and dull. Besides, he wouldn't go out with anyone so quick after me. We were together three years, ya know."

Jason's gut clenched. Had she really been such a bitch all the years they were together, and he'd failed to see it? He watched in fascination as Ryder approached his smirking ex-girlfriend, a glint of unholy amusement lighting up his bright blue eyes. The man was up to something.

"Well, hey, sweetheart. You're very beautiful, aren't you?" Ryder's gaze traveled up and down Chloe, and Jason watched as she preened and moved closer to him. "Jason must've been six fools to Sunday to let you go, huh?" No surprise Chloe would be on him like jelly over peanut butter. Ryder was an extremely good-looking man.

Her giggle, once cute, now grated like nails on a blackboard. "Thanks. How do you know him?" She jerked her thumb. Apparently he didn't even rate a name when she flirted with another man. Jason held in his laughter. What would she do when she found out she was flirting with a gay man?

Ryder leaned closer. "I'm sure Jason could never replace someone like you as a girlfriend." She moved closer to him until her breasts pushed up against his chest. Ryder continued to murmur into her willing ear.

Connor leaned over and whispered to Jason. "Are

you brave enough to play along with him?"

A worm of worry crept through him. "Why, what's he going to do?"

Connor shushed Emily's giggles to answer. "Ryder will take things to the extreme if you play along with him. He and I have done some pretty funny stuff to prove a point or to piss people off."

"I guess I'm game." To a degree, he thought warily, but it was too late to back out now.

Chloe's nails were doing the scratch and walk up Ryder's chest. She grabbed the top button of his shirt when Ryder closed his hand over hers. "Oh, honey, I don't think so."

A familiar pout tugged down her full, glossy lips. "Why not?" She dragged a long red nail over his hand. "We could go somewhere and discuss it."

"Wait for it," Connor muttered in his ear.

Jason braced himself for the unknown.

Ryder brushed her hands away. "Because, honey, I'm gay. And I have a hot boyfriend." He turned and pierced Jason with those bright blue eyes. "Right, Jase?"

What the fuck?

"Are you willing to play along?" Emily's breathy voice touched him like a caress, but he was more drawn to the man now standing in front of him. And with everyone around him, his brothers and friends, people from the neighborhood, he stepped up to Ryder with no hesitation at all.

"Got that right."

Unashamedly, Ryder slid his arm around Jason's shoulder and pulled him close "Don't worry. I'm not going to kiss you. I wanted to shake the bitch up a bit." Ryder's mouth barely touched his ear, and they might not be kissing, but the trembling sensations in his body caused by the mere nearness of Ryder's lips left Jason dizzy with uncertainty and never-before-dreamed-of desire.

Chloe wasn't the only one shaken up, it seemed.

"Eww, Jase." Chloe took a step back. "What're you, like gay or something?"

Jason tensed, suspecting the next thing to come out of her mouth would be something stupid and homo-phobic. Liking Ryder as much as he did, he had no desire to jeopardize their budding friendship to spare Chole's feelings.

"Not that I owe you any explanations, but Ryder's a good friend. So keep that mouth of yours quiet and walk away if you're going to say something offensive or obnoxious."

"Whatever." She tossed her curls and licked her lips. "I mean it's not like I'd be surprised or anything if you were, 'cause now I'm with a real man, and he knows how to keep me satisfied." She drew a long red fingertip down the valley between her breasts.

"Glad to hear." If Chloe thought her words hurt him, or that he missed the feel of her body next to him at night, she'd be dead wrong. They might have been together for years, but since their split, she'd barely crossed his mind. If she stood naked before him now she couldn't be any less enticing.

Jason turned his back and with Ryder by his side returned to the bar and the beer John had waiting for him. Emily and Connor joined them as well.

"No offense, man, but what the hell were you doing with someone like that?" Connor waved a taco chip around as he spoke.

Embarrassed, Jason took a drink, forestalling his answer. While he liked Connor and Emily, it was Ryder, strangely enough, to whom he directed his explanation. Jason couldn't get rid of the feeling of Ryder's lips touching his skin or the strength of his arm around his shoulders.

"Uhh, we met young and sort of fell into dating each other. It became a habit, I guess."

"A bad one, from the looks of it." Ryder slouched by the bar and dug a chip into some salsa. "For me, I prefer my own company and my dog's, rather than being with someone I don't enjoy spending time with."

"You spend too much time alone, though, Ry." Emily's gaze traveled between him and Ryder. "Maybe you and Jason could go running together. You could take the dogs."

"Em—" Ryder began, but Jason, before he could stop himself, cut Ryder off.

"That sounds like a great idea. I'm into it."

Emily's smile beamed triumphantly, while Connor stared at him, his sharp eyes narrowed in thought. But for Jason, the only person whose opinion mattered was Ryder's.

"What do you say, Ryder?"

Ryder shrugged. "Sure. I'd love the company."

Chapter Seven

"WANT A WATER or a beer?" Ryder let Pearl off her leash and she scrambled to the kitchen, Trouper in her wake. He could hear the noisy slurping of the dogs as they each took a well-deserved drink. Before they left for their run, he and Jason had put out a bowl of water and food for Trouper so he wouldn't have to share.

"I'll take a beer, thanks. All this running we've been doing helps me keep in shape better than lifting weights ever did."

Jason ran a hand down his tightly muscled abdomen and Ryder swallowed hard, imagining Jason's body under him...on top of him. He opened the refrigerator, took out two bottles and handed one to Jason without commenting.

"Liam and I always thought building muscle was the best, but I seriously lacked in my cardio." Jason uncapped the bottle and took a healthy swallow. Ryder watched Jason's throat move and wanted to lick the strong cords of his neck. Damn. He turned his back and wrenched off his own cap and gulped down the beer without tasting.

For the past week, since that uncomfortable evening at the bar where he'd met Jason's ex-girlfriend and played that game on her, Jason had joined him on his nightly run with Pearl. He and Trouper would meet up with Ryder and Pearl at the rescue, then either drive to the Brooklyn waterfront and run through Brooklyn Bridge Park, or head to the city and run along the path by the West Side Highway. Afterwards, they'd pick up either a pizza or some other take out and go hang out at Ryder's apartment to watch basketball or hockey. Ryder convinced himself he was using this time to make sure Jason qualified as a good match for the rescued puppy, ignoring how much he truly enjoyed spending the time with Jason.

"You're fine; I don't think you have to worry."

"Well, I like keeping in shape and the running is helping. Maybe when the weather gets better you'll come further into Brooklyn and we can hit the trails in Prospect Park."

The fact that Jason thought that far ahead should have comforted Ryder, but instead he began to doubt himself. While he loved Connor as a brother, his first responsibility was to Emily and their marriage, not to Ryder's broken heart. And one could never have enough friends. But Jason was that deadly combination of looks, intelligence and kindness, all wrapped up in a gorgeous package, and Ryder couldn't help his attraction.

"Yeah, sounds great." He pointed to the bags Jason carried which held the eggplant and chicken cutlet parm heroes they'd picked up on their walk back to his apartment. "But if we keep eating like this after running, we're gonna need to do this forever, 'cause we're defeating our purpose."

Jason put the food on the coffee table and flopped down on the sofa. "I'm fine with that. With Liam hot on the dating scene and John busy with the bar, I've sort of lost my usual crew." His laughter sounded a bit uncertain. "And to be honest, I'm not that into hanging out at clubs and chatting up women anymore. I never was too much, but after spending time with Connor and Emily, it would be nice to have what they have, y'know?" He picked up the remote and turned on the game.

Ryder joined him in the living room but chose the club chair off to the side and propped his legs up on the coffee table. He didn't want to sit too close to Jason. "Yeah, but I don't expect to find that. What those two have is something special; I don't think I've ever seen two people so perfect for one another."

The game forgotten, Jason held his gaze with those mesmerizing eyes. "Sounds like you haven't found the right person."

There went that flip of his heart again and Ryder, knowing how easily he could fall for Jason and how easily it would ruin the potential for a lasting friendship, kept his voice as nonchalant as possible.

"Yeah, maybe. But the last thing I'm looking for is a relationship. I have too much personal stuff going on and that takes precedence."

"Oh, yeah? Anything I can help with?"

"Nah." Ryder had little desire to get into his family dynamic and ruin the evening. "Let's eat before the food gets cold and the dogs decide to help themselves." He pointed to Pearl who sat at his feet with a hopeful gleam in her eyes. "I found this one helping herself to my Chinese take out the other night." He scratched her chin and she licked his hand. Ryder had no idea what he'd do if he didn't have his dog. Since he rescued her, Pearl had become his late-night confidante and his confessor. It was in her willing ear that he could whisper his fears of being alone, and his attraction to Jason. Best of all she loved him unconditionally. Sometimes he wondered who had rescued whom.

Jason slid the sandwiches out of the bag and tossed him his. They sat in companionable silence, occasionally slipping Trouper and Pearl bits of food. When they'd finished, Ryder stood to collect the garbage.

"Here, give me your stuff and I'll toss it." Ryder held out his hand and Jason pointed to the seat next to him.

"Can you sit for a second? I feel like we need to clear the air about something."

His heart racing, Ryder joined him but sat a safe distance away. Acutely aware of Jason's overwhelming physical presence from the first time they met, Ryder struggled hard to not fall for him—no more straight guys looking for a secret gay fling. Instead, he forced a smile.

"What's up?"

"Well, at the bar when you met my ex and you kind of led her on that the two of us were in some kind of relationship—"

"Did that bother you?" His heart plummeted. "I'm sorry."

"No, not at all." Jason ran his hand through his hair. "I really don't give a shit what Chloe thinks. But ever since then you've seemed kind of, I don't know, off? And *that* bothers me."

Because I don't want you to know how I feel. Like I want to kiss you every time I see you but know I can't.

"I thought it would be fun to see her reaction."

"And it was. It didn't bother me in the least. But see, I've never had any gay friends so I don't want to do or say anything wrong that might offend you." Jason's dark look searched his face and Ryder schooled his expression to remain neutral. "Like that first time at the construction site. I know you got pissed at me and we started out on the wrong foot. I don't want to end back up in that place again."

When Jason had started talking, for a crazy minute Ryder had hoped Jason might say that he was bisexual and had feelings for him. He should have known better. Jason had never given him any indication he was anything other than what he looked like: a good-looking, nice straight guy. This must be Jason's way of letting Ryder know that even though he approved of the game they played that's as far as it went. He wouldn't ever be interested in Ryder as anything but a friend.

"No problem. I'm not pissed at you and like I said, I like having the human company to go running. Pearl is great, but sometimes you need someone to actually answer the questions you're asking, you know?"

JASON UNDERSTOOD EXACTLY what Ryder meant. "Yeah. And I like running outside, even though it's cold. Makes me feel more alive."

Ryder smiled but said nothing as he gathered up the rest of their trash to take back into the kitchen. Jason watched him from beneath lowered lashes while gnawing at his lower lip. He'd never been the best at expressing himself, and had almost bungled that conversation.

Sighing, he turned back to the television, but didn't pay attention to the screen. How could he talk to Ryder when he didn't even understand what was going on himself? Being with Ryder and spending so much time with him brought Jason back, ten years earlier, to a place he'd never planned to revisit. He'd managed to persuade himself that night had been nothing more than a little too much alcohol and college-boy hormones. But now? Jason didn't need a drop of alcohol to notice Ryder's blue eyes sparkling in the sun, or the play of muscles in his strong thighs as they ran together.

What was his excuse now, at twenty-eight?

"Idiot," he mumbled.

"What did I do?" Re-entering the living room, Ryder bumped his foot and tossed him a bag of chips. "Look, I even got your favorite kind—sour cream and onion." He shuddered. "I can't believe you eat that crap. It's full of chemicals."

"It's what keeps me young and well preserved." He tore open the bag and grabbed a few chips, then stuffed them in his mouth. Anything to keep from staring at Ryder. What the hell was happening to him? Every nerve ending in his body sizzled with awareness. Like that first time he saw Ryder at the construction site, Jason's heart pounded and his breath caught in his throat.

Did Ryder suspect? Doubtful, for on the outside Jason appeared his usual happy go lucky self, while inside his head confusion reigned. Spending so much time with Ryder left Jason a conflicting mess of emotions he'd never anticipated or experienced and he had no idea what to do.

"You've gotten awfully quiet. Everything okay?" Ryder's voice brought him back to awareness.

"Uh, yeah, sorry. I was thinking about something."

Deliberately ignoring Ryder's skeptical look, Jason continued to stuff the chips into his mouth. What should he do, tell him? And tell him what? That even when Jason was home, he wondered what Ryder was doing? That he'd never found anyone so easy to talk to about his life, his fears and dreams? That his smile was beautiful, yet Jason still saw the dark sadness lingering in his eyes? Fuck.

What the hell was he supposed to think about that?

And more importantly, what should he do about it?

The Nets scored and he made a half-hearted attempt to act interested, while he continued to wrestle with his thoughts. He hadn't been out on a date with a woman since he and Chloe broke up and, Jason realized staring unseeing at the television, he had no desire to meet anyone either. Each time Liam attempted to set him up, or double date, Jason came up with a litany of excuses as to why he couldn't go. Too tired from work, numbers to go over, or any host of other reasons that had Liam mumbling about Jason being an old man and a hermit.

But the real reason? To himself Jason confessed he'd rather be here, with Ryder and the dogs, than at a bar or a club. Jason didn't want to be with a woman, or any other man. Only Ryder. He crumpled the empty bag of chips and tossed it aside.

Sooner or later, he'd have to capitulate and go out with one of the women, if for no other reason than to keep Liam from suspecting something else was afoot. Jason could hardly wrap his own head around it; he couldn't imagine talking to Liam about his conflicted sexuality. Afraid? Scared shitless.

"If you'd rather go home, I understand. Sometimes I'm not fit for human company myself and need to be alone."

"No. I—I don't want to be alone." How could he could spend an entire day surrounded by people and still be lonesome, except when he was with Ryder? Besides he'd only go home and think about Ryder. A never ending dilemma of anxiety.

"Sorry. I'm being a lousy friend, I know." Jason searched for something, anything to stop thinking about Ryder as anything *but* a friend. His gaze lit on the video game console and the stack of games.

"The Nets are losing. Let's play." He snatched up a controller and tossed one to Ryder. "I used to crush Liam at this."

"Not me." Ryder swung his legs down from the coffee table and turned on the game player with the remote. "Prepare for your ultimate defeat."

Jason wondered if he'd already lost the war inside his head.

Chapter Eight

THE BEST THING in Ryder's life was that he and Landon, in addition to spending every Wednesday evening together for their brothers' night, managed to circumvent the no-texting-or-calling moratorium set up by their mother, as Ryder got him a pre-paid phone. Month-to-month and untraceable, it proved the perfect solution to their problem. He'd also given Landon a key to his apartment, and there was nothing he liked better than coming home to the television blaring and Landon stretched out on the sofa with Pearl, a litter of junk-food bags surrounding him.

Jason's adoption of Trouper had also gone smoothly, and the puppy settled down as king of the house. Before he'd brought the dog home, Jason had bought out the pet store's supply of chew toys and treats. That dog was one lucky fellow.

With or without Emily and Connor, Ryder had begun to hang out at Drummer's after his day had finished. It had a good, homey feel to it with classic rock purring out of the speakers and excellent, never-ending bar food. He liked John, who never pressed him for inane conversation if he saw Ryder had a bad day; John would nod and pass him a beer with no questions asked and an understanding smile. Jason's brothers were fine, although the younger one, Mark, liked to try and psychoanalyze him a bit too much, and he'd already learned to ignore Liam's less than enlightened remarks about current events.

But mostly he liked hanging out with Jason. The times Jason didn't join him on his run, Ryder suspected he had a date. It didn't surprise him. Jason was a normal guy, and Ryder figured he wasn't sitting at home by himself every night. What did surprise him was how much the thought of Jason out on a date bothered him. He tamped down the irrational stab of jealousy that centered in his chest on those nights and went for an extra-long run with Pearl instead. They were friends, nothing more, and Ryder was determined not to fall for a straight guy.

And all that was picture-perfect until he came home one night, anxious to see Landon, planning his ultimate defeat at *Call of Duty*, and the apartment was dark. Dropping his backpack, he heard Pearl's nails clicking in the wooden floor.

"Where is he, girl? What happened?"

He flipped on the light, and entered the living room, spying the note on the coffee table. His blood turned to ice as he recognized his mother's elegant, precise penmanship.

Keep away from my son.

Devastated, Ryder slumped to the floor, hugging Pearl to his chest. In the back of his mind he knew the good times spent with his brother had all been an illusion. Stupidly, he'd fooled himself into believing one day he'd be able to go home again and be accepted with loving arms. He envied the gay men and women he'd seen interviewed on the television, talking about how their families accepted them for who they were, loved them no matter what. He'd never know that pleasure.

The times he'd been allowed to spend with Landon were even more precious to him, now that they were gone. Tears fell unchecked on Pearl's fur as he cried without shame, knowing he'd lost a part of his heart and his soul.

"What am I going to do, girl? It hurts so bad." He almost couldn't catch his breath. His cell phone rang, but he let it go to voicemail. The one person he wanted to talk to was now out of his reach. It rang again, and he didn't bother to check; he turned off the ringer.

Ryder lay down on the sofa. A thought came to him that if Landon still had his phone, he'd be able to text him. With raised hopes, he checked his phone, only to see three missed calls from Connor and Emily's number. He turned the ringer back on but didn't bother returning the calls. Much as he loved his friends, he couldn't pick himself up to call them back.

He must've dozed off, because the next thing he knew, Emily was kneeling beside him, shaking him.

"Ryder, sweetie, are you all right?" A hazy fog hung over his eyes, and he blinked hard to clear his vision. He should've known Connor and Emily would come to check on him. They'd swapped keys years ago in case of an emergency.

"Wh-what's going on? What time is it?" Ryder struggled up on his elbows and squinted at his watch. "Shit." Remembering Landon was no longer going to be there, he broke down in tears. "He's gone, guys. She took him away, and she won't ever let him come back."

After a long talk and some soul-searching, Connor persuaded him to go out to Drummers, even though he felt like crap. "Come on, man. The game is on, and John said he was doing wings five different ways." Though Connor teased, his concern was evident.

"Why don't you and Em go by yourselves? You don't need me. I'm in no mood to socialize." He rolled over and closed his eyes. Every text he'd sent Landon had been returned as undeliverable. His mother must've discovered the phone and disabled it somehow.

"Ryder, please. You can't sit here by yourself. Maybe if we all put our heads together, we can come up with another way you and Landon can see each other." Emily's sympathetic face hurt his heart. He knew she grieved over his mother's unfair treatment of him. She put her hand on his shoulder, comforting him with her warm presence. She had a point.

He pulled himself up and shrugged. "Okay, but don't expect me to be great company."

Connor smirked. "I'm going for the wings, man. John makes some awesome sauce."

Shaking his head, Ryder got out of bed to shower and change. Only Connor could put a smile on his face. And Jason. Inexplicably his body tightened and his blood raced. He missed Jason's company. Once dressed, he took Pearl out for a walk and fed her, giving her one last scratch behind the ears before leaving, wondering how he could be so miserable about Landon, yet at the same time, excited to see Jason again.

Connor found a parking spot right outside the bar. He cackled with glee. "A perfect night is when you find a spot right away." He grabbed Emily's hand. "Come on, babe. Ry, let's rock and roll. The wings, they are awaiting."

One would think the man hadn't eaten in a week the way he carried on about the food. They entered the bar, and Ryder's spirits were lifted immediately by the warm and raucous welcome they all received. Connor naturally made a beeline for the much-discussed wings. Emily, who had a personal champion in John, kissed the blushing bar owner hello first, then greeted their other friends.

"Ry, over here." Ryder turned to see Jason beckoning him over. He shouldered his way through a knot of people, greeting the now familiar faces he'd been hanging with for several months. Glad that Emily and Connor had forced him to come, he strengthened his resolve to find a way to see his brother again. Tonight he'd try to enjoy himself.

"Hey, dude, what's up? How's Troup?" Ryder hadn't seen the little guy in a few days and missed his puppyish exuberance. The little mutt never failed to bring a smile to everyone's face with his antics.

A smile broke across Jason's face. "Ahh, he's great. I took him over to my parents' house yesterday, and the girls fell in love with him. He's a real charmer." He plunked himself down at a table, indicating Ryder should join him. "I'm gonna take him over there some mornings when I know I'll be late on the job."

"You could bring him to my apartment if you want, and he could hang out with Pearl," said Ryder, keeping his voice casual. "Of course that's if you're still doing a job close by, like you are now." Mallory Bros. Construction had scored a condo conversion on the Lower East Side of Manhattan, so he knew Jason was traveling into the city every day. "I could give you an extra key and let Clarence know to let you up, if I'm not home."

Jason seemed uncertain. "I don't want to put you out or anything."

Ryder shrugged. "It's cool. No big deal. Emily and Connor have keys in case I'm ever stuck somewhere and Pearl needs to be taken care of."

"Okay, thanks." Jason smiled at him. "How about a beer?"

Ryder agreed, and Jason left for the bar to get their drinks. Emily slid into his vacated seat.

"Hey, baby." He squeezed her fingers. "I have to

thank you for forcing me to come out tonight. You were right."

A smile lit up her face. "I'm glad, sweetie."

He and Emily sat quietly for a moment before she spoke. "You really like Jason, don't you, Ry?"

"He's become a great friend. Sure, I like him."

Lowering her voice, she touched his hand. "I see how your eyes follow him across the room. You look wounded, because you think happiness is impossible for you. Since you guys started hanging out, you're the happiest you've been in years. It's more than friendship for you, isn't it?"

Ryder opened his mouth, then snapped it close. Jason leaned against the bar to talk to John and flirted with a pretty redhead who waited to pay for her drink. The overhead lighting cast his face in half-shadows, outlining the planes of his cheek and jaw. His dark, curling hair brushed his neck, touching the collar of his shirt. Faded jeans hugged his muscular legs, and Ryder eyed the curve of his ass as he propped his leg up on a stool, bending down to listen to the woman. It shouldn't surprise or upset him to see Jason with a woman, but the heart never followed the direct instruction from the brain. It was like a child turning his back on his elder and wiser parents, declaring he would do what he wanted and no one could stop him.

"No." He shook his head, more determined than ever to shield himself from the pain falling for a man like Jason would bring to his heart. It was as inevitable as the wind and as harsh as the brightness of the sun on a crisp winter's day. And in the end, he'd be left once again, devastated and alone.

Emily's wise eyes studied him for a heartbeat. "The road leading to happiness is never the straightest one. The obstacles and curves it throws in our way make us wiser and stronger." Her warm hand held his, fingers curling around his palm to give his hand a comforting squeeze. "You will find happiness, sweetie. You're at a curve right now and need to pick a path."

"Emily, you're talking in riddles. You sound like one of those New Age gurus." Jason returned with the beer, along with a plateful of food for them. "Thanks, man."

Under lowered lashes, he studied Jason's profile. The blunt, strong hands of the man fascinated him. He'd seen those strong fingers stroke his dog with tender care, as well as haul heavy Sheetrock panels. Ryder's mood darkened as he imagined those same powerful hands gripping the headboard above his bed as Jason, naked, sweaty, and calling out his name, pounded into him. Smothering a frustrated curse, he shoved a chicken wing into his mouth and chewed.

Emily excused herself after shooting him a frustrated glare and returned to Connor's side.

Ryder drank down his beer, then casually asked, "So, did you get her number?"

"Nah." Jason shrugged and drank his beer. "Not my type."

Surprised, Ryder said nothing, choosing to drink his

beer and eat the wings and sliders Jason had piled on his plate rather than talk. Idly he listened to the TV, which was tuned to one of the music channels. All at once he froze, hearing a familiar voice, then stared in disbelief at the screen, watching an interview of music's up-and-coming producers.

Matt. His former lover. The bottle of beer slipped from his nerveless fingers to crash on the floor. "Shit."

Jason jumped out of his seat. "Ryder, are you okay? What's the matter?"

Ryder didn't answer. How could this be? Matt, looking healthy and happy without a care in the world, beamed out at him from the screen "Shh." He waved his hand for Jason to be quiet. "Let me listen to this." The interviewer posed a question concerning Matt's rise in the industry within the past year.

Staring at the face of the man he'd once loved, Ryder's heart broke open all over again as he waited for the answer to the question.

"I was in a bad relationship for a long time. When I hit rock bottom from all the drugs, I knew I had to change my life. I changed my diet, my mind-set on life, and met my girlfriend. With her love and help, I won my battle. We married last month, and I've never been happier."

Feeling a hand on his shoulder, Ryder jerked his concentration from the screen and met Connor's sympathetic eyes. Many a night he'd spent with Connor, getting drunk after he and Matt broke up. That was the great thing about his friend. No judgment, simply a shoulder to cry on and someone to drink with, who kept the beer coming. Someone who knew him as well as he knew himself.

"How could he say that load of crap? Bad relationship? The man was high all the time. I begged him to get help every single fucking day, but he brushed me off." He reached for Connor's beer and downed what was left in the bottle. "I need to get drunk. This has been one hell of a day."

He pushed himself away from the table and headed toward the bar, Connor following. "Ry, slow down."

Was he kidding? "John, let me have a beer, and keep 'em coming." After downing half the bottle, Ryder placed it back on the bar and faced his friend, arms folded. "What are you gonna tell me? That it was a long time ago and I should be over it by now? That I'm better off without him?"

"If we're being honest, aren't you?"

Perversely, he wanted to pick a fight with Connor, who was only trying to help. But he didn't want to be rational and calm. He wanted to scream, yell, and break something.

"So time heals all wounds?" The bitterness in his voice disgusted him. How pathetic he sounded. Shouldn't he have gotten over Matt by now? But it wasn't Matt, rather it was the realization that his love had never been returned or appreciated. Why did he allow himself to be used by men? He picked up the beer and finished it, holding out his hand for the next one. A decidedly unsteady hand, he noticed.

"It does, if you let it."

"You know, my heart doesn't have a use-by date. There's no expiration for my feelings when you can say time's up, you've mourned long enough." Another drink and another half bottle gone. He was getting good at this. Hazy from the beers, he swayed, then braced himself by leaning on the bar.

"Hey, Ry, look at me." Connor patted his cheek, and Ryder met his friend's unflinching, honest green eyes. "You know you're like my brother, right?"

Choked up, he could only nod.

"So don't punch me when I tell you to grow a pair of balls and move on. That shithead used you for a year, and he's gotten on with his life. He's had no trouble forgetting you, so find someone else and forget him." Connor gave him a thin smile. "You know they say living well is the best revenge."

Emily tugged on Connor's sleeve. "Babe, I don't feel so good. I need to go home." She gave him an apologetic smile. "I'm sorry; it's been a really long day."

"Don't apologize. Go ahead, you and Connor. I'm hanging for a while." Ryder slumped against the bar and toyed with his beer bottle. Jason came to stand by his side.

"I can take you home, Ry." Jason's solid presence sent out danger signals to his already overstimulated senses.

"I can grab a cab. 'S all right." Desperate to keep his

distance from the man who'd invaded his thoughts but would never be interested, he fought to stand straight and failed miserably.

"Cool it, man. Sit and chill for a while." Jason pointed to John. "Give him water."

His mouth tightened with anger. Everyone believed they knew what was best for him, like he was some kind of kid. Ryder's breath caught as Jason's arm draped over his shoulder.

"Shut up and drink your water. Then I'm taking you home."

Oh damn, he was so screwed.

Chapter Nine

RYDER REFUSED TO leave for another hour. He became testy when John tried to cut him off, but when the bar owner threatened to kick him out, Jason got Ryder to agree that for every beer, he'd drink a glass of water. At least there was another liquid other than alcohol going into the man's system. Jason also forced him to eat a few bites of a turkey sandwich.

"What happened? Why's he getting so trashed? It's not like him, from what we've seen over the past few months." Jason pulled Liam aside to a table away from the bar, and he filled him in on what he knew, that this guy Matt had been Ryder's boyfriend and a drug addict. Now he was married to a woman, and in cleaning up his act, he blamed their relationship for his troubles.

"I guess Ryder feels lied to, 'cause he thought they had a serious relationship. He'd been in love with the guy for a year." Jason shrugged. "It's gotta hurt to hear this guy say their relationship was bad and the reason he became hooked on drugs."

Liam glanced over at a dejected Ryder, still sitting at

the bar, shoulders slumped. "That's seriously fucked up, man. I mean, I've never known anyone who was gay, but Ryder's cool."

Mark, who'd also been listening, while at the same time keeping an eye on Ryder, coughed out a laugh. "Not that I don't blame you for wanting to smash that bastard in the face, but how would you know if someone was gay unless they told you? And the way people like you react, why would they tell you when there is still so much prejudice?" Uncomfortable, Jason felt the weight of his younger brother's provocative question. "Do you feel uncomfortable being friends with a gay guy, Jason? Like people might think you were gay too?"

There was something behind Mark's interrogation, Jason decided, but he couldn't put his finger on it. Being the psych student that he was, Mark never said anything that didn't have meaning behind it. Jason didn't have the time or inclination to figure out his complicated feelings for Ryder—it was almost one in the morning, and he needed to get Ryder home.

He jumped up from his seat and stretched out a huge yawn. "That's stupid. Like I'm gay by association. Besides, I don't give a shit what people think of me, and I don't care who Ryder sleeps with. If they think I'm gay because of my friends, fuck 'em." He headed toward the bar. "I'll catch up with you guys tomorrow. I promised Connor I'd take Ryder home."

He slipped into the seat next to Ryder, who failed to

acknowledge him. Trying to lighten the mood and cheer him up, Jason bumped shoulders with him. "C'mon, Ry, let's go. It's getting late, and I'm sure you want to go home and sleep it off."

Ryder faced him, his eyes so full of pain Jason flinched. "I was a good guy, Jase, y'know? I thought he loved me; he tole me so. Now I don't have him, don't have my brother, and my parents don' want me." He knocked back his glass of water, then squinted into it. "Even John doesn't like me anymore 'cause he won' give me another drink. Says I'm drunk when I'm not."

Ryder leaned over, almost toppling into his lap. Jason grabbed him around the waist before he fell on the floor, and held him upright. "C'mon, buddy, let's get you up and outta here. Time to go home." Still holding on to his swaying body, Jason tried but couldn't ignore the firm play of muscles underneath Ryder's shirt and the light, clean scent he always carried on his skin.

"Hoo-kay, boss. Le's go." He pulled away, walking unsteadily toward the door. Jason called out a good-bye to everyone and hurried after Ryder.

Ryder stood outside, blinking and peering down the street. Jason took his arm. "This way, Ry. Come on." Jason led Ryder to his truck and helped him inside. After buckling him into the seat, Jason stood and observed him for a moment. Ryder lay back against the headrest, eyes shut, that amazing hair spread out behind him. His breath came out in soft puffs. All his earlier pain seemed to have been wiped clean from his face, leaving him looking young and vulnerable.

With shaking fingers, Jason reached over, poised to touch Ryder's face. Realizing he stood in the public street, he lurched away from him and slammed the door shut. Jesus, what the hell was he thinking? Ryder lay there drunk and upset, and all he thought about was himself. Jason slid into the driver's seat and opened the windows, allowing the crisp night air to flow into the truck. That plus the Stones singing "Satisfaction" from the car stereo brought forth evidence of life from his seemingly dead-drunk passenger.

"Mmm. Love this song. Story of my life." Eyes still closed, but looking less white and strained, Ryder smiled faintly. "How much longer before we get to my apartment?"

Jason glanced at the clock on the dashboard. "Hmm, at least twenty minutes."

"Wake me when we get there, 'kay?" Jason froze as the top of Ryder's head leaned on his shoulder, brushing his chin. A warm breath sighed into his chest as Ryder settled into him, making himself comfortable for the ride back into the city.

Half an hour later, Jason pulled up in front of Ryder's building. He put a tentative hand on Ryder's head, smoothing down the thick silken strands of hair between his fingers. He wriggled out, leaving Ryder sleeping, and approached the doorman.

"I have to help Mr. Daniels upstairs. Is there anyone who can park my truck for me?"

"Certainly, sir." The doorman who'd previously been introduced as Clarence picked up a house phone and spoke quietly into it. Within moments a young man wearing a porter's uniform appeared.

Perhaps he was used to tenants coming home in less than stable condition, as Clarence handled the situation with brisk efficiency. "Mr. Mallory, if you give Shane here your keys, he'll park the truck while you take Mr. Daniels upstairs. I'll have your keys waiting for you when you return."

After thanking the doorman, and with Shane's assistance, Jason helped Ryder out of the truck. He'd woken up, thank God, so he could walk on his own two feet, although he was unsteady and uncommunicative. Jason allowed the porter to help him until he got to the elevator.

"I'll take it from here, thanks." He gave the guy five bucks as a thank-you for his effort. "I'll be down later for the truck. Clarence said you'd leave the keys at the front desk."

The young porter smiled. "I will. Thank you, sir. Please tell Mr. Daniels I walked his dog tonight and fed her earlier." He held the elevator door open for them. "Good night, sir."

Jason wished him good night and, with his arm still around Ryder's waist, helped Ryder into the elevator and punched the button for the sixteenth floor. Ryder said nothing, merely leaned against the wall. The elevator settled, and the door opened.

"Come on, we're here." Jason touched Ryder's shoulder, and his eyes opened.

"Hey." Ryder cleared his throat. "You can go home. I can make it from here."

Jason pushed him out of the elevator before the doors closed on him. "Don't be an asshole. I'm coming inside with you."

Ryder yawned, then shuffled and wove his way down the hall. After two missed efforts, he fit the key into the lock, and they finally made it inside the apartment. Pearl met them at the door, whining and yelping. Ryder mumbled about taking a piss as Jason played with Pearl and gave her fresh water.

When he looked into Ryder's bedroom, he saw the guy lying across his king-size bed, unmoving. Ryder hadn't bothered to take off his pants, socks, or shoes, and had even kept his jacket on.

Exasperated, Jason stalked over to him. "Come on, man, get undressed." First he took off his own jacket, then removed Ryder's. He pulled off Ryder's sneakers and socks and was debating whether or not to remove anything further, when the phone rang. Ryder lay unmoving on the bed, seemingly passed out cold.

The phone continued to buzz. Late-night phone calls were never a good thing. As his mother said, *"Nothing good happens after midnight on the road or on the phone."* With some trepidation, he picked it up.

"Hello?"

He heard a quick intake of breath, then a voice that

sounded more whisper than speech. "Ryder? Is that you?"

"No, it's Jason. I'm a friend." He sat down on the edge of the bed. Who could this be? Maybe Ryder had a boyfriend. He really didn't know anything about the guy's personal life.

"He never mentioned you before. How long have you known each other?"

Jason suppressed a smile. This guy, whoever he was, sounded like a nosy mother rather than a jealous boyfriend. "I adopted a dog from the rescue, and he, Connor, and Emily hang out at my friend's bar."

"Oh, yeah, he told me about that."

He heard whispering in the background, and Jason had the distinct impression that whoever this was, he was trying to hide the conversation. "Who are you?" Jason glanced over at Ryder, lying curled on the bed, muttering to himself.

"I'm his brother, Landon. I-I wanted to speak to him. We haven't talked in a long time."

Jason's heart broke for the kid. He couldn't imagine not being able to talk to his brothers or see his family. "Listen, Landon, he's asleep now. He had a little too much to drink, so I drove him home. Is there any way he can reach you?"

"No. I snuck away with my friend's phone, but he's gotta leave and needs it back. I thought..." His voice dwindled away, the disappointment evident.

Oh hell. Poor kid. Jason wished he could help him

and Ryder. An idea suddenly clicked in his mind. "Hey, Landon, Ryder told me you're interested in architecture and design, right?" He and Ryder had talked a lot about Landon; Jason even knew where the kid went to school.

"Yeah, so? I gotta go in a sec." Now Landon sounded like a normal impatient seventeen-year-old.

"Meet me at the coffee shop on the corner at Seventy-Third and Second across from your school, tomorrow at four. I have an idea for you and Ryder." Jason had no idea why he needed to involve himself in this situation, but after seeing how desperately unhappy his friend looked tonight, and now hearing how miserable this poor kid sounded, he wanted to do something to help.

"What? Okay, I gotta go. Sure."

In the background Jason heard someone yelling, "Give it to me, Daniels. Let's go." The phone went dead.

Jason dropped the phone on the bed. His idea had merit, and he knew he could make it work. Closing his eyes for a moment, he lay back on the pillow.

❧ ❧ ❧ ❧ ❧

DESIRE FLOODED THROUGH Jason as, in a light doze, he curled himself around the warm body lying next to him. Instead of the soft curves of a woman, he hugged the bulk of well-developed shoulders and biceps. As he slowly awakened, the dim light filtering in through the half-opened shade revealed he was in Ryder's bed. He must have fallen asleep after speaking with Landon.

Ryder lay, for want of a better word, cuddled in his arms. Their bodies pressed into each other, chest to chest, hip to hip. The heaviness of Ryder's erection pushed against his own alarming hardness. In the presence of glaring daylight and normal behavior, he would have jumped away. But here, in the sanctuary of this bed, it all seemed so right. Like where he was supposed to be.

As if watching his body from above, Jason trailed his hand down Ryder's arm and caressed its way up the strong planes of his sculpted chest. It traced the jut of Ryder's cheekbones, then cupped his bristly jaw. He'd have thought the stubble of hair on the man's face would be off-putting, yet inexplicably, his lips drew nearer, coming to rest at the tender spot beneath Ryder's ear. That clean, irresistible scent of him, plus a light tang of sweat, set his senses reeling. Without a second thought, he pressed a kiss to Ryder's jaw, then swept his tongue over the man's neck to taste him. Temptation. He needed more; he craved it. Jason sucked at the tender skin beneath Ryder's ear, the blood pounding in his head. This. This was what he'd wanted to do from the first time he saw Ryder. With only the two of them here now, Jason could finally admit it to himself.

"What? What's goin' on?" Ryder's breath wafted by his ear, but Jason chose to ignore the question, concentrating instead on savoring the man next to him. He hummed his pleasure as his tongue tickled Ryder's earlobe, then nipped and nuzzled the strong cords of

Ryder's neck. He was in foreign territory as to what would make a man feel good, so he kissed him as if were kissing his girlfriend.

Obviously his tongue and lips were in the right place, as Ryder moaned, rolling his hips, thrusting his cock directly against Jason's. Their bodies rocked together, humping and rubbing, as every nerve ending in Jason's body centered around the point of friction they created between them. Ryder, eyes wide open now, stared at him in total shock.

Jason forestalled any anticipated protest, hungry and needy to continue physical contact. It was something he'd never imagined, yet right now, he couldn't tear himself away from this bed and this man if a bomb exploded around them. He took Ryder's face between his hands and brushed their lips together. "Shh. Let me, please." The words came out almost as a groan as he nibbled and licked Ryder's neck. The intimate little noises coming from Ryder sent Jason's cock jerking painfully against his zipper. Jason slid on top of Ryder, shifting so that their cocks rubbed against each other through their jeans. Blood rushed through him, heat pooling in his groin. He bucked his hips against Ryder's in a desperate move to create more friction. Face-to-face, Jason could stare at the man who'd been invading his dreams for months.

To Jason's surprise, Ryder looked neither pleased nor happy, but rather confused and a bit fearful. Even in the dimly lit room, Jason could make out the disbelief on his face.

"Jase, what the fuck is going on? What are you do-ing here?" His sleep-roughened voice wary and tense.

"I have no fucking clue," he whispered, right before he bent down and brushed Ryder's lips, tasting Ryder's mouth for the first time. From his cock and his balls straight to his heart and his brain, a sizzle of electricity shot through Jason, and all he knew was this driving force—an insatiable desire to kiss and be kissed. But only by this man. Jason cupped Ryder's jaw, slanting his mouth across the other man's. The urge to claim him grew stronger, to suck and lick those firm lips, as he slipped his tongue inside Ryder's mouth. Their tongues tangled, and they tore at each other, teeth scraping and clashing as the rising hunger to possess overtook him. Their breathing grew harsh and labored in the silence of the bedroom as they devoured each other. Nothing in his life prepared him for Ryder's lean body writhing beneath him, as his probing tongue ravaged the inside of Jason's mouth.

These were not sweet kisses. No pretense it might be a woman if he closed his eyes. Lust took over, all-consuming and overpowering, like a conflagration, burning him up alive. Jason's insides liquefied, all that heat and blood pooling to his dick, which grew harder and thicker with each swipe of Ryder's tongue in his mouth. The pounding of his heart beat a matching tattoo to the throbbing in his dick and the pulsing of his blood. Body and soul, connected.

Jason pulled Ryder closer, tangling his fingers in Ryder's silky hair. The softness of the strands played in sharp contrast to the unfamiliar raspy stubble against Jason's chin and the driving, powerful thrusts of Ryder's tongue. Ryder was fucking his mouth and Jason couldn't help but moan with pleasure as their lips slid against one another. He shifted downwards, nipping and sucking at Ryder's neck, completely undone, helpless with want. He returned to the man's amazing mouth, almost snarling in his need and hunger, as Ryder clutched his back and shoulders in a grip so tight Jason was certain he'd sport some interesting bruises. Ryder shifted, sliding his legs from around Jason.

A strangled curse escaped Ryder's mouth, and Jason pulled back when he felt those hands pushing him away. Shaken and dazed by the overwhelming sensations zinging around inside him, he leaned on his elbow to stare down at his friend. In the shadowed light of the bedroom, Ryder's mouth gleamed, wet and passion-swollen while his eyes remained dark and unreadable.

Pale streaks of moonlight hit Ryder's grim-looking face. "I don't know what game you're playing, Jason, but it needs to stop."

Jason couldn't believe what he heard. Game? What the hell? That was not the reaction he expected. Shit, he didn't know what to expect. Holy hell, he'd kissed another guy, and his body's reaction was like *nothing* he'd ever anticipated. His balls still ached, his dick throbbed hard as a rock, and even now, when some

FELICE STEVENS

rational thought managed to return to his brain, he couldn't blame it on sleep; he still wanted to shove his tongue in Ryder's mouth and kiss him senseless, regaining that fire.

"I'm not playing a game. I admit, I didn't intend to sleep here. I closed my eyes for a moment." He fell back against the pillows, his hammering heart slowing down to its regular steady beat. "But as for the kiss, I'm not apologizing. I don't know why it happened, but neither of us looked like we had a problem with it."

"Look. Just 'cause I'm gay doesn't mean I sleep around. I'm selective in who I sleep with and monogamous when I have a relationship. But"—Ryder took a deep breath, staring hard into his face—"I'm not a freaking sideshow act, and I don't plan to be an experiment for you to practice whatever feelings you think you have or need to work out in your head. Trust me, you don't want this life."

Jason's face burned. What the hell had he done wrong? He'd never intended this to happen. "I didn't mean—"

"No, of course you didn't *mean* to do it. But I've had my heart stomped on enough already, and I don't need it anymore. Thanks for bringing me home; I appreciate it." He lay back down and closed his eyes.

Well, that was that. Jason knew when he was being dismissed. He gathered up his jacket and slipped it on. Before he left, he studied Ryder—his long, loose-limbed body curled like a question mark on the bed. He

114

hesitated, then blurted out, "I never meant to offend or hurt you. I hope you know that. And I hope we're still friends." When Ryder didn't answer, he left the bedroom, gave Pearl a pat good night, and closed the door silently behind him.

The city traffic gave him a chance for some introspection on the ride home. No matter what Ryder thought, Jason knew what happened between them in Ryder's bedroom had nothing to do with drunken curiosity and everything to do with reality. A reality Jason had been ignoring, and thwarting for years, if not his whole life. The attraction toward Ryder was more honest than any he'd felt for a woman he'd dated or slept with. And more fucking scary.

The scent of Ryder's aftershave clouded his senses; he could still feel Ryder's hot and hungry lips on his. Jason pounded the steering wheel in frustration, not at the taxi that cut him off, but at the thought he might've screwed up his friendship with Ryder, and the potential of something more. Something real. He needed to speak to Ryder to prove to him that what happened in the shadows of the night wasn't a dream to be forgotten in the clarity of next morning's sunlight.

It wasn't until he crossed the Brooklyn Bridge that he realized he'd forgotten to tell Ryder his brother had called and the plan he'd come up with.

Chapter Ten

RYDER DIDN'T NEED a clock to know it was morning. Warm beams of sunlight hit his face and back as he lay in bed with his eyes closed, waiting to die. The hammering inside his head was like a fist banging on a door—insistent, hard, and unceasing.

He opened his eyes and squinted at the clock. Shit. Ten o'clock. He never slept this late. From the side of his bed, Pearl gave him a disappointed look, as if she knew what had happened the night before and how fucked up his life had become in a heartbeat.

Luckily today he worked the afternoon shift at Rescue Me. It took a major effort to haul himself out of bed. After staggering a few steps he stood still, waiting for his head to clear. He bent down, bracing his hands on his thighs, and took some deep breaths. The slight nausea passed, but he needed a piss, to brush his teeth, and to get some major caffeine injected into his system right now.

When the banging didn't stop, he realized it *was* the door. Who the hell was here so early? He allowed himself the wild hope that it was Jason, and they could continue what they started last night, but he quickly dismissed that idea. First, he had no intention of ever allowing *that* mistake to happen again, although if his cock had anything to say about it, that wouldn't be the case, as it twitched and hardened at the thought of Jason. No fucking way. *Down, boy.*

He hoped his sour thoughts would deflate his hard-on as he went to see who the hell was bothering him.

"Hold on." When he looked through the peephole, the sight of Connor's cheery grin greeted him. Fantastic. Ryder yanked open the door and growled without even bothering to say hello. "You better have some fucking coffee with you if you're here so early."

"You know you love me." Connor bumped his shoulder and went straight for the kitchen. All negative thoughts about his best friend flew out the window when Ryder saw the two extra-large cups in his friend's hands and a paper bag under his arm. A warm vanilla smell hit his nose. Nothing, not even sex, would be better than coffee at this moment.

"You are correct when you bring me nectar of the gods." He accepted the cup from Connor and took a sip. He loved that instant when the heat of the warm coffee spilled through his body. "Ooh God, I do love you for this." He moaned and took another sip of the hot vanilla-flavored brew.

"Come over and give me a kiss, then." Connor grinned and made kissy noises. "I like a lot of tongue."

He laughed and took fresh bagels out of the bag, put them on plates, and got the cream cheese out of the refrigerator. "Em is working this morning, and I wanted to come by and see how you were doing after last night." He cocked his head, staring hard. "You okay? You have a funny look on your face."

Ryder's face heated, and he took another sip of coffee, more so that he didn't have to subject himself to Connor's probing gaze. The guy was an excellent lawyer, and his bullshit meter was almost always perfect in detecting when someone was lying.

"Yeah, I may have had a bit too much to drink last night, after seeing Matt."

"So I recall," said Connor dryly. "What a bastard." Connor swore, swiping his cream cheese onto his bagel. "It was a totally shitty, asshole thing to say."

Ryder shrugged. "Whatever." He finished his coffee and forced himself to eat some of his bagel. "I need to walk Pearl and take a shower. Stick around, and I'll go back with you to the office. I'm working this afternoon for a while anyway."

"Sure. I'll walk Pearl for you and feed her."

Connor's words came out garbled with the bagel in his mouth as he put on Pearl's leash. Twenty minutes later, when Ryder returned from his shower, Connor had finished rinsing off his plate, and Pearl had powered through half a bowl of food. Freshly showered and shaved, and feeling almost human, Ryder pulled on a blue sweater over a white button-down and his favorite comfortable jeans. There was something to be said for not having to put on a suit to go to work. He checked and saw the marks Jason had left from the night before. Warmth flooded through him at the recollection of Jason's mouth on his, but he pulled a scarf around his neck to hide the bruises—the last thing he needed was for Connor's sharp-eyed gaze to spot them.

"Thanks for walking her. Let me finish my breakfast, and then we can roll." He sat for a few minutes, chewing his bagel and sipping his coffee, while random bursts of memories from last night exploded in his mind. Still shocked at Jason's behavior, he allowed himself a brief fantasy of continuing where they'd left off, wondering what Jason looked like underneath his clothing.

He could sit here all day, dreaming of Jason's beautiful body and talented tongue. God, he needed to stop. After stuffing his keys and wallet in his pockets, he grabbed his coat from where it hung off the doorknob. "Let's stop somewhere first and pick up some lunch and bring it back to the office. The dogs are also running low on treats, and we need some snacks and stuff."

Connor eyed him. "You certainly look better than you did when I came in."

"I feel better too. Nothing like a good shower," he admitted. He pulled on his down jacket. "And coffee." He drained the last of his cup.

They left the apartment, Pearl in tow. He liked taking her with him to the office to show people what wonderful pets pit bulls could make if treated and trained correctly. Plus, she loved the attention from everyone there and the playtime with the other dogs.

"Good morning, Clarence." He smiled at his doorman, who bent down to pet Pearl.

"Good afternoon, Mr. Daniels, and you too, Mr. Halstead." Clarence gave Pearl one final pat. "I hope your friend got home safely last night. He left quite late."

"Uh, yeah, he's fine. Thanks. I'll see you later." Shit. Damn. Ryder winced, as his secret was exposed. He caught a glimpse of Connor's smirk.

"So, what was that all about? I know Jason took you home." Connor tried to play nonchalant, but given past experience, Ryder knew he was in for an interrogation.

Trying to keep it casual, Ryder flipped down his sunglasses, hiding his eyes from Connor, who was now in full lawyer-interrogation mode. "Yeah, he did. It was no big deal."

"You guys have gotten pretty close lately, huh?" Connor reached over and took off Ryder's shades. "Don't try that. I know you too well."

"Oh, fuck you." But even to Ryder, the curse sounded halfhearted, and Connor wouldn't take offense. He grabbed his sunglasses back. "Yeah, we're friends. So are you and Emily with him. And everyone else. So what?"

"I don't know; there's something different. I said it to Em the other night. It's nothing I can put my finger on." Connor stopped in front of their favorite Thai place. "Want me to grab some pad thai and curry? I'll get it while you wait outside with Pearl."

Happy to get a reprieve from the conversation, Ryder agreed and waited outside. In less than fifteen minutes, Connor was back with several bags.

"Okay, so want my take on Jason and you?" His friend's bright green eyes bored into him as they walked to where the car was parked.

Like he had a choice in the matter. "There is no Jason and me. We. Are. Friends. Nothing more."

Ignoring him like he usually did, Connor kept right on talking. "The way I see it, you like the guy but won't let yourself get close to him, because for starters, he's not gay, and you don't want to fall for a guy who isn't gay."

They reached Connor's car and climbed in, Pearl jumping into the back seat. After they buckled in and started the drive to Brooklyn, Connor picked up the conversation where he left off. "But I noticed something."

Ryder stretched out his legs. "Do tell." He smirked. "It's not like you need my permission to talk."

Connor grimaced, his voice unusually solemn. "I said to Em the other night, and she agreed—Jason watches you." Ryder caught his side-eyed glance. They entered the traffic for the bridge. It was stop-and-go all the way across the span. Ryder could see the Statue of Liberty and the new Freedom Tower rising into the sky. Damn, he loved this city. No matter how many times it got knocked down, it picked itself up and came back better than ever. He could take a lesson from its spirit.

Changing the radio station to something more classic rock from Emily's Top 40 hits, Ryder tried to downplay Connor's observation. "I don't know what you mean. We're friends. We hang out, watch the game. Sometimes he'll bring Troup over, and we'll take the dogs out when we go running. That's all."

Finally free of the bridge traffic, they eased into downtown Brooklyn on their way to the rescue office located in Bushwick. He stared out of the window so he wouldn't have to watch Connor's face.

"Yeah, yeah. But I'm saying he *watches* you. Not like a friend, but like someone who's interested in you as a man." Connor turned the car into the lot behind their building, which they shared with a bodega and an auto supply store. "I know what I see." He hopped out of the car, taking the bags of food with him, leaving Ryder, nonplussed, to follow with Pearl.

They entered the office, where Emily sat, talking on the phone, her face alive with excitement. She said good-bye to whomever she was speaking with and hung up.

"Hi." She kissed Ryder, and her husband, then bent down to hug Pearl. "Ooh, I smell Thai." She took the bags out of Connor's hands and put them on the table, then turned around with a wide smile.

"Guys, guess who that was on the phone." Her eyes sparkled.

"No idea, babe. Who?" Connor greeted Laurel and Hardy, giving them, as well as Pearl, each a treat from the bowl on the desk.

"It was the president of the Brooklyn Chamber of Commerce. They want to give us a service award for all the help we've given the community by rescuing and helping the dogs while still being respectful of the home owners and developers. He thinks we can turn it into a big fund-raiser for Rescue Me." She hugged Connor. "Isn't that great?" After dancing across the room, she grabbed Ryder around the waist. "I know it must be partly because of how great a job you did getting the dogs out that time from the site Jason was working on."

At the mention of Jason's name, Ryder's stomach did a little flip. The memory of their kissing and rubbing against each other on the bed last night rose so strongly in his mind his face burned.

"What's going on? You're blushing. Ooh, did something happen between you two?" She pounced on Connor, who had reentered the room. "Did you talk to Ryder about Jason?"

"Come on, Em, knock it off. Nothing's going on. He took me home 'cause I was drunk. That's it." No way would he allow her to drag any information out of him. Besides, he knew what the score was. The guy had some beers in him and probably hadn't gotten laid in months, so when he fell asleep, he must've thought he was in bed with a woman. By the time they were fully awake, they were too into eating each other's mouths to stop right away.

It had been a long time for him without a lover, and he wasn't about to shake up his carefully constructed life to allow a straight guy in who was looking to play on the gay side until he found a girlfriend. Been there, done that. Ryder had enough of being in second place with other men, or no place when it came to his family. Everyone in his life, except for his brother and these two friends, had let him down. While he'd never denounce who he was, being gay had never been easy for him. That was why he preferred to be left alone. If he was alone, he couldn't get hurt. Jason Mallory, while he was the temptation of a lifetime, was too dangerous to be anything more than a friend. Getting closer to him was a certain guarantee to having his heart kicked to the curb again.

The door opened behind him, and the dogs barked and whined. Ryder's nerves shot to high alert as Emily's blue eyes gleamed with delight.

"Jase, it's so nice to see you. What are you doing here? Aren't you supposed to be on-site today?" Ryder turned to watch Emily give the man a hug and kiss. "Want to stay for lunch? Connor, as usual, got enough pad thai to feed a small country."

Jason squatted down to greet the dogs, who swarmed around him. Laurel and Hardy now accepted him, as he'd spent some time here before adopting Trouper, and when the two big pit bulls jumped on him, they sent him sprawling to the floor. He fell down laughing as they licked his face.

In a flash, Ryder recalled Jason licking his neck, sucking at his skin. The faint bruises on his neck tingled and desire swamped him, recalling the heaviness of Jason's cock through his jeans as they frantically rubbed and humped together. The thrust of his probing tongue, their wet mouths searching, frantic and greedy, hot breaths merging had Ryder achingly hard. Jason's lips tasted delicious—all full and soft, yet firm and demanding.

Shit. Not two minutes before, he'd resolved to keep the guy at a distance, yet here he was having dirty fantasies about him. He had to stop. His dick ached, and Ryder knew from the laughter in Connor's damn knowing green eyes his attempt at nonchalance toward Jason didn't fool his smart-assed friend in the least.

"Hey, Jason, how's it going?" Ryder accepted licks from the dogs as he extended his hand to help the guy up from the floor. Jason's wary eyes flashed at him as he took his hand, gripping it tightly for a moment before withdrawing it once he was on his feet.

"Uh, can we talk a moment, in private?" Jason stood close enough for Ryder to feel the tension rolling off his body. His smoothly shaven jaw clenched tight, a muscle ticking in the hollow by his ear.

Another surge of pure lust jolted through Ryder, which he immediately and viciously smothered. "Uh, well, I just got here…"

Emily, the matchmaker, pushed them into the back

office. "Go, go. We'll set up lunch. It's slow so far today, Ry. No calls. Connor and I can start planning the Chamber of Commerce thing." She winked at him, even though he tried giving her his best evil glare. "Take your time, boys." She slammed the door behind him.

He sighed and faced Jason. "So."

Jason kicked the floor. "Umm, how's your head this morning? I'm thinking you must have a wicked hangover." The room they were in was pretty small, without much space to maneuver around. Jason backed up and leaned against the desk.

Remaining by the door, Ryder shrugged. "Not so bad. Guess all the water I drank at the end helped, and Connor gave me some aspirin before he left the bar. Thanks for staying and looking after me."

"No big deal." Jason's blue eyes pinned him so that he couldn't look away. "I didn't come here to talk about your drinking habits."

Ryder raised a brow. "No? So why are you here, then?" He crossed his arms. "Last night I thought I said everything that needed saying."

Still glaring at him, Jason moved a step closer. "I know you did, but I didn't get a chance to answer. You dismissed me like I was a stranger. I thought we were friends." He raked his hand through his hair as his voice, full of frustration, rose a notch. "Look, I didn't plan on it happening. It surprised me as much as you, but I thought you knew me well enough to know I wouldn't fuck around with you."

Ryder tried to ease Jason's agitated state. "It's fine. Let's forget about it, all right?" He gave him an uncertain smile. Better this way. They could work through Jason's uncomfortable feelings, and as for his own yet-to-be-reckoned-with desires, he could push them back into that black box where he kept all his life's disappointments. Right now it contained his parents' treatment of him, his inability to see his brother and the affairs with Josh and Matt. Jason would be one more depressing addition.

Jason cocked his head and narrowed his eyes. "I don't think you understand." He took a step closer. "I'm not sorry for kissing you."

Jason's soft, husky voice sent a shiver through Ryder and he backtracked a few steps. "I am, though. I'm not looking to teach someone to be gay. You either are or you aren't, man, and you're straight." It pained him to push the guy away, but he wasn't about to sacrifice a friendship for casual sex.

Jason snorted. "You don't really know shit about me. If I was perfectly straight, would I have dreams about you?" His blue eyes took on a glint Ryder had never seen before as he continued. "Dreams that have you on your knees sucking my brains out through my cock. Dreams of me sucking you."

Ryder retreated until he ran out of space and found his back up against the wall, his eyes still caught up in Jason's mesmerizing dark blue regard. All the air seemed to have been sucked out of the room.

"No one's ever had this effect on me, not any woman I've ever dated or slept with, none of my friends. Not even the guy I once fooled around with in college." Jason swallowed, a heavy, nervous gulp, then huffed out a self-conscious laugh, all the while never breaking eye contact. "You didn't know that about me, did you? I've never told anyone until now."

Ryder stood mute, in a state of suspended belief that Jason stood before him, saying these things to him. Jason—bisexual? Was that what he wanted to say? That explosive piece of information Ryder knew had never been shared with anyone before warmed his heart. Jason shared his secret with him, but Ryder remained uncertain what it ultimately meant to their friendship. His heart beat a wild, stuttering rhythm while blood pounded in his head.

As if he couldn't bear to face Ryder with what he was about to say, Jason turned his back to him. His normally steady, calm voice shook somewhat, betraying exactly how deep his uncertainty ran. "I don't know what I'm doing here. Am I gay now, 'cause I dream of you, your mouth, your tongue *in* my mouth? Or, am I bi? God, I can't believe I'm even saying this, but it's been making me crazy for weeks now, and I'm not sure what's happening to me anymore." He tried to laugh, but it came out choked. "I'm kinda lost at sea here, floating around without a paddle. You know"—a red flush stained the back of his neck—"sex with my ex-girlfriend was never that good. When I look back, it was always unsatisfying, a way to get off quick." His whisper sounded like a shout to Ryder's ears. "Maybe it's why I've never thought of settling down. Maybe I knew something was missing."

He ran his hand through his hair, still turned away, then braced his hands against the desk. "I'm not doing anything to hurt you, Ry, but you gotta believe me when I tell you I'm not fucking around here. I'm as surprised and confused as you."

Dumbfounded by Jason's confession, Ryder attempted to regain his equilibrium and soothe Jason's rattled senses. The guy was still his friend. "Hey, why don't you turn around and look at me?"

Jason turned, his faced reddened, eyes full of caution and fear.

"We're friends, first, no matter what you think you feel for me otherwise. I'm flattered you think you have these feelings for me, but having a sex dream about a guy doesn't make you gay. Neither does a one-time experiment in college. From what I remember, it's pretty common. Don't let it make you crazy." Ryder forced himself to laugh, his voice catching in his throat like sandpaper. Maybe, if his life weren't such a fucked-up soap opera, if his parents accepted him and he hadn't been scraped off the bottom of Matt's shoe and tossed aside like garbage, maybe then he could envision trying for a relationship with someone as special as Jason, letting him into his heart. Not an option, so these hurtful, troubling thoughts got squashed down into that black box of disappointments.

"Have you ever had a sex dream about a woman?" Jason's halting voice sounded doubtful but curious.

Ryder couldn't lie to the guy. "No, but I've always known I was gay."

Someone banged on the door. "I'm coming in. Put your clothes on." The door opened, and Connor's smiling face appeared. The smile died when he caught Ryder's scowl.

"Uh, food's getting cold..." Connor's voice trailed off.

"Be there in a sec." Ryder made an impatient gesture. "We're finishing up."

Connor opened his mouth, but Ryder speared him with a look that promised all sorts of horrible things would happen if he remained in that doorway. Or continued to speak. Connor put up his hands. "Oohkay, see you in a few." He shut the door behind him.

Jason seemed to have pulled himself together and calmed down. "Listen, the real reason why I came over is I forgot to tell you last night your brother called, and I spoke with him."

All thoughts of their prior conversation fled as Ryder jumped on Jason with questions. "What did he say? Is there anything wrong?" He approached Jason, his stomach churning. If his parents were hassling Landon, he was going to make sure to do everything in his power, legally and maybe a little illegally, to see his brother again. Full-blown warrior mode kicked in as he struggled with his impotence to protect him. No one was more important in his life than Landon.

"Cool down, Thor. Everything is status quo, but while I spoke with him, an idea popped into my head, and I wanted to run it by you before I mention it to him." As he spoke, Jason grew more animated, his voice rising with excitement. "I thought since you said he was interested in architecture, he could come on-site at the project we're working on now, on the Lower East Side. He can shadow me or Liam and help us with the plans, to get some hands-on experience. And you could maybe stop by and visit on the pretense to say hi to us and see him." His blue eyes glinted bright. "What do you think?"

Ryder stood stock-still, rendered mute with shock. "You'd do that, still, after what happened last night and what we talked about today?" Shame coursed through him, as well as guilt. "I think it's amazing of you to offer, and no matter how badly I want to see my brother, there's no need for you to involve yourself in my family problems."

"No worries, Ry." Jason passed by him on his way out the door. "That's what friends are for."

Ryder followed him out of the office, contemplating what he'd said, excited at the chance he now had to once again be back in his brother's life, and thankful Jason still wanted to be his friend.

Chapter Eleven

J ASON EXITED THE train at 77th St. Bitterly cold for March, the wind swept down the block taking people's hats with it, and he congratulated himself on planning to meet Ryder's brother inside the coffeehouse and not on a corner somewhere. He arrived a few minutes before four o'clock and, seeing that Landon wasn't yet there, ordered his coffee, sat down, and waited. Ryder had shown him several pictures of the kid, so Jason knew what Landon looked like: basically a younger, thinner version of Ryder.

He sipped the hot, steaming coffee, keeping his eyes trained on the door as his mind wandered back to the afternoon he'd spent at the rescue. The four of them had shared lunch; then he'd watched as they began to coordinate for the fund-raiser for Rescue Me. He was impressed with their organizational skills and their ability to pull together notable philanthropists from the neighborhood, as well as many owners of local business-es and restaurants. Emily could charm anyone to contribute their time, and Ryder and Connor took care of all the legalities of the tax implications of charitable filings, and the rental of the space for the fund-raiser.

The door opened, ushering in a gust of chilly air and several napkins fluttered across the small, round table he sat at. After retrieving them, Jason watched Ryder's brother enter the coffeehouse. He realized while he knew what the kid looked like, from the pictures Ryder had shown him, Landon had no idea who he was meeting.

"Landon, hey, over here." Jason raised his hand, waving him over.

The teenager approached him, eyes hooded, somewhat on his guard. No welcoming smile graced his face. He looked around, first to the line of people waiting for coffee, then back to Jason, a frown tugging down the corners of his mouth.

"I thought Ryder would be here." His shoulders slumped, and his voice shook with discouragement. He blinked rapidly, but Jason caught the sheen of tears in those melancholy blue eyes. Jason had a sense of what Ryder must've looked like as a teenager, all long limbs and angled cheekbones. Coupled with those startling eyes and thick, shining hair, Landon was a devastatingly handsome kid.

Ahh, shit. "Come sit down. Ryder was too afraid your mother would find out and punish you, so he had me meet you."

Landon dropped into the small chair, pushing his backpack under the table. After refusing Jason's offer for a drink, he asked, somewhat harshly, "Who are you again, and what do you want?"

"Ryder and I are friends, like I mentioned on the phone. Several months ago I adopted a puppy from the rescue and we all became friends—Ryder, Emily and Connor." Jason steeled himself as he explained his scheme. "I know you and your brother are being kept apart, and it's killing him. He hides it well, but he's miserable and refuses to allow himself to move ahead with his life unless and until you are part of his again."

Landon nodded, his silky golden hair falling into his eyes. Brushing it back, he no longer sounded angry, merely sad and curious. "My mother can't handle him being gay and wants to forget he exists. When she isn't bad-mouthing him to me, she has people watching me, so I can't stay here long. My dad says nothing at all, but I barely see him as it is. Ryder and I are caught in the middle, as usual." He shredded the napkins before him into a pile of brown paper. "Where do you fit into any of this anyway?"

Jason quickly filled Landon in on his plan. "So I think if I have you over at the site, you can actually help our company. It'll be a win-win-win. We get an intern; you get to see your brother and also get something to put on your résumé for college."

He could see Landon becoming more and more excited as he outlined his plan.

"Yeah, I really think this could work." Landon's brow furrowed, and his face screwed up momentarily. "I still don't understand, though. You haven't really known Ry that long, and you're such good friends?" His mouth curved up in a slight smile. "Are you guys dating? I knew he was interested in someone, but he wouldn't tell me the details." Happy expectancy brightened Landon's dejected attitude. "He's a great guy and the best brother."

"We're friends, that's all."

Landon looked unconvinced. "Well, whatever. I don't care who you are as long as I get to see my brother. Nothing's been right since my mom went crazy and refused to let him come home." He ducked his head, and Jason watched him surreptitiously brush at his eyes.

Right at that moment, Jason decided no matter what he had to do, he was going to make sure Ryder and his brother would overcome their mother's attempt to keep them apart. Having a close relationship with his own sisters and brothers, he couldn't begin to imagine not having the support of his family. It was terrible for Landon, but at least he had the comfort and familiarity of his home. For Ryder, though, he'd lost both his home and his family, everything familiar and dear to him.

"Hey, Landon, I promise I'm going to make this work. On Monday, come to the site, and I'll make sure Ryder will be there too." Jason scribbled the address of their work site on one of the napkins Landon hadn't torn to pieces and gave it to him.

"Cool." Landon checked his watch. "Shit, I gotta go,

or my mom will probably have the cops out looking for me or something. Um, like I said, I still don't really understand why, but thanks for doing this." He flashed a smile. "I'll see ya Monday."

Jason gave him a fist bump. "See you then." He watched the boy hurry out, disappearing into the evening crowd on Second Avenue. Happily sitting back in his chair, he wanted to let out a cheer of accomplishment. Instead, he picked up his phone and texted Ryder. *Spoke to Landon. Coming by to tell you how it went.*

He jumped out of his chair and hurried out the door. The normal rush-hour madness had begun to build, forcing him to weave his way through the crowds and down the stairs to the train.

About half an hour later, Clarence let him up to Ryder's apartment. Before he had a chance to knock, Ryder opened the door and pulled him inside.

"So? Tell me how it went. First of all, how did he look?" Jason could tell Ryder had already had a drink. Not drunk, merely relaxed and in his happy place.

Jason unzipped his jacket and tossed it on the chair. He settled on the couch, and Ryder, wearing sweats and a T-shirt, sat next to him. Damn, the guy always looked good, but tonight he looked like a male model for a sleepwear ad. The sweats hung on his lean, narrow waist, and the T-shirt stretched across his muscular chest and broad shoulders. A wedge of pale golden skin gleamed above the top of his pants, winking at him. Jason chewed the inside of his cheek, forcing his mind away from his disconcerting thoughts of how hot Ryder looked. Instead he concentrated on recounting his meeting with Landon. "He looked good. Pissed as hell at your parents. And as concerned about you as you are for him."

Ryder nodded. "And he agreed to work with you guys, right?"

When he nodded, a huge grin split Ryder's face.

"That was so freaking smart of you, Jason. I really can't thank you enough, man." His lips twisted in a grimace. "So damn ridiculous that we have to sneak around like this. I wish... Ah, fuck it." He leaned back on the sofa and closed his eyes.

Poor guy. "Hey, Ry. It'll all be good. Things are starting to work out, right?" The memory of what happened between them in Ryder's bed flashed through his mind and his blood sizzled. Jason moved closer to Ryder, studying his profile. A frisson of excitement rolled through him.

"I suppose so, but I wish it didn't have to be this way. It's so unfair to put the kid through this because they have a problem with me." Ryder's eyes opened, and Jason locked onto that bright blue gaze. "They have no idea how hurtful their behavior is to him."

Impulsively, Jason put his hand on Ryder's shoulder. "Hey, and what about you? You count too, you know. Look what all of this is doing to you. I know you worry about Landon, but he looked like a pretty well-adjusted kid to me." He tightened his grip. "Who worries about you, though?"

Ryder licked his lips. "I guess Connor and Emily. They've stood by me and will always have my back."

Jason shifted near, pressing his thigh into Ryder's. "I'm on your side too. You know that, right?" He held his breath as Ryder lifted his hand. Was he going to push him away again? This wasn't like the night Jason took Ryder home. Jason wasn't half-asleep, and Ryder wasn't drunk. Ryder's warm hand landed on his own, patting it.

"I know. I don't know why, though. I certainly haven't been that nice to you." He smiled slightly.

That spark of excitement exploded into a full-fledged fire within his blood. Without a second thought, Jason leaned over and kissed Ryder on the lips.

Ryder's eyes widened, but he didn't pull away. "I thought we decided this was wrong."

Jason settled himself more comfortably next to Ryder. "No, you decided. I think it's a good idea." He kissed him again. "A very good idea." He cupped Ryder's jaw and brushed Ryder's lips with his own. "This may be the best idea I've had in a long time, as a matter of fact."

Jason caught Ryder's face between his palms, tracing the jut of Ryder's cheekbones with his thumbs. "You say it's an experiment but I'm not so sure. I've thought of little else today except for how much I wanted the chance to kiss you again. Now it's time for you to stop thinking and kiss me." Jason captured Ryder's mouth with his. For several minutes they kissed, Ryder's lips warm against his own. With a firm, deliberate slide, Jason slipped his tongue into Ryder's mouth, sweeping into its velvety heat. Ryder tasted like fine chocolate—sinful, rich, and impossibly sweet. Tongues touched and breaths merged, and the world tilted on its axis as he clutched at Ryder's shoulders, grabbing on to his muscled arms. So different from a woman, but not wrong, no, never wrong in his mind.

And finally that memory, the one he'd never dared allow into the light of day, clawed its way to the surface. It was a recollection of stumbling back to the dorm with his friend Brian Leary, both of them a little drunk from a freshman fraternity rush party. Face-planting on Jason's bed, Brian asked if he could crash with him, and he agreed. When he woke up in the middle of the night, though, Brian's mouth was pressed to his in a tentative kiss. Instead of pushing him off, Jason returned the kiss with enthusiasm. To his surprise and shock, he became tremendously aroused, and he and Brian dry humped and rubbed each other until they both got off in their boxers. Jason might have continued exploring those feelings, but in the days following the incident, Brian ignored him every time he brought up that night. Not long after, Jason met a girl whom he started dating and having regular sex with, and he'd put Brian and that kiss out of his mind until recently.

But the man before him was unforgettable. A kiss from Ryder was not one to be forgotten. Not that he wanted to. Ryder groaned and tipped his head back, revealing the strong, corded lines of his neck. Christ, he was beautiful. Jason needed him. Now. Growling with supremely restrained desire, he licked Ryder's thick neck, tasting the man who'd come to occupy his thoughts lately. Jason sucked and kissed his way from Ryder's jaw to his chest, then returned to Ryder's mouth, hungry, needy, and dizzy with a desire he wasn't certain he understood.

The next thing he knew, Ryder flipped him onto his back and hovered over him. "You want me to say it? Okay, I will." Ryder leaned down and nipped at his mouth. Jason shuddered, his body aching, his cock hard and full in his jeans.

"I want you. Fuck, I'm dying for you. I don't think I've ever wanted someone so badly in my entire life. I've tried not to think about you and to push you away, but I can't fight it any longer; it's killing me. I want to bury myself deep inside you and make you scream so loud and so hard the walls will come crashing down around us. There, I said it." Ryder kept kissing Jason, teasing him, brushing his mouth tenderly over Jason's lips, his cheeks, his jaw. Ryder licked down his neck, biting, sucking, and nuzzling. "Now say it back to me. Tell me what you want." Ryder seized Jason's mouth with his own, his tongue invading, sweeping, and searching. Their teeth clashed, chests heaving. Jason writhed and whimpered with need. Oh God, he was going to explode.

"Tell me," Ryder demanded as he licked Jason's ear, sucking the lobe into his mouth and pulling on it. "You've pushed me as far as I can go, and I can't say no anymore. You want this, want me?" Ryder's lips and tongue were everywhere, invading his mouth, his ear, the hollow of his throat. But still, Ryder didn't touch him, wouldn't press that rock-hard body against him and give him the friction, the hardness he so desperately craved.

"Fuuuuck, yes, God, I want you. Touch me, please," Jason whined, begging into Ryder's neck. Adrenaline rocketed through Jason, sending his heart ping-ponging in his chest.

Without warning, Ryder stood and held out his hand. A smile quirked the corners of his kiss-swollen lips. Jason loved the way Ryder looked, hair all tossed about, thoroughly debauched and sexy. "C'mere."

Jason took his hand and found himself pulled up tight in Ryder's arms. "Let's do this the right way. Not hurried and quick on a sofa." They walked to the bedroom but remained standing by the bed. Neither made a move to lie down.

Shit. Was he ready for this so soon? Kissing was one thing but faced with the prospect of getting full on naked with another man, Jason suddenly wasn't so sure. He swallowed, gulping down his nerves. "Uh."

Ryder bent close to him, whispering softly. "Don't worry. You trust me, don't you?" Ryder kissed that secret spot behind Jason's ear, dragging the wet trail of his tongue down Jason's neck. An ache, sweet yet painful, grew within Jason and he trembled under the pinpricks of nerves running riot through him.

"Do you trust me, Jason?"

Held within Ryder's arms, he peered up into his friend's face. Trust him? He'd better. This was life-changing for him, like a fucking volcanic eruption of epic proportions. He opened his mouth, but no words came out, so he merely nodded. Shivers racked him as Ryder tucked him closer into his hard chest.

A warm palm cupped his face, the thumb stroking his cheek. Jason was one step away from breaking down and falling apart in Ryder's arms. Another shiver rolled through him.

"Hey, listen to me. Relax. I won't do anything you don't want me to," Ryder murmured, calm and strong, one hand caressing Jason's face, the other circling his back with soothing strokes.

What did he want? He had no fucking clue. Now that the time was here, with Ryder standing before him so open and honest, he had to be honest with himself. He licked his dry lips, suddenly shaky with nerves that popped up all over the place. "I don't know what I'm supposed to do or, um…"

Helplessness was not a feeling he normally experienced. He was used to being in control, giving orders. But here, he was in so over his head he was completely lost. He was hurtling down a runaway rollercoaster without a seat belt. Death defying and dizzying.

"Shh. I'll take care of you." Ryder smoothed back his hair. "I love your hair." He dragged his fingers against Jason's scalp, tugging at the curls. "So damn soft and beautiful. Do you know the first time I saw you, I wanted to grab you by it and kiss your gorgeous mouth?"

His nervousness now replaced by overwhelming desire, Jason groaned and pressed himself against Ryder. He loved kissing Ryder. "Do it now, then." He grabbed Ryder around his neck. "Kiss me. I can't fucking stand it anymore."

Ryder pushed him down on the bed, caging him between his arms. "Don't you want me to touch you?" Their lips touched, and Jason bit back a moan as he arched his body.

"God yes," he ground out, frantic to keep Ryder's lips on his. But Ryder seemed content to tease him with tantalizing, soft kisses.

"Where do you want me to touch you?" Ryder's warm breath wisped over his throat. "Here?" Ryder kissed Jason's collarbone, gliding across Jason's neck, nipping and sucking as he went. "I'm going to leave a mark so you remember you're mine." Ryder bit down on his shoulder, sucking the skin into his mouth.

Jason cried out and writhed as his cock thickened, pressing painfully against his suddenly too-tight jeans. He'd never been so turned on in his entire life. "Please." He strained upward, trying to touch Ryder, push up against him to get that needed friction, but Ryder remained out of reach.

"Should I touch you here?" Once again, those torturous lips skimmed the shell of his ear.

Jason whimpered. The powerful need to touch and be touched by Ryder scared him. He pressed his erection through his jeans, feeling the dampness where, in his excitement, he'd already leaked through his boxers to the denim.

"Or here?" Ryder's lips kissed Jason's hand. The hand that now stroked his dick through his jeans.

Jason's heart stood still before it resumed thundering as Ryder popped open the fly, then dragged down the zipper. With his teeth.

Holy shit.

The feel of Ry's mouth on his stomach, the damp gusts of hot breath so close to his painfully engorged cock, almost caused him to come on the spot. He barely noticed Ryder pulling off his sneakers and yanking down his jeans as a tingling began in his balls and his body trembled and shook.

"Shit, that was the sexiest fucking thing I've ever seen." He squeezed his dick to forestall the prickling down his spine that always preceded his orgasm. Ryder hadn't taken his eyes off him, and he could see the rapid rise and fall of his chest and hear the effort it took him to take each breath.

"Do you want me to help you with that?" Ryder indicated his hand, now holding his dick, which rose above the waistband of his boxers, the wet tip peeking out.

His hand faltered for a moment. Did he? Before he answered, Ryder took him in hand, holding him. Jason's dick swelled, leaking another burst of liquid from its flushed head.

His brain might not be sure, but his body knew what it wanted. Meeting Ryder's gaze, he jerked a quick nod, gasping, "Don't stop."

Ryder's face broke out in a smile that chased away the sadness lurking in his eyes. "I knew from the first you'd be trouble for me. But I couldn't stop thinking about you, wanting you, even though I tried." He bent down and stole a swift kiss. "No turning back now, right?" His hand began to move in long strokes, and Jason could no more tell Ryder to stop touching him than he could stop his own heartbeat.

"No. No turning back."

Chapter Twelve

RYDER SPOKE THE truth when he said he knew Jason would be trouble for him. Sitting next to him on the sofa, he hadn't been able to take his eyes off the man's narrow waist and fine ass, the T-shirt stretched across broad shoulders, and faded jeans he wanted to tear off. How was Ryder supposed to turn away from Jason now, as he lay beneath him on the bed, gasping for breath? Jason's thick cock pulsed hot and heavy under his hand. From their first heated kiss, Ryder wanted nothing more than to rip off Jason's jeans and slide his mouth onto his dick.

Turning back was a joke. He wanted Jase, wanted every gorgeous inch of him. He tugged off Jason's boxers, watching his cock spring free. It jutted up proudly, as if waiting for Ryder's touch. His breath caught in his throat at the thought of taking it in his mouth.

"Ry?" Jason's voice broke into his thoughts. When he met Jason's eyes, Ryder's heart softened as he once again saw the uncertainty in his lover's face. "I, uh, don't really know what I'm supposed to do here." Jason bit his lip, and Ryder grinned. God, this guy was adorable.

"It's okay. I'll take it from here. I promise to make it good for you." Ryder bent over Jason, giving him a kiss on the lips that he meant to be quick, but the slight tremor in Jason's voice, coupled with the insecurity in his eyes, made him slow down to kiss him properly. The way he deserved. "Your eyes get me every time, you know?" Ryder took Jason's face between his hands and ravaged his mouth. Their tongues met and thrust against each other, not frenzied this time but slow, tender and sweet. This kiss stole his soul and invaded his heart. Jason tasted of warmth, passion, and hope. Everything Ryder had been missing in his life. A driving hunger and need rose within him to make sure Jason would never forget his first time. To have him here in his bed, to touch and kiss him was nothing short of exhilarating, awesome, and utterly terrifying. This step would change everything, but it would be easier to stop a train racing out of control than to keep from touching and loving Jason.

No turning back.

They kissed, hot, wet and searching, and Jason re-laxed beneath him. Ryder gazed down at him with fondness. "Up." Jason lifted his arms up and Ryder tugged off the long-sleeved T-shirt he wore, revealing wide shoulders and muscled arms that spoke of countless hours of physical labor. Jason was no pretty boy content to sit back and let others do the dirty work at his construction sites. Silky dark hair covered his broad chest forming a perfect happy trail down to his straining shaft.

Ryder bent down and licked the beautiful cock bobbing in front of him. The smell of Jason surrounded him, and Ryder breathed deeply as he licked at the root, wetting the springy curls of his groin. He slid his tongue around the head, then engulfed him in his mouth, taking him all the way to the back of his throat, drawing him in deep with a hard sucking force.

"Oh, Christ," Jason cried out, almost coming off the bed. His eyes rolled to the back of his head as he sank back onto the pillows.

Spurred on by Jason's cries of pleasure, Ryder licked at his cock, lapping at the liquid that seeped from the head, swirling around the sensitive underside, all the while continuing to stroke the base. He drew his tongue upward to the tip, keeping a soft yet unyielding pressure on the sensitive skin. Using his saliva and Jason's fluid to create the wet, slick friction necessary, Ryder stroked Jason, smooth and easy from root to tip. The heady scent of musk and man filled his senses, and Ryder could feast on him all day long.

Quivering and breathing heavily, Jason looked like a blissed-out pagan god, his naked, muscled body all warm and enticing, laid out for an offering.

"Ry, don't stop. You're killing me." Jason's moans turned into whimpers as his hands reached out for

Ryder's.

God, those sexy little noises nearly made Ryder come undone. His heart twisted, and right then Ryder knew, despite all the walls he'd put up to protect himself, the ship had sailed. He was a goner for this man.

"Fuck." Jason thrust his hips faster. He mumbled inarticulate words as his head thrashed back and forth on the pillow.

With his hand still jerking Jason's cock, Ryder licked down the hardened length to his balls. He nuzzled, then rolled one into his mouth, then the other. Jason's harsh breathing and muttered cries spurred him as he nibbled at the slant of his hip bone, then took a nip of his thigh. When Ryder sat up on his knees, it was only to grasp Jason's cock more firmly before once again taking it deep in his mouth, sucking, tasting, swirling, then swallowing him down to the root.

Jason's hips bucked, and he slapped at the bed, grabbing the comforter, twisting it into knots. Ryder reached up and seized his other hand, entwining their fingers, holding on for dear life.

"Ryder." Jason's sob resonated against the walls of the bedroom before he exploded in his mouth and down his throat. Ryder continued to lick and swallow Jason's pulsing cock, until it softened and finally slipped free of his mouth. Sitting back on his heels, Ryder anxiously searched Jason's face for a sign of distress or uncertainty.

"Hey. How do you feel?"

Sleepy-eyed and smiling, Jason snuggled down under the covers. "Never better. Gonna take a nap for a little, okay?" He heaved a contented sigh and fell asleep. Ryder sat for a few minutes, listening to his steady breathing.

Never mind no turning back. Ryder was so far gone it was scary.

﹐ ﹐ ﹐ ﹐ ﹐

AFTER JASON'S ORGASMIC meltdown, Ryder left him sleeping while he walked Pearl and picked up a few things at the supermarket and drugstore. It was nice to think of someone waiting for him when he returned home, especially when that someone was Jason, all sleep warmed and disheveled in his bed. His body hummed into overdrive, reminding him he'd neglected to take care of his own needs. There were no regrets, as he didn't believe in being a selfish lover. It was Jason's first time with a man, therefore his feelings and needs were paramount.

As he walked, hunched against the cold, brisk chill of a mid-March evening, Ryder had no illusions about where this relationship between Jason and himself was going, even as arousal simmered in his veins. Having lived as a straight man his whole life, Jason was most likely disillusioned from the breakup with his longtime girlfriend and looking to try something new. He dismissed the one time Jason mentioned with that guy from college. Ryder didn't hold it against him; hell, he knew the score when he let the guy kiss him this evening.

It was so cold even the basketball courts lay silent tonight. Ryder remembered he and Jason were supposed to go to Drummers later to hang out. How would Jason act in front of his friends and family now?

Don't be an asshole. You don't have a relationship because you gave the guy a blowjob. Of all people, you should know better than that.

There comes a point where you become tired of the loneliness and need a human touch, a caress to make you realize you still exist as a person. His friends were the best people in the world, but they couldn't replace the aching void within him. Everybody needed to feel loved, be wanted by someone else, even if only for a fleeting moment.

He turned down his street and entered his building. "Hey, Clarence. How are you this evening?"

"Good evening, Mr. Daniels. Bit of a chill still in the air tonight."

"Yes, indeed. I'll see you later."

Both his hands and his feet ached from the numbing cold, and he couldn't wait to get inside to the warmth of his apartment. He opened the door, heard the shower running, and smiled to himself. It really was nice to come home to another person. He dumped his coat on the chair and stood in front of the open refrigerator, putting away the milk he'd bought, when he heard a noise and turned around. Jason stood in the doorway, naked, with only a towel slung around his slim hips, drops of water clinging to his broad shoulders. "Hey, you." An uncertain smile chased on his lips.

Ryder swallowed. "Hey, yourself. I stepped out to get a few things." The man looked good enough to eat, all damp and sweet smelling.

"No worries." Jason leaned up against the counter. "You know, I thought about it, and this isn't right."

Here it comes. The brush-off. Ryder had prepared himself to be disappointed but hadn't expected it to happen so soon.

"What..." The words died on his lips as Jason pushed him up against the counter, muscling into his face.

"I asked you before who takes care of you, and from what I see it's no one." To Ryder's shock, Jason unwound the towel from his waist and dropped to his knees in front of him, dark blue eyes glinting bright with wicked humor. He reached up with one hand and yanked down Ryder's sweatpants, which fell in a heap around his ankles. "I'm gonna take care of you tonight."

"You don't have to." But Ryder's protest fell on deaf ears as Jason palmed him through his boxers. His dick responded, jerking full, hard, and thick, twitching under Jason's fingers.

"Have to, want to," Jason mumbled, pushing down Ryder's boxers, allowing his dick to spring free. It bobbed right in Jason's face, and he hesitated only a second before he swiped his tongue over the head.

"God, you taste amazing. I knew it." He gave another lick, and Ryder grabbed the counter behind him to keep from falling to the floor.

"Shiiit." He could hardly draw a breath. In all his life he'd never seen anything so erotic as this beautiful man, naked and glistening wet, kneeling before him, lips wrapped around his cock. His body shuddered with desire as Jason gripped him.

"You don't have to do this. I don't want to rush you...God." He bit off a moan as Jason wrapped his hand around him and licked the head of his dick, gently sucking it, flicking his tongue all around the swollen, sensitive tip.

"You're not rushing me. I haven't been able to think about anything else for the past few weeks. Am I doing this right? I want to make it good for you."

Right now, with Jason's wet lips tight like a vise around him, Ryder didn't give a shit about anything else except Jason's insanely talented mouth and tongue. Ryder's head fell back as he spread his stance.

Jason slid Ryder farther and farther into his mouth, swallowing Ryder's cock down his throat. Ryder closed his eyes as the sensation of Jason's swirling tongue flowed over him like warm honey. He moaned and cupped the back of Jason's neck with his hand, guiding him, urging him to move faster, harder, deeper.

Through hooded eyes, Ryder observed Jason working his own erection. That sensual tableau coupled with the feel of Jason's mouth on his cock set off a fluttering at the base of Ryder's spine. It had been almost a year since Ryder had been with a man, and he wouldn't last long, if the way his balls drew tight and his strong and quick thrusting were any indication.

"Fucking hell." How Ryder managed to keep his footing, he'd never know. He erupted in Jason's mouth before pulling out, still coming in spurts against Jason's chest and chin. Ryder sank to the floor, and together they stroked Jason to his own shattering completion. The scent of sex and sweat rose around them, hazy and thick. Ryder leaned over and kissed Jason, loving the fact that he could taste his essence on the man's skin and the inside of his mouth. He licked his face, then kissed his lips again.

"Hey, that was pretty fucking awesome." He took the towel Jason had rested on and wiped them both up.

Jason simply nodded, wrapping his arm around Ryder. "I need another shower now before we go out tonight. Wanna join me?" His grin was a promise of all things wicked.

Ryder kissed the corner of his mouth. "Let's go." He jumped up and snapped the towel at Jason's very fine-looking ass.

Chapter Thirteen

J ASON WALKED INTO Drummers with Ryder that night around eight thirty. He grinned and bumped against him with his arm. "Good thing there's lots of food, 'cause we kind of missed dinner." Faint patches of red stained Ryder's cheeks.

They'd spent almost half an hour in the shower, and Jason could honestly say he'd never come so hard in his whole life. The recollection of a naked Ryder kneeling at his feet, with all that slicked-back hair and steamy water spraying over his gleaming body while he sucked him to oblivion was enough to set off another raging hard-on.

"Asshole." The softness in Ryder's blue eyes tripped a beat in Jason's chest. "You'd better not speak so loudly if you don't want people to find out."

Jason didn't like it but agreed. "Yeah. I know it sucks, but I don't want to say anything until I tell my parents and the rest of my family."

Ryder touched him on the shoulder. "Hold up a sec. Are you sure you want to tell your family about yourself, about us? It can wait until you have time to come to grips with it."

Jason disagreed. "No, I don't want to wait. There's nothing to come to grips with." An edge of concern crept into his voice. "Are you having second thoughts about this?" Now that he and Ryder had given in to the blaze of attraction between the two of them, he didn't think he could ever go back to the way life was before. The thought of how they'd spent the past several hours sent a wave of heat and lust through him that had him biting back a groan of desire.

"It's not a matter of second thoughts. It's you coming to terms with identifying yourself in a new way. Dealing with the looks from people, their snide comments." Ryder's mouth tightened, hard lines bracketing his face. "Family and friends not being supportive." That haunted expression Jason hated to see entered Ryder's beautiful blue eyes. "It isn't going to be as easy as you might think. Are you willing to tell them you're now with a man and face that unknown?"

"Hey, I know you've had it rough." Jason wished he could hold Ryder and give him the comfort he so needed. His heart ached for Ryder and his continued estrangement from his family. Jason knew his own family would be supportive, and as for his friends, fuck 'em. If they couldn't accept who he was, then he didn't need them. "My family won't have a problem with it."

Sure, he was a little surprised at his brother's initial reaction months ago to meeting Ryder and hearing he was gay. But now they were buddies and often watched the basketball game together, just the two of them. Jason knew they'd planned on going to several Yankee games once the season started up again.

"Come on, before Connor eats all John's food." He winked at Ryder and casually squeezed his arm. It was going to be hard keeping his hands off this man, knowing all the smooth golden skin that lay beneath the clothes. After years of an emotionally dead relationship, he sensed his body coming alive, like a plant bursting through the ground to reach the warmth of the sun. Ryder was his sun. He warmed his soul. Jason would be damned if he'd let anyone kill what he and Ryder had.

Jason slid onto a bar stool and greeted his friends. "Hey, John, let me have a beer." He smacked at Connor's hand and grabbed the last slider off the plate. "Damn, man. You need to get checked for a tapeworm."

"I'm a growing young man, I'll have you know." Connor slapped him on the back and went to greet Ryder. Jason watched the two men talk and joke around, happy to see Ryder relaxed. He failed to realize anyone had sat down next to him until Emily spoke quietly in his ear.

"You're together, aren't you? You and Ry. I mean like a couple."

His hand gripped his beer a bit tighter. Shit, Ryder wasn't kidding when he said Em was perceptive. His expression a mask of neutrality, Jason took a deep breath before he swiveled around to face Emily. "Why would you say that?"

She huffed an impatient sigh. "I've known that man for years, and I've always been able to see through him, his bullshit, and all that guilt he piles on himself." A smile warmed her face as they watched Ryder and Connor pretend argue over who knew what. "As soon as he walked in here, I could tell something was different. And I think that something is you."

He opened his mouth to protest, but she held up her hand. "You don't have to say anything, 'cause you must have a reason for not wanting to yet." She leaned forward, all trace of humor wiped clean from her pretty face. "But know that if you hurt him, you are dead to me and Connor." Without waiting for an answer or even a reaction, she slipped off her seat and left him to join her husband.

"What the hell was that about?" Liam slid into Emily's vacated seat. "I heard something about dead to her and Connor. Is she gonna sic those big dogs on you?" Enjoying his own joke, Liam elbowed Jason, his hearty laugh booming over the bar.

"You're hilarious, man. It was nothing." Jason drank down his beer. "So, I have to tell you that I took on Ryder's brother as an intern for us. Kid's a high school student, but he's interested in architecture, so I figured he could learn, and we could have someone around to be like a gofer, as well as show him some of the ropes." He rolled the bottle around in his hand, inexplicably nervous about Liam's reaction.

"Huh." Liam's eyes flickered from him to Ryder, then back. "How come you didn't think to talk to me about it ahead of time? We're partners, I thought."

"It's not like we're paying him, so it doesn't cost us anything." Jason hated how defensive his voice sounded. It was time, however, to tell his brother the real reason for taking on Landon. "Besides, I figured it would be a way that Ryder and his brother could get a chance to see each other. I've told you what a bitch their mother is. So everyone wins here."

Liam's dark eyes darted between him and Ryder again. Jason knew he suspected something else was going on but couldn't figure it out. "You've really gotten involved in Ryder's life, Jase. I know he's a good friend, but this is kind of above and beyond, dontcha think?" Those dark eyes pinned him until he was forced to look away, unwilling at this point to go any further.

"Not really. Think how you'd feel if you couldn't see Mom or Dad or any of us, and hadn't for months?" Obviously it was a sobering idea, as Liam's expression turned from suspicious to contemplative.

At Liam's sigh, Jason relaxed a little, knowing his brother understood. "Yeah, that would suck. I forgot how shitty they are. It's okay. I don't really have a problem with it." He finished his beer, then leaned closer. "So listen, I met this hot lady, and she has a friend. Wanna double-date? I saw the friend's picture on Facebook, and she's also a cutie."

Shit, fuck, crap. How was he going to get out of this

one? He and Liam had occasionally double-dated, but hadn't in a while, not since he'd begun spending so much of his free time with Ryder. "Ahh, when were you thinking? 'Cause I'm kind of busy now."

"Yeah? What are you doing that's more important than spending time with a gorgeous woman?" demanded Liam, looking like there could be nothing at all that could ever top that.

What could he say? Spending time with a gorgeous man—naked and in bed? Yeah, right. He sighed his agreement. "All right, fine. Make sure you tell me when."

Liam busted out a grin as he punched in the numbers on his phone. "Hey, Courtney, it's Liam. Yeah, my brother said yes, so how about we meet you in, like, half an hour at the restaurant? Sounds good? Great, see you soon." He ended the call. "Right now, buddy boy." Liam called over to John, "John, we're heading out. Jase and me have dates."

Fuck. He didn't want to leave Ry here, but he couldn't say no either. It would be too suspicious to bail on his brother and a date to hang out with his friend. Helpless, he slid off the stool and caught John's eye. His friend shrugged.

"You don't look too happy, Jase. Something going on?" John's perceptive gaze searched his face. Out of all of them, John was the quietest, rarely revealing his feelings, but for some reason, Jason knew he could trust him to understand.

"You'll be around sometime? Maybe we could talk."

John didn't bat an eye. "Always here for you, man. You should know that." They gave a quick fist bump, and then Jason turned to an anxious Liam. "Christ, Liam, hold on. You sprang this on me with no warning. I have to say good-bye to everyone. Unlike you, I have manners."

Liam flipped him off, which Jason chose to ignore, joining Connor, Emily, and Ryder. "Uh, hey, guys. I gotta take off. It seems my asshole brother set me up on some blind double date." He fixed Liam with a death glare. His brother ignored him and made a "hurry up" motion with his hand. "I'm sure he thinks he's going to get lucky tonight, even though I'm not in the mood."

Connor merely smiled and said, "Have fun," his attention drawn back to the game on the screen. Emily, on the other hand, shook her head and turned her back on him. Truthfully, he didn't really give a shit what they thought; he was only concerned with Ryder. And if Ryder was feeling anything like him, he'd be disappointed, annoyed, and a little angry. Instead, Ryder gave him a weak grin.

"Go on. Liam looks like he's going to pop you one if you don't leave already. Talk to you whenever." He spun around on his chair to face the television screen and with that, Jason was dismissed.

He stood there a moment, his gaze boring holes into Ryder's back, willing him to turn around even though he knew the man was too proud. What was the point anyway? He couldn't say the truth out loud, that he'd rather be here with him than anyplace without him. That he knew it wasn't going to be easy being together, at least until he could tell his family. Jason vowed before the weekend was out, he'd have that talk with them.

Turning on his heel, he barked at his brother, "Let's go and get this over with."

Liam matched him stride for stride as he stomped out of the bar. "What the hell are you so pissed about? I get you a date with a hot woman, and you act like I did something wrong. What's the matter, Ryder jealous?"

Jason stopped dead in his tracks. "What the fuck's that supposed to mean?"

Liam snorted. "Jesus, you're dense. Anyone can see the guy's got the hots for you." They reached Liam's car and got in. "I mean you have to see it. I like the guy and everything, but it would creep me out to think a friend of mine wanted to suck my dick and all."

Oh shit, Jason was so not having this conversation now. What the hell would his brother say if he blurted out, *Never mind a friend. How would you feel knowing your brother spent the afternoon having mind-blowing sex with a man including him sucking and having his dick sucked?*

Definitely not the conversation to have in a moving vehicle.

※ ※ ※ ※ ※

RYDER PICKED AT the label of his beer bottle and

yawned. Between planning the fund-raiser for the rescue and doing some legal research on whether a landlord could break the lease and kick a tenant out of his apartment if he owned a pit bull, he was bone tired. The weekend had flown by, and now he was vegetating on his living room couch, feet up, relaxing while watching college hoops. It was time for March Madness, and it was all basketball, all the time. Typical Sunday afternoon. Except that he hadn't seen Jason since he'd left Drummer's with Liam and had only one hurried-sounding text from him that there was some emergency on-site, and he'd try to stop by if he could. The disappointment stunned him. Here Ryder was, minding his own business, no need for a romantic entanglement, when he got swept off his feet and pulled under the tide so completely he was drowning.

His phone buzzed, interrupting his musings, and his heart quickened when he saw the text was from Jason. *Did you eat? Feel like Chinese?*

A smile broke out as he texted back. *Sounds great, but give me time to get dressed.*

The phone buzzed immediately. *Don't bother; I like you better undressed. Open your door. Now.*

He jumped up and ran to the door, Pearl at his feet. After unlocking it, he flung it wide open to see Jason and Trouper. The two dogs barked, no doubt happy to see each other, and took off running down the hall, leaving him staring at an exhausted, rumpled Jason, who looked like he hadn't slept in days. He had at least a two-day stubble on his chin, and his hair flopped over his brow, tousled and messy, like he'd rolled out of bed. Ryder's heart turned over at the sight.

God, he could eat him alive.

"Hey, you. Come on in." Ryder took Jason by the arm and dragged Jason inside the apartment. With his foot, he kicked the door shut behind him. He didn't let him go as he took the bag of food and put it on the small side table. No matter how exhausted he looked, the sight of Jason standing before him, so large and overpowering, intoxicated him.

"Hey, you. I'm sorry I was MIA, but there was a problem—"

Ryder cut him off with a passionate kiss, sending a heartfelt thank-you to heaven that there was no hesitation on Jason's part as they tangled tongues. He pushed off Jason's jacket and pulled his shirt out of his jeans, never breaking contact with his mouth.

With trembling fingers, he slid off Jason's belt. "I don't care. You're here now." He took Jason by the hand and led him into the bedroom. "Let's get you cleaned up. Then I'm going to kiss every fucking perfect inch of you."

Jason's blue eyes flared darkly with heat. He tugged his shirt over his head, unlaced his boots, and shucked his jeans, then followed Ryder into the bathroom. Ryder had already gotten naked and turned the water on as Jason stepped into the shower.

"I missed you. Let me take care of you, babe." He pressed up close to Jason, every dip of muscle and curve of bone imprinting itself on Ryder's body.

Jason groaned and leaned up against the wall, already hard and huge. As Ryder pumped the bodywash into his hand, he watched Jason relax in the heated spray. He rubbed his hands together, forming silky suds. Perfect. The soap spread in glossy bubbles over Jason's chest and stomach. A ripple ran through those tight abdominals as Ryder spread the gel over Jason's torso. He rinsed him off with the handheld attachment and leaned over to kiss the flat little nipples.

A loud moan resonated in the glass-enclosed shower. After pumping more gel into his hand, he grasped Jason's cock as well as his own and, with slow, deliberate slippery strokes, began to jack both of them off.

"Oh shit, oh fuuuck..." Jason sagged and might have fallen to the floor of the shower had Ryder not been holding him against the wall with his body, pushing him, crowding him so that they were flush up against each other, cocks rubbing and sliding together as the hot water continued to sluice over them.

"How does that feel, babe?" he whispered in Jason's ear, kissing that sweet tender spot by his jaw. He made sure his hand never stopped pulling and tugging at their cocks as Jason began thrusting into his hand, harder and quicker, mumbling under his breath.

"Don't stop; don't ever stop touching me." Jason panted as his fingers clutched and slipped against the tiles. "Feels so fucking good. Shit, what you do to me." He leaned his head back against the wall, hair drenched, stubbled face all wet and gleaming, eyes closed, mouth open and breathing hard.

What a beautiful fucking sight to behold. A spike of lust shot through Ryder and he plunged his tongue into Jason's mouth. Their tongues warred with each other as his hand wrapped around their cocks and deliberately increased the friction and pace of his rubbing and pulling. Sparks tingled up his spine, and his vision blurred. His heart thundered hard and fast as he sensed the rush of his impending orgasm. Before he could catch his breath it was upon him, and he jerked and pulsed out endlessly against Jason's stomach. Ryder's chest heaved, and he slumped against Jason, still stroking his cock.

Not a minute later, Jason spilled himself between the two of them. Ryder could feel the throbbing of his cock as it ejaculated, snuggled up tight against their bodies. Jason's head fell down on Ryder's shoulder in a dead weight of exhaustion.

Ryder rinsed both of them off, patted Jason down, and put him in a terry-cloth robe his mother gave him one long-ago Christmas, when she still considered him her son. With his arm around him, he pushed him toward the bed and took off the damp robe, leaving it to lie on the floor. His mouth dried at the sight of a nude, sleepy Jason. Devastating. The man looked so sweet and cuddly. Something hard inside Ryder broke open, awakening long-dormant desires, and his heart twisted.

This was new, this overwhelming happiness. He

pulled down the covers, pushed Jason into bed, and slid beside him, remembering as he lay back on the pillows that tomorrow he was going to see Landon, all because of this man lying beside him in bed. He owed him so much. Ryder couldn't help but smile with contentment as he lay soaking in Jason's heated, drowsy presence by his side.

The late-afternoon sun sent warming fingers of light across the bed. Out in the hall, he could hear the jingling of the dogs' collars as they played together. Jason rolled over and put his arms around him, spooning him, kissing his cheek. Sleepy and satiated, Ryder stroked his arm. "Come on, Sleeping Beauty, take a nap. The food will keep."

Chapter Fourteen

"D AMN IT, THIS was supposed to be done last week. Didn't the Buildings Department tell us that we'd have the permits? Where the hell are they?" Jason raised his gaze to the ceiling and took a deep breath. God help him, if they didn't get these permits, they were so screwed. Spying Landon hovering at the doorway, he waved him in. He mouthed, *Take a seat*, and gestured with his chin to the chair in front of the desk.

Landon slouched down in the chair, dropping his backpack on the floor. Frustrated with the runaround, Jason lost the little patience he had left. "Look, I don't care about the bureaucratic bullshit. Fix it." He clicked off and tossed the phone on his desk.

"Uh, problems?" Landon glanced up at him from under the fall of his bangs. The kid looked so much like Ryder it made Jason realize how much he missed the man today. They hadn't had a chance to speak since early this morning, after spending the entire night wrapped around each other. He had to be at the site early, and Ryder had a meeting with the city's Small Business Association.

He rubbed his face with his hands. "It's so frustrating dealing with the government. They don't realize we need things, like yesterday, and when they promise it'll be ready and then it isn't, it royally screws us up."

"Maybe I can help. After all, that's why you want me here, right? What if I go get what you need? That way you don't have to wait for them to send it to you."

Satisfaction shot through him. "Yes, that would be excellent. Let me give you the specifics—address of the Buildings Department and the person you have to see." Jason fumbled through some papers on the desk. Finally, after some muttered curses, he found a copy of what he had filed. "Here. Take this and show it to them. Say you work for me, and don't let them give you the runaround. Here's my cell phone number if you need to call me." He checked his watch and saw it was only two o'clock. "How come you're out so early? You didn't skip class, did you?"

"Nah, man. I get out early on Mondays. You want me to go now?" Landon was bent over his phone, concentrating on entering all the information, when a sound from outside caught Jason's attention.

The day improved dramatically when he saw Ryder lounging in the doorway of the office. It was the first time Jason had seen him dressed up, looking corporate in a business suit, and it was all he could do to restrain himself from hopping over the desk and grabbing him.

The man looked dangerously edible. The sleek navy suit sat on his lean runner's body with grace and style, showcasing his broad shoulders and narrow waist, while the pure white shirt and bright blue tie enhanced his unbearable hotness. Ryder's eyes brightened when they caught sight of Landon, who had yet to realize he was there.

Hey, you. Jason mouthed the words, knowing instinctively that Ryder wanted to surprise his brother.

Ryder winked at him, mouthing back the same greeting.

Landon, finally finished, slipped his phone back in his pocket. "Okay, so I guess I should get ready to go, right?" He reached down to grab his backpack.

"You have a few minutes. The office doesn't shut down until four thirty. There's someone I want you to meet. He says he knows you, but he's kinda shady." Jason couldn't keep the grin from his face any longer. One thing he'd never had was a poker face. He couldn't lie for love or money.

Landon turned in his chair, and when he saw Ryder, he jumped up and ran right into his brother's open arms. "Ry."

The kid sounded so broken and emotional. Jason didn't want him to feel embarrassed, so he decided to give the two brothers some time to themselves. As he passed Ryder, who still held on to Landon for dear life, he squeezed his arm and whispered, "I'll be outside when you want to find me. Take all the time you need."

Ryder nodded, and Jason left the trailer, closing the door behind him. He'd picked up his coat on the way out, but luckily it was one of those Spring-is-right-around-the-corner, March days. The air blew warmer, and the endless sky soared bright blue, free from any clouds or threat of rain.

He wandered inside the lobby of the soon-to-be completed building, noting the clean workmanship while listening to the crew yelling out jokes to each other in Spanish and English. They'd put together a good group of people who knew how to get the job done. Liam's loud voice could be heard above all the others as he good-naturedly ordered them to pay attention to their work and stop talking about women and sports.

A grouping of chairs stood against the wall, and Jason dropped onto one of them, stretching out his legs, still thinking about Ryder and his reunion with his brother, when Liam joined him, choosing a chair next to his.

"You're looking pretty serious, bro. Is something bothering you? Is that why you bailed early on our double date?"

Liam's concern only increased the guilt Jason carried over not confessing his relationship with Ryder. Now was as good a time as ever, he decided. After all, he had no shame, no reason to hide it.

"Nothing's bothering me. I was thinking about Ryder and his brother."

"Oh, yeah, I forgot. Is the kid here?" Liam checked his phone and answered a text, talking to himself. "That Courtney, man, she is sweet and gorgeous. I'm seeing her again tonight." He shot Jason a quick glance. "Want to try it again with her friend? I'm sure she could arrange it."

"Landon's here with Ryder. I left them to hang out awhile in the trailer. Then Landon's going to go over to the Buildings Department and pick up those permits for us." This time spent together with his brother would help Ryder so much toward healing how broken apart he still was inside over his parents' rejection.

"Okay, good. So are we set for tonight, then? I'll let Courtney know to tell Jen." Liam was poised to text, when Jason put a hand on his arm.

"Uh, no, I'm not interested in her, sorry." The nerves made his hands shake, and his heart started racing.

"What, are you nuts? She's hot. What more could a guy want from a woman?" Liam stared at him as if he had two heads.

The blood pounded in his head. *Go on. Say it already.* "Uh, well, the thing is I'm kind of seeing someone else." Lame ass.

Liam's face creased with confusion. "What? You're kidding. Who?" His voice grew loud, demanding an answer.

"I never planned for it to happen, but I know it's the right thing for me." He faced Liam, holding his gaze, searching his dark eyes for understanding. "I want to know I have your support."

"What the fuck are you talking about, Jase? Oh, no." A light seemed to dawn on Liam's flushed, angry face. "You're not back with that bitch, Chloe, are you? Tell me she isn't pregnant. That'll kill Mom."

In the darkest moment of Jason's life so far, leave it to Liam to make him laugh. "No, you dumbass, I'm not back with her. Never."

Liam fell back in the chair, exhaling a loud and long sigh. "Thank the Lord. Then what the hell, man? Who is she?"

Ryder and Landon interrupted them. Landon had his backpack slung over his shoulder and his phone in hand.

"Uh, hey, Jason, I'm going down there now. I'll pick up what you need and bring them back as fast as I can." Landon looked at Liam.

"Oh, right, you guys never met. Liam, this is Ry's kid brother, Landon. Landon, my big brother, Liam." Jason watched them shake hands, but his regard was solely on Ryder.

It killed him to have Ryder standing so close to him and having to pretend they were mere friends, when he could still taste the man on his tongue and feel the touch of Ryder's hands stroking his body. Waking up this morning to find a warm and naked Ryder curled around him, all that smooth golden skin begging for his mouth to lick and kiss, was a feast for his soul. He wanted more, though, now. He wanted him low and filthy, hard and hot in his mouth, begging, whimpering, completely undone.

He met Ryder's passion-filled gaze. Heat sizzled between them and Jason would swear Ryder knew. Knew his dirty, secret thoughts. An aching need to touch and be with this man again slammed into him. Jesus, he'd better get control of himself, or he'd be running to the portable toilet to jerk off. His hands fisted with frustrated impotence.

"Hey." His gaze touched Ryder, but it was enough to catch his smile.

"Hey. I'm going to go downtown with Landon. I'll catch you later." Ryder said good-bye to Liam, and the two left.

Liam remained standing when Jason sat down, his large body tense, dark eyes narrowed.

"What's the matter; didn't you like Landon?" With arousal still vibrating through his body, it took Jason a few minutes to notice Liam's antagonistic stance.

He knew.

Jason's whole body stiffened as he prepared for what would be the mother of all confrontations.

Liam stood still, arms crossed, his heavy, harsh breathing the only indication of his anger. "Look me in the eye and tell me right now. Tell me I'm wrong, and then we'll laugh about it and go have a beer. But I need to hear you say it."

Though fear clutched at Jason's throat, he surprised

himself and managed to speak in an almost casual tone. "Why don't you ask me the question first?"

"Tell me that guy didn't get to you, that he's not fucking you." Liam's raspy voice begged. "Shit, I can't believe I asked you that. Forget it; I'm sorry. Of course he's not." He huffed out a shaky laugh. "I know he wants in your pants. That's what they do."

Jason's blood ran cold. Here it was. Moment of truth. "Would that upset you so much? If I came out and told you I was gay? Would you stop being my brother, not talk to me?" His speech was deceptively calm, considering how he shook and sweated in his jacket. "Wouldn't you still love me?"

Another nervous laugh. "Don't fuck with me. You can't be gay. You dated Chloe for years and had other girlfriends."

"But you didn't answer me. What would you do if I said I was gay? Or bisexual, actually since, as you pointed out, I've dated women in the past? And this has nothing to do with Ryder and everything to do with us as brothers."

"Why are you doing this? You want to play an April Fools' joke on me early, is that it? Okay, ha fucking ha. You got me. Not funny."

Jason stared into the fearful, confused eyes of his older brother and knew he was going to shatter his world. "I'm sorry," he whispered. "I'd hoped you would be okay with it."

"What the fuck are you talking about?" Wild-eyed

now, Liam backed away.

"Ryder and I are together." He'd climbed hundreds of feet in the sky with only a thin rope and a prayer, but coming out to his brother was the single scariest thing he'd ever done in his life.

"No." Liam pushed his hands through his hair. "No fucking way. You had girlfriends, lots of them. You screwed women. You don't go from liking pussy to sucking dick. It…it doesn't work like that." He jumped to his feet. "No brother of mine is a faggot. Let me call Courtney; she'll set you up, and you'll see. You'll want to be with a woman." He pulled out his phone.

"No, don't. Listen to me, please." Jason put his hand out to stop his brother.

"Don't touch me," Liam snarled, pulling away from his touch.

The pain from the disgust and loathing in Liam's eyes choked Jason. As long as he lived, he'd never forget the heartbreak of his brother's rejection. He dropped his hand, thankful his breathing, to his great surprise, came steady and calm. "I see." At least his shaking legs were able to hold him as he stood, anxious to get as far away from Liam as he could. First, he had to tell him what rested in his heart.

"You know what, Liam? Growing up, I always looked to you as my champion, the person I wanted to be most like. Not Dad, but you. I thought you knew everything." It was the end of Jason's hero worship of Liam. He'd never be able to look up to his big brother again. Not after this. "It's hard to deal with it when your dreams are shattered, and everything you thought true was a lie." He drew in a deep breath, brushing away the tears that started falling.

"You're disgusted and ashamed of me because I want to be with a man. That's my life and how I am. There's no choice there. And you want to know something?" His voice broke. "I'm ashamed to call you my brother because you choose to be a bigoted, fucked-up, homophobic asshole. I'd rather be me than you any day."

He didn't wait for a response, and left Liam standing there as he walked away. He returned to the trailer, pulled out his phone, and texted Ryder.

I need you. Can you come to my house at 5:30?

Five minutes later, his phone buzzed.

What's wrong; what happened?

This wasn't something to tell over a text.

Shit went down with Liam. And other stuff.

Ryder's response was immediate.

I'll be there.

Right now he wondered if Ryder was the only one he could count on in this world. He had so much to say, so much to tell him. But face-to-face. Tonight he'd bring him home to meet the rest of his family. He thought back to what Ryder had said the first time they were together, and repeated it in his head like a mantra to hold on to.

No turning back.

Chapter Fifteen

I T WAS CLOSER to six o'clock by the time Ryder returned home, changed, picked up Pearl, and drove to Brooklyn. Traffic was its usual bitch, and by the time he pulled into Jason's driveway, his head pounded, ready to explode. He leaned back against the headrest to gather his thoughts and, once again, for about the hundredth time, wondered what had happened to force Jason to send out a distress signal.

"Come on, girl." He snapped on Pearl's leash, unwilling to let her free in an unfamiliar area. Although he'd been to Jason's home a few times, more often than not they'd hang out at Ryder's apartment. He suspected it was because Jason didn't want to have to explain who he was in case his family dropped by.

Before he reached the door, it opened, revealing an agitated Jason in a T-shirt, faded jeans, and bare feet. Pearl spied Trouper and ran inside, but Ryder remained on the stoop, staring at the unhappy man in front of him.

"Hey, you."

Jason opened the door wider. "Come on inside."

Ryder stepped into the warm house. "I hope you have beer ready for me, 'cause it was a nightmare over the bridge—"

The words died in his throat when Jason's mouth closed over his. He managed to slam the door shut when he found himself shoved up against the wall, flattened by Jason's hard body. There was nothing he needed to do but close his eyes, accept the probing tongue, and enjoy those strong, rough hands rubbing against him.

Ryder laughed, hugging Jason tight before letting go. "Mmm, if this is why you needed me, why not let me all the way in the house and we can get comfortable." Getting no response, he opened his eyes to see Jason standing before him, head bowed and chest heaving, those normally sure, strong hands clenching and unclenching into shaking fists.

Uh-oh. Something really bad had happened. "Hey, Jase. Look at me." When Jason continued to stare at the floor, Ryder cupped Jason's jaw and lifted his face so he could stare into his eyes.

Ah, hell.

Fury wound its way through Ryder as Jason blinked away his tears. He'd bet his last fucking dollar Liam had made some stupid comment about gays. Because of his own parents, Ryder understood Jason's upset all too well. The only thing he could do was be there for him, listen to him, and try to take away his pain until they figured out how to handle the situation. Together. If

Jason still wanted him, that is. Deep in his heart, the fear lived on that one day Jason would return to his life as a straight man, leaving him alone and devastated. If that happened, nothing would remain behind of him but scorched earth.

"Hey, you. Eyes to me." He brushed his hand through Jason's silky dark hair. "Jase, please." Ryder caressed Jason's bristly cheek with the pad of his thumb. "You're scaring me. Please, talk to me."

Jason stopped examining the floor, finally meeting his eyes. Pain replaced his normal cheerful expression, and his dark blue eyes stared straight ahead, vacant and haunted. "He hates me, can't stand the sight of me anymore."

Ryder strained to hear. "Who, babe? Liam?"

Jason nodded. "I told him, Ry. I told him about us. I didn't want him to keep trying to fix me up with women. I tried to talk to him, but he said such vile, disgusting things." He shuddered, and Ryder held him close—close enough to feel the steady beat of his heart.

"You're so goddamn brave, and I'm so proud of you." Ryder continued to hold him, rubbing soothing circles on his back. His lips found Jason's hair, and he kissed him. Nothing sexual, but an attempt to heal and comfort him.

"If he could have spat on me, he would've, you know? I mean, I always knew he wasn't the most enlightened person, but I'm his brother, goddamn it. How could he look at me like I was something dirty because I have sex with the man I love?"

Ryder stilled, his hand faltering on Jason's back. He remained silent, absorbing the hurt and sorrow pouring out of the man he held within his arms, while inside he reeled from the impact of the words Jason uttered.

"The man I love."

He was under no illusion Jason believed he was in love. It was something that slipped out, like a child might say in haste and anger to his parents to make a point. Still, hearing it rocked his world, because he knew he was head over heels in love with Jason.

"Don't let it get to you, Jase. There will always be haters. I've learned to deflect their negativity."

Jason turned an anguished face to him. "But how do you deal with this? It's like the ultimate betrayal. Your family should always love you no matter what, right? I'm still the same person I was before he found out, so why should it matter?" A sob broke free, and he swiped away the tears. "I don't know how you've pulled through without anyone by your side."

Jason's hand touched his cheek, then swept the hair from his face. "I think you must be the strongest man I've ever known, and I'm so proud you're mine." He rested his head in the cradle between Ryder's neck and shoulder.

Ryder tightened his arms around Jason, too overwhelmed to do anything but nod and hold on for dear life. Here he was supposed to make Jason feel good, but instead, he was the one being comforted.

"Don't think about me. I'm here for you. I have to think Liam will come around once he's had a chance to think about it." Much as he hated Jason's brother right now, he wasn't going to bad-mouth him. The two were close, and if Liam didn't apologize soon, Ryder planned on paying him a visit.

Jason pulled away and threw himself down on the sofa. "I don't give a shit anymore. You wanna know something?" He patted the seat next to him, and Ryder sank down but kept his distance. Jason didn't need sex; he needed understanding and whatever advice Ryder could give him.

"What? Tell me whatever you want. I'm all ears." Ryder slipped off his coat and found a place for it over the end of the sofa.

"There was always something missing every time I was with a woman. I enjoyed being with them, but the sex was never, you know..." Jason broke off, and it tickled Ryder to see his face turn red.

Oh, it was fun to tease him. "What? Tell me." He stretched out his foot and rubbed Jason's thigh. "Was it better than how we make each other feel?"

"Hell, no." The denial was instant and certain, and Jason's deep blue eyes crinkled with amusement. "Damn you, Ry, I know you're kidding me. But I'll say it out loud. I don't mind." Jason reached over and took his hand. "No one has ever made me feel like you have. The sex is amazing, but it goes much deeper than that; I hope you know it. Does it mean I'm bisexual? I don't presume to have all the answers. What I know for certain is that I want you. I need you in my life."

Although touched by Jason's declaration, Ryder remained practical. He was, after all, aware of how things could go south in a hurry, and ultimately, Jason would never give up his entire family if they refused to accept his sexuality. Nor should he. Ryder would step aside rather than have Jason ostracized from his loved ones.

"I know, but you're too close to your family to allow what we have to destroy your relationship with them. They're too important to you, and I understand that."

"Don't be a jerk. Put your jacket back on, and let's go."

An irritated, bossy Jason was a sexy Jason, and Ryder was fast becoming turned on. He'd like nothing more than to stay home in bed, showing him exactly how much he wanted him and his body. "Aren't we staying here? Where are we going?"

Jason had already pulled on his jacket. "I want you to meet the rest of my family—my sisters and my parents." He whistled for the dogs, and they came skidding back into the room, barking and excited.

Alarm shot through Ryder. "Are you kidding? After what happened today, you really think this is the best idea? Don't you think you should talk to them alone first and tell them about yourself before springing me on them?" Ryder knew he sounded panicky, but what if they blamed him for turning their son gay? It could get very ugly, very fast.

Jason held out his hand. "I need your support and want you by my side."

Who was Ryder kidding? Whatever Jason needed Ryder would gladly give him—his support, his friendship, and most of all, his love. Despite all the walls and the warning bells, he'd fallen for Jason. From the moment they'd met, he couldn't shake him from his thoughts. Some inevitable string continued to reel him in, closer and closer until here they were, at life's turning point. Wherever Jason went, so did he. There was never any doubt.

No turning back.

He took his lover's hand. "Okay. Let's do this."

Less than twenty minutes later they pulled up to a sprawling Victorian house in a quiet tree-lined neighborhood he'd never imagined existed in New York City. Large and well maintained, the homes all boasted large plots of land and comfortable front porches. They painted the perfect setting for young, well-to-do families starting out.

They put the dogs on their leashes and got out of the car. "How long have your parents lived here?" Ryder studied the brick facade and gorgeous stained-glass windows that graced the front of Jason's parents' home.

"My father's parents bought it in the early 1960s when it was dirt cheap. My parents have lived here since my grandparents passed away. They keep talking about selling and moving to Florida once my youngest sister graduates high school, but we know better and laugh at them. They'll never leave." Jason bumped his shoulder. "Who knows, maybe one day we'll buy it from them."

Ryder gulped down a nervous laugh. "Yeah." Shit, he was shaking. He'd never met anyone's family before. What if they were all like Liam and hated him on sight for what they thought he'd done to their son, or their brother? "Um, so before we go in, tell me your sisters' names again."

Jason took him by the shoulders, forcing him to meet his eyes. "Stop worrying—it'll be fine. My parents aren't like Liam. They're much more liberal. I don't know where he got his narrow-minded ideas from, but I swear not from here. Nicole is older—she's going to college in the fall. Jessica is still in high school. We call them Nic and Jessie. You already know Mark. My dad is Anthony, and my mom is Helen." Jason pulled him by the arm. "Let's go."

Trouper recognized where he was and whined to be set free. Ryder had no intention of letting him off leash, so he followed Jason up the brick steps and waited while Jason opened the door with his key.

"Mom, Dad, anyone home?" Jason called out.

"Jason, is that you, sweetheart?" an older woman's voice called out. "I'm coming."

Ryder could hear the chatter of conversations farther on in the house. At Jason's instructions, he let the dogs off leash, and they scampered to the back of the house, Pearl happily following in Troup's wake. As Jason and he shed their coats, a man's deep voice yelled out. "Jase, what's this? You took in another one?"

The man whose voice Ryder heard came striding down the hall, a broad smile on his face. "Hello, son." He hugged Jason, then turned to Ryder. "Ryder, right? Jason told us all about you. Glad you could join us."

Oh, not quite everything, I'll bet.

Ryder couldn't help but laugh as that thought popped into his head. "Hello, sir. It's nice to meet you." Darkly handsome with the same blue eyes as Jason, Anthony Mallory's handshake was firm and his smile welcoming. It wasn't hard to imagine this was how Jason would look when he reached his age.

"What's this 'sir' nonsense? I'm not interviewing you for a job. Call me Tony." Jason's dad clapped him on the back. "Here's my wife now. Helen, come meet Jason's friend, Ryder. He's the one who rescued our Trouper."

"Oh, hello, so nice to meet you, Ryder." Her dark eyes held his, and he sensed an instant chemistry with her. She had a kind, sweet face, one you wanted to unburden all your problems to and have her give you a hug to make it all better. "We've heard so much about you from Jason, and we love our little Trouper." She bent down to pet him and laughed as he jumped up on her. Pearl stood behind him, eyes bright and tongue hanging out. "Is this your dog?"

Beckoning Pearl, Ryder made the introductions. "Yes, this is Pearl. She and Trouper are fast friends." He smiled as Jason's parents made a fuss over his dog. She loved it and, after a few minutes, followed Troup out of the room as if she'd always lived there.

Helen wiped her hands on a dish towel. "Let me clean up, and I'll join you all in the family room. Tony, go with the boys. Jessie and Nic are already in there, fighting over what movie to watch."

Tony chuckled. "Those two girls will be the death of me. If they aren't fighting over clothes, it's over boys. Do you have any brothers or sisters, Ryder?"

They continued walking through the wide hallway to the back of the house. Everywhere he looked, pictures of school graduations, birthday parties and family vacations covered the walls. Beautifully restored to its Victorian splendor, the house boasted the original parquet floors, crown molding, and fireplaces in every room. The entire home radiated warmth and love—so different from the sterile, perfect atmosphere his mother had accomplished in decorating their family apartment. Each piece of furniture and knickknack meant something and was more than a showpiece.

"To answer your question, yes, I have a younger brother. Landon is seventeen. You certainly have a beautiful home here, Tony. I never knew such houses existed in Brooklyn." Ryder stood in the doorway to what must be the family room. It boasted original wood-framed French doors that opened to a huge, almost thirty-foot room. A sixty-inch flat-screen television resided above a massive stone fireplace. Several comfortable couches and chairs were arranged for optimal viewing of the screen, with sturdy antique tables set with platters of sandwiches, fruit, and salad.

"Thank you. We've enjoyed every moment in this house. I couldn't imagine living anywhere else." Tony stepped through the doorway, and everyone in the room stopped talking, waiting expectantly for him to speak.

"Welcome to movie night at the Mallory house. I can't guarantee you a great movie, but there's never a dull moment here, that's for sure."

Ryder shook his head and caught Jason's eye. The damn fool was actually laughing. Suddenly, Ryder saw the humor in the situation, even if he was still scared shitless.

Oh, you have no idea.

Chapter Sixteen

J ASON STEPPED FORWARD to make the introductions and watched with amusement as his sisters checked Ryder out. Sure, the guy was gorgeous, but to see his sisters' faces light up and eye him up and down like he was a dress on sale was almost too comical.

Jason put his hand on Ryder's shoulder and steered him over to the girls. "Ry, this is Jessie and Nic. Jessie is starting high school, and Nic is a senior. She'll be going to Cornell next fall."

Ryder smiled at them both. "Great school, Cornell. Do you know what you want to study?"

Nic pushed her long dark hair out of her face. "Oh, I don't know yet. I haven't decided on a major, but maybe prelaw, since I love to argue." She stared at Ryder with frank approval. "What do you do? Do you work with Jase?"

"No, I'm a lawyer, but I work full-time now for the pit bull rescue where Jason got his puppy. I handle their legal work and their rescues, which is how I met your brother."

"I didn't know you were a lawyer, Ryder. Jason never told us." Helen must have come in behind them and had now taken a seat next to Mark. "That must come in very helpful with the dog rescue. I watch that show on television where people go to jail for abusing their animals, and that makes me so happy. It should be a crime to abuse any animal."

Jason relaxed, thrilled to see how comfortable his parents made Ryder and how well they all got along.

And then Liam came in and the shit hit the fan.

"Hey, hope I didn't miss—" He stopped short and looked around the room, his face hardening when he saw Ryder. "What's he doing here?" There was no mistaking the sneer in his voice. Jason tensed.

"Liam. What's wrong with you?" His mother's shocked voice echoed in the otherwise quiet of the room. "Ryder is a friend of your brother and a guest here."

"A friend of my brother, huh?" Liam spun around and faced him with barely restrained contempt. "Is that what they're calling it these days?"

"Shut up." Jason advanced on Liam, fists clenched. "I have nothing to say to you and even less desire to hear your mouth."

"What's going on here? Are you two fighting about something?" His father sounded bewildered.

"Go on, Jason, tell them. Destroy your parents. Or are you afraid?" Liam's face twisted in an ugly grimace of anger.

How could this man be the brother he so loved and admired? Jason searched for Ryder, only to find him standing pale and shaking by Nic and Jessie. *Oh God, how could this have spun so far out of control so fast?*

"It's okay, you know. Whatever it is, I'm sure it isn't as bad as he's making it out to be," Mark, who'd come to stand behind him, whispered in his ear. "I'm with you, no matter what."

Jason took a deep, shuddering breath. "I need everyone to sit down. I have to talk to you, and before you ask, I'm fine. I'm not sick or anything."

"Sick in the head, if you ask me," muttered Liam.

Mark stormed over to him and, to Jason's amazement, grabbed Liam by the shirt and, breathing hard, stood nose to nose with him. "If you don't shut the fuck up right now, I'm gonna bash your face in." His mother gasped, and Mark, shooting a glance over to her, muttered, "Sorry for the language, Ma."

She remained silent, sitting with her hand to her throat, looking scared.

Mark let go of Liam and nodded to Jason. "Go on, Jase."

Jason elected to sit by his mother and took her small, shaking hand in his. "For a long time now, I haven't been happy. I dated a lot, and even though I went out with Chloe for all those years, something was always missing."

"You haven't met the right girl yet, honey. You're still young, though." His mother patted his hand.

She's so sweetly naive. He stole a glance at his father. He seemed more thoughtful and tuned in to the tone of the conversation. "Uh, that's not the problem, Mom. I'm doing this wrong. I don't want you to think that this is something that happened out of the blue. It's been with me for many years, but it's only now that I realized it."

Nic put her hand up to her mouth. "Oh my God. Jase, are you gay?"

He let out his breath and nodded. "Yes. I didn't want it to have to come out like this, but—"

"But now that he has a boyfriend, he thinks everyone will be fine with it and welcome them both with open arms." Liam stood in the center of the room, his face red with anger. He pointed at Ryder as he continued shouting. "Well, we don't accept it. I knew this guy was trouble from the moment I laid eyes on him. I told Jason he was after him, and Jason laughed at me. And now look at him. For Christ's sake, he brought his lover, a pervert, to meet your daughters, Ma. Tell him to leave, and then we can get back to normal." He sat down in a club chair and smirked.

"You should leave." Jason's heart jumped in his throat, and he thought he might vomit. It never occurred to him that his mother wouldn't accept him. Over the pounding of the blood rushing to his head, he heard his mother continue to speak.

"If you can't speak to your brother civilly and with respect, you should leave. I won't allow you to talk to

Jason like this. To think I raised one brother to behave like this to the other. It breaks my heart." With wonder in his eyes and a heart full of hope, Jason tore his gaze from the floor to find his mother smiling with tenderness at him. "I will never turn my back on one of my children, never. I love you, Jason, no matter who you love."

His father, sounding older and gruffer than usual, broke into the conversation. "You say you've felt like this for many years, but how? You were with that girl."

"Ugh." Jessie shuddered. "What a horror she was. I'm not surprised you're gay after being with her."

Out of the mouths of babes. The tension broke as Ryder choked back a laugh, and everyone else joined in. Everyone except Liam and his father.

"Dad." Jason left the couch to sit by his father. "Are you gonna be okay with this?"

"Well, you can't expect me to jump up and down with joy over it. It's not that I'm antigay or anything, but never to have children, no grandchildren?" He shook his head. "The happiest days of my life were when you and your brothers and sisters were born. You'll never get to experience that."

"Not true, Dad." To Jason's surprise, Mark interjected himself into the conversation. "Many gay couples adopt children now or use a surrogate to have a baby for them. Let me ask you a question." His blue eyes shone with honesty and Jason's heart swelled with pride as he watched his younger brother. "What would you tell me if I got married and my wife couldn't have children? Or if I was the one who was sterile? Wouldn't you want us to adopt or try some other way? If your only problem and concern is having children, then I think we'll all be fine, except for Liam the asshole over there."

He'd never been prouder of his brother. This was how he'd hoped his family would react. With understanding, compassion, and unconditional support. He grabbed Mark, wrapped his arms around him, and hugged him hard and long. "Thank you," he whispered. "I love you."

"Love you too, man."

"So Ryder is your boyfriend, Jase?" Jessie sat, twisting a strand of her long brown hair round and round her fingers, her big blue eyes wide as she looked from him to Ryder.

"Yes, Jess, he is." He left his father's side to kneel by her chair. "We've been friends for two months now, but just recently it's turned into something more." He heard Liam's derisive snort in the background. "Does it bother you, honey?"

To his relief, she gave an almost imperceptible shake of her head, slanting a curious look at Ryder from the corner of her eye while giving him a shy smile.

"I'm leaving. This is ridiculous." Liam stormed out, and Jason heard the front door slam.

His mother winced, then sat back, disappointment radiating from her, while his father said nothing, a stoic yet unreadable expression on his face.

Nicole sat, a miserable expression on her face. "It's so unfair."

Perplexed, he perched himself on the arm of her chair and gave her shoulder a little squeeze. "What's unfair, cookie?"

"Ryder. He's so hot. How come all the good-looking guys are gay?" she asked, her dark eyes all mournful. "As long as you're happy, I don't care at all. Now can I at least kiss your boyfriend hello?"

He rolled his eyes. "Glad to see nothing has changed. Go ahead. Welcome him, Nic."

She hugged Ryder, who still seemed stunned by the entire event. "Welcome to the family, Ryder. We're crazy, but you'll find that out soon enough for yourself."

"Nicole, please. You'll scare the poor man away." His mom waved a hand to Ryder. "Come, Ryder, sit by me so I can get to know you better." His mom patted the seat next to her and proceeded to take Ryder under her wing. She had an inner eye for the wounded and probably sensed Ryder's internal turmoil. There was nobody better at putting people at ease and soothing their hurts, and she was the one everyone turned to for comfort.

He always knew his mom was amazing, but to see her accept him and Ryder so easily almost brought him to tears. His dad, he suspected, would have more of a problem with the situation, as he remained quiet, no doubt still stunned by what he'd heard. Jason wanted to put it all out in the open so they could talk about it. He and his dad had always been close, and if this was going to be a problem, the sooner they could work on it meant the sooner they would reach a solution. "Do you want to talk about it? We can go to the kitchen where we can have some privacy."

His dad nodded. "Yeah, I think we should."

He walked out, his dad following behind him. When they got to the kitchen, he opened the fridge and took out a beer. "You want one?"

His father shook his head. "No offense, but I need something a little stronger to handle this." He took a bottle of scotch from the cabinet and poured himself a neat shot.

"Why don't you ask me what you want to know so we don't get caught up in all the misunderstanding and bullshit?" Jason swallowed his beer and sat down at the long, weather-beaten kitchen table. He'd spent so much of his childhood sitting at this table it only seemed appropriate to be here for this, the most important conversation of his life.

"I guess *how* is the main question. How, after all these years, do you suddenly realize or think you're gay? Isn't it something you would know all along? And you've had girlfriends so what does that mean?" Relieved to see his father wasn't angry, merely bewildered, Jason gathered his thoughts together to try and make him understand.

"It means I'm still working it out in my head. I'm bisexual. It wasn't something I ever wanted to speak about, but this isn't my first experience with a man. In college, there was an incident that, had I chosen to pursue it, might have changed my direction even then. I dated women simply because that's who I allowed myself to be attracted to. I never thought of another man until I met Ryder. The attraction was instantaneous and impossible for me to ignore or fight. And I didn't want to, if we're going to be perfectly honest. What I said before was true." He gulped his beer, embarrassed even at his age to discuss his sex life with his father. Kinda weird. "It's never been great with women. It always felt like I was going through the motions to get to the end result."

"And with this man?" His father coughed and took a quick drink.

Oh yeah, his father was uncomfortable discussing his son's sex life. But it wasn't because Jason was having sex with another man. Growing up Jason always talked to Liam about sex, not his father. That's what big brothers were for, or so he thought. "We haven't, uh, gotten that far yet in our relationship, but everything about it, about him, is different. He's always on my mind. I wonder what he's doing during the day, and I worry about him getting hurt when he goes out on calls to rescue the dogs. I'm proud when he goes to court and wins a victory for the business." He stopped to catch his breath for a moment and then whispered, "He makes me happy, Dad."

His father sipped his drink, then looked him in the

eye. "How do his parents feel about him and you?"

"They kicked him out," he answered softly, almost as if Ryder's pain was his own. Which, in fact, it was. "He hasn't seen them in well over six months, and even though he pretends it doesn't matter, I know how devastated he's been. It's only recently that he's been able to see his brother again, since his mother cut off all communication between the two of them. Landon is seventeen, and I gave him a job as an intern with the firm. Ryder saw him today, and now he'll stop by and get a chance to see him all the time."

His father's faced grew stone cold. "What a terrible thing to do to your child."

"Yes, it is, isn't it? Rejecting your flesh and blood because of who they love?" He met his father's troubled eyes across the table.

"I would never reject you. I'll always love you. I'd hoped you know that. It will take me some time to wrap my head around it. As for your brother Liam, he's a different story."

Jason set his jaw. "I don't want to talk about him."

A noise from the hallway drew his attention. Ryder stood in the doorway. "Uh, Tony, the girls want to start the movie, but they say they can't unless you're there to give the okay." He fidgeted, unable to meet Jason's eyes. It was so unusual to see a normally confident Ryder so unsure of himself. Not in control.

"Dad?" Jason took his father's hand. "Are we okay?"

His father smiled. "We're better than okay. We're

the same. Same as we ever were." He left the kitchen, but not before giving Ryder an awkward pat on the shoulder.

Jason stood and held out his arms. "C'mere."

Ryder hesitated, looking over his shoulder. "Are you sure?"

It took Jason less than five seconds to cover the distance to where Ryder stood. He cupped his cheek and kissed him on the lips. "Don't worry about it. I think it's going to be fine."

Ryder put his arms around him. "Your mom is unreal. She made me feel so welcome. Everyone did. I wish…oh, never mind. It doesn't matter." Jason heard Ryder's pain, and his heart squeezed. Although he tried to hide it, Ryder had never gotten over his family's rejection. No matter how they treated him, they were still his family, his blood. Jason knew one day he and Liam would have to come to terms with their mutual anger and disappointment. But right now, he needed to reassure Ryder.

"It *will* work out, Ry. You have to believe that one day your mom and dad will come back into your life and accept you. And if they don't, then you have my family to claim as your own." There was unexpected joy in knowing his family for the most part had readily accepted him and Ryder.

"You're incredible." Ryder kissed him on the cheek. "I'm so lucky to have you."

Jason touched Ryder's cheek. In his mind, he was

the lucky one to have found a man like Ryder. "Will you stay with me tonight? Be with me? I feel like it's a whole new beginning for us, and I want to be yours. Completely." A slight shiver raced through him, and he ached to have the deep, ultimate connection with Ryder.

A sweet smile broke over Ryder's handsome face. "I'd love to."

"Ahem." They broke apart, laughter coming from the hallway.

"Nicole." Jason spied his sister waiting outside the kitchen door and wanted to wring her neck.

"What? I wasn't spying, honest. Mom and Dad want you guys to come in and eat already." She whispered as he and Ryder walked by, "That was really hot, by the way. You two are adorable together."

"Nicole." His warning fell on deaf ears as she laughed her way down the hallway.

If only his problem with Liam could be solved so easily.

Chapter Seventeen

RYDER AND JASON left the Mallorys' house around eleven at night, with promises to return for Sunday dinner. After settling the dogs into the back seat, it was a quiet ride home.

They pulled into the driveway, and Jason opened the car doors to let the dogs out before they locked up for the night. Once they were all safely ensconced in the house, Ryder raided the refrigerator for a beer, then collapsed on the sofa. "Oh my God, I can't believe this day." He'd gone from the high of spending time with Landon to the low of hearing about, then seeing for himself Liam's homophobic rant and betrayal of Jason, back up to the biggest high of his life—acceptance from Jason's family. He'd hung out at Drummers enough with Mark to know he'd accept Jason's coming out, and the girls were sweet and funny. The reaction from Jason's father scared him the most, with the potential to be as horrible as Liam's but he had to give it to the man; although Tony acted uncomfortable, Ryder knew he tried because he loved his son.

Jason's mom was the best. Perhaps she was shocked and disappointed, but she didn't show it, acting gracious and caring, like a mother should. He closed his eyes, willing away the memories of his mother's hateful words in his ear. *Abnormal, deviant, perverted.*

"Hey, Ry, what's the matter? You were sitting there with such a smile on your face, and then, all of a sudden…"

Jason dropped down next to him, his dark blue eyes tender, then reached over to brush the hair off his face. "You were thinking of your parents again, weren't you? I've seen you do that. One minute you're fine, and then your eyes get that distant and sad look, as if you're running unhappy conversations in your head."

Obviously he wasn't as adept as he thought in hiding his emotions, but Ryder didn't want to talk about it. That was what he always did, ignore or deflect. "What's the point in talking about it? They're never going to change, and I should accept it. At least now, I'll get to see Landon."

He put his bottle down on the coffee table and drew Jason into his arms. "Thank you for doing it. I know you don't really need anyone to help you. You did it for me, and that means more to me than anything." He kissed Jason, loving the rough stubble of his evening beard. The kiss started out soft and sweet, lips touching, tongues licking, but it didn't take long before the delicious slow ache kindled into a fire.

"How about we move this to the bedroom, okay?"

He stood and took Jason's hand, drawing it around his waist. They stopped every few feet to kiss and caress each other, and by the time they reached Jason's bedroom, he knew if they didn't slow down, their lovemaking would be over before they'd had a chance to begin.

"Shh, let me undress you, 'kay?" The man was glorious in his passion, those blue eyes glazed and unfocused, full lips parted, broad chest heaving. Utterly desirable and all his.

Ryder pulled the sweatshirt over Jason's head and undid his jeans. As he removed his own clothes, Jason stripped as well so that they stood together, naked and aroused. Ryder watched as Jason's cock jerked and swelled to an impressive hardness, tiny pearls of moisture leaking from the head. His mouth watered, and he couldn't help but grab him close and, using that delicious wetness, rub their cocks together in a sensual, naked dance. The slickness of their mingling liquids and the hardness of their aching shafts left them gasping for air.

"Get on the bed." Ryder pushed him down, and Jason scrambled to the center of the king-size bed, lying spread-eagled. His body was a smorgasbord of erotic delicacies, and Ryder intended to feast on every part. After straddling Jason's body, he grasped both their cocks and began to stroke and rub them together, continuing the friction as he took Jason's mouth in a hungry kiss. The man overpowered all his defenses, and

FELICE STEVENS

Ryder knew, with the little presence of mind he had left, that he had fallen so deep and hard for Jason he could never let him go. He groaned and licked his way down Jason's straining neck, nipping and biting him, tasting his sweat and his skin.

He bit down on Jason's muscled shoulder, then kissed the reddened mark, hearing the quick intake of breath, knowing it turned Jason on by the corresponding jerk of his swollen cock against his abdomen. "Mine, all mine," he mumbled as he continued tonguing his chest, drawing the little nipple into his mouth.

"Oh God, Ryder." Jason moaned loudly, his hands holding Ryder close, hips bucking. "Want you so bad. Please, now." He writhed underneath him, begging and gasping, Jason shifted, trying to climb from under him.

"Not yet, babe. I want to hear you scream for me." Ryder brushed his fingers over Jason's erection, loving the feel of that heated flesh against him. Bending down, he swiped his tongue across the silken tip, causing Jason to thrust his cock and his hips upward in swift movements. Ryder swirled his tongue around the full head and sucked in all that delicious male taste of Jason.

"Ryder, please," Jason moaned, begging for more.

With a wicked smile, Ryder let go of Jason's cock, giving it one last kiss. "Not loud enough. Besides, I want you inside me."

There was no sound in the room as even Jason's ragged breaths grew still. Ryder bit back a smile. "Do you want that too?" He crept back up Jason's body to stare deep into his lover's eyes. The longing and need in them nearly caused his heart to stop.

"I want to be inside you. I've wanted it for a while." Jason kissed him, his tongue tracing Ryder's lips. "Show me what to do. I want it to be perfect for you."

His sweet guy. Ryder kissed Jason's rough cheek and, in a hard and demanding voice, ordered him. "First, get the lube and condoms."

Jason scooted over to the night table and pulled open the drawer, grabbing the small bottle and a strip of condoms. He returned to Ryder's side, putting his hand on Ryder's cock.

"I've dreamed so many nights about this moment. I want you so badly. I'm afraid I won't last inside you." Jason's hand moved in long, loving caresses, stoking his fire as he nuzzled his neck and ear. Ryder writhed with yearning as Jason's questing mouth suddenly seemed to be everywhere on his body—breathing hotly in his ear, nipping at his jaw, sucking at his nipples.

Taking a deep breath, Ryder halted the movement of Jason's hands on his cock. "It's been so long since I've been with anyone, since I wanted anyone." He licked his lips, eying Jason's cock. His body clenched with the thought of Jason inside him. As Ryder wound his arms around Jason's neck, he whispered into the corner of his mouth. "You changed me from the moment I met you, and made me willing to take risks I never dreamed imaginable."

He waited, then smiled. "Make love to me, Jason."

JASON UNSNAPPED THE top of the container of lube and trickled some of the slippery gel onto his fingers. He tossed aside the bottle and took in the sight of Ryder lying before him like a golden god. "Tell me what to do. I don't want to hurt you."

"You won't. I promise."

Ryder's quiet voice and gentle smile reassured him, as he kissed the curve of Ryder's neck, then trailed his fingers down the crease of his ass. With a tentative touch, Jason pushed the tip of his index finger into the tiny opening. When Ryder shivered, growling low, he stopped, concerned and worried. "Did I hurt you?"

"No, don't stop." A flush crept over Ryder's face as he moaned with undisguised pleasure.

The desperate strain in Ryder's voice thrilled Jason as he continued the slide into his lover's body until his finger was buried deep, tightly held inside soft velvet heat and wetness. Excited and turned on, Jason stroked himself with his free hand.

"Jason, God, don't stop. Please."

With his head thrown back in abandon, teeth worrying his lips and his hand stroking his cock, Ryder looked turned on and blissed out. Jason sank a second finger next to the first, stretching the small, snug opening.

His own cock, stiffer than it had ever been, pulsed with need. Because he wanted to please this wonderful man, he'd watched some man-on-man videos over the past few weeks, trying to learn how best to pleasure a lover. Now that his initial nerves were dispensed with, he stroked Ryder's firm thighs, reaching up to gently tug his balls and tickle the sensitive skin behind them.

Ryder jerked, causing Jason's fingers to spread apart even more inside. He stretched his fingers wide, then pushed them in, curling upward until he touched the small knot of tissue he'd only read about. He brushed his fingers across it and listened to Ryder wail his pleasure.

"Oh God, Jason, please." Ryder bit back a moan, eyes squeezed shut, his hand jerking his cock with hard tugs. The pleading grew heavier and rougher. "Need you, babe, please."

Jason removed his fingers, tore open the condom wrapper with shaking hands, sheathed himself, then poured more lube over his erection. He positioned the head of his cock at Ryder's impossibly small opening. A moment of uncertainty stopped him.

Jason glanced up, and Ryder's dark, hungry gaze had him mesmerized, the desire so open it took his breath away.

"Do it, Jase. Slowly push yourself in. I can't wait to have a part of you inside me." He gave him a lazy smile. "Don't you know by now how much I love you?"

Pure joy filled Jason, and his heart tripped with happiness. He pressed a swift kiss to Ryder's lips, then whispered against his mouth, "I was so scared at first. I was overwhelmed by everything. Overwhelmed, overpowered, and in way, way over my head."

"And now?" Ryder's luminous eyes shined, even in the dimness of the bedroom.

Jason kissed him again, resting his forehead against Ryder's. "And now I love you more than I ever thought possible. I'll do anything to keep you happy."

"Then get on with it, babe. Make us both happy." Ryder smiled against his cheek.

Jason pushed the head of his cock into Ryder's opening and felt the resistance, but hearing Ryder's soft cries and gentle urgings, continued to push through the tight barrier. He stopped at his lover's hiss, then continued on past that ring of muscle, sinking himself into a man for the first time. His aching cock was gripped tight, clutched in a velvet slide of hot pleasure. He knew for certain, once he was inside Ryder completely, this was where he was meant to be.

"Move, please," Ryder whispered, and Jason lifted on his hands and pulled out halfway, then pushed back in. Remembering Ryder's extreme reaction when he hit his prostate, he tried to aim for that pleasure spot once again. The head of his cock rubbed against the spongy knot, and Ryder moaned his passion. He stroked that angle, relentless in his desire to please, while underneath him, Ryder writhed and begged, scrabbling at the bedsheets, calling out in unintelligible gibberish as his hips frantically bucked up against him, slotting him deeper and deeper inside. Jason reached down and pulled on Ryder's straining cock, stroking rough and fast. Within minutes, Ryder arched and exploded, jerking endlessly all over his abdomen and chest. The thrill of having Ryder shatter beneath him, knowing he'd given this beautiful man such joy, rushed over him in a blinding wave of passion and heat.

He pounded into Ryder's body, unrelenting in his need to claim him and become a part of him forever. Jason gritted his teeth as he drove himself deeper inside Ryder. He thrust harder; his body trembled and a tingling radiated up his spine. His balls drew tight, and sparks appeared in his peripheral vision. "Ryder." He sobbed as he grabbed Ryder's shoulders, digging his fingers into the skin, sliding himself inside as far as he could.

All at once his orgasm hit, roaring through his body, engulfing him in hot white light, driving him forward to collapse in a sated, puddled mess on top of Ryder's sweat-slicked body. His dick pulsed and throbbed as he emptied himself into the condom. After several minutes, when Jason discovered he could once again move, he slipped out of Ryder. After disposing of the condom, Jason slid back into Ryder's arms, flinging a leg over his hip to snuggle close. Ryder pulled him closer.

"Hey, you." Ryder kissed him, then searched his face, concern clouding his eyes. "How do you feel?" They rolled on their sides, bodies still touching. Ryder's hands kneaded his back, and Jason arched into the incredible sensation, moaning his pleasure. "Can I assume you feel okay about everything, still?"

Jason forced himself to stay awake long enough to kiss Ryder and pull the covers they'd kicked off earlier over their exhausted bodies. "I feel better than okay. All thanks to you." He snuggled into Ryder's arms. "I hope I didn't disappoint you."

Ryder remained quiet, his arm tight around Jason's shoulders. The even sound of his breathing led Jason to believe he'd fallen asleep. As Jason was about to drop off himself, though, Ryder spoke.

"I didn't realize how being with the right person could change your world and your outlook on everything, but you have to know you rescued me from myself. You've made everything in my life so much better from the moment I met you."

Jason said nothing, listening to Ryder speak from his soul.

"All I ever wanted was to be loved. Being with you tonight, though, forced me to admit that I'd never really been in love before. I'm in so deep with you, Jason, I don't ever want to let go."

Jason trailed his fingers over the strong muscles of Ryder's back. "Tonight, telling my family and having you by my side seemed as natural as breathing. No one's ever cared about me like you have, and I don't know how I got so lucky, but I'll never let you go now. Even if my family hadn't accepted me being gay, I would choose you."

They hugged tight, and the sticky feel of their bodies alerted Jason to the fact that they needed to shower.

"Dude, come on, we're gross." Feeling energized, he jumped out of bed, slapped Ryder's ass, and winked. "Bet you'll be sore for a while."

He laughed until Ryder manhandled him into the shower, turned on the water, and got on his knees. Then it was no laughing matter at all.

Chapter Eighteen

TRY AS HE might, Ryder couldn't keep a smile from his face the next morning as he walked into Rescue Me with Pearl. Connor sat at his desk, surprising him; during the week he normally worked at legal aid.

"Hey, what're you doing here?" Ryder chose a muffin from the box Emily had on her desk. "Shouldn't you be downtown?" He bit into a cranberry and hummed his appreciation. "God, these are good." After another bite and a sip of coffee, he sat at his desk and checked his calendar. The soreness in his ass reminded him of the night spent with Jason, and as he shifted in his seat to get comfortable, he couldn't help grinning. Waking up with Jason, having breakfast, and doing all their mundane morning tasks had him imagining how it could be if they ever lived together.

"Hey, dream lover. Get your head out of your ass, or whoever's ass it's been in." Connor stood before him, snapping his fingers to get attention.

"Hmm? What is it? What do you want?" He checked his phone to find a text from Jason.

Landon will be here at 4. Dinner later then Drummers? I want to talk to John.

He immediately answered. *I'll be there at 5 so Landon can work. Everything else sounds great.*

Try as he might, Ryder couldn't quite hold back a smile from touching his lips. Connor pounced all over him like a cat on a mouse. "You got laid. Hallelujah. Emily, did you hear?" Connor called out. "The man finally got laid." Connor cackled with glee as Ryder peered at his best friend in disgust.

"I didn't get laid, you asshole."

Emily sat down on his desk, scrutinizing his face. "You do seem different, sweetie. Care to share with your best friends?" Connor stood behind her, sliding his arms around her waist. "You tell us your secret, and we'll tell you ours." She kissed Connor's cheek.

Instantly, he was on alert. "What's going on? What secret?"

Connor stared him down. "Uh-uh, man. You first."

He could feel the heat creep up his face. "Jason and I are a couple."

Emily squealed, and Connor laughed. "A couple of what?" He snickered, and Ryder rolled his eyes as he accepted Emily's hug.

"Your husband is such a jerk."

"I know. Ignore him like I do. When did this all happen?" She bounced up and down on her toes. "I knew you were perfect together."

"It's all pretty new, but I met his family last night. Everything was fine, except for Liam." It still hurt replaying Liam's hurtful words. He'd thought they were all right with each other, friends even. Never once had he ever thought Liam actively hated gay people. "He was pretty awful."

"Guy's a fucking prick." Connor swore viciously. "I always knew he felt like that." He came over and hugged Ryder. "I'm happy for you, man. Jase is cool and a great guy. But I never knew he was gay." He cocked an inquiring brow.

"There was some guy in college, but it didn't lead anywhere, and he never pursued any other relationships with men. I don't even care. I'm happy." Ryder's two friends grinned back at him. "So what's your secret, you two? I don't think I've ever seen such mysterious smiles on your faces."

Emily looked at Connor, then back at him. "We're going to have a baby." She placed her hands over her still-flat stomach. "In about six months or so." Her face flushed pink. "You're going to be an uncle."

Letting out a whoop of congratulations, he picked Emily up and hugged her hard. "I'm so happy for you, baby. You're going to make an amazing mommy." Connor stood watching them, a smile on his lips. Ryder hugged him close. "Hey, Daddy." Their baby would be so lucky to have a man like Connor as a father.

Connor turned white as chalk. "Oh shit. I'm going to be a father." He wobbled and grabbed the back of the chair. "I gotta sit down."

Ryder busted out laughing.

Emily whispered to him, "He fainted in the doctor's office when we found out. He's such a wimp."

Ryder laughed until the tears rolled down his face. His joy reached no bounds.

*　*　*　*　*

"SO THE VENTS have to be placed here; otherwise the smoke and cooking smells from the restaurant will be drawn back into the building, right?" Landon pointed to the blueprints unrolled on the desk.

"I don't think the people would appreciate paying however many millions of dollars for their lofts and having them stink like yesterday's dinner." Jason grinned at Landon.

The kid was smart. He asked the right questions, never complained when asked to do something menial, and always showed up on time. A great assistant. The fact that Ryder was his brother was irrelevant for work purposes, except that Landon's presence assured Jason he'd get to see his boyfriend. His lover. He couldn't help the goofy grin he knew was plastered on his face. The happiness in his heart glowed bright for anyone who cared to notice. Even the crew made cracks about it, joking, "Bossman must be in love," or "Look at that grin. He must be getting some."

His cock twitched with interest as he replayed last night in his mind. In his deepest fantasies, he'd never dreamed that making love to a man would bring the pleasure it had. All the years with Chloe and other women were like a drop of rain in a puddle—nothing lasting, no one ever standing out. One night with Ryder and he couldn't erase the feel of his lover's tongue sliding in and out of his mouth, or wrapped around his dick.

Last night, when he'd entered Ryder's body, it had a sense of rightness, of belonging. He could still feel that grasp and pull of Ryder's body, drawing him in farther and deeper and hotter...

"Uh, Jason? Everything all right?"

He jerked back to the present, his breathing strained, and—*oh shit*—a rock-hard erection straining against his zipper. Embarrassed, he cleared his throat and moved behind the desk. "Er, yeah, sure, fine. I'm, ah—"

"Thinking about your girlfriend, from the look of it." Landon snickered, rolling up the blueprints and placing them back in their protective tube. "She must be hot to get you so worked up."

He glared at Landon. "Shut up. You're only seventeen. Don't even think I'm gonna talk to you about sex." He took the blueprints from Landon and replaced them on a special rack he had built to hold them. He checked his watch. "Want to come with me for a walk-through on today's work? I can't believe it's almost finished."

Landon jumped to his feet. "Definitely. I can't wait to see what it looks like inside." He grabbed his backpack. "Ryder said he'd be here around five, and

then we'd hang out until you guys were ready to leave."
He hesitated a moment. "Sorry about the girlfriend
crack."

Jason decided Ryder had better tell his brother they
were together as soon as possible. It wasn't fair to the
kid, especially now that Jason's family knew. Besides, he
liked Landon and didn't want to keep anything from
him. He didn't think Landon would have a problem
knowing that Jason and Ryder were lovers.

"No, I'm sorry I snapped at you. I overreacted.
You're seventeen, not a little kid. Let's go, then." He put
on his jacket. "It's getting warmer every day, thank God.
This winter was a bitch. Ready to go?"

"Oh, shit."

Jason turned to see what the problem was. A white-
faced Landon stood frozen, staring at the screen of his
phone. "Trouble?" Whatever it was couldn't be good.
He'd never seen the kid so scared.

"My mom," he said, lifting his blue-eyed gaze to the
ceiling, then him.

Jason could see fear etched in his face. What kind of
woman inspired such panic in her own child? Then he
remembered how she'd treated Ryder, and he understood.

"Sh-she's here, outside, and wants to talk to me. I
know it's a trap. She must suspect something or know
that Ryder and I have been seeing each other again." He
smashed the door with his backpack. "Why can't she
leave us alone? He's my brother. I'm never gonna stop

wanting to see him."

Jason glanced away from the stark plea in the boy's eyes. Why couldn't his brother feel like Landon? "Don't worry. You're here working, and Ryder isn't due for almost an hour. We can deal with her, and she'll be gone before he gets here."

Landon rolled his eyes. "She's sneaky and smart, remember. I know she's up to something." He picked up his backpack. "Let me go meet her before she decides to come in."

Well, there was no way in hell he was letting Ryder's mother onto his site and not being there to meet the bitch. He needed to lay eyes on the woman who had rejected her son so callously simply because he was gay. Once again, he thanked God for his mother, who loved him no matter what. Even if she didn't understand his choices, she stood by him, the way a mother should.

"I'm coming with you."

Landon's eyes flared with alarm. "No way. She'll eat you alive. You'll see, she'll make you somehow tell her about Ryder." A pale sheen of sweat dampened his face, and his voice quavered with nerves.

Jason scoffed. "Shit, better men than your mom have tried to bully me. Big ugly construction workers." He patted Landon on his shoulder. "Don't worry. I can handle her. Come on."

They walked out of the trailer, and Jason spotted her immediately. Small, stick-thin, and pale blonde, Mrs. Astrid Daniels exuded disapproval from every pore of her fine-boned body. Jason shuddered.

"Damn, that's your mom?" He shivered again and swore a cold wind swept through his body at the mere sight of her. The woman had no warmth to her at all. Amazing that she had birthed two loving children like Ryder and Landon.

Landon didn't bother to answer him, choosing instead to confront his mother head on. "Mom, what are you doing here? I'm working."

She ran a disapproving eye over Jason, then turned to her son. "I am aware. I'm not certain this is the right atmosphere for you. You needn't be here, with all these rough men and dangerous equipment. If you wanted to work, your father could find you a job at the firm."

Jason didn't give Landon a chance to respond. He turned on his charm and gave her the "meeting your girlfriend's mom" smile. "Mrs. Daniels, what a pleasure to meet you. I'm Jason Mallory, owner of the firm, and I must thank you for allowing your very talented son to work here as a high school intern. I'm amazed at how helpful he is, and I know I have only you to thank."

"Well, yes, but I'm not sure it's—"

"This will be an excellent extracurricular activity for his college résumé, and I know he's learning so much, right, Landon?" His hoped the kid would catch on and play along.

"Yes, Mom. Mr. Mallory is showing me how to read blueprints and learn all about the internal structure of various buildings. I know this will help me with my grades as well, since we discuss theories based on physics and other aerodynamic problems."

Jason laughed inside. Kid was good on his feet. He had to hand it to him. Mrs. Daniels, however, was no fool.

"How did you even meet my son? Mr. Mallory, did you say your name was?" Her eyes narrowed. "Where are you from?" The snobbery oozed out of her. "You don't live in Manhattan, do you?"

"No ma'am. I live in Brooklyn. My firm works with many high schools to give the kids a chance for hands-on experience in the field of construction or architecture." It was doubtful she'd check with the high school to learn that was a bald-faced lie.

"But you aren't an architect. You're nothing more than a glorified construction worker, are you?" Her lips curled in distaste.

Oh, the woman was a bitch. But it was four thirty, and he needed to make nice and get her out of here before Ryder came.

"I have a degree in architecture from Syracuse University, ma'am. My brother and I started this construction firm. So I guess you could say I'm both." He put his arm around Landon. "Your son's never on the physical site of the building when the men are working. He's either here in the office, or at the Buildings Department, or other city agencies when I need assistance. I'd never put his safety in jeopardy."

Her nose wrinkled as she gave a disapproving sniff.

"Landon, this all seems rather menial to me. Couldn't you find something in an office where you wouldn't have to grub around with all these people?" She gestured to the group of men who were on their break, sitting around laughing and telling jokes. "You'd really be much better off working in a corporate environment like the one the firm provides. After all, one day you'll be working there."

"Mom, I really like working here. And it isn't for too much longer." Jason watched Landon attempt to reason with her for approval. "Once finals start, I won't be working. Plus, I have all my SAT stuff to do. So really, it's only for, like, another month or so."

Jason could virtually see her brain searching for a reason to forbid her son to come, but she couldn't come up with a viable response to Landon's well-thought-out plan. "Very well. I'll allow this for one more month. Then I think you'll have acquired enough 'experience' or whatever it is you think you're getting here." Those thin lips of hers pinched with distaste.

At least she had a heart concerning one son. "Thank you, Mrs. Daniels."

"Yes, well, Landon, isn't it time for you to come home? I have James here with the car. You can ride home with me." A black sedan waited by the curb.

Shit, no. "Ahh, we weren't finished for the day, Mrs. Daniels. Landon has one more thing to complete here, and then I promise I'll send him home in a cab myself, as I know you wouldn't want him on the subway after dark." He held his breath, waiting for her answer.

She raked him with another disapproving, icy glare. "I can't imagine what you have him doing so late in the day, but very well." She turned the full force of her frost-bitten glare on her son. "Dinner is at seven thirty. I expect you to be there. Your father will be joining us tonight. He's invited his old friend who is on the admissions committee at Princeton. Make sure you aren't late." She gave him a curt nod. "Mr. Mallory." Then she was gone.

They watched the driver hold the door for her as she entered the car, then drive away. After the sedan disappeared down Broadway, he chuckled. "God almighty, kid. Too bad you aren't old enough to drink. 'Cause you sure deserve one after that."

"Yeah, right?" Landon huffed a brief, strained laugh; then his whole demeanor changed. A brilliant smile broke over his face as he waved at a tall figure walking down the block. "Over here," he called.

Ryder.

Jason's heartbeat quickened at the sight of his lover. Once again Ryder wore a suit, but this time it was a dark charcoal gray. He'd paired it with a crisp white shirt and a green-patterned silk tie. The man was nothing short of mouthwatering. Jason frowned, noticing plenty of women and quite a few men checking Ryder out.

Yeah, that's right. All that is mine.

Jason's hands itched to run through the golden,

shining hair flopping over Ryder's brow. His face heated recalling how only last night he grabbed Ryder by that gorgeous mane as he slammed into his perfectly shaped ass. Lost in a sexual fantasy, he jumped, startled when Ryder called his name.

"Yo, earth to Jason. What's up, man? You were a million miles away." Ryder's laughing face and wink let him know he knew exactly what Jason was thinking. "I hope it was something special."

Jason smirked back at Ryder. "Nothing big."

The three of them returned to the trailer, and Jason made Ryder a coffee and gave Landon a bottle of water.

Landon stood watching the two of them, a perplexed look on his face. "Can I ask you guys a question? And I hope you don't get mad at me."

Jason shrugged. "Sure, go ahead."

Landon licked his lips. "Are you two together, like as a couple? The only reason I'm asking is that you looked so happy to see Ry today, and Ryder always talks about you so much." His voice trailed off as he looked at both of them.

Jason quirked a brow. "Ry?"

Ryder cleared his throat. "I wanted to wait until things were settled between Jason and me, but now that it's all good, yeah, Jason and I are together. You're sure you're all right with it?"

Jason stood by Ryder's side, a supportive hand resting on his shoulder. "You're still okay working here, right?" He'd really hate to lose the kid.

Landon broke out in a big smile. "I think it's cool. Jason's a great guy, and I'm really happy for you." Tears prickled in Jason's eyes as the brothers hugged. This was the best of all possible outcomes. He pushed aside thoughts of Liam and his own disappointment.

"Landon." He suddenly remembered Mrs. Daniels' visit. "Tell Ryder about your mother."

Ryder's face darkened as Landon recounted the afternoon visit.

"But honestly, I think she left being okay with me being here. Don't worry." He checked his phone. "Shit, I gotta go home and get ready for that stupid dinner."

Ryder hugged him. "It's okay." His face fell. "Um, does Dad ever mention me or talk about me? Ever? Like even when Mom isn't around?"

Jason's heart broke all over for him.

Landon shook his head. "He's never home. I think this is the first time he'll be home for dinner in over a month. The few times I did see him, he looked really sad and tired."

"I'd be sad too, if I was married to your mom. No offense, but God, that woman is arctic." Jason shivered. Astrid Daniels could freeze water with a look.

Landon agreed. "Yeah, tell me about it." He hugged Ryder. "It was great to see you. Tomorrow too?"

Ryder nodded. "Yep, provided the slave driver you have for a boss doesn't work you too hard."

They all laughed, and Jason received a shock when Landon gave him a fierce hug good-bye, whispering in his ear, "I'm really glad you're with Ryder. You're the best." He picked up his backpack and ran out.

Ryder's arms slid around him. A warm breath drifted over his neck as Jason relaxed in his embrace.

"You are the best." Contentment spread through him, as Ryder nibbled on his ear, sending an electric shock directly to his groin. "I thought about you all day while I was in court." Ryder's husky voice set Jason's blood on fire. "Instead of my case, all I could think of was how I wanted you in my mouth."

An inarticulate sound escaped Jason's throat.

"I wish the door had a lock." As Ryder continued to rain kisses on Jason's neck and jaw, his hand moved under Jason's sweater to caress his back.

The naked hunger on Ryder's face was palpable. "There is," said Jason, his voice rough with desire.

Ryder's blue gaze darkened. "Go do it. Now. Lock the door."

Jason scrambled and locked the door. "Ry." He couldn't take another step, his legs shook so. In one long stride, Ryder was there, hard up against him, pulling down Jason's zipper, freeing his engorged cock from his jeans.

"God, do it. Do it now." Jason moaned, gripping the doorknob behind him.

Ryder smirked. "Not so fast. I need to enjoy this view." He went down on his knees and yanked down Jason's pants and boxers. Ryder held the base of his cock, squeezing it hard. He licked Jason's balls, then transferred his attention to the drops trickling from the tiny slit at the tip of his erection.

Jason cried out, jerking his hips forward, trying desperately to find Ryder's mouth. "Suck me already, or I'm gonna come all over your face."

Ryder's eyes gleamed with delight. "Save that thought for tonight." In one fluid motion, he engulfed Jason's dick into the heated cavern of his mouth.

Stars flickered before Jason's eyes, and he began thrusting, fucking Ryder's hot, wet mouth. "I can't hold on too much longer." Whatever Ryder was doing with his tongue should be illegal, he thought in a haze of lust as it wrapped around his cock. It took every ounce of strength not to scream the trailer down as the suction, heat, and friction drove him to the edge of oblivion.

Ryder's fingers massaged his balls and slid toward his ass. "Inside me, please, please." Jason heard himself begging, shameless with greedy desire, but didn't care. "Now, goddamn it. Do it." He moaned loud and long, arching into Ryder's hand, hungering for his finger, his lips, anything to end the need scorching within him.

A fingertip brushed up against his hole, circling, then entering the tight opening the tiniest bit. That was all he needed, and with a shout, Jason exploded, emptying himself in Ryder's mouth. It was the most blinding orgasm he'd ever had, incinerating his senses and his ability to think. When he came to, Ryder held him close.

"You're beautiful when you come, you know that?"

Jason's face heated. "That was intense." The heady scent of their bodies mingled with the smell of sex as he nuzzled into Ryder's chest. Jason yawned, then stretched, curving his arms around his Ryder's neck to press a kiss against the still rapidly beating pulse in his neck. "It's never been like this before with anyone, ever."

Ryder's arms tightened around him as he managed a weak chuckle, then returned the kiss. "Let's get you cleaned up and grab some dinner. Remember, you said you wanted to talk to John about us." He kissed him again, smoothing his hair back.

Jason would love nothing more than to spend the entire night in bed, underneath Ryder, but that would come later, after he spoke to John and told him he and Ryder were together.

His heartbeat quickened, praying John wasn't going be like his brother Liam.

Chapter Nineteen

I T WASN'T WITHOUT some trepidation that Jason entered Drummers that night. Even though he had all his friends and Mark around him, he knew very well that Liam could turn the scene ugly in a hot minute.

He and Ryder took a seat at the bar. It was crowded, what with March Madness nearing its close. John approached, an easy smile on his face. "Hey, guys. The usual?" At their nods, he uncapped a beer for Ryder and slid it over. "Dude, I finally got your favorite on tap. You want that, or you still want the bottle?" He smirked. "The way your boys from Syracuse are playing, maybe you need a whole pitcher for yourself."

"Shut up, man. I'll take it on tap." Jason grabbed some sliders and pushed the plate over to Ryder. Mark hurried in, cheeks red from the cold, his arm around a young blonde woman. A few minutes later, Connor and Emily arrived. Her face glowed with happiness. Jason jumped off his seat and pushed his way through the crowd until he reached them.

"Hey, Ryder told me the news." He bent down and

kissed Emily, then hugged her. "I'm so happy and excited for you."

Emily returned his hug. "Thanks. I'm so happy for you also, honey. I knew you two were perfect for each other. I saw it the first day we met you."

Connor came and hugged him too. "Ryder's been my best friend since law school, and he's the greatest guy I know. His heart is so full and open; that's why he can't understand people who treat him like shit, because he would never be like that himself." No one knew Ryder better than Connor, so to have his approval meant everything to Jason. "You've been so good for him, Jase. He's never been as happy as when he's with you. The breakup with Matt was bad, but when his parents turned their backs on him, I worried he might do something drastic."

How lucky Ryder was to have a friend like Connor. Jason had thought his brother would be like that, steadfast, always having his back. Thank God at least Mark stood by him, but losing Liam was like losing one of his limbs—the ache still remained, even though the physical part of the body was gone.

"I'll never hurt Ryder," Jason assured them both. "I love him. He's the best thing that's ever happened to me."

Emily wiped the tears from her eyes. "That's all we ever wanted for him. To find someone to love and to be as happy as we are." She sniffled and fumbled for a tissue.

"She's so emotional lately." Connor's mock whisper had Emily glaring at him. "Must be all those hormones."

"Ooh, wait till I get my hands on you." Emily grabbed her husband, and Jason couldn't help but laugh.

"You're in trouble now, my man."

Connor smirked. "She gets horny when she's feisty. I'll reap the rewards later at home." He ducked when Emily tried to smack him.

Jason beat a hasty retreat, leaving the warring couple to kiss and make up, and returned to Ryder, who'd been joined by his brother Mark and the girl.

"Hi." He and Mark briefly hugged, and he waited for an introduction.

"This is Julie." Mark smiled at the young woman. "She and I are in the same psych class, and when I saw her wearing a Nets shirt, well, you know I had to ask her out."

Her light laugh rang sweet. "Big Nets fan here. I'm so thrilled they're back in New York now." She took a sip of her drink. "Ryder was telling me about the pit bull rescue. I'd love to help out after classes and on the weekends if you need me."

Ryder draped his arm around Jason's shoulder. This was the first time they'd gone out together as a couple. Instead of fear or shame, warmth and contentment settled within Jason at the thought that he would be going home with him. Every single night. A shiver ran through him as Ryder's hand idly stroked his shoulder. The acceptance by their friends and family made the night seem almost celebratory. If Liam could only understand him and share in his happiness, his life would be complete.

He slipped his arm around Ryder's waist. "That sounds great, Ry, doesn't it? I know you guys need help now that you're preparing for the fund-raiser." He took the beer Mark handed him. "I'll do whatever I can to help."

"Me too," Mark joined in. "Whatever you need, I'm there. I love Troup. He's a great dog."

"Well, what do we have here, a queer convention?"

Jason's heart sank at the sound of Liam's sneering voice. He tensed and withdrew his arm from around Ryder's waist. "Keep moving, Liam. No one is asking for your opinion."

Ryder whispered in his ear, "Don't let him get to you. He's trying to make you angry. Rise above it." He squeezed his shoulder.

"Make sure you listen to your boyfriend, Jason. Is he the master in the bedroom too? What do you guys call it, a top?" Liam snickered, then walked up to the bar. "Yo, John, gimme a beer."

John stood behind the bar with his arms folded. His hazel eyes blazed, fierce with anger.

"No."

Liam's grin faltered; then he laughed. "Quit fucking with me, man. Give me a beer."

John braced his arms on the bar. "I said no. See the sign?" John pointed to the sign over the bar that read MANAGEMENT RESERVES THE RIGHT TO REFUSE SERVICE TO ANY PATRON.

"I'm refusing."

Liam sputtered in his rage. "What the fuck? What did I do?"

"You're a fucking jerk, the way you talked to Jase. So unless you're willing to apologize and act like a decent human being, you can walk the fuck out of my bar."

"Don't tell me you're okay with him and this queer."

"Shut the hell up, you goddamn asshole." John's large fist banged, causing several glasses to fall to the floor and shatter. The entire bar quieted down. "Do you know what you're doing, treating your brother like this? It's so fucking wrong to speak to anyone like this, but your own brother, your flesh and blood?"

John grabbed a picture off the wall, and Jason's heart skipped. "Ah, shit."

Ryder leaned over. "Who's that?"

Jason whispered back, "That's Eric. John's older brother. He died in his first tour in Afghanistan three years ago." He blinked back tears. "He was a great guy, and John's only sibling—his only family, actually, since his parents died years ago."

"Shit." Ryder scrubbed his face with his hands. "That's fucking awful."

John shoved the picture under Liam's pale face. "Do you remember my brother, Liam? Of course you do. *We fucking worshipped him.* Remember how we toasted him right here three years ago and told him that bar stool would be waiting for him when he came home? Do you?"

Liam nodded.

"But he isn't coming home. He isn't ever fucking coming home, and he'll never sit there again. And every day I open this bar, and all I want is for Eric to walk through that door, laugh, and tell me it was a joke, and I can wake up from this fucking nightmare that he's gone, and I never had a chance to say good-bye and tell him I love him."

Jason could hardly see through his tears and heard Emily weeping. Ryder put his arm around him, and the wetness on Ryder's cheek mixed with his own.

Mercilessly, John continued. "My brother died alone in a strange country with no one around who loved him. So now I want you to tell me that you're going to turn your back on your brother, one of the nicest fucking guys I've ever known, and walk out of his life and never speak to him again because you don't approve of who he sleeps with. And what the fuck happens if he gets hit by a car when he walks out of this bar tonight, and you never have that chance to say you're sorry or to say good-bye and he dies alone? Do you want the last memory between you and him to be your anger, your hatred?"

John's chest heaved as he pushed his face into Liam's. "Are you going to be able to live with yourself? Because I'm gonna fucking tell you, you won't. I had the best relationship with Eric, and I almost put a gun to my head to end it all because I couldn't stand the pain of his death. Will you be able to live with your pain?"

John beckoned Jason, and after taking a deep breath, he walked over, standing next to Liam. "Do you love your brother, Jase?"

He nodded. "No matter what he says to me, he'll always be my brother."

John turned to Liam, who, to Jason's shock, stood white-face and devastated. "And you. Do you love your brother? Or are you willing to throw it all away because of your ignorance and stupidity? What's happened to you? The man I've been friends with since high school would never behave like this. Are you willing to say good-bye to Jase forever? Are you willing to risk it all?"

The only noise in the bar was John's heavy breathing. Liam's head bowed, and his shoulders shook. Jason put his hand on Liam's shoulder. "Hey, Liam. It's okay."

Liam shook his head. Jason put his arms around his brother, holding his breath in case Liam pulled away from him, praying that he didn't.

He didn't.

There wasn't anything else he could do, except hold on to Liam, his heavy body, damp with sweat, racked with the effort of containing his sobs.

"I'm sorry." The words wrenched out of his mouth, guttural and laced with anguish. "Oh God, Jase, I'm sorry. I'm a fucking idiot. Don't walk out on me. I couldn't deal with losing you, like John lost Eric. Please. Don't hate me."

There was no joy here in flaying Liam apart. His humiliation would run deep and strong for a while, but that was Liam's cross to bear. The best Jason could do was try to regain the bond of family there was between them. It would take time to mend the rift, as what Liam had said to Ryder and him was so devastating and hurtful. But, if his brother was willing to make the effort to change, he would make the effort to help him.

"I don't hate you." It was true. He couldn't hate his brother, even if he didn't understand why Liam felt the way he did. "You've made it hard for anyone to like you these past few weeks, though."

Liam's mottled, tear-streaked face flushed a deeper red. He opened his mouth as if to speak, then shut it and shook his head, scrubbing his hands over his face.

"Let's go sit over here." Jason led him to a table in the corner. He sat with his back to a scowling Ryder. He knew Ryder would be annoyed with him for forgiving Liam, but he'd deal with it later. This wasn't so simple. It was his brother. He had to give him a second chance. "Why don't you talk to me now? No one else can hear us."

Liam slanted a look up to him as his fingers began to

systematically crumble the chips inside the basket on the table. "I dunno. It was so weird. One minute you're banging Chloe; the next you're kissing a guy." He swallowed hard. "I don't understand you."

"I'm not asking for you to understand me. I'm asking you to stand by me. Support me. Continue to love me. Who I choose to love isn't a group project. You don't get to decide what's right for me." Jason grabbed the basket away to focus Liam's attention. "I'm not even asking you to like Ryder or approve of our relationship." Liam's eyes flickered behind him to where Ryder stood with everyone else, and Jason waited until his brother's concentration returned back to him. "But this is who I am, and who I'm going to be with. You don't ask my approval for who you date or sleep with; I'm not asking for yours. I ask only that you be civil and not make nasty comments."

Liam hesitated, then asked, "Are you really in love with him?"

Without any hesitation, he nodded. "Yeah. I am, very much so. And he is with me. We fit. I don't know how else to put it. When I'm with him, I'm the happiest I've ever been. So whether you like it or not, Ryder's here to stay, and you need to make peace with that. Got it?" He glared at him.

"Trying to be a hard-ass, huh?" Liam paled. "Oh shit, I didn't mean it that way. I'm sorry."

Jason burst out laughing. "Actually that was pretty funny. I know you didn't." He stood, anxious to get back to Ryder. "We're all good, right?"

"Yeah. You know I'm an idiot sometimes. I'll make the effort, I promise."

"That's all I wanted." Liam stood, and they hugged each other. "I'll catch you later." Jason returned to the group, where they pounced on him with questions. Everyone but Ryder, who leaned against the bar, pensive and remote.

Jason excused himself to join Ryder. "Hey, you." He touched Ryder's shoulder. "Why so quiet? Everything all right?" It was unusual now for Ryder to brood and be distant.

"I don't know, Jase. Is this a good idea, you and me? I'm driving a wedge between you and your brother. I know your father doesn't really understand or like our relationship, and I'm sure, as sweet as your mom is, she'd rather you settle down with a nice girl and have babies." His haunted eyes stared across the room. "I've really fucked up your life."

What a shit storm this night was turning out to be. "You know what isn't a good idea? Being here with all these people right now. Be with me, and let me show you how right we are together." More than ever, he needed him. Tonight. The rapid pulse beating in Ryder's throat signaled how affected he was.

"Don't you want to stay and hang out with every-one?" Ryder's voice shook.

"I want you inside me." Jason put out his hand. He watched Ryder's eyes widen, then glow with rising passion.

Ryder gulped down the rest of his beer and took Jason's hand. "Good night, everybody." They practically ran out of the bar, to the grins and catcalls of their friends and family.

Chapter Twenty

T HEY HELD HANDS throughout the entire car ride and kissed like lovesick teenagers at every light, drawing honking horns from cars filled with women and sometimes men, giving them the thumbs-up. Ryder couldn't give two shits who saw what, as long as he got Jason home and in his bed as soon as possible.

"My parents have Troup since I knew it would be a long day, so we can go to yours, okay?" Jason steered the truck onto the Gowanus Expressway, toward the Brooklyn Bridge. The magnificent skyline of the city, dripping in twinkling lights, rose in front of them as they made the curve onto the BQE.

"Mmh. Sure. Sounds perfect." Anything that involved Jason in his apartment for the night was more than fine with him. The only thing he could think about was Jason, stretched out on his bed or on top of him, riding into oblivion. And though he spoke bravely, Ryder wanted to make Jason's first time perfect for him. It was going to hurt and feel strange, so he was willing to do anything he could do to ease his discomfort.

He remembered his own awkward and painful first time, in college. It became easier, but sex had never satisfied anything more for him than a physical urge. Not even with Matt, whom he thought he loved. Being with Jason now, he understood what Connor meant the night he told him he was going to ask Emily to marry him.

"It's hard to explain, man, but you know how it is when you find that last piece of a puzzle and it's completed, and it finally makes sense? That's how she makes me feel. Like I make sense and I'm finally whole."

Jason was his puzzle piece. By some chance in this crazy big city, one little dog had brought them together. He leaned over and kissed his cheek as they headed into the city. "I love you."

Jason grinned. "I love you too."

Luckily they made all the lights on Houston Street, and it wasn't long before they pulled into the garage under his apartment building. He'd gotten Jason a guest parking pass to make it easier for him to park his truck in Ryder's garage. Jason gave the keys to the valet and told him it was for overnight parking, and the young guy smirked.

Ryder wasn't in the mood for any more bullshit tonight. Stepping into the guy's face, he challenged him. "You have a problem with something?"

The valet paled and scuttled away from him. "No sir."

"Good." He turned around. "Let's go, Jase."

He and Jason waited for the elevator that would take them to the first level, and it seemed an eternity before the doors opened. They stepped inside, and no sooner did the doors close than he pushed Jason up against the wall and took possession of his mouth. Their tongues met and clashed; their lips pressed and sucked until his heart pounded so hard he thought it would explode out of his chest. He reached down and cupped Jason's hard-on, rubbing and squeezing it through his jeans.

"If you don't stop that, I'm gonna come in my jeans, making this an early night."

"Oh, babe, if you think you're only gonna come once tonight, you're in for a surprise." He stuck his tongue in Jason's ear, delighting in the moans that echoed in the small elevator chamber. "I'm gonna make you come so many times and so hard you won't be able to crawl, never mind walk."

Jason's cock jumped beneath Ryder's roving hand, and his whimper only served to make Ryder suck his ear and neck harder. He pulled away when the bell rang, leaving Jason dazed, confused, and quivering from head to toe. Tucking Jason into his side, with his arm wrapped around him, Ryder walked past a smiling Clarence.

"Good night, Mr. Daniels, Mr. Mallory." Clarence tipped his hat. "Have a good evening."

"Good night, Clarence." Jason, he saw, could only muster a smile. They entered the elevator, where Ryder once again, flattened him against the wall and proceeded to kiss him senseless.

"Do you want to know what I'm gonna do to you, hmm?" He licked his way down Jason's neck, biting and scoring his skin as he held him pinned up against the elevator wall, chest to chest, cock to cock. Ryder rolled his hips against Jason's, rubbing at the hardness straining to break free. Jason's breathy moans played like music to his ears.

"I'm going to suck and kiss your mouth until I steal the breath from your body. Then I'm going to lick you from your neck down to your toes." He squeezed Jason's cock, feeling the jeans grow damp under his questing fingers. The elevator dinged for their floor, and he half dragged, half pulled a stumbling Jason to his door.

Once they were inside, the bedroom door shut in the face of a disgruntled Pearl, Ryder pushed Jason down on the bed and straddled him. "After I finish kissing you, I'm gonna fuck you so hard into this mattress you might end up in the apartment beneath this one." He grinned at the feel of Jason's cock jerking under him, and he pulled down the zipper. "Let's get naked. Now."

He stood and shucked off his clothes, watching as Jason did the same. Soon he stood before Ryder, fully and magnificently nude and his mouth watered at the sight of Jason's heavy erection. Ryder couldn't wait until it was his turn to be inside Jason.

JASON NEVER GOT tired of seeing Ryder naked. From the first, there was something about the man's golden skin and smooth muscles with their dusting of blond hair that kept him in a perpetual state of arousal whenever they were together. The thought of Ryder's cock inside him sent his head spinning with a combination of fear and desire. His ass clenched.

"Ry." He reached out a hand to Ryder. "Hold me?" Now that the time had come, he trembled with a bout of unexpected nerves.

"Hey. Look at me." Ryder cupped his face so Jason was caught in his mesmerizing, bright blue gaze. "Are you nervous?"

Jason jerked an embarrassed nod.

Ryder pulled him down on the bed and slid his arms around him. "Don't be. We don't have to do anything if you don't want. I'm happy to have you here to hold all night, if that's what it comes to."

"I don't want you to be disappointed in me."

"Disappointed in you? Jason, you've changed your whole life for me. I'm in fucking awe of you and your courage. The way you brought me into your home and made everyone, even your father, accept me was unreal. You stood up to your brother, the man you work with and looked up to your whole life, and told him you're gay and you chose me over him." Ryder shook his head. "I could never be disappointed in you. You're fucking amazing. However, I'd never have let you choose me over your family."

"But—" Jason started to speak, but Ryder cut him off.

"Family is always the most important thing. I'm glad Liam came around, but I couldn't live with myself if I caused dissension between you and your family. Luckily, we don't have to concern ourselves with that anymore." Ryder kissed him, and as always, it only took the simplest touch of his lips to stoke the simmering fire inside him. Jason's cock swelled further, leaking all over his stomach. It knew what it wanted, even if his brain didn't want to process it.

"Go with your heart," Ryder whispered against his mouth. "Let it guide you. Whatever you decide, I'm not going anywhere unless you're with me." Ryder rained kisses on his lips, cheek and jaw. "I'm here for the long haul, and it will take more than not having your sexy ass tonight to get rid of me."

Jason kissed him back, the need for Ryder building within him.

Ryder growled and rolled on top of Jason, straddling him. Jason's cock twitched and grew as Ryder licked his lips. "Look at you. So fucking gorgeous and so fucking mine."

Ryder kissed his lips. "Mine." He licked down Jason's neck and chest, nipping and sucking at his nipples. "All mine."

Jason twisted under him. "Shit." His body sought Ryder's hardness, greedy for the friction to bring him relief.

"Not yet." Ryder moved down his body, kissing his stomach and the springy curls at the base of his jutting cock. "Fuck, you smell so good. I could eat you."

"Fuuuck me."

But he didn't. Jason moaned, begged, and pleaded, but Ryder tormented him with kisses and licks down his thighs and the backs of his knees.

"Please, fuck me, damn it; I'm gonna die." Jason whimpered, grasping to hold on to Ryder, but he moved out of reach.

"Do you want me inside you, Jase?" Ryder touched his ass, sliding a finger between his cheeks. "Do you want my cock in here?"

Jason couldn't speak; he moaned his assent.

Ryder chuckled low. "I'll take that as a yes. I'm going to make you ready for me, all right?" He bent over and kissed him. Jason grabbed hold of him around the neck and plunged his tongue deep into Ryder's mouth, needing that connection. They spent several minutes kissing.

"Don't worry. I'll take care of you." Ryder's touch was as gentle as a butterfly wing against his cheek.

Jason heard the bottle of lube snap open, and seconds later, one of Ryder's fingers probed his opening, sinking inside, stretching and invading. The clever, twisting finger curled and slid within his passage. A slight burn and sting accompanied it, but Jason barely registered it as Ryder's second finger joined the first, sending a different type of heat throughout his body.

The gentle sweep of Ryder's fingers imprinted them-selves on his soul.

"How's that feel?" Ryder whispered in his ear.

"Okay, a little strange, but—Oh holy shit—"

Ryder's questing fingers bent, then brushed a spot, sending blinding fire through him. His body bowed off the bed as Ryder continued to stroke the spot that caused such painful pleasure.

"What. The. Fuck." He panted, unable to catch his breath as wave after wave of desire crashed through him.

Ryder manipulated those wicked fingers inside him until he couldn't remember his name, and he begged for release as he thrashed his head on the pillows.

"You're ready, Jase. Do you want this?" Ryder kissed him back to reality. "If it's yes, climb on me and lower yourself. That way, you control it." Ryder tore open the foil package and slid the condom down on his cock. Jason watched him stroke himself and his ass clenched with need.

He straddled Ryder, who helped him steady himself. The blunt head of Ryder's cock nudged at his opening, and Jason tried to relax, but his heart pounded too hard.

"I'm going to put myself in. Then seat yourself slow and easy, bearing down." Ryder held on to his hip with one hand, then grasped himself with the other. He pushed the head of his cock inside, and Jason ground down on his jaw, squeezing his eyes shut. The burn and stretch hurt, and he gasped with the initial shock of the intrusion of Ryder's cock, yet as the first tight ring of muscle was breached, allowing Ryder to slide farther and farther inside him, the searing pain became replaced with a feeling of completeness. Soon he was fully seated on top of Ryder, knees straddling his body.

Ryder grinned at him. "You did it, babe. Now when you're ready, move up and down."

Jason took a deep breath and lifted a bit, then slid down, the strange, achingly full feeling remaining. He continued, lifting higher each time, bracing his arms on either side of Ryder's head.

"Keep going." Ryder panted.

He leaned forward, changing his angle, and there it was again. That sizzling-hot firestorm of desire bursting throughout his body, incinerating his skin from the inside out. He continued the slide up and down on Ryder, gliding on his stiffness, which stroked him in that spot over and over again. Whimpering, he grabbed on to the headboard to give himself traction. Nerve endings ablaze, his vision blurred, and he cried out as Ryder gripped his hip, working him into a frenzy of passion and lust.

"Look at me, Jase," Ryder urged.

Jason opened his eyes and watched Ryder stroke him as he rode his cock, hurtling toward oblivion. He moaned, pounding himself up and down, their sweating bodies slapping against each other.

Ryder thrust himself up inside him, and the white-hot flame burst through him as he cried out in his completion. Jason split apart into a thousand shattered, electrifying pieces, only to come back to earth, redefined and realigned. As he collapsed on Ryder, he climaxed, arching up into him, spurting hot and wet all over his chest and stomach.

Jason had no idea how long they lay there. The smell of sex, mingled with the scents of their bodies, surrounded them. Thankful all his body parts still worked, he slipped off Ryder and watched him dispose of the condom, wincing at the unfamiliar soreness in his ass.

Ryder chuckled. "You'll ache for a few days, but I hope it was worth it." The smile faded from his face, and his voice sounded anxious. "Are you all right, really? Did I hurt you?" Real concern resided in his eyes. "I wanted to make it good for you."

Jason took Ryder's hand in his and kissed the palm. "Why don't we shower, and I'll show you how good I really feel?"

Ryder caressed his face. "Look at me and know I love you. That even when we're apart, I'm with you. Do you see it and feel it? Do you know you're all fucking mine?"

Jason couldn't answer, only nod. The entire experience overwhelmed him.

Ryder's blue eyes shone as he leaned over and kissed him on the lips. He jumped out of bed and headed for the bathroom. "You mean everything to me."

Jason's chest tightened, and he fell back onto the pillows. The course of his life had taken so many turns in the past several months; he'd hardly had a chance to catch his breath. It didn't seem possible that he no longer could foresee a life without Ryder, and that scared the shit out of him. The one thing he'd always prided himself on was the control he maintained at his job and with the people around him.

With Ryder he had no control at all.

"Are you coming?" Ryder called. "The water's getting cold."

"I'm coming." He'd deal with his confusing thoughts later—a vision of a naked, wet Ryder was not to be ignored.

Chapter Twenty-One

"PLAYING HOOKY FROM work, huh? I don't think I've ever seen you here during the day." John poured Jason a beer and one for himself. "Cheers."

But Jason didn't feel cheerful; in fact, he felt like shit. Instead of answering John he stared morosely at his glass, watching the foamy head settle, wishing he could disappear into its snowy depths.

"Jase, what's up?" John set his glass on the bar, concern etching deep lines in his forehead. "I don't think I've ever seen you so upset."

"I think I fucked up." Not think. Jason knew it. And knew he had no idea what to do about it either.

"How? Talk to me." John came from around the bar and led him to a two seater table in the corner. At this time of day the bar was empty; even the cook wouldn't show up until later in the afternoon.

"You don't mind me talking about this with you? Some guys—"

"I'm not some guy. I'm your friend before anything. It doesn't matter to me if you're sleeping with a man or a woman, as long as you're happy."

"I'd been with Chloe for so long, the relationship was easy." At John's smirk, Jason shrugged. "Okay not easy. Maybe simple was better. I knew what to expect."

"And with Ryder you don't?"

Taking a careful sip of his beer, Jason struggled to put words together that would make sense.

"I honestly have no clue what I'm doing. It's like a tightrope walk with no safety net underneath. I knew it wouldn't be easy, but damn." He swallowed half his beer, struggling to find the right words. "Everywhere we go, if we show the slightest bit of affection toward each other you wouldn't believe the looks we get—cabbies, the checkout girl at the deli…so many people. I thought I could brush it off but it's hard, man." He chugged down another gulp.

"Most worthwhile things usually are."

Jason glanced up sharply; John's neutral expression stared back at him steadily.

"Can I ask you some questions?"

"Of course. Anything, you know that." Jason leaned back in his chair.

"Are you having second thoughts because your relationship is with another man, or is it Ryder?"

"I'm not sure." Those spoken words sent a knife through his heart.

"Sure of what? That you love Ryder? Or that you're willing to embrace a whole new way of life? Because it is. You can say you're cool with it and don't need labels to define you and all that other crap, but the fact remains the same. You're a bisexual man, in love with a gay man. People are gonna judge you based on that alone."

Hearing John say the words didn't bother Jason. He loved Ryder. But is love always enough? "What if I let Ryder down? I do love him; compared to any of my relationships prior to this, now that I'm with him I know I was going through the motions."

Jason spoke the truth. So much had happened in the past few months, he'd hardly had a chance to breathe. First breaking up with Chloe, then falling so hard and so fast for Ryder, and the crisis with Liam, Jason hadn't had a moment to himself to take stock of all the changes in his life.

"Why would you let him down?"

"I don't know what I'm doing. I'm figuring it all out as I go."

"Love doesn't come with a how-to manual. Most people don't know what they're doing; they only know who they want to do it with."

Jason chuckled. "For someone who's never been in love, you sure seem to know what you're talking about."

John's expression dimmed and his lips twisted in the painful semblance of a smile. "How do you know I've never been in love?"

The laughter died in his throat. "Uh, well I've never seen you with anyone, or heard you mention a woman, so I assumed…" He gave John a weak, apologetic smile.

"I'm sorry."

"It's okay. I never expected the person I loved to return my feelings, so I learned to deal with it a long time ago. But that doesn't mean I don't know how it feels. You want their happiness before yours. You strive to anticipate their needs, never let them down and always try to be there for them if they need you."

"Yes." Jason leaned forward to press his point. "Ryder's been hurt so many times before. What if I hurt him? I'm not sure he could recover."

"What if you don't and love him forever instead?"

Surprised at John's insight, Jason held his dark gaze. "I'm afraid."

John smiled faintly. "It takes a lot of courage to admit that. Most people can't. Or won't."

Jason scratched the surface of the old wooden table with his fingernail. "I know that this relationship is it for me. The way Ryder makes me feel..." His face grew hot when he realized what he said to his straight friend. "I'm sorry. I know you don't want to hear about my sex life."

"It's okay. You'd be surprised what I hear."

"Bartenders make great confessors, huh?"

John returned his grin with a tight smile of his own. "Sort of. But more important is you're my friend and I'll always be here for you."

"What if I end up not being able to satisfy him? Or worse yet, what if I really don't love him? I've never been in love before, how do I know if it's the real thing?" Eminently frustrated, Jason pushed away his now empty glass.

"Do you honestly think you're going through a fad and your feelings are going to fade?" The phone rang, but John ignored it. It stopped then started up again immediately. "I'm sorry," he said. "With no one else here I have to answer that. Be right back."

John's departure gave Jason a chance to think. His feelings for Ryder fade? Impossible. The sex last night had been the most intensely personal experience of his life. Feeling Ryder inside his body, even now the mixed pleasure and pain brought so many emotions to the forefront, Jason could barely think straight or speak coherently. He needed to get out of there and be alone.

Still on the telephone, John held out his hand but Jason ignored it and waved goodbye. John meant well but a few of the things he said required more thought than an off-the-cuff answer, no matter how well-intentioned the question. He hopped in his truck and headed home to think, relishing the thought of uninterrupted peace, something he hadn't had in forever.

Jason pulled into his driveway and cut the engine but didn't go inside, choosing to sit and remember Ryder and him together on the night he came out to his parents. How sweetly comforting Ryder had been with him in the aftermath of his blowup with Liam. How scared and nervous he'd been to tell his parents he was in love with another man. The first time he'd said to

Ryder, said to *anyone* that he loved them. The first time he made love to Ryder.

"Fuck." He pounded the steering wheel with his fist then exited the truck, hitting the alarm button on the key remote. The house seemed strangely quiet when he entered it, then Jason remembered Trouper was staying with his parents; he'd planned on spending long days at the construction site and didn't want the puppy by himself for so long. It hadn't taken Jason long to get used to having another living creature in the house with him and as he wandered through the rooms, he missed the jingling of Troup's tags and the click of his claws on the floorboards as he followed him around.

A cold beer would do wonders right now and after taking one from the fridge, Jason went to the living room and collapsed on his comfortable sofa. Memories of Ryder kissing him assailed his senses and he shook his head, as if that would be enough to dislodge them.

What John had said to him in the bar before the phone call interrupted them resonated deeply with Jason. Could he ever love another man—kiss him or have sex with him, or was it because that man was Ryder? He set the bottle down and flipped over on the sofa, his stomach churning with anxiety. For years he'd buried the memory of that one drunken night he'd fooled around with his college friend. It had never disgusted him, nor had he been ashamed; he'd allowed it to die and he then got swept up in dating women. Being in construction didn't put him in the path of many gay men, and Jason simply went with the flow and dated women exclusively.

The moment he met Ryder his outlook on relationships changed. From the first, they'd had this connection his brain may not have picked up on, but his body most assuredly did. Jason wanted to know everything about Ryder, his life before they met, and all the relationships he'd had. Ryder's pain over his parents' mistreatment became Jason's and he railed against a society that would treat a person the same as an unwanted dog because of who they loved. Admittedly Jason had never given much thought about gay rights before meeting Ryder but even he knew the difference between right and wrong.

His phone rang and his heart skipped a beat when he saw Ryder's number. Jason knew he couldn't talk to him now and didn't answer it. Fuck, he was being a dick—but Jason knew if he heard Ryder's voice he'd be persuaded to see him and everything would get swept under the rug. He didn't have the heart to talk to Ryder about this; Ryder would assume Jason regretted having sex or even being together, and that wasn't it. He didn't know what was wrong; there was all this shit floating around in his head and until he worked it out he needed to be alone.

When the ping of a text came through a moment later, he shut the phone off, preferring not to know how much he was hurting Ryder with his silence. Another layer of guilt to pile on to the growing list of "Fucked up things Jason did today."

His doorbell rang. Shit. With his truck in the drive-way announcing he was home, no way could Jason not answer. Feeling like a condemned man no matter who waited outside, he walked to the door and opened it, shocked to find Liam waiting on the porch with a frown.

"Liam? What're you doing here?"

"I could ask you the same question."

Liam brushed past him as he entered and Jason closed the door and followed his brother back into the living room.

"I didn't feel too well, so I figured better take the day off and shake whatever I might be getting." He hoped his smile convinced Liam and he could send him on his way.

"You always sucked at lying." Liam stretched out on his sofa and picked up Jason's forgotten beer. "Now sit your ass down and tell me what's really going on. You have a fight with Ryder?"

They may have made up, but Jason had no inten-tion of discussing his male lover with his brother. "No we didn't, everything's fine." He sank into the club chair positioned catty corner to the sofa.

"Bullshit." Liam finished off half the beer in one swallow. "I know you; who knows you better than me? No one. Something's bothering you. Now give." Sadness darkened his normally wide-open face. "You're still mad at me, I guess. I know I was a bastard and it'll take you a long time to believe me, but I'm sorry for everything I said. I'm still wrapping my head around it, don't think I'm not, but I only want you to be happy." His blunt, work-roughened fingers toyed with the edge of the peel on the beer bottle. "If being with Ryder makes you happy, then go for it."

The bit of shine that had dulled on his relationship with Liam over the last few months picked up a sparkle again. The fact that Liam had taken the trouble to leave work and come to see him proved to Jason they'd make it back to where they once were, perhaps even stronger.

"Do you think I'm making a mistake?"

Shocked didn't begin to explain Liam's face. "Are you fucking kidding me? After everything you said to me last night? You think you're making a mistake? What the hell are you talking about?"

"I've never been in love before." Helpless and unsure of putting his feelings into words, Jason decided Liam would be the one person to tell him if he was wrong or not. "How do I know if I really love Ryder or if it's…" Embarrassed, he found he couldn't continue.

"Sex?"

He jerked a nod, but kept his gaze trained to the floor.

"Don't be a dumbass. What, you think I don't know you're having sex with him? You're not spending your time together holding hands, that's for sure."

He couldn't help but smile at Liam's pathetic attempt at a joke. "I mean yeah, the sex is amazing. No one's ever made me feel like Ryder."

"It's more than that. Even I can see it and I'm oblivious to that kind of shit."

"You can?" Jason finally looked at Liam, who wore a faintly amused smile.

"Yeah. That's how I guessed in the first place. You two have this weird kind of connection whenever I see you together. Like you need to be near each other or something whenever you're together. It's a vibe; I don't know how to describe it."

Jason understood. He felt it as well. From their first meeting, he sensed Ryder was meant to be an important part of his life. Things between them may have started off inauspiciously in that abandoned house on his construction site, but from that day on, Ryder had never been far from his mind. No one, man or woman had ever had that kind of emotional and mental impact on him.

"But is that love?"

"Think about what you had with that Chloe. Your relationship with Ryder isn't even in the same ballpark."

With every woman he'd dated, Jason had waited for that spark to ignite, to feel the passion he'd heard his friends talk about when they discussed sex with their girlfriends. When it didn't happen for him, he assumed he hadn't found the right girl yet and left it at that. But from that first impulsive kiss the night Ryder got drunk over his ex-boyfriend, he'd been a fire in Jason's blood, fanning the flames of a desire he never thought possible.

Making love to Ryder and giving himself over so completely and intimately last night, Jason knew he'd been irrevocably altered. Ceding over such control and power to any another person prior to this relationship seemed unimaginable, yet with Ryder there was never any question. What he wanted, Jason wanted as well.

"I tried to explain it to John before and told him I was afraid."

"Afraid of what?"

"I don't know." He jumped up, needing to be mobile. "Failing Ryder in his expectations of me, failing myself if I let Ryder down as his lover. See, I was the one who persuaded Ryder to start the relationship. He never wanted to get involved. So if I screw up, it's all my fault."

"Jesus, Jase that's a shitload of guilt you're dumping on yourself for no reason." Liam retuned to playing with the neck of his beer bottle. A smile tugged at his lips. "Want to know what I think?"

"Yeah."

"I think you're in love. Like really in love and you didn't see it coming and it's hit you. *Bam!* Like a big fucking Mack truck right in the face and you have no fucking clue what to do about it. You thought you'd end up like Mom and Dad with the wife and kids and house but now it's a different story and you don't have a plan."

Dumbfounded, Jason stared at Liam. "Wow, that's pretty insightful."

Liam smirked. "Mark made me read some of his psychology mumbo jumbo. I still don't understand half of the shit he says, but this is pretty obvious even to me."

Jason returned to his chair and fell back into it with a whoosh of his breath. "Maybe you're right. I thought I knew what was going to happen in my life. Now I don't have a clue."

"Sometimes it's better that way. You know?" Liam stood and went to the kitchen and tossed the beer bottle in the recycling bin. He returned and to Jason's surprise slung an arm around his neck. "For the last few years you've been miserable, but we all left you alone to work your shit out. Now that I think about it, I've never seen you happier than when you're at Drummers hanging out with Ryder and his friends. I never claimed to be the most enlightened guy; I like my beer, pizza and my ball games and didn't let politics and all that shit get to me. But yeah, I'm selfish. Now that it's affecting my brother, I'm involved. Who's gonna tell you that kind of happiness is wrong? What gives them that right?"

"I love you, man." Jason hugged Liam, grateful for a family willing to listen and accept.

"I love you too. Don't let your head play games. Sometimes you gotta go with your feelings."

Liam left and for the rest of the evening, Jason sat in the darkness thinking about life, love and Ryder. The entire night passed and he didn't go to bed—he sat on the sofa, playing devil's advocate with his life. Coming out to his family had been the hardest thing he'd ever had to do, but their reaction gave him hope. And if he could get Liam to see two men could be in love, surely he'd be able to walk through any firestorm that might arise in his professional life. He left his phone off, wrestling with his conscience. His silence hurt Ryder for certain, yet if they spoke his resistance to push through this himself and come out stronger and healthier in the end would crumble. Jason needed to work on himself alone. Never had everything he'd ever wanted all been so close within his reach.

He'd have to be a fool not to grab hold tight.

Chapter Twenty-Two

SOMETHING WAS WRONG. Almost two damn days and no Jason. Two long days since the man who'd stolen Ryder's soul had walked out of his apartment after they'd made love, and not a single word, phone call, or text. It could only mean one thing.

Jason couldn't handle being gay.

Once again, Ryder had given his heart, only to have it ripped from his body and shredded. What had he done wrong? They hadn't quarreled or had a bad word cross between them. After the confrontation with Jason's brother in Drummers, it had been a night of passion and love. Or so he'd thought.

"I'm a fucking jerk, Pearl, aren't I?" He lay on the couch; Pearl sat beside him with her head in his lap. She licked his hand as he fondled her silky ears. "I thought he was different, but I've never been a good judge of character." For what seemed like the hundredth time, he checked his phone, feeling like a silly teenager with his first crush. Nothing.

Against his better judgment, he hit the speed dial

he'd assigned to Jason, but like all the other calls he'd made, it went straight to voicemail. Since he'd already left several messages to call, Ryder didn't bother to leave another message. He had some shred of pride to cling to and had no intention of begging Jason to come back to him. Obviously for Jason, things had gotten too real, too fast. Maybe Liam had met up with Jason afterwards and they had a heart-to-heart. Jason might've realized the enormity of what he had done and had regrets.

Ryder pressed his fist against the hurt in his chest, attempting to soothe his aching heart. How could he have let his guard down so easily? It had taken him so long to recover from Matt and protect himself, only to be swept away by Jason's magnetic gaze and sweet, caring nature. By disregarding all the warning bells his brain sent him, he'd set himself up for heartbreak.

"Asshole."

He wasn't yet willing to admit if he meant Jason or himself.

Pearl whined and wriggled up to lick his face. "I know, girl. I owe you another walk, don't I?" At the mention of the magical word, she leaped from his side and trotted into the kitchen to get her leash. If it wasn't for her, he'd never leave his apartment, preferring to lie on the couch like a slug and mope.

"Okay, girl. Let's go. The fresh air will do us both some good." He didn't bother to shave. No one would care, and he certainly didn't. Ryder recognized he was in the beginnings of full-fledged breakup mode, but fuck it. He thought he'd finally found a man who loved him. He was entitled to sulk and get drunk. He took Pearl out for a walk and then came back to the apartment, and against his better judgment, checked his answering machine to see if Jason had called. Nothing.

Despondent, Ryder decided to order some food and hole up for the rest of the night. After eating and cleaning up, he went to throw out the trash, but when he opened the door, there Jason stood, with his hand up, about to knock.

"Uh, hey. How are you?" Jason shifted under his glare.

He looked terrible, Ryder assessed, his blue eyes dull, the skin under them bruised as if from lack of sleep, and his face could use a good shave. Maybe it was wrong to feel satisfaction at the despair he sensed within Jason, but Ryder didn't care. "I'm fine. Why wouldn't I be?" Ryder bared his teeth in a sham of a grin. Pearl, the traitor, jumped on Jason, licking him madly, her tail wagging like a crazy metronome.

"I need to talk to you." Jason attempted to put a hand on his arm to restrain him, but Ryder sidestepped his touch.

"What's there to say? You've obviously had a change of heart since our night together, and because you're a nice guy, you think you need to come here in person to break it off with me." Leaning up against the door frame, he kicked his sneaker at the marble threshold. "Let me make it easy for you. It's over. I didn't want to get involved seriously with anyone anyway, so—"

"Oh, shut up and don't be an idiot." Jason shoved him back inside the apartment, Pearl in tow. He kicked the door closed behind him. Ryder didn't have a chance to object, as he found himself pinned up against the wall by Jason's hot, hard body. "Listen to me, please."

Mulishly, Ryder stuck out his jaw. "Fuck you. No."

With an angry growl, Jason slammed the wall with his hands, caging him in between his arms. "Ryder, it isn't what you think. I want to talk to you."

"Too fucking late." Ryder spat out his words, the hurt over Jason's disappearance bubbling to the surface and overflowing. "I wanted to talk to you the past two days, and you shut me out. Not one fucking text. You couldn't be bothered to answer me to let me know you were okay?"

"I needed some time to take stock of all the change and upheaval in my life. Can't you understand?" Jason slid his arms over Ryder's shoulders, holding him close.

"No. I can't. You don't treat someone you supposedly love with absolute silence. Just go. You're only making it worse." Ryder bit his lip, overwhelmed by Jason's nearness, his deep blue eyes and intoxicating warmth. This was the man he dared to dream might be his forever. Realizing he was about to lose that crippled his ability to think straight and remain calm.

"Ryder, please listen to me." Jason's mouth hovered by his ear. "There's so much I need to tell you."

Summoning the last vestige of strength he could

muster, he crossed his arms defensively in front of his chest. "Screw you. I listened to you crying out my name when I was inside you. I listened to you telling me never to leave you." Giving Jason a shove, he pushed away from him. "I've listened enough. Now get the fuck out and don't bother me anymore."

He strode away toward his bedroom, but a heavy hand clamped down on his shoulder, halting his progress.

"Don't do this to us." Jason's hand slid to take his neck in a possessive hold, his fingers searing like a brand on Ryder's skin.

"Me? You're calling *me* out for this? *I'm* not the one who went into hiding. I was here. Where were you?" He didn't care that he shouted. He pulled away from Jason's touch.

"I'm sorry. I know I fucked up by shutting you out. But if I talked to you I'd want to be with you." Jason advanced on him but Ryder sidestepped him and went back to the living room.

"You're supposed to want to be with me if we're together." Ryder made sure to keep his distance, placing the sofa between them.

"I needed to work shit out in my head."

"You're not getting it. It isn't only about you if we're together. I care if you're hurting. That's what being in a relationship means. It's working things out together." He sat down on the sofa. "Your pain becomes my pain as well."

"Don't you understand, Ry? If I spoke to you, I'd break down. I've never been in love before—with anyone—man or woman. I figured it would happen eventually and I'd find someone who'd make me happy. But you blindsided me and I can't imagine life without you. Fuck, I can't even breathe without you. It fucking scared me to death because I thought I knew who I was, and what my life would be like. Then you walked in and there went everything I knew." Jason joined him on the sofa. "Suddenly the only real thing in my life, the only future I could see was you."

Staring into Jason's tortured face, Ryder felt himself softening. No one had ever said those words to him before. They came from Jason's heart. Ryder wanted so much to believe Jason, yet the events of the past few years had made him into a jaded, almost bitter person. So instead of giving Jason the forgiveness Ryder knew he waited for, he said nothing.

"Please Ryder. Please forgive me."

"I don't know if I can."

"Why not? We love each other and should be able to work through my mistake."

"Maybe my mistake was letting you into my life."

Stricken, Jason stood and pulled him up into his arms. "Don't say that. Don't ever fucking say that."

Ryder tore away from Jason. "Do you know what it was like to lay in my bed with the sheets smelling of you, of us, and call you, only to get no answer?" He walked away blindly heading to the bedroom, planning to shut himself inside.

Jason followed, pushing him down on the bed. "I'm so sorry. I hated what I did to you. I sat in my house by myself and every time you called or texted it nearly killed me 'cause I knew I hurt you by not answering, yet I couldn't see another way to work through the shit inside my head. But I get it now—I know that a life without you is no life at all." Standing over him, Jason tore off his jacket and unbuttoned his shirt, flicking open the buttons. "I love you." When he finished, he left it on, hanging open. "I'm staying." Without ever taking his eyes off of Ryder, Jason unbuckled his belt and slid it out of its loops, then toed off his sneakers. "And I want you."

As excited as he was at the sight of an aroused Jason in his bedroom again, Ryder pushed himself away, farther up the bed. "You can't come here after total silence for almost two days and expect to fuck me."

It seemed Jason didn't get that memo, as he unzipped the fly to his jeans and pulled them off. He jumped on the bed, crawling up to Ryder, an intent, hungry look in his eyes.

"I don't want to fuck you. I want to love you." Jason reached out to him, but Ryder scrambled away, rebuffing his touch.

"You gave up your right to touch me in this bed when you disappeared without a trace." Little did Jason know his body burned for him. Determined to keep his distance, Ryder refused to allow his emotions to overrule his heart this time.

Jason pounded his fist in the bed. "I'm sorry. I was an idiot. I panicked and got so scared and thought it all was happening too fast." He crawled closer, and Ryder continued to move backwards, until he hit the headboard. "I lost control of my head, my heart—my life. Please don't tell me I blew it, Ry. I love you. I fucked up for a while I know, but I came back to you, to us."

"Please, Jase." Ryder licked his lips as he gazed into the burning eyes of the man he so desperately loved. "I don't think I can do it."

Stricken, Jason moved on top of him, his big body straddling Ryder's thighs. "No, don't say it. Punish me, hit me, curse me. I'll take it all, but don't break it off. I love you."

Ryder's breath caught in his throat. Never had anyone laid himself so completely bare to him. Could he forgive him and learn to trust him again? "I-I don't know. What if it happens again?"

Jason's lips brushed his. "I won't let it. I know what I want."

"And what did you end up with? What do you want?"

"That it's all shit without you. No matter what the world is going to throw at us, we'll face it together. I can't go back to being alone. I need you."

It all sounded nice, but Ryder needed more reassurance than simple words. "You left me alone for almost two days. Didn't you think I might need you? Imagine how you'd feel if you were me."

Jason fell back on the bed, staring up at the ceiling. "I stayed home from work and spoke to John and Liam."

Ryder almost choked. "Liam? That's who you talked to instead of me?"

A smile tugged the corner of Jason's lips. "He's kind of become our champion. Right away he saw our connection."

Narrowing his gaze, Ryder rolled over on his side. "Yeah? That didn't stop him from being a total prick."

"Give him a break, he's trying." Jason sat up and in the shadows of the bedroom Ryder studied his profile. Whether in bright sunlight or the darkest night, Ryder would always be able to find Jason.

"So you talked to Liam. So what? You should've been able to talk to me."

Jason shook his head. "Not about this. We talked about my past and what I thought I wanted out of life. You never saw me with my old girlfriends—Liam did. Better than I ever could, he saw what I was missing from my life."

"What?"

"You." Jason rolled on top of him, leaving him breathless. "Love."

Ryder's breath caught in his throat. "Yeah?"

"It's hard to know what you're missing until it disappears. But when you weren't there, Ry?" Jason leaned down and nuzzled his neck, and Ryder couldn't help but arch into his touch. "It was like the other half of me, my heart was missing. Let me in again. Let me come home."

Ryder couldn't speak. Could he dare trust him? "Undress me." He sat up, pushing Jason off him, his gaze hard and hot. "Now."

Jason grinned. "Okay, babe."

"I wouldn't smile if I were you. By the time I finish with you, you'll be lucky to crawl away."

Jason's grin faded at his ruthless smile. Ryder might have decided to forgive him, but Jason needed to learn to never take his love for granted again.

Ryder pulled off his shirt and lifted his hips as Jason popped the button of his jeans and unzipped his fly. "Take them off."

Jason complied, and Ryder took in his glazed eyes and rapid breathing when it revealed he wore no boxers or briefs. It seemed Jason got very turned on by his going commando. "Now take off all your clothes."

He lay back, stroking himself as Jason ripped off his shirt, boxers and socks. Jason's body never failed to excite him, and from the size of his erection, he was pretty damn excited as well. Ryder reached out and swirled his fingers over the slick, wet head of Jason's cock, then brought them to his mouth and sucked them.

"I love the way you taste." Jason's loud groan caused Ryder to smile. "Kiss me."

He had no idea a man as large as Jason could move

so fast, as he found himself pinned to the bed, his mouth taken in a ruthless kiss. Jason's tongue swept inside his mouth, and their tongues fought and tangled with each other until they gasped for breath. Their cocks rubbed together, slick from the precome that leaked from them both.

Ryder's control was slipping fast. "Get the condoms and lube from the drawer." Jason grabbed at the drawer and pulled out a strip of condoms and a small bottle.

"Let me inside you, Ry, please," Jason begged, blue eyes darkened to almost black, his face damp with sweat. "I want to make love to you." His hand drifted down between their bodies to grasp their cocks and rub them together.

"Is that what you want?" God, it felt so good to have Jason's hands on his dick. His excitement grew as he massaged the smooth, heated skin of Jason's back and squeezed his firm ass. A whimper escaped Jason's lips.

Their bodies entwined, becoming a sticky slide of tangled arms and legs. "Please." Jason's teeth nipped Ryder's jaw as his hips rolled and his fingers dug into his shoulders.

"Do it," Ryder gritted out. "Fuck me, now." He couldn't hold back, not with his mouth tormented by Jason's lips and tongue. Jason's fingers, now cool and slick from the lubricant, teased and probed him. One of his thick fingers sank into him, beginning its wicked stretch, soon joined by a second digit.

Ryder could do nothing but hang on as Jason's

intent, dark blue gaze focused on him, drawing him deep into his depths. "I'm sorry, Ryder. I never meant to hurt you. You know that, don't you? I promise to never fuck up again."

Ryder couldn't think about anything while Jason's fingers were creating such sweet, blissful havoc within his body. "Inside me, now," he gasped, wild with lust.

Jason withdrew his fingers, then ripped the foil package with his teeth, rolling the condom down on his erection. He slicked himself up and wasted no time in nudging the thick head of his cock at Ryder's entrance.

Ryder pushed down, accepting the sting of Jason's cock as it slid into his body. He moaned loud and long. "All the way."

Jason thrust into him, pushing himself in fully, until he was firmly seated inside. "Move, Jason." Ryder grunted his order, anxious for the friction to continue. "Move, now."

Jason complied, gritting his teeth as he angled his thrusts, snapping his hips while never breaking eye contact. "Say you forgive me."

The glow of passion kindled to an inferno as Jason continued stroking inside his body. Ryder struggled to hold on to his sanity as his body drew tight, vibrating with the onslaught of his orgasm.

Jason pled with him. "Say it already." As he dipped his head down to kiss him, Ryder met him halfway.

"I forgive you." Their mouths met, and the kisses turned sweet and loving.

Then Ryder's orgasm hit like a cascade of sparks exploding throughout his body, the fiery embers showering down inside his blood. He cried out in his happiness at having Jason back in his bed and in his life. The taste of Jason in his mouth, his aching body stretched to the limit, Ryder's life had never been more complete, more real than at this moment, when he knew his heart had at last found its home.

When he returned to some semblance of normalcy and Jason pulled out of him, getting rid of the condom, Ryder pushed Jason down on his back and took his cock deep within his throat while sliding slick fingers inside him.

And when Jason climaxed, Ryder withdrew his fingers, and kissed Jason, even as he lay soaked with sweat, breathless and twitching. "Don't ever leave me again. Talk to me, don't run away and shut me out." Jason didn't open his eyes, merely nodded, and curled up into a ball.

Ryder laughed, slipped under the covers, and cuddled next to him, holding him within his arms.

Chapter Twenty-Three

SITTING AT HIS desk in the office late one April afternoon, enjoying the feel of the sun on his back as it streamed in through the windows, Ryder took a break from his computer screen to make a cup of coffee and relax. The fund-raiser was only a month away, and things were progressing right on target. They'd rounded up a slew of sponsors who promised to donate gift certificates for local restaurants and boutiques, as well as some big-name celebrities who lived in Brooklyn and were very involved with animal rescue. Hopefully the fund-raiser would generate awareness and money to staff the office for Rescue Me properly, and work on educating more people.

How different this year was than last, when he was half out of his mind with grief over the demise of his relationship with Matt. It wasn't until Jason became a more permanent part of his life that Ryder knew what true love meant. After Jason's freak-out and disappearance, he'd become an eager pupil, willing to give as well as receive, and it was rare that a morning went by without Ryder waking up to find Jason's mouth on him, bringing him to a breathtaking climax, or simply spooning him, burrowing against his body, holding him tight. His hot, wet kisses and firm hands touched Ryder with such gentleness, it nearly took his breath away, and Ryder was more than happy to return the favor.

The sounds of Jason puttering around the kitchen, watching television, or taking a nap on the couch made his apartment the home Ryder had always wished for. But Jason brought so much more than love into his life; he'd given him back his brother. In the late afternoons, no matter how busy he might be, Ryder always made time to meet Landon, even if only for a quick coffee or a snack, to catch up on their lives. Sunday evenings were spent with Jason's family, for dinner and watching movies. Helen's warmth and compassion had him unburdening the pain of his parents' rejection while enjoying the acceptance into Jason's loving family.

Since Emily had announced she was pregnant, she and Connor had him and Jason over for dinner once a week, to catch up and relax away from the office and all the craziness of planning for the gala. Last week, when they were all standing around the kitchen, she took his hand and placed it on her stomach. After a moment, he'd felt it. A little ripple, like the flutter of a butterfly's wing against his skin. He'd smiled with openmouthed wonder, then exchanged glances with Jason, now daring to dream of a day when maybe they too might have a family of their own.

He shuffled through the paperwork on his desk, sipping his coffee, and spent the next hour securing more sponsors and donors for the fund-raiser, then he heard the front door open. Laurel and Hardy growled and stood, flanking him on either side. Normally, people didn't drop by the office, so he shushed them and stood to see who it was. A tall blond man with his back to him studied the posters for the fund-raiser.

"Can I help you with something?" Ryder leaned against the doorjamb, petting the top of Laurel's head, then reaching down to scratch her ear.

The man spun around and gave him a slight smile. "Hi, Ry. Long time no see, huh?"

He'd always heard the phrase "heart dropped to the knees," but until now he hadn't experienced it. "Matt?" He couldn't do anything but stare at the man before him, the almost shrill sound of disbelief ringing in his voice. "Is that really you?"

Matt laughed and nodded. "In the flesh. You look great." His hooded amber eyes darkened as they stared at each other. "Fantastic, actually." He licked his lips.

"What do you want? Why are you here?" Ryder remained standing, not offering his former lover a seat, coffee, or any encouragement to stay.

"Can't a friend stop by to see how you're doing?" Matt took a step closer but stopped when the dogs started up their growling again. "Call off your killers. I'm not here to hurt you."

Ryder's discomfort grew as Matt continued to eye

him like a piece of meat. What the hell was this about? The man had a wife and a baby on the way, if he remembered correctly. "No, I'd say you accomplished that already. Oh, and let's not forget that interview a few months ago about the 'bad relationship' you had that your wife saved you from." His lips twisted in a grimace of a smile. "Thanks for that."

"Oh, come on, you know I didn't mean it. I had to say that for Abby's sake." At his questioning look, Matt explained. "My wife. She knows all about you, about us."

"There's no us, remember? You decided the drugs were more important than I was to you and left. I carried on with my life. End of story." He gestured toward the door. "Now if you've nothing else, I'm very busy, so—"

"I miss you." Matt's soft voice hung in the air.

Shocked, Ryder struggled for an answer that wouldn't sound too harsh, then gave up and decided full steam ahead. "Fuck off. I'm sorry for you, then. I don't miss you. I've moved on." There wasn't any need for niceties or to pretend a friendship that wasn't there. Did Matt think they'd be lovers turned friends, going out for the occasional cozy brunch or dinner? He had no desire to be friends. Where maybe last year his heart would have still held out hope and he'd have been overjoyed to hear these words, now they meant little to nothing.

"Come on, don't lie to me. I know how much you were hurt when I left. But we can have it all back, now."

Matt took a few hesitant steps closer until Ryder could smell the lemony scent of his aftershave and see the desire glowing in his eyes.

"Christ you're a married man, and I—"

"She doesn't have to know, and she wouldn't care anyway. The marriage was a mistake. I got drunk one night and ended up in bed with her. When she told me she was pregnant, I felt, you know, obligated. But I don't love her."

The man couldn't speak the truth if his life depended on it, but again it didn't matter to Ryder. "Leave me alone. I'm in a relationship now and have no desire to be your friend, never mind your back-door lover." The past had truly been exorcised from his soul. Nothing remained except pity for a man whose shallowness outweighed his own vanity, believing he could charm his way back into Ryder's life and his bed so easily. Matt was like that marshmallow fluff he teased Jason about eating. No substance, only the crash and burn of the sugar high that made you sick to your stomach once you'd eaten it.

The thought of Jason brought a smile to his lips, which Matt jumped on, misunderstanding.

"I knew you'd want me back. You were so in love with me. You couldn't have forgotten how good it was when we were together." Matt grabbed the back of his neck, pulling him close to kiss him.

Ryder wrenched free. "Get the fuck off me and get out." The dogs sprang to their feet, barking, completely on the defensive. Ryder needed to calm them down, which meant removing Matt from the scene. They were as protective of him as they were of Emily and Connor and had that innate animal sense, knowing when the object of their affection felt threatened. "I said get out. There's nothing left for you here. I'm with someone now and happy. Try and make something out of your marriage. Don't come back to me again, because the next time they won't be as pleasant." He gestured to the two dogs, whose collars he was hanging on to. Laurel and Hardy were quiet now, but Ryder sensed the coiled tenseness of their quivering muscles.

Matt blanched, a trickle of sweat ran down his forehead, flattening his long sun-streaked hair. He looked nothing like the highly stylized man who'd breezed in earlier, overly confident his overtures would be welcomed with open arms. His cockiness had been replaced by something Ryder had never seen in Matt before. Fear.

"Please leave." Ryder urged him, a little gentler now. "There was never anything real between us." Turning his back on the man had never been easier. He should be thankful to Matt, because if he hadn't been treated like dirt, he never would have recognized what a truly healthy relationship should be. A man like Jason was the real thing, and the love they shared meant everything to him. It had taken him a while to realize he was worth it, but now he had the love of his life, his dearest friends, and a family who accepted him, even if his own didn't.

As he watched Matt walk to his waiting car, it was as if his life had separated into two parts, before Jason and after with only a few people remaining constant through both—Connor, Emily, and Landon. Now, along with Jason and his family, Ryder's persistent struggle to gain acceptance from his parents was no longer a burden he had to carry. It wasn't acceptance he wanted from his parents, he understood; it was their love. That wish unfortunately, wasn't as easy for him to put aside.

Hardy jumped up and licked his face. "Come on, you two terrors. Let's find you some treats for a job well done." They danced around his legs. He'd just finished washing his hands when the phone rang.

"Rescue Me. How may I help you?" He tucked the phone between ear and shoulder while he dried his hands.

"May I speak with Mr. Ryder Daniels?" It was a pleasant-sounding woman's voice, but not one he recognized.

"Speaking. What can I do for you?" He sat down at his desk and entered his password to unlock the computer.

"My name is Patty Walsh. I'm a senior partner at Everett and Winston. We met at the zoning board meeting a month or so ago."

Ryder searched his memory and came up with a picture of a woman in her early fifties, tall and thin, with an easy smile. "Yes, I remember. How are you?" He had absolutely no idea why she'd be calling him. E&W

was a premier boutique law firm in the city. They liked to take on many socially conscious cases, but aside from seeing the partners at the zoning board meetings he'd attended and a few other times he'd appeared at various city agencies, he had little contact with them.

"I'm well, thank you. Mr. Daniels, I'd like to know if you could come to our office for a meeting tomorrow."

Obviously she was not one for small talk. "Can you tell me what this is about? I'd like to be prepared for the meeting."

"Oh, it's nothing you need to prepare for. Shall we say ten o'clock?" Her amused voice raised his curiosity to an even higher peak.

"That's fine, but—" She had hung up. Damn. What was that all about? He sat wondering about it until he heard the door slam, and Mark's girlfriend, Julie, entered the office. She'd begun volunteering after that spectacular night at the bar when Liam and John had their fight.

"Hi, Ryder. Are you the only one here?" She reminded him of Emily: smart, sweet and funny. Jason's brother Mark adored her.

"Yes, and I'm leaving early. It's slow, and I have my cell if you need me." He added the appointment tomorrow to his calendar and turned off the computer. "Hopefully it will stay this way. We haven't had any dog-sighting calls in a while."

She put her bag on the desk. "Don't worry. I know

how to get in touch with you if anything happens. Besides, Emily left me the numbers of some more vendors to call, and I have my friends putting up the posters about the fund-raiser in stores all over Brooklyn and downtown Manhattan." She flicked her long hair over her shoulder and pulled a granola bar out of her bag, unwrapping it as she spoke. "Are you seeing Landon?"

The surprise must've shown on his face, as Julie laughed at him and explained. "Mark told me how Jason cooked up a way for you and your brother to see each other." Her face softened in sympathy, and Ryder understood why Mark was so smitten with her. "I think it's wonderful how close you and your brother are. I'm sorry you have to sneak around to see each other, though."

He bent down and kissed her cheek. "Thanks, sweetie. Yeah, I'm off to see both of them now. I figured to get in a little early and hang out with them since it's slow now. Once it's closer to the time for the fund-raiser, it'll be crazy."

She shooed him out. "Go ahead then. Go on. I'll talk to you later."

He grabbed his leather jacket and ran out of the office, anxious to surprise his brother and Jason.

Chapter Twenty-Four

J ASON VIEWED THE completed building with unabashed pride. It wasn't only the money they'd made from the project; the thrill of seeing the MALLORY CONSTRUCTION sign on the building site was the culmination of the dream he and Liam had talked about and planned—to run a business together. The Sunday he and Ryder had taken his parents for a drive to show them the work, his father hugged him, and his mother's smile beamed bright as the sun.

"We're so proud of you and Liam for what you've accomplished." His father had swiped a hand over the tears spilling from his eyes. He touched the sign with their name printed on it. *"You're so young to have accomplished so much already."*

It was one of the best days of Jason's life, next to meeting Ryder. Nudging Landon with his shoulder, he pointed down the block. "Look who's here." He couldn't help the silly grin on his face when he caught sight of his boyfriend walking down the block. No matter where he was, Ryder attracted light, creating a golden aura that drew people toward him. Jason remembered how sad he'd looked when they first met, his luminous blue eyes dim and haunted.

These days, an exuberant joy followed Ryder, Jason noted, watching his confident, easy stride. A thrill shot through Jason, knowing Ryder was his. The passion and love they shared was something Jason never dreamed existed in those cold lonely years he dated Chloe. Each day built upon the next, weaving together a life built not only on physical love, but trust, friendship, and respect.

"You really care about him, don't you?" Landon's gaze flickered from him to Ryder, the same blue eyes as his brother's, only more serious.

"Yeah. I really do. And you're still okay with it, right?" Jason constantly worried that for some reason Landon would have as hard a time dealing with his brother being gay and in a relationship as Liam had.

"Yeah, of course. Why wouldn't I be?" Landon punched Jason on the shoulder. "Maybe one day you'll be my brother-in-law." He smirked, then greeted his brother as he approached.

Jason didn't smile back, but merely stared at Ryder as he hugged Landon. Jason would love to marry Ryder sooner rather than later, but he wasn't sure if Ryder would want to take that step so fast. First, though, he wanted to make every attempt to try and reconcile Ryder with his father. His mother was a lost cause as far as he was concerned.

"Hey, you. That's a really serious look on your face."

Ryder brushed his lips to Jason's. "I hope whatever it is, it isn't something upsetting."

He shook himself out of his unsettling thoughts. "Not at all. I was showing Landon the finished building. Isn't she beautiful?"

Ryder put his arm around him and gave him a brief squeeze. "It's amazing. I'm so proud of all you've accomplished. What jobs do you have lined up next?"

"I actually am glad to be getting back into the smaller one-and-two-family home rehabs as well as doing some condo conversions. Liam and I managed to snag some good contracts that should keep us busy all summer long."

"That's great, babe." Ryder chuckled. "You're working hard, and here I am playing hooky from work. I figured I could get a chance to hang out longer with you guys today."

Jason checked his watch. He hesitated. The way the trains ran at this time of the day, it could take an hour to get uptown. "I have some errands to run uptown. Why don't you guys hang out, and I'll come back? I'm expecting a delivery around four. Can you stay for it, Landon?"

"Sure," Landon agreed. "I can hang out and show Ry what I worked on with you."

Jason gave Ryder a kiss good-bye, then left to take the train uptown.

IT WAS CLOSE to four o'clock by the time Jason emerged from the subway at Grand Central, and his nerves started kicking in. Was he doing the right thing? When he first thought of the idea, it seemed to be, but now that he was about to step headfirst into the fray, he wasn't so sure.

But then he remembered last Sunday's dinner with his parents and why he'd come up with the idea. He'd heard Ryder confiding to his mother that it was his father's birthday and during the week he'd tried calling to wish him a happy birthday, only to be rebuffed by his mother.

If Jason had a gun, he would've had no qualms about shooting that bitch through the head.

He swallowed his fear and rode the elevator up to the forty-fifth floor of the impressive but cold-looking steel monolith of a building that housed the law firm of Daniels and Montague. A twinge of anxiety nibbled at him as he studied himself in the ceiling mirror. He certainly didn't belong here in this corporate land of suits and ties and knew he looked out of place in his button-down shirt, jeans, and work boots. Well, fuck it. This was who he was, and Ryder loved him. But knowing Ryder had been forced to give this all up almost made his mother's snobbery understandable now. The prestige, wealth, and power of his family put him on a different planet than Jason came from. Hell, a different galaxy. These were the people in the society pages and multimillion-dollar homes.

Jason had once jokingly asked Ryder how he afford-ed his apartment, considering he worked for a nonprofit. He regretted it immediately, noticing how uncomfortable Ryder became, before he admitted that after his grandmother died, she'd left him a large amount of money that allowed him the freedom to work and live how he wanted.

The elevator stopped and whooshed open, revealing a glass-fronted office with men and women in suits, bustling about looking important as Jason thought lawyers often did.

The sight of Alexander Daniels standing tall and lean by a secretary's desk, greeted Jason as he stepped off the elevator. Jason had looked up his picture on the Internet, but now in person, Jason could see the striking resemblance between the older man and his two sons. An air of weariness and ineffable sadness surrounded the man.

Here goes nothing.

Jason pushed open the glass doors and strode through the puzzle of desks, coming to stand by Ryder's father. "Mr. Daniels, I'd like to speak with you."

The alarmed secretary pinned him with a fierce glare. "Who are you, young man, and what are you doing here?" She looked to her boss. "Should I call security, Mr. Daniels?" Her hand hovered over the phone, an anxious mother lion protecting her cub.

"What is it that you want, young man? I have no appointment with you, correct?" The man might look drawn and sad, but his voice rang with a quiet strength that commanded respect and attention.

Jason eyed him, not with fear but with determination. He decided he was very stupid or very much in love. He preferred to think the latter.

"No, sir, you don't."

"I'm sorry, then, but I'm very busy." Daniels turned away.

"Too busy to speak about Ryder?"

That got him the attention he deserved, as the man whirled around, his face drained of color. "He's all right, isn't he? Nothing's happened to him?"

And in that moment Jason knew how very much Alexander Daniels cared for his son. It was there in the sweat beading on his brow, the paleness of his face, and the fear and longing in his eyes. Eyes, Jason noticed, the same luminous blue as Ryder's and, like Ryder's, revealed every emotion fighting within him.

"Can we speak somewhere in private, please?"

Daniels nodded, beckoning with his hand as he strode toward the back of the office. "Come with me. Jane, hold my calls."

"Yes, sir." To Jason's surprise, she flashed him a small smile before turning back to answer the ringing phone. He hurried after Daniels's retreating back, following him down the labyrinth of hallways, closed doors on either side.

Finally, they came to a door marked PRIVATE. Daniels unlocked it and gestured for him to enter. Jason seated himself at the small conference table and waited for Ryder's father to join him.

"What are you here to tell me about my son? How do you know him? He's not sick; at least tell me that." Although Jason felt for the man, hearing the strain in his voice, he had to remember this was Ryder's father, the man who threw his son out and cut him off from his family simply because he didn't want to be embarrassed.

"Ryder's fine and has no idea I'm here. My name's Jason Mallory." He locked gazes with this formidable man. "I'm the man who's in love with your son, and I'm the luckiest man on earth because Ryder loves me back. No matter what you and your wife did and said to him, he can't and won't change who he is. And I thank God for that, because it means that we can be together. I'm not here to plead his case as to why you should accept him because he's gay."

"Now wait a minute, young man." Daniels's hand reached out, but Jason drew away.

"I don't want to wait a minute or an hour. I'm here to tell you that what you're doing to him is breaking his heart. He loves you and his brother, and God only knows why, but I think he even loves his mother, no matter she's been keeping him and Landon apart."

"What are you talking about? Ryder doesn't want to see Landon. My wife told me he couldn't even be bothered to come home for Thanksgiving. He was too busy with his friends." Daniels stood, his face no longer pale but flushed with anger. "She said she called and begged him to come home, but he laughed and said we didn't fit in with his lifestyle. He especially didn't want to see myself or Landon because he knew how much we'd disapprove of him."

Was this a joke? "Didn't you try and contact him yourself, sir, and find out what was going on?"

"N-no. I didn't I'm afraid." Daniels dropped into his chair, his face red. "I've never been close with my family. The only thing I know how to do is work and make money. It's all my father taught me. My wife took care of the boys—"

"Oh, she took care of them, all right," said Jason, his laugh bitter and hard. "Do you know how much your children crave your love? They're desperate for you to show them any attention, but you aren't home to ever see that."

"I'm trying to make sure they have everything they need."

"What they need is you, not your money." Jason slammed his hand down on the table. "Ryder has nightmares and is haunted by the fact that his father doesn't love him because he's gay. And Landon's crying out for you to spend some time with him, to know him. Grab this time with him; he's a great kid."

"How do you know Landon?" Daniels asked.

"He's worked for my construction company after school for a while now. One day he'll make a fine architect."

"Architect?" Ryder's father stared at him. "I had no

idea Landon was interested in architecture."

Jason couldn't keep the harsh sarcasm from his voice. "Of course you didn't. How could you? You don't know a single thing about either one of your children, but I bet you can recite how much money this place took in last year." He couldn't believe he had the nerve to talk this way to one of the most prominent lawyers in New York City. But all it took was remembering Ryder's anguished face and self-doubt, all caused by this man and his careless disregard.

"I've never stopped loving Ryder. I didn't understand why he wouldn't join our firm; I still don't. It's his heritage, his legacy."

Jason scoffed. "But only if he's straight, right? You can't accept him because he's gay. He's become one of the city's foremost animal-rights attorneys. Did you know that? He and his friends are running a huge charity fund-raiser next month and have already raised over two hundred thousand dollars for Rescue Me. He did that, him and his friends, all by themselves. It's what he's passionate about. If you'd only take the time to find out about your son, you'd realize what a special man he is."

"I'll admit I was shocked and a little sad when he told us he was gay. But only because I knew how much hate there is in the world and how hard it was going to be for him to make his way." Daniels's phone buzzed, but he ignored it.

"I'm sorry, but that's a bunch of BS if you ask me.

It's only been hard for him because he's had to do it alone. Until now, of course. If that were the case, you and your wife wouldn't have ostracized him and prevented him from seeing his brother." Jason leaned back and folded his arms over his chest.

The buzzing of Daniels's phone continued; then Jason's vibrated, but he chose to ignore it as well.

"That's not true. My wife would never keep the children from seeing each other." But Jason knew he'd insinuated a kernel of doubt in the man's mind, and his voice sounded less sure of itself than it did in the beginning of their conversation.

This was going nowhere. "Look, Mr. Daniels, I wanted you to know that Ryder misses you, all of you. I'm telling you he wants his family back. But if you and your wife don't want to see him, that's fine. Because he has me now, and my family to turn to when he needs support. They love him and accept us as a couple." He stood and walked to the door. "Please don't keep him from his brother, though. They love each other. Soon Landon will be off to college, and you won't be able to control him as much as you can now. Do you want to risk the chance of losing both your sons because of your pride and your prejudice?"

He turned the knob and opened the door. "Good-bye, sir." He didn't look back, shutting the door carefully behind him. With a shake of his head, he walked past the windows of the conference room that framed the hallway. He couldn't help but see through the half-opened blinds, Daniels still sitting where he'd left him, his head cradled in his hands.

It was all up to Ryder's father now. From now on, the only person Jason was concentrating on was Ryder.

Chapter Twenty-Five

RYDER GAVE HIS brother a congratulatory fist bump. "I have to hand it to you, I didn't think you were serious about this stuff." Landon had finished explaining the blueprints he'd unrolled on Jason's desk, and the animation and excitement on his face filled Ryder with a sense of pride. The flooring and solar panels Jason's crew installed made it one of the newest "green" buildings in the city.

"I love it, and Jason's a great teacher. I'm going to use what I learned here to make my portfolio for when I apply to colleges next year." Landon rolled up the prints, then slid them back into the tube. He clicked on the computer screen and brought up Jason's new website. "Look, I helped him and Liam with this the other day."

Ryder tensed at the mention of Liam's name. Though they'd made up, he still resented what Liam had put Jason through and wasn't sure he could trust him, even with Jason's assurances. For Jason's sake, he kept quiet, though. "Looks great." He checked his watch and wondered where Jason had to run off to in such a hurry. When he heard footsteps outside the trailer, he smiled. "That must be Jason now. Guess whatever he had to do didn't take too long."

Anxious to get home and spend some quality alone time with his lover, he opened the door before Jason could, a wide smile on his face. "Hey…" The smile died on his lips as he came face-to-face with his mother.

"I knew it." His mother's pale blue eyes flayed him as she spat out her words. "I knew all along something was going on here, but I couldn't catch you sneaking around until now." She pointed one of her perfectly polished nails at Landon. "This is how you repay me for everything I've done for you? You deliberately disobey me and go behind my back to see him."

"My name's Ryder, Mom. I'm your son too, re-member?" Ryder stepped closer to Landon. Although he hadn't seen his mother in almost a year, she looked the same as she had the last time he stood before her. Pale, thin, and angry. Always angry. Her eyes narrowed until they were nothing more than slits in her frozen face. He wondered how she took in enough oxygen through her pinched nose and tight lips. Everything about her screamed *hands off, don't touch.*

"Sometimes I wish I could forget."

The absolute viciousness of her statement rocked him. Before he had a chance to catch his breath, Landon spoke.

"What kind of mother are you? How can you be

such a miserable bitch?" Landon placed a trembling hand on Ryder's shoulder. "I love him. He's my brother, and nothing you can say or do will ever make me feel any differently."

Tears slid down Ryder's face. What a man his brother was turning out to be, even if he was forced into this untenable situation far too early for a kid of seventeen.

"I love you too, and I'm so proud of you." Ryder hugged Landon. "Maybe you should go, though, before she gets even angrier."

"No." Landon's jaw set in a mulish thrust. "I'm going to be eighteen soon. She can't tell me what to do and who to see anymore."

"Now you listen to me, young man. I'm your mother. I didn't raise you this way. You think it's fun now to go slumming? You won't think so when we cut off your allowance. Your trust fund doesn't kick in until you're twenty-five. Your father and I have a reputation to uphold." She flung open the door so hard it banged back on its hinges. "Let's go."

Landon stayed put. "I'm not going. If you want, you can throw me out too. Is that what you want, Mom, to lose both of us?"

His mother's eyes filled with panic. Ryder made one last-ditch effort to reason with her. "Why can't we work it out where I don't have to see you and Dad, since you both have such a problem with me, but Landon and I can still see each other?" He forced a smile. "Is that too much to ask?" Her eyes flickered from him to Landon. "Do you hate me that much? Hasn't the punishment gone on long enough?"

Her lips pursed as if she smelled something rotten. "I don't hate you, Ryder. But I can't accept it, and your father and the firm can't afford to be tainted by your associations. I don't want Landon exposed to your life. You have a partner?" She swallowed, looking supremely uncomfortable.

He nodded. "I'm in a relationship, yes."

Before they had a chance to continue, the door opened, and Liam blustered in. "Hey, Ry. What's shakin'?" He stopped dead as he caught Ryder's eyes. "Uh, sorry to barge in. I didn't know you had company. I thought it was only you and the kid in here."

Ryder caught his mother's horrified glance. "Tell me this is not the man you're with." He almost laughed at the pleading sound of her voice. The sight of Liam, fresh off the site in dirty jeans, heavy boots, and a sweat-dampened work shirt that clung to his thick biceps, freaked her out and sent her scuttling to the opposite side of the trailer. The clean scent of the outdoors mixed with the smell of sweat from his skin. He looked every bit the common construction worker his mother had been deriding and feared. If Ryder were a mean person, he'd play a rotten trick on her and pretend Liam was his lover, but he doubted Liam would play along.

To his surprise, Liam answered. "Who are you?" He stepped all the way inside the trailer, closing the door behind him. It was a relatively small space and crowded now with the four of them. Liam stood next to Ryder, and if he didn't know better Ryder almost thought of it as a show of solidarity on the man's part.

"It's my mother, Liam."

Light dawned in Liam's eyes. Ryder still assumed the two of them were on somewhat rocky ground. Even though Jason had told him of Liam's support when he'd disappeared those two days at the beginning of their relationship, he and Liam barely talked about anything of consequence since that highly emotional night at the bar. Liam was, however, clued in to his life enough to know about the problems with his parents.

"So, Mrs. Daniels, you've come to say hello to your sons. They're great guys, aren't they?" To Ryder's shock, Liam draped a heavy arm around his shoulders. His mother's lip curled in disgust.

"May I presume, young man, you are Ryder's…partner?" She shuddered as she spoke the words.

"No, you may not presume anything. I'm Liam Mallory, and Jason, my brother, is his boyfriend." Liam's arm around his shoulder felt strangely comforting to Ryder.

"I can't believe you and your family condone your brother's abnormal behavior." Ryder stared at his mother and wondered at her capacity to love anyone, if she could talk this way about her own flesh and blood. Her brittle voice and stiff posture made him think of childish stick figures. They held no life or emotion, acting as mere placeholders for the flesh-and-blood pictures they sought to portray.

Ryder pushed off from Liam. "Mom, enough already."

Liam advanced on Ryder's mother, jabbing a none-too-clean finger in her shocked face. "Look, lady. Ry here may have to put up with your shit, but I don't. To be honest, no, I didn't like it at first. But it doesn't matter what I like, right? There's only one thing that matters to me in this world, and that's my family. If my parents and brothers and sisters are happy, then so am I."

Liam caught him by the shoulder with a meaty hand and held on tight. Ryder couldn't move if his life depended on it. "This guy has made my brother happier than I've ever seen him. It's like every fucking day is Christmas morning when you see them together. You should get down on your knees and thank the Lord Ryder's found someone to love who loves him back."

Liam stormed toward the door, then stopped and turned back. "And don't think for a minute Jason doesn't care for him. My brother adores him, loves him, and would give him the fucking moon if he could. So stay the hell away from them and let them be happy." He slammed the door behind him and left.

Ryder gaped, staring at the door after Liam's outburst. Never in his wildest imagination would he have believed Liam to be his champion. Now, instead of the coldness and pain of his mother's rejection, the warmth of finally hearing Liam's complete acceptance flowed through him, giving him the happiness and inner peace he never thought he'd be granted. Only his father's recognition and declaration that he still loved him could make him feel better, but since that would never come to pass, Ryder remained content.

His mother gathered her handbag and opened the door. "What a common man. I hope at least his brother has more class, but I'll assume not." She shut the door carefully behind her. The sound of her footsteps receded.

Sometimes there was no place for words, where silence was more of a friend. He and Landon sat down, each of them staring off into space. The realization he and his family would never reconcile no longer suffocated him, paralyzing him so that he couldn't think or see straight. His brother wasn't ashamed of him, and that was really all he needed. He'd have to get used to it and had, for the most part. Having Jason and his family's acceptance of them as a couple made his own parent's rejection easier to deal with. Thank God Jason had the most wonderful loving family, especially his mom. Now with Liam coming to terms with his and Jason's relationship, they could forget the past, forget his parents' abandonment, and move forward with their lives.

"Hey, I texted Jason and told him what happened." Landon nudged him with his foot.

"Did he answer?" Ryder pulled out his own phone,

but he had no text from Jason. Strange. They always told each other where they were going to be during the day.

He heard footsteps outside, and he braced himself for round two with his mother, but when he opened the door, it was only the delivery person Landon was waiting for.

After placing the box on the desk, Landon checked his phone again. "Yeah. He said he's on his way back. That was sent a few minutes ago, so it should be, like, fifteen more minutes."

Good. He couldn't wait for Jase to get here so they could go home. Tonight more than anything he needed to feel his Jason's arms around him, anchoring him with his love. They planned to go to dinner at Connor and Emily's. He wanted to tell them about Matt's visit and get their take on the meeting he had tomorrow with the partner from Everett and Winston.

The doorknob rattled, and Jason came storming inside.

"Hey, you." Ryder gave his lover a weak smile.

"Are you all right? Shit, and Landon was here too. Was it really awful?" Jason threw his jacket on the table and came close to peer into Ryder's eyes. "I'm so sorry you had to go through that by yourself."

Ryder put up a hand. "We weren't alone. Believe it or not, Liam came in and blew my mother out of the water."

Landon stood up and grabbed his backpack. "Yeah,

he was great. Really shut her up. I gotta go now, though." He gestured to the package on the desk. "Jason, there's the delivery you were waiting for. I entered it in the system."

"Thanks." Jason patted him on the back. "Will I be seeing you again?"

"I'll text you and let you know the plan." Landon turned to Ryder. "I'm definitely coming to the fundraiser. Nothing they can do or say is gonna stop me."

Ryder pulled Landon into a hug. "You're the best. And don't worry. No one's going to keep us apart anymore." A smile tugged at his lips. "You'll be happy to know Jason's sister Jessie will be there, and she's cute. She's heard a lot about you, so I'm sure you'll have a good time." He smirked as Landon flushed a deep red and left the trailer, mumbling under his breath about dumbass brothers.

Jason's arms came around him, holding him against his solid body. He could feel the play of muscles in Jason's arms under his shirtsleeves as they held him close, and shivered when Jason's warm lips kissed his neck.

"Now that he's gone, tell me the truth. Was it awful? Was *she* awful?" Jason's firm hold and soothing kisses relaxed him, emptying his mind of all the tension and pressure of the past hour.

"It wasn't that bad, babe. I told her I didn't care anymore about her and my father's approval, as long as I got to see Landon." He turned in Jason's arms to face him. As always, the tenderness in Jason's blue gaze tripped his heart, setting prickles of electricity through his arms and down his spine. This feeling inside went so much further than mere sex or lust.

"I love you, Jase. I love you so much sometimes it scares me. And if I didn't think I'd have everyone within a city block hearing me scream this trailer down, I'd show you right now how much I fucking love you."

Jason's wicked grin matched his own as the need and hunger rose within him. It only took two steps for Jason to lock the door and unbuckle his belt. "The crew's gone for the day, and I don't give a shit if the entire city hears you call my name when I bury myself inside you." He reached into his pants for his wallet and pulled out a condom. "I keep this in case we want to have a quickie somewhere. Like now." His grin grew broader.

Ryder's dick twitched as Jason unzipped his pants and dropped them. He didn't even bother taking off his boots. Ryder reached out a hand, but Jason knocked it away.

"Turn around, undo your pants, and drop them." Jason's seductive voice rumbled low and authoritative, causing Ryder to shiver. "Do you know how many hours I've spent fantasizing about you bent over this desk and what I'd like to do to you?" He growled and bit down on Ryder's shoulder, then licked the sore spot.

Ryder moaned and struggled to undo his pants with shaking hands.

"Here, let me." Jason brushed aside Ryder's trembling fingers with a strong hand, and yanked down his pants and boxers. Ryder was so hard and so turned on already he knew it wouldn't take long for him to come, as Jason's rough hand grasped his cock and began to stroke.

"Jase, now. Do it. Right now."

Hearing the crinkling of the foil, he spread his legs wider, bracing against the desk. Jason scrambled into his desk drawer and pulled out a little tube. Within moments, Ryder felt slick fingers probe his opening, enter, and twist. Whatever Jason whispered in his ear made no sense to him at all, as the wicked machinations of those clever fingers, slipping and sliding, twisting and snaking into his channel, set his brain on fire.

"Jason." He pushed against the digits inside him, whimpering with ecstasy as Jason brushed his prostate again and again.

"Ready?" Jason stood behind him, smoothing his rough hands over Ryder's ass.

"Yes," he gasped. "Jase, please."

With one strong thrust, Jason entered him, then immediately pulled back, only to push forward again. Pleasure bloomed as Jason invaded his body, his thick cock turning Ryder's insides into a quivering mass of jelly. With unerring accuracy, Jason thrust inside him again and again until with a choked cry, Ryder came undone, torn apart by the sensations rocketing through his body.

"Jason." The walls echoed around them; the shock and awe of his orgasm ripping through him as he spilled into his hand. Ryder sensed immediately when Jason climaxed, from the rigidity of Jason's body, his desperate grasp as he pulled Ryder close, and the wispy, stuttering breaths against Ryder's shoulder.

They lay half-slumped against the desk until the sharp edges began to dig into Ryder's thighs. "Jase, I gotta move."

"Why?"

Ryder smiled at the testy grunt. Jason liked nothing better than to cuddle up and take a long nap after lovemaking, but they had to leave here soon, get the dogs, and go to their friends'. "Come on, get that gorgeous rear in gear. We're having dinner at Connor and Emily's." He pushed up, laughing as Jason cursed under his breath.

"Shit. I wanna go home and get into bed. With you." Waggling his dark brows, Jason leaned in for a kiss. "Sure I can't convince you to cancel on them and come home with me?"

After wiping his hands with some napkins he found on the desk, Ryder pulled his pants up and tucked in his shirt, watching Jason's eyes follow his movements as he straightened his clothes. "Chill out, lover boy. You'll have to be satisfied with the quickie we had until later." Ryder laughed, then took Jason's face between his hands. "You're mine. I know I tried to hold back at one point, but never again. I love you so fucking much it hurts to breathe sometimes, 'cause I'm afraid I'm gonna fuck it up and you'll leave me." He put his hand on Jason's neck to pull him closer. "Don't give up on me. I need you to be there when it gets too dark sometimes."

The room seemed even smaller now, as all that mattered was the two of them standing toe to toe.

As their foreheads touched, Jason cupped his hand around Ryder's neck, his rough thumb stroking a calming pattern on Ryder's skin. "I could never give up on you. There was never any choice once I met you. From the first time I saw you, I knew you'd be mine."

Ryder struggled for breath, then rested his lips against Jason's cheek for a moment before kissing his mouth. "Let's get going. The sooner we get there, the sooner we can leave."

Chapter Twenty-Six

DINNER WAS THE usual chaotic affair at Connor and Emily's brick townhouse in Carroll Gardens. Knowing they were expected and the door would be unlocked, Jason put a hand on Ryder's back and followed him inside, only to be greeted by the couple's two large dogs, their whip-long tails wagging. The canines exchanged a series of excited barks and woofs with Pearl and Trouper before all four skidded away to the rear of the house.

Connor's eyes lit up when Jason and Ryder entered the kitchen. "Save me. She wants to kill me."

"Can I have his iPad, Em?" Ryder leaned over and kissed her on the cheek. "Pearl stepped on mine yesterday, so it would save me a trip to the store."

"I'll take his car." Jason cradled the bowl he carried in the crook of his arm and snitched a stuffed mushroom from a platter. After chewing, he gave Emily his own kiss. "I love those old sports cars."

Emily laughed and put down her kitchen weapon. "He's been a pest all day. *Don't stand on your feet too long. Are you sure you don't want a drink of water? Make sure you eat your fruits and vegetables.*'" She wrinkled her nose at them. "It's like living with my mother all over again."

He and Ryder shared a look, then burst out laughing. "Why, Connor," he gasped through his snickering, "you old mother hen, you."

"Oh, screw you," muttered Connor. He sat on the counter, never taking his eyes off his wife.

While Ryder busied himself getting beers out of the refrigerator, Jason put down the large salad bowl and pulled up a stool at the kitchen island. He loved Connor and Emily's house. Warm and cozy, it wasn't one of those huge, rambling brownstones, but a three-story brick townhome with two large rooms on each floor and a garden out back. No matter that there were plenty of rooms, everyone always congregated here, in the kitchen. Emily had the walls painted a creamy pale yellow to contrast with the glass-front dark cherrywood cabinets. The counters were poured concrete, and the floors were the original hardwood plank.

She loved to cook and have guests over and had a huge restaurant-style stove and refrigerator, as well as a long scrubbed-wood farmhouse table. Jason sniffed with appreciation as the tantalizing aroma of her homemade sauce filled the air.

"What's for dinner?" He pointed to the bowl. "We brought salad."

Connor's face brightened. "Good, she'll eat her

greens now, since you brought it. If it was me, she'd probably throw it away."

"Or dump it on your head," she cooed. "And to answer your question, Jase, eggplant parmigiana." Her deceptively sweet tone set Ryder off in gales of laughter.

"Guess the honeymoon period is over, my brother." Jason accepted a beer and shared a smile.

Connor shot them both evil, dark looks. "Wait, Jason. One day this bastard will do something to piss you off, and then you'll see how it feels."

Jason continued to chuckle, stealing another stuffed mushroom. After taking a bite, he poked Ryder with his elbow, offering him the rest. When Ryder failed to respond, he poked him again. "What's wrong? You look kind of weirded out."

"Um, I need to tell you guys something."

Jason had never seen Ryder so nervous. He glanced at Connor, who shrugged.

"Go ahead. What's the matter?" Figuring to offer him comfort, Jason put his hand on Ryder's arm, but instead of relaxing, Ryder tensed and drew away. "Ry, what's going on? You're making me nervous."

"It's nothing bad. It's just that, um, Matt came to the office today."

Emily dropped the ladle she'd been holding, splattering hot tomato sauce all over the floor. "Shit, damn. Did I hear you right?" Her worried gaze first searched Connor, then landed on Jason. "You know about him, right?"

Still stunned, he nodded. "Yeah. After the time he gave that interview on television." He slid off the chair next to Ryder and stood before him. "Why didn't you say anything earlier? What did he want?" A cold, panicky thought burst out of his mouth before he could censor it. "He wants you back. I know it. I'm sure he came on to you. Did he kiss you? Did you let him?"

"Jesus Christ, Jase, stop." Ryder slammed his hand down. "How can you even think I'd want him after everything we've talked about?"

From the corner of his eye, Jason watched Emily take Connor's hand and leave the room, but it barely registered. "You loved him, though. And you left in such a bad place with each other, with nothing resolved. Maybe seeing him today brought back all the feelings you once had for him."

Ryder put his arms around him, holding him close. "What I once had with Matt was an unhealthy relationship based on me giving and him taking. I don't ever want you to put us and what we have together on the same level as that."

"Why didn't you tell me you'd seen him?" Jason's heart rate slowed as Ryder's words sank in.

"I know I should've called you right away, but then I got another call, and after everything that happened with my mother this afternoon, frankly, it didn't seem that important anymore."

"Did you have any feelings when you saw him again? Don't worry about hurting me. I need to know."

He'd crash and burn later if Ryder admitted he still cared about Matt. The guy lived an exciting life and Ryder had been so in love with him. Worse, he'd been Ryder's first love. Someone special.

"The only feelings I have are pity and a little disgust at myself for allowing Matt's needs and wants to take over my life." Ryder kissed his cheek. "Don't you understand how much you mean to me?" Ryder pushed him up against the counter until their eyes locked. "I always tell you, you're fucking mine, but baby, I am fucking yours until the day I die. You own me."

Jason slumped against Ryder and held on for dear life. "God, Ry, I got so scared for a minute. I didn't know what to think. All I saw was the sky crashing down on top of me when I thought of you with him."

"Oh, babe, I can't guarantee I won't make mistakes, but from when we first met, it's only been you, and only ever will be you." Their lips met, and Jason's world settled back on its axis with the smooth, sweet slide of Ryder's tongue in his mouth. Jason kissed him for a few moments before pulling away, meeting Ryder's bright blue eyes with his own.

"Don't keep things from me, though. We've had enough of that shit already." Grumbling and still annoyed, he paced the floor in front of the table. "Is there anything else you haven't told me?"

"After Matt left, I got a call from the senior partner at a very prestigious firm in the city. They want to speak with me tomorrow morning." Ryder placed the salad in the refrigerator.

"What about, do you think?"

Ryder shrugged. "Who knows? Maybe they want to offer me a job. I'll find out and promise to tell you right away." He raised his brow. "Is that okay with you?"

"Would you take it? A job there, I mean." It had never occurred to Jason that Ryder might one day leave the rescue to practice law again.

"Not sure. If I could handle it where they'd let me do the animal-rights work, maybe." Ryder drank his beer. "I've never thought of going back to a firm, but it might be nice, if we could swing it at the office."

There was a sudden shriek and a loud thump from the living room. Ryder beckoned, and together they crept inside. There, sprawled out on the sofa and locked in each other's arms, were Connor and Emily, oblivious to anyone but themselves.

Jason chuckled as they tiptoed back to the kitchen. "All is forgiven, as usual." Taking up the bread knife, he began to slice the crusty Italian bread, stealing the end piece.

"How do you think she got in her situation in the first place?" Ryder smirked.

"I heard that," an outraged voice called out from the living room.

Jason couldn't stop laughing as he helped set the table.

AT TEN O'CLOCK the next morning, Ryder entered the offices of Everett and Winston. While not as large or as venerable as his father's law firm, it was prestigious enough in its own right to pick and choose from the best and brightest law students, including former clerks to US Supreme Court justices.

After being offered coffee and water and turning down both, Ryder waited close to ten minutes before a young man, most likely a first-year associate, came by to escort him to the senior partner's office. He was shown in and introduced to the woman he'd spoken with on the telephone. There was one other individual in the room, aside from the associate, whose name, he learned on their walk to the office, was David.

"Mr. Daniels, this is Stewart Clinton, another senior partner with the firm."

"Nice to meet you, Daniels. I know your father quite well." Clinton's handshake was firm and quick. "Let's sit down." They all sat around a conference table.

Ryder's smile faltered for the moment. "Nice to meet you as well." And he left it at that. If Clinton noticed any awkwardness, he failed to let on.

"Now, then, may we call you Ryder? I'm Patty."

"Of course." Ryder preferred using his first name. Only athletes and presidents should go by last names, in his mind. "I'm truly at a loss to why I'm here."

Patty smiled at him. "Here at Everett and Winston, we've always prided ourselves on being on the cutting edge of the legal community. We were one of the first law firms in the city to tackle sexual discrimination against LGBT individuals in the workplace and in the schools, and we also have a very strong family law and women's rights division." She took a breath and a sip of water.

All very interesting as background information, but nothing new anymore. Those divisions, while once unique, were now a big part of most general practice firms. Still, he listened with a polite smile on his face.

Stewart spoke next. "Ryder, we're aware of the work you and your friends do for the dog rescue and are quite impressed with the arguments you made before the zoning board and the other city agencies where we've seen you speak. You're very passionate about this cause, aren't you?"

"Yes, I'm very dedicated to the rescue and to the dogs."

Stewart stroked his chin. "Do you own one of these dogs?"

"I do indeed, and my partner rescued one as well." Ryder clicked on his phone to bring up a picture of Pearl and Troup, showing it to Stewart and Patty.

"We are also aware," Stewart began again, "of the fund-raiser you're having. We plan to attend and, once again, commend you on your ability to raise such interest and money."

"Thank you both, but I'm not quite sure why I'm here, still."

Patty handed him a folder. "Inside here is a new

division we are creating in the firm. An animal-rights division. Not only for dogs, you understand, but for all animals and for the people who care for them. We would like you to start it up and are prepared to make a very generous offer." She sat back in her chair.

Ryder glanced at the paperwork, stunned by the offer. He found three sets of eyes staring at him when he looked up. With a weak grin, he hefted the papers. "I need some time to digest this, talk it over with my partner and the other founders of the rescue."

"We understand, Ryder. But we can't underscore how serious we are about this effort and you spearheading it." Patty came from behind her desk to stand next to David, the associate. "David here is also interested and has asked to be included in the new division."

Ryder shifted his attention to the young man, returning his friendly smile. "It's something I'll give plenty of thought to, but as I said, I'm afraid with the fund-raiser I can't give you an answer until after that date."

Stewart stood then, a sure sign the interview was finished. "I look forward to the fund-raiser. All three of us are going, so we'll see you there." He shook Ryder's hand. "David here will show you out."

Ryder said good-bye and walked out with David at his side.

"So how long have you worked with the rescue?" David held the door open for him. "Is that where you met your partner?"

"I've worked there almost three years, but Jason and I have been together a few months."

They reached the elevator, and David pushed the button, then leaned up against the wall, apparently content to wait with him. "I hope you come on board here. It's a great firm and a very friendly work environment."

The elevator dinged, and the doors whooshed open. Saved by the bell. "It was nice to meet you, David." They shook hands. "I hope to see you at the fund-raiser."

"You definitely will." David gave him the same wide, friendly smile.

The elevator doors closed, and Ryder skimmed through the folder, impressed with their work. They'd thought of everything. They offered an extremely generous benefits package, and they'd done their homework on the pending legislation on animal rights. This opportunity had come out of the blue, but he wouldn't make any decision without first discussing it with Emily, Connor, and Jason. He'd never leave the rescue in a lurch. None of this would be decided until after the fund-raiser. Emily was stressed enough, and he refused to add to her anxiety. Not that he'd have a choice. With Connor hovering around his wife like an angry wasp ready to sting anyone who dared approach her, it wasn't high on his list of priorities.

As soon as he left the building, he texted Jason. *I finished.*

He received an immediate text back. *Can't wait to hear.*

Maybe it would be easier to raise awareness for the rescue if he took this job, he thought, slipping his phone into his pocket. He'd talk to Jason about it. An idea popped into his head, and he grinned happily to himself. He stopped and pulled out his phone to text Jason again. *Playing hooky this morning. Bringing coffee. Be naked or be sorry.*

Chapter Twenty-Seven

T HE NIGHT OF the fund-raiser had arrived, and Ryder bordered on panic, unable to sit or stand still for more than a few moments before jumping up, remembering an errant detail he thought he'd forgotten but of course hadn't. The stress and emotions of all the planning caused him, Connor and Emily to be unusually snappy with one another for the past few weeks and he hated it.

"Hold still, babe. I can't tie your bow tie if you keep fidgeting." Jason kissed Ryder's neck, flooding his body with warmth.

"Try keeping your fucking lips off me if you don't want me to move." Ryder yelped when Jason nipped his ear.

"Stop that and calm down," Jason growled.

Those wicked lips, however, continued to move across Ryder's neck as Jason's tongue dragged tantalizing patterns along his skin.

"Calm down?" Ryder's voice rose, incredulous at Jason's demand. "If you want me to stop, then keep that fucking tongue off my neck. I swear to God it's like a lethal weapon." He moaned when the wet tip of Jason's tongue entered his ear.

Those destructive evil lips pressed against his skin quirked up in a smile. "That was your ear, not your neck, if we want to get technical."

"What the hell, Jase?" Twisting away, Ryder held up his hands in self-defense. "You're killing me tonight. I can't afford to be so, so…" He shrugged, helpless with inexplicable feelings of anxiety.

Jason's arms came around him, pulling him close. "I'm sorry. I thought it would settle you down, not overexcite you."

Ryder breathed in Jason's familiar warm scent, and his muscles relaxed, the tension releasing from his body. They stayed that way, forehead to forehead, holding each other as Jason's strong, sure hands massaged his back in soothing circles.

"I don't know why I'm so tense," Ryder admitted, straightening up and yanking at his tuxedo jacket. "I guess we've been planning this for so long the fact that tonight's the night overwhelmed me for the moment."

"Understandable. I know you'll be fantastic. My whole family is so excited, Jessie especially." Jason checked his reflection in the mirror. He too wore a tuxedo and had confessed to Ryder it was the first time he'd worn one since his high school prom. That necessitated a shopping trip to Madison Avenue, where Ryder gifted him with a sleek designer tux. At first Jason had objected when he saw the cost, but after he accepted it as a belated Valentine's Day gift, it was obvious how much he enjoyed wearing it. Ryder had caught him touching the soft, smooth wool of the jacket, visibly preening at its luxurious feel.

Ryder chuckled. "Who are you kidding? She's as excited to meet Landon as she is about the fund-raiser." His heart beat faster at the sight of Jason. "You look gorgeous. I'll be the envy of everyone there tonight."

The buzzer rang, and when Jason answered, he heard Clarence's voice announcing their car was waiting downstairs. They both grabbed their wallets, keys, and phones, and after securing the dogs on their leashes, headed out. Once in the car, Jason took his hand. "Are you really that nervous? You speak in front of strangers all the time about this stuff."

"True, but never in front of you guys, and our family. And who knows who else will be in the audience." The collar of his shirt strangled him, and Ryder tugged at it to try and breathe a little easier. "This is so damn important to us. And then there's the job offer, which I still haven't mentioned to them." He scratched Pearl's ears. "I've never kept something this important from the two of them, and I kind of feel like I'm betraying them somehow." Pearl licked his hand as if she knew he needed extra comforting and reassurance.

Jason leaned over and kissed him on his cheek. "You aren't. Emily's so crazed right now it would only add to her stress level, and Connor would probably kill you."

Of that he had no doubt. He hadn't spoken to Emily in over a week, so there hadn't really been an opportunity for them to talk. Connor was so distracted by the pregnancy that he didn't notice Ryder's silence. "I want everything to go smoothly. You never know who might be in the audience. This night has the potential to change everything."

Jason laid his head on Ryder's shoulder. "As long as you're with me, I don't care what happens."

Ryder couldn't help but smile as he kissed the top of Jason's head. "That's a given, babe. Together forever."

❀ ❀ ❀ ❀ ❀

THEIR CAR GLIDED to a stop across the street from the Green Building on Union Street in Carroll Gardens and Ryder spied the food trucks they hired busily dispensing lobster rolls, barbecued brisket sandwiches, gourmet grilled-cheese sandwiches, and spring rolls and dumplings to the crowd. They'd provided a smoothie truck for those who didn't want anything alcoholic from the two bars set up inside the space. For dessert one truck provided cotton candy and the other, old-fashioned ice cream treats. Judging by the long lines, the trucks were the big hit Emily had predicted.

"Ry, this looks amazing." Jason squeezed his hand as they stood on the sidewalk surveying the scene. The party planner Emily worked with had outdone herself. Standing outside they could see thousands of twinkling white lights showering down from the ceiling and, coupled with the music from the pianist and violinist they'd hired, it created an overall dreamlike, magical atmosphere.

"Guys, over here." Connor waved at them from the front door.

Ryder nudged Jason and tugged Pearl's leash. "Let's go. I need to mingle, and I want you with me." His heart lurched at the happy grin that spread across Jason's handsome face. He must have done something right to get so lucky to have found Jason.

A much-more-relaxed-than-usual Connor had his arm wrapped around his sparkling wife. Emily, now visibly pregnant, with that glow only expectant mothers had, threw her arms around Ryder as soon as she spotted them.

"Oh, Ry, you look gorgeous, sweetie." She kissed him and turned to Jason. "You too, honey. My two gorgeous men."

"Hey." Connor cleared his throat. "What am I, chopped liver?"

She brushed him off with an airy wave of her hand. "I live with you. It's different." Ryder knew better and smiled at the warm kiss she planted on Connor's lips. Seemed like everything between the three of them reverted to normal, now that all the planning was done and the event was in full swing.

He turned to Jason. "Let's put the dogs outside with the others and mingle." The four of them made plans to meet up in an hour to coordinate the speeches. He and

Jason made their way to the back, stopping to greet acquaintances and chat as they walked past.

"Jase, Ryder, over here," Jason's sister Nicole called over the din of voices. Ryder took Trouper's leash from Jason. "Why don't you go over there and say hi while I take the dogs out to the garden? I'll be right back."

Jason nodded. "Okay." He leaned over and kissed him. "Don't be long. I don't want anyone else taking you away from me." He winked and threaded his way through the crowd to greet and join his parents, brothers, and sisters.

Whatever nerves or hesitation Ryder might have been harboring evaporated. He had the man he loved, the surrogate family who loved and accepted him, and his friends. Pearl and Trouper happily joined Laurel and Hardy in the makeshift dog run, and after spending a few minutes playing with them, he hurried back inside to join Jason and his family. On the way over to them, he spotted Landon entering the building and waved him over.

"Hey, I'm so glad you made it. What did you tell Mom?"

Landon's face tightened with anger. "I told her I'm going out and hopped in a cab. I didn't wait for her to answer." A strange look crossed his face. "Dad and her have been fighting a lot, late at night when they think I'm asleep. Something about her keeping secrets from him and stuff."

Ryder had no interest. "I wouldn't worry. Mom's a

master manipulator, and I'm sure she'll talk her way out of whatever it is." By this time, they'd reached the crowd of Jason's family. Aside from his parents and siblings, Ryder noticed Liam had brought a date, and Mark, of course, was there with Julie.

"Ryder." Helen hugged him and kept her hand on his arm. "We're so proud of you and everything you accomplished here."

"Thanks. It's been a tremendous amount of work but I think it's a success."

The acknowledgement and pride in Jason's eyes warmed Ryder's heart as he gazed around the packed room. They'd never know how their willingness to embrace him into their family had, in a way, taught him the power of forgiveness and love. They were a family built on that bedrock, which was why Jason and Liam were able to bounce back and create a bond even stronger than before.

And as much as his own parents hurt him, Ryder knew he would accept them back into his life if they'd make an effort to understand him and show him he was loved. Until that time arrived, his happiness would be found here, within the circle of these people who loved him unconditionally.

Landon met Jason's family and was quickly surrounded by Jason's mother and sisters. Inwardly Ryder couldn't help but laugh at his brother's panicked expression. Kid didn't have a chance against those three, and he was much too well-mannered to walk away.

Besides, Jessie was adorable. It might be a good thing for his brother to have a girlfriend and concentrate on something else besides his miserable family situation.

"Hey, Ryder." Liam clapped him on the shoulder. "I'd like you to meet Courtney." The petite woman shook his hand, greeting him with a warm, friendly smile.

"I'm so happy to finally meet you. Liam talks about you and Jason all the time."

Ryder arched his brow. "You do?"

Liam put his hands up. "Only good things, bro. Come on, you know we're good, right?" His dark eyes met Ryder's.

Ryder hugged him. "Yeah, I'm kidding. We're cool." And they were. Ever since the incident with his mother at the construction site, Liam had been nothing but a staunch supporter of him and Jason, finally understanding that he was in Jason's life to stay. Forever, if Jason felt the same way he did.

"Hey, Ry, I'm gonna take Jessie outside to meet Pearl, okay?" His brother's gaze remained fixated on the pretty sixteen-year-old, and Ryder couldn't blame him. With her hair bouncing over her shoulders in smooth brown waves and her big blue eyes, not to mention the sparkling black cocktail dress that made her look like she'd stepped off a Paris runway, Jessie Mallory looked as beautiful and fresh as an April morning.

A smile quirked his lips. Considering how many hours Jessie spent with Pearl on Sundays when he and

Jason came for family dinner, he wondered how she'd manage to make Landon believe she'd never met his dog before. From the way his brother couldn't take his eyes off her, though, he guessed it didn't matter.

"Go ahead, you two, but I'm making my speech in a few minutes, and I don't want you to miss it." He patted his brother on the back. "Behave yourself. She's only sixteen."

"Yes, Mother." Landon smirked, then grabbed Jessie's hand and hurried outside.

Shaking his head with a sigh, he accepted a drink from Jason. "Thanks."

"Don't worry, Ry. Landon's a good kid. I think it's cute." Jason took his hand and squeezed it.

Ryder relaxed. What was he worried about? They were young kids, and Landon was responsible. At a tap on the shoulder, he turned around, a smile on his lips at the ready to greet a guest.

It was Matt. With a pregnant blonde woman.

He froze.

"Hello, Ryder." Matt drew forward the woman next to him. "This is my wife, Abby. This is Ryder, sweetheart. He and his friends here run the rescue."

"Hello, Ryder." Her open, friendly demeanor indicated to Ryder that Matt had most likely lied and had never disclosed the true nature of their relationship to his wife. Still holding Jason's hand, he made the introduction.

"Welcome, Abby. It's nice to meet you. This is my

partner, Jason Mallory. Jason, this is Matt Hawkins and his wife, Abby."

Matt and Jason greeted each other with stilted nods, Jason saving his usual friendly personality for Abby.

Matt's eyes focused on his and Jason's entwined hands. "So have you two been together long?"

"Long enough," Jason answered, his voice clipped. Ryder hadn't seen him this angry and upset since the confrontation with his brother.

"I didn't expect you, Matt. Why are you here?"

At least Matt had the grace to look embarrassed. "My production partner is a big fan of pit bulls. When he heard about this fund-raiser, he was bummed he was in Canada and couldn't make it, so he asked me to make an appearance and a donation."

Jason's hand squeezed his. "Emily's trying to get your attention, Ry. It's time for your speech."

"Thanks, babe." Ryder leaned in and pressed his lips to Jason's ear. "Don't let him fuck with your head." Then he kissed him on the mouth. "I love you." Making his way through the crowd, he nodded to Landon and Jessie as they returned, hand in hand from the dog run. He finally reached the makeshift stage and climbed the steps, standing next to Emily and Connor.

The night they had strived for all these months had finally arrived and from the throngs of people, it looked to be a success. The crowd hushed, and Emily took the microphone. The stage stood about five feet off the floor, so they had an overview of everyone there, numbered at Ryder's guess, anywhere from one hundred and fifty to two hundred people.

"Thank you, everyone, for coming tonight to support Rescue Me. With the assistance of my husband, Connor Halstead, and dear friend, Ryder Daniels, I started this service to help these wonderful dogs who have been so misunderstood by society. It all begins with the training. Like a child learns from his or her parent, a dog learns from its master. If you give them love and treat them well, they'll return the favor in kind, tenfold. A dog is one of the most loving animals on earth." She handed the microphone over to Ryder.

He took it and smiled at the crowd. "Good evening to you all, and thank you. Over the past three years, we have rescued hundreds of dogs from abandoned homes or yards, fostered them, and placed them with loving families. I took one in, and my partner adopted one almost six months ago." He found Jason in the crowd, standing next to his family and Landon. "It was how we met, actually."

The crowd laughed, and several women sighed. He continued. "Unfortunately, not all stories have happy endings. Many dogs we find are so badly abused they're near death, or have been so brutalized that they are unadoptable. We have no choice but to have them put down. It is our hope that the practice of using these dogs, or any dogs for the purposes of fighting, including bait dogs, will be outlawed and the owners prosecuted to the fullest extent of the law."

From the corner of his eye he saw Stewart Clinton, Patty Walsh, and the associate, David, by the bar, listening to him. "We need laws to protect the animals from these criminals, for that's what people who train these dogs to fight are." People were still walking in, paying for their tickets at the door. "There is so much prejudice against these dogs…" His voice caught in his throat as he spotted the tall, straight figure of his father enter the building. "Uh, and…" He couldn't help but track his father as he made his way through the crowd to come to stand near the stage, beaming up at him with quiet pride in his eyes. "We need to make sure we do all we can to protect these animals who can't protect themselves." Dazed, he sought out Emily and Connor. *Help me*, he mouthed beseechingly.

"Take the mike from him, now," he heard Connor murmur to Emily. As if in a trance, Ryder walked off the stage, the crowd parting before him like he was Moses in the Red Sea, until he stood before his father. Behind him he heard voices and instinctively he knew they belonged to Landon and Jason, but he never took his eyes off his father.

It had been close to a year since they'd seen each other and it pained Ryder to see how much his father had aged. Swaths of gray dominated his once-golden hair, and lines of fatigue scored his cheeks and brow.

"Dad." He needed to clear his throat several times, as he couldn't seem to find his voice. "Why are you here?"

"I deserve that and more, I know, son. But can we speak, please? Or if you don't wish to speak to me, would you listen to what I have to say?"

What happened to the strong, sure man he knew as his father—the man who made grown men quiver in their shoes with a mere piercing glare? The man before him sounded broken, his voice a bare whisper, so Ryder had to strain to hear. His hands trembled, and his bruised, sad eyes shone with a suspicious glassy sheen.

"We can speak right here. There's nothing to hide. As a matter of fact, there's someone I'd like for you to meet." Ryder glanced over his shoulder and waved Jason over. His voice hard with defiance, Ryder made the introduction. "This is my partner, Jason Mallory. Jason, this is my father."

"Hello, sir." Jason stuck out his hand, and to Ryder's surprise, his father, without any hesitation, gripped it, shaking it firm and strong.

"Hello, Jason. Nice to see you again."

Feeling as though he were in an alternative universe, Ryder looked from his father to Jason. "When the hell did you two meet?" His voice trembled with confusion and disbelief.

"The day your mother came to the trailer, I was at your father's office trying to get him to see how wrong he was about you." Stupefied by Jason's admission, Ryder watched his lover and father converse in a congenial manner, as if they were meeting for a beer.

Picking up the thread of the story, his father continued, "After that, I went home and confronted your mother. All along she'd claimed you didn't want to be a part of the family anymore. That you'd rather be with your boyfriend than with us. I thought maybe you would show up for Thanksgiving dinner. I wanted to see you so badly, but she said…" His voice caught, and he put a hand over his eyes, like a shield from his pain. His father's breath hitched; then he continued. "She said she begged you to come, but you refused. You didn't want to see us, to see me."

Landon broke in. "That's a lie. Ryder always wanted to come home, but she wouldn't let him unless he became what she called 'normal.'" Landon's voice cracked with emotion. Ryder wanted to comfort his brother but couldn't process all this at once.

"You really wanted to see me? You wanted me to come home?" Ryder held his breath, waiting, hoping.

"I've failed miserably as a father and as a human being for you to think otherwise." His father's voice escaped in a great whoosh of breath. "God help me, you're my son, and I love you, both of you." His gaze traveled to Landon, coming to rest back with Ryder. "I never, I swear to God, never wanted you to leave the house. Ryder, your mother lied to both of us, and I'm sorry to say I fell for it."

His father came closer and put his hands on Ryder's shoulders. In all the years he could remember, the one memory he didn't have was his father's touch.

Until now.

"Please forgive me. I know I've made horrendous mistakes, and I can't erase the past, but will you allow us to move ahead for the future? Together as a family?"

Jason took his hand and whispered in his ear, "Everyone deserves a second chance."

Ryder remembered Jason and Liam's problems and how now they were closer than ever. He opened his arms to his father and hugged him, feeling his arms encircle not only him, but drawing in Landon, until the three of them embraced. In the background, he heard clapping and cheering but didn't care.

His father let him go, and Jason's arm slipped around his waist, holding him firm. "You did the right thing. You have such a wonderful heart for love and for forgiveness. Now you can have your entire family around you and be happy."

Ryder touched his forehead to Jason's, leaning into the familiar, beloved warmth of the man he loved beyond anything. "It's only because of you, and what you've given me." He took Jason's face between his hands. "Thank you for loving me and giving me back my life."

"I love you too." Jason hugged him hard.

Taking his father's warm, slightly trembling hand within his, he pulled him toward the back of the room. "Come with me, Dad. There's a group of people I want you to meet." Along with Landon, he and Jason led his father to where Jason's entire family stood, waiting expectantly. And though tears streaked her cheeks,

Helen possessed the biggest smile he'd ever seen.

"Everyone, this is my dad." Meeting his father's gaze with his own, Ryder smiled. "Dad, meet your new family."

Chapter Twenty-Eight

THE SKY ROSE above the ocean, a lick of azure blue against the rolling, gray waves. Morning had arrived in East Hampton, yet the sun already beat hot against the sand, sending shimmering waves of heat down the beach.

Ryder leaned against the weathered deck of the beach house, watching the gulls skim the surface of the water. Tiny sandpipers danced along the shoreline, darting in and out of the tide, and further down the beach he saw Pearl and Trouper playing tag in the surf. Connor and Em's dogs were there as well, flopped down on the sand next to Ryder's father, who stood like a sentinel on the edge of the shoreline.

The past year with his father and brother had been the best time of their lives as a family. He, his father and Landon spent weekends reconnecting and sharing their lives. With the full support and love of his father Ryder joined Daniels and Montague and created an animal rights division within the firm, recruiting eager associates and several partners as well. They were all cognizant of how a different client base—one with money and power to effectuate change—could help their cause.

The iced coffee tasted cold and deliciously nutty, and Ryder placed his mug back on the railing, watching his father walk further down the beach toward the dunes in the distance, the dogs scampering in his wake. Hopefully one day his father would find love, but, as he confided to Ryder last month, his marriage to Ryder's mother was over. Grimacing, Ryder shut his mind to thoughts of his mother, as he wasn't willing to spoil his wedding day.

In the distance, he watched the workers preparing the lawn in the back of his father's estate for the reception in the early evening. They planned for the ceremony to take place on the beach and a row of white chairs stood stacked at the ready to be lined up on the sand. He and Jason had chosen the July 4th weekend as the perfect time to celebrate their wedding. What better day than Independence Day to hold a ceremony enabling them to marry like any couple in love?

Large white tents had already been set up on a portion of the lawn next to the house, and a dance floor had been laid down. Ryder had no problem envisioning his friends abandoning the closed in area and heading back down to the beach later that night to party on the sand. That's what he and Jason intended to do.

Since childhood, the beach had been one of Ryder's favorite places in the world. It allowed him to become

FELICE STEVENS

one with himself; at peace with all the emotions running through his body once he realized he was gay. He'd lie on the sand, heart pounding, and practice coming out to his parents in his head.

Even knowing how cold and distant his mother had been all his life, Ryder never believed she'd cut him dead and stop loving him. The violent, negative reaction from her to his coming out set him on a self-destructive course for his future relationships until he met Jason. And yet, even knowing how happy and in love he and Jason were and that they were getting married, she continued to reject him. Even Landon had left her, choosing to move into his father's new apartment when he came home for visits or vacation. Now she truly was alone. Still, a tiny piece of him had held out hope she would show up today and accept him once and for all.

Stop being an asshole. She'll never come.

Strong arms encircled his waist from behind, and a warm breath wafted past his ear. "Hey you. Why're you up so early?"

Ryder sighed and leaned back into Jason's chest. "Hey. Couldn't sleep. I always come out here in the early morning to look at the ocean." He could feel the press of Jason's early morning arousal in the crease of his ass, and he rubbed himself up against the hard length.

Jason's hands crept lower, stroking Ryder's stiffening cock, cupping his balls. A low moan escaped Ryder. "What're you doing?"

Jason's teeth nipped Ryder's earlobe, then traveled

down his neck. "If you have to ask, I've been neglecting you." He licked down Ryder's neck and stroked him faster, until Ryder thrust his hips up into Jason's hands, groaning out his pleasure.

"Let's go back to bed, babe." Ryder turned around to face his soon to be husband. "I want you naked and inside me."

Jason's dark blue eyes glinted but instead of agreeing, he pinned Ryder up against the deck. "Uh uh. No way. I didn't come to the Hamptons to sit inside. I want to fuck you outside, with the sun beating down on us and the smell and sound of the ocean."

Ryder's breath caught in his throat at the intensity of Jason's stare. A smile curved his lips. "That's pretty romantic for a big tough construction guy." Jason bent over and his mouth covered Ryder's, crushing their lips together in a deep possessive kiss. Their tongues tangled together, breaths merging.

A union of two souls into one.

"I don't care what you call it." Jason's breath rasped heavy as his lips moved across Ryder's jaw, licking and sucking at his neck. "I love you, and I don't care who knows it. Now shut up and let me taste you."

Jason hooked his fingers in the waistband of Ryder's thin athletic shorts and yanked them down. They slid over Ryder's hips to fall in a puddle around his ankles. His cock sprang free, jutting up toward his stomach, its flushed head already gleaming with wetness. Ryder groaned as Jason knelt in front of him and licked up the length of his straining cock. His large hands held Ryder against the railing, while his thumbs teased slow circles around the slant of Ryder's hipbones.

"Shit, Jason." Ryder's head fell back as Jason's mouth enveloped his cock in one hot, wet slide. A trembling began deep within Ryder as he planted his feet wide, steadying himself so he could remain upright against the onslaught of Jason's wicked, roving lips.

Jason's tongue played havoc with Ryder's cock, one moment teasing the slit at the tip, the next curling around the shaft itself. He moved faster and faster up and down Ryder's length, and Ryder couldn't help thrusting himself in and out of Jason's mouth. For a moment he opened his eyes and watched his cock sliding in and out between Jason's full lips, gleaming wet in the sunlight. The sensation of Jason's flickering tongue, and the slight scrape of his teeth was almost too much to bear. The man was a fucking god with his mouth, and Ryder closed his eyes again, wanting only to feel.

Like a rollercoaster in descent, the rush came upon him, his body tightening in preparation for his orgasm when Jason inserted the tip of a thick, wet finger inside his ass. Ryder bucked up, thrusting deep into Jason's mouth, crying out, uncaring who might hear him.

"Fucking hell." He erupted, shooting down Jason's throat, feeling as though his cock was being swallowed whole. Ryder reeled, and if he didn't have the hard wooden railing behind him, he knew he would've collapsed.

After swallowing every drop, Jason leaned back with a smirk on his face. "Better now?"

Under his early morning stubble, Jason's face flushed red, and his dark blue eyes shone bright with desire. Ryder saw the sheen of perspiration on his naked, tanned shoulders.

After pulling up his shorts, Ryder sank down next to Jason and kissed him on his cheek. "Better than better. But you look like you need some taking care of yourself." He indicated the bulge in Jason's sweatpants. "I can't leave you like that."

Jason pulled Ryder into his arms, ignoring him. "I bet you were thinking about your mother, right? Look, babe, if she doesn't come today, it's her loss. You have everyone else who loves you here, right?"

Ryder stiffened, then laughed, but there was no humor in it. "Yeah, all except the one person who's supposed to love me, no matter what. Kind of ironic, right?" The one point of contention between him and Jason in the planning of their wedding was Ryder's insistence on sending his mother an invitation. Jason had been dead set against it, but Ryder invited her anyway. Jason hadn't mentioned her silence until now.

"I know you think I'm an asshole for still wanting her to show up. But she's my mother, Jase. No matter how horrible she is, I thought she'd come around."

Jason jumped up and pulled Ryder to his feet. "Maybe she'll surprise you yet. But if she doesn't, you have my mom who loves you, and my sisters. Hell, even Liam loves you now." Ryder let Jason lead him inside the house toward the bathroom. They shed their clothes along the way, until both were naked. Jason turned on the shower and they stood under the warm spray together.

"As long as you love me, I don't care." Ryder whispered to Jason.

"I do and I will. Forever." Jason pressed him up against the shower wall, kissing him until he could barely remember his name.

❖ ❖ ❖ ❖ ❖
THE WEDDING

At five o'clock the sun shone bright, although the intense heat of the day had dissipated somewhat. A simple canopy stood on the sand, draped in white with vases of white calla lilies at the base. Seventy-five guests sat on the beach, listening to strains of Vivaldi playing in the background. Connor Halstead and his wife Emily walked down the aisle, Emily holding their baby son Jack in her arms. Jason watched as his sisters, Nic and Jessie followed, their pretty faces shining with excitement. He thought Jessie was almost as happy to see Ryder's brother, Landon, as she was to be in the wedding.

"Look at your brother, Ry." Jason nudged Ryder. "He can't take his eyes off of Jessie."

Ryder laughed. "Don't blame him, she's gorgeous."

Jason joined him and laughed until he saw Liam walk down with his girlfriend Courtney. A year ago he never would've believed he and Liam would be at this point, yet the huge grin on Liam's face and the thumbs up sign he gave all the guests almost brought tears to Jason's eyes. He was so damn lucky to have the family he had. A fierce wave of protectiveness for Ryder and all the hurt he'd endured rose over Jason. Without a word, he grabbed Ryder and kissed him hard. "I love you. Never doubt it for a minute, no matter if we get angry at each other or have shitty days. I'll always love you." His voice shook, rough with emotion.

Ryder's bright blue eyes flickered then gleamed. "I know. And I love you too. Nothing can or will change that." He hugged him back. "Now let's go get married, so I can make you legal."

Jason held Ryder's hand as they walked down the aisle and finally stood with the judge under the canopy. It was perfect. The setting sun's rays painted a rainbow of colors across the horizon and the gentle pounding of the surf blended in with the soft violins. The judge cleared her throat and waited for silence.

"Jason and Ryder have written their own vows and wish to share them with you, the most special people in the world to them." She looked at him and smiled. When Ryder's father introduced them, he'd liked her right away. She was warm, smart, and funny. "Jason, you're up first."

He faced Ryder, his heart pounding. Ryder had

never looked happier or more beautiful. His golden hair blew in the gentle breeze and his bright blue eyes glittered. More important to Jason, Ryder's face radiated peace and serenity. It was now a rare occurrence to see the dark shadows that once resided there.

"You know I'm not big with words, so I'm going to speak from my heart." Jason took Ryder's hands in his. "Ryder. I once told you that you changed me from the moment I met you. But I don't think so. I was merely waiting until you came to rescue me from a lonely half-lived life. I never thought one person could bring so much joy and happiness to everyone he meets but that's what you do. You made me believe in love again, because as soon as I met you I knew I could never let you go. You're stuck with me for life now, babe. I love you, forever and always."

Ryder blinked, and cleared his throat. Jason squeezed his hand.

"Jason, falling in love with you enabled me to chase away the darkness and bring light back into my life. And because of you, my father and I reunited, and my brother and I have the best relationship in the world." Ryder hugged his father who stood next to him under the canopy, then faced the audience. "I love you, Landon."

"Love you too, Ry." Landon called out.

Tears burned behind Jason's eyes as Ryder took both his hands. "Jason, your love gave me the strength to not only face my demons but conquer them. The love I have for you exceeds anything I imagined. You are my partner, my lover and my heart. And because of you I get to have a whole new family who I love like my blood and who accept me. I love you."

The judge smiled. "I've rarely seen a couple so perfect for each other in all the years I've performed the marriage ceremony, and I have no qualms in stating unequivocally I know Ryder and Jason will have a long and happy marriage."

"Kiss each other already!" Connor's voice broke into the judge's speech. The congregation broke out into laughter.

The judge laughed. "Very well. By the powers vested in me by the State of New York, I now pronounce you married." She pointed to Connor. "Are you ready, Connor?" Placing a gentle hand on each shoulder she stated loud and clear for everyone to hear, "You may now kiss each other."

Jason took Ryder's face in between the palms of his hands. "I love you, babe. No turning back now, remember?"

A beautiful smile broke across Ryder's face. The words he'd said to Jason the first night they made love never meant more than they did at this moment.

"Never. Love you too." Ryder captured Jason's mouth, stealing his breath and his heart as he had from the start.

Jason held on tight to Ryder and didn't let go until he heard the cheers and whistles of their friends and family. Heat warmed his face and he reluctantly pulled away, giving Ryder one last, soft kiss on his mouth.

"Hey, husband." He smoothed the pad of his thumb over Ryder's full lower lip.

"Hey yourself." Ryder smiled, then raised their clasped hands over their heads and to applause and cheers, called out. "We did it, everybody." They walked back down the aisle and stood, accepting the congratulations of their friends and family. Jason caught Ryder's gaze sweeping over the crowd, looking futilely for the one person who failed to show. His mother.

Jason would not allow that bitch to destroy Ryder and ruin their wedding. "Time to party, babe." Jason accepted two glasses of champagne from the waiter and passed one to Ryder. "Look who came to wish us well." He pointed down the end of the aisle.

Ryder peered around him and laughed out loud. There, at the end of the aisle, sat Trouper and Pearl. Connor and Emily's two huge black pit bulls, Laurel and Hardy sat behind them. All four dogs wore flower-covered collars, their heavily muscled bodies a sharp contrast to the delicate beauty of the blooms. In her mouth, Pearl held a squeaky, heart shaped toy with the words "Just Married."

🐾 🐾 🐾 🐾 🐾
THE WEDDING NIGHT

THE PARTY LASTED for hours. As expected, the guests all ended up on the beach dancing under the stars. With their pants rolled up to their knees and their shirts unbuttoned, he and Jason relaxed on one of the blankets, an open bottle of champagne between them. They took turns taking swigs from the bottle, stealing kisses in between.

Sitting under the stars, the surf pounding on the shore and all his friends and family around him, a sense of peace and contentment spread through Ryder like warm butter melting on toast. He watched Landon slow dance with Jessie, smiling to himself as he caught them stealing a sweet kiss. Thankfully, it seemed Landon would have a better experience with his first love than most. Jessie was a doll.

Connor and Emily swayed together, and Ryder only hoped he and Jason would have as strong a marriage as his best friends did.

"They really are perfect together aren't they?" Jason whispered in his ear and kissed his cheek. His breath smelled champagne-sweet, and coupled with his heat and the salty tang of the ocean, a powerful throb of lust rose within Ryder.

"You're perfect." He pushed Jason down on the blanket and began kissing his face. "Every fucking inch of you is perfect." Ryder nipped the strong line of Jason's jaw, then licked down to the pulsing beat along his throat. "Let's go inside. I want to fuck you so badly I'm about to do it right here in front of our friends."

He heard Jason's breath catch in his throat. "Are you serious?" In one fluid motion, Jason stood, grabbed the bottle of champagne, and took Ryder's hand. "I'm fucking dying for you. Let's go."

Ryder thought they'd be able to get away without anyone noticing, but he should've known better.

"Sneaking out early you two? Where do you think you're going?" Connor's laughing voice stopped them both in their tracks. Damn him. Just once he'd like to get something by those knowing green eyes of his best friend.

"Ahh, we're gonna say good night." Ryder crossed the sand to his best friends and kissed Emily on her cheek. "Good night, baby. Thanks for everything. I love you. Try and keep him on a leash."

Emily hugged him hard, then Jason. "I'm so happy for you, sweetie. I love you guys so much." She leaned back into Connor's arms. "We've got the dogs for the night so don't think about anything."

They bid their family good night and Ryder hugged first his father, then Landon. "Love you, buddy. Thanks for always sticking by me."

"Together forever, Ry. You, me and now Jason and his brothers and sisters." Landon grinned back at him. His brother now had reached Ryder's height, and Ryder wondered if he and Jessie would stay together when he went off to Cornell in the fall. Only time would tell.

"Where's John?" Ryder heard Jason call out, surrounded by his brothers. "I want to thank him and say good bye."

"I saw him talking to the bartender before. They

went back inside the house I think. Knowing him, he's probably talking business."

Impatient to be alone with his husband, Ryder pulled Jason away. "See you in the morning everyone." The two of them ran up the slope of the beach toward the separate guest house they were using for the night. No way was Ryder staying in the same house as his family and especially Connor. Knowing his best friend, he'd probably come busting in at 4 am yelling "Fire."

And Ryder had plans for the night that didn't involve anyone but him and Jason. "Come on. Let's get inside and get in bed." He opened the door and pulled Jason inside, fumbling for a light switch. A solo lamp turned on, lending low, mellow light to the living room. Ryder didn't stop to appreciate the rustic beams of the cottage or the flowers set on the table, but he did grab the bottle of champagne sitting in an ice bucket, then dragged Jason to the back of the house and into the bedroom.

"Damn you're bossy now that we're married. Are you gonna be like this all the time—"

Ryder threw Jason down on the bed and straddled him. "I've been hard for you all day, and seeing you lying there all dark and sexy tonight makes me want you more than ever." He pulled off Jason's shirt and undid his belt, sliding it out of the loops. Jason remained silent, his eyes gleaming in the semi-darkness of the cottage. Only faint moonlight streamed in through the windows, touching the pure white sheets, gilding the bed silver. He tore off his clothes, leaving them in a heap on the floor.

Right now, Ryder's thoughts were only for Jason, lying all warm and half-naked underneath him. "Lift up for me." Jason complied, and Ryder slid off the thin linen pants Jason wore, along with his boxers. At the sight of his husband's thick erection, another stab of lust rolled through him. "You're so fucking gorgeous."

Still Jason said nothing, merely lay back with a half-smile curving his lips. Ryder took that as an invitation to take control, and bent down, engulfing Jason's cock in his mouth. He swirled his tongue about the head, then slid his lips all the way down the thick shaft. Jason's skin smelled of musk, a slight tang of sweat and summer warmth.

Love made all the difference. Ryder kissed his way up Jason's broad chest, the familiar taste of his skin like food for the soul. He'd sacrifice everything for Jason—this wonderful, giving man who brought joy with him everywhere he went. Ryder slicked his cock up with the lube he'd taken out earlier and slid into Jason's body. As he entered that tight heated passage, Ryder once again experienced that sense of completeness, the knowledge that Jason was a part of him and they were two halves of one whole.

The passion simmering between them spiraled out of control, as it always did when they made love. Ryder shut down to everything, falling into mindless desire of being inside Jason. He thrust hard and sharp, snapping his hips over and over again. Jason writhed beneath Ryder, clutching his shoulders, lifting his knees up and yanking Ryder against him.

"Harder." Jason panted, shifting so Ryder could sink deeper inside. "Now."

Ryder complied, and with the sweat pouring off both of their bodies, he plunged into Jason again and again until the ultimate ecstasy engulfed him and he shattered. The force of his orgasm slammed into Ryder and his cock stiffened then pulsed, spurting hot inside Jason's body. Electric aftershocks buzzed pleasurably through Ryder's nerves and he collapsed on top of his husband with a sigh of contentment.

Several minutes passed before Ryder returned to his senses, then he rolled to his side and took Jason's swollen cock in hand. It only took a few strong pulls before Jason came hard, groaning out his pleasure loud and long, his creamy white essence spilling through Ryder's fingers. Ryder loved that Jason was a noisy lover and didn't consider him well loved unless the walls echoed with his loud cries.

They lay together, both breathing hard, unwilling or unable to move. After a moment Ryder, finally able to walk, got up and went to the bathroom where he cleaned himself off, his legs still trembling from the after-effects of their lovemaking. With a damp towel in hand, Ryder returned to their bed and wiped off Jason's chest and stomach.

"Umm, that feels good, babe." Jason moaned, then

surprised Ryder by pulling him into his arms and kissing him. "I'll never get enough of you. I remember the first time I saw you sitting in the truck. I got hard just looking at you." He laughed and continued his lazy exploration over Ryder's sensitive flesh, kissing his jaw, his breath hot in Ryder's ear. "You're still the sexiest man alive, and I can't keep my hands off you when you're nea me." Once again Ryder's body began to stir and quiver with desire as Jason began to lick his sensitive nipples. "You fucking slay me."

"Don't ever stop touching me, wanting me. My mistakes made finding and loving you all the more special. Now and forever, babe. This is only the beginning." He turned into Jason's embrace, returning his kisses, and Ryder knew for certain that this was where his life began, and all that went before had merely been a prelude to this moment.

Epilogue

"DADDEEE." RYDER HELD out his arms as one-year-old Gemma pulled herself up by the table leg and took an unsteady step toward him, chubby arms outstretched, her round, bright blue eyes wide with excitement.

"Come, baby, come on." She took a few more steps before he swept her up in his arms, smothering her with kisses, falling in love with her sweet baby scent all over again. Jason stood behind him, videoing her on his cell phone.

"What a big girl." Emily clapped her hands, letting go of three-year-old Jack's hand. "Look at Gemma, Jack."

He pursed his little lips. "Gemma's a baby." With that pronouncement, he caught sight of his father and took off after him at top speed, screeching with delight as Connor picked him up to throw him in the air over and over again.

Ryder continued to snuggle his little girl, blowing raspberries on her stomach as she shrieked with laughter.

Today was her first birthday, and he marveled at the changes in his life over the past two years.

After he and Jason got married, they found a surrogate who agreed to carry a baby for them, and a year later Gemma was born. Never in his life had he known such happiness existed. This little girl had made his marriage a true family in every sense of the word.

"Dude, where's the birthday girl? Ah, there's my favorite niece." Liam burst into his parents' kitchen and grabbed Gemma from him, tickling and kissing her.

"Idiot, she's your only niece." Jason hugged Liam. "Hey, Courtney, can't you keep him in line?" He kissed his brother's fiancée while Ryder greeted Mark and Julie, who walked in behind them.

"How's Landon, Ry?" Mark bent down to pet Pearl and Trouper, who ran into the kitchen from the backyard.

"He's good. He and Nicole are driving down from Cornell this weekend to see the family." Landon still dated Jessie, who was graduating high school this year and planned to attend Vassar.

After Ryder took Gemma from Liam to change her diaper, he carried her into the family room where everyone had assembled. As soon as Gemma saw her grandmother, she began to squirm, reaching out to her.

"Nananana." Her sweet baby voice brought a smile to everyone's face. Although Helen held Gemma, Tony couldn't resist sneaking in a few kisses. Many a Sunday afternoon found Grandpa Tony snuggled in his lounge chair with baby Gemma, the two of them fast asleep.

The doorbell rang, and Ryder's father entered with Denise, the woman he'd begun dating after his divorce became final last year. Alexander Daniels immediately gave his granddaughter a kiss, then greeted his son and Jason.

"Ryder, what did you think of that decision from the court on that case of yours?" Although Ryder now worked at Daniels and Montague, he didn't give up working at Rescue Me, continuing to volunteer there on the weekends. After the initial fund-raiser brought in so much recognition, they were able to hire a full-time staff. The donations and contributions kept them afloat, especially with a hefty contribution from his law firm, and the benefit had become a yearly event they all looked forward to.

"I was happy the judge put him in jail. Bastard deserved it for what he did to those animals." He greeted Denise with a warm smile. He liked her tremendously and hoped she and his father would eventually marry. From his mother, he heard nothing and for the most part Ryder had learned to let go of the pain. Maybe one day in the future they would reconcile, maybe not. He went in search of his husband.

"Hey, you." His breath caught in his throat when he saw Jason, leaning up against the refrigerator, looking devastatingly handsome in a blue polo and faded jeans. His black, silky hair curled around his neck. Ryder pressed a kiss to his mouth, never getting tired of the spark of lust that flared at Jason's touch.

"Hey, you," Jason answered, "I have good news. Mom and Dad are going to take Gemma and the dogs for the weekend. That leaves us all alone."

At the thought of a weekend alone with his husband for the first time in over a year, Ryder's heart beat a bit faster. He loved Gemma to distraction, but getting up for those late night feedings were a bitch for both of them, as they shared the burden equally. Neither he nor Jason would trade the sleepless nights for the world. That baby meant everything to them. "What should we do, babe?" He pressed up against Jason, inhaling his familiar warm scent.

"Oh, I'm sure we'll think of something," Jason teased, kissing his neck.

Hand in hand they walked back through the house to their family, and Ryder smiled, remembering the day he'd gone to a building site to rescue a dog. Who knew he'd be rescued too?

The End

Coming Winter 2016

REUNITED – Ryder and Jason's story continues. Read the first chapter now!

"DADDY!"

Four-year-old Gemma's plaintive cry split the night. Ryder Daniels squinted open an eye to see the time on the digital clock next to his bed. 3am. Shit. Nothing good ever happens at this hour of the night, or morning if he wanted to get technical. Maybe it was a bad dream, even though Gemma rarely woke up at night anymore. They'd gotten lucky she'd slept through the night since she was eight weeks old.

He settled down beneath the comforter, preparing to fall back asleep. Jason moved closer to him and Ryder slid his foot down Jason's leg, relishing the scrape of his hairy leg. As long as he was up, it shouldn't be a total loss and Ryder kissed Jason's naked shoulder, licking up his strong neck, feeling the steady pulse of life beneath his lips. Jason's sighs spurred him on and Ryder smiled to himself, unsure whether his husband was even awake, but he didn't let that stop him from palming Jason's ass and giving him a hard squeeze.

"Daddy, please. Come."

Damn. No use. Fully awake now, Ryder slid out of bed, immediately missing Jason's solid warmth. Longingly he gazed back down at Jason splayed out in the center of the bed. He'd collapsed after they put Gemma to sleep last night, barely able to stifle his yawns longer enough to eat dinner. Mallory Brothers Construction had taken off in the past few years and though he and Liam had hired several other architects and construction engineers to help alleviate the load of work they took on, Jason still tried to be as hands on as possible. His latest project found him traveling between Long Island City and Brooklyn, which meant a long commute to and from the site every day.

"What's wrong?" Jason mumbled, his face buried in the pillow. "I had a dream someone was copping a feel." He turned his cheek on the pillow and mustered a tired smile. "Thought I was gonna get lucky."

"It was me, but Gemma woke up before I could make your dreams come true. Go back to sleep, babe." Ryder leaned down to kiss Jason's stubble-rough cheek. "She probably had a bad dream."

"Mmm. Well hurry back. I was dreaming of the beach and you were my hot cabana boy." He wiggled his ass. "I'm ready to get oiled for my massage."

Ryder snorted and rolled his eyes. "You're insane." But he couldn't help kissing Jason's smooth shoulder again. "Be right back," he whispered against Jason's skin, but all he received was an sleepy answering sigh.

Both Pearl and Trouper waited outside the bedroom

door, ridiculously bright-eyed and awake for it being the middle of the night. Both dogs kept him company, trailing behind him on his trek down the hall to Gemma's room.

He pushed open the half-closed door to Gemma's room and even though she'd woken him up out of a deep sleep, Ryder couldn't help but smile at the sight of her sitting up in her little toddler bed, rubbing her eyes. Gemma had been so proud when she'd graduated from her crib and insisted on picking out the bedding. Naturally dogs played a big part in the design. Her numerous stuffed animals slept with her every night, surrounding her like a fuzzy protective zoo.

"Hi, baby girl."

"Not a baby, Daddy." She pouted, and Ryder watched her round eyes fill with tears. "My head hurts and I feel funny."

The dogs padded over to her and pushed their faces onto her mattress, whining slightly until she petted them. Ryder crossed the room and knelt at her bedside.

"Funny, how? Funny like throw-up funny, or funny another way?" He smoothed his hands over her strawberry-blonde curls, resting his fingers along her soft cheeks, relieved she had no fever at least. It never ceased to fill him with wonder that his and Jason's love had contributed to the creation of this little person, and her life was their responsibility. Ryder loved Gemma so much it hurt his heart sometimes simply to look at her.

"Funny like things are all spinny and I feel sick." A

fat little tear escaped to roll down her cheek. "I'm scared." She hiccupped a short breath.

Ryder sat on the shaggy rug next to her bed and patted the mattress next to her. "How about you lay back down and I stay right here and tell you a story until you fall back asleep. But if you still don't feel well in the morning, I'll have to take you to see the doctor. How's that?"

Yawning, she nodded. "Ok." She lay down and he covered her with the fluffy pink comforter and kissed her forehead. Without opening her eyes, she spoke. "I want Pearl and Trouper to stay too."

At the sound of their names, the dogs gave a gruff little bark, and lay down next to Ryder, like two large sentinels. Ryder couldn't help but laugh; both huge dogs were nothing but putty in the Gemma's hands. From the moment she'd come home with them from the hospital, Pearl and Trouper made Gemma their priority, as if they knew how special she was. Wherever she could be found, they were there with her and Ryder couldn't be sure who loved whom more.

"Of course. All three of us."

"I wanna hear how you met Daddy Jay."

"You've heard that story a hundred times." Ryder stretched out his legs. "Aren't you tired of it?"

"Please?" She let out a huge yawn. "Cause it has Trouper in it."

How could he resist? "Ok. Aunt Emily and I got a call from your Uncle Liam who said they'd found some dogs when he had Daddy Jay were working on some buildings. I was still working full time at Rescue Me then and Aunt Em and I went to see what we could do to help."

"And Daddy Jay thought you and Aunt Emily were married. That's so funny."

It was. Ryder will never forget seeing Jason for the first time, standing in his work clothes in that parking lot of his construction sight. When their eyes met, the immediate, electric connection rocked his core. He'd never experienced that with anyone and from that moment on, Ryder's life changed forever.

"I know. And then I found the dogs, including Trouper who was a little puppy, and we brought them back to the rescue. A few days later Daddy Jay called and wanted to adopt Trouper."

"Trouper and Pearl are best friends like me and Shanice." Her eyelids fluttered closed. "Shanice is coming to play tomorrow, Erica said."

Erica, their housekeeper and sometimes babysitter had been with them since Gemma's birth. When Ryder and Jason found out she would have to put her own child in day care to work for them, they insisted she bring little Shanice with her. They secured Shanice a place at Gemma's pre-school and the two little girls became inseparable. Ryder couldn't stop laughing when Shanice shyly told him that Gemma had "lent" one of her daddies to her for Father/Daughter day at school, since Shanice's father had died when she was only a baby.

"That's nice. Since it's Saturday, maybe we can all go to the park."

"Okay." Gemma yawned and closed her eyes. Her even breathing after a few minutes had passed indicated she'd fallen asleep at last. Ryder glanced down at Pearl who gazed back at him with intelligent eyes, her tail wagging furiously against the rug. "You want to stay here with her?" Trouper had already planted himself on the opposite side of the bed, resting his muzzle on the mattress. He hadn't taken his eyes off of Gemma.

With a whine, Pearl licked his hand and Ryder scratched her head. "Okay girl. You and Troup watch over her and come get me if she wakes up again." He received an answering lick, then Pearl circled the rug and sprawled out, settling in for the night.

Careful to keep quiet, Ryder walked out of Gemma's room on the balls of his feet, leaving the door halfway opened on his way out. Back in his own bedroom, the illuminated dial of the clock shone 3:37. Sighing, he slipped back into bed.

"Ry?" Jason cracked open one eye. "What was wrong?"

Ryder settled under the comforter, relishing the feel of Jason's warm feet tangling with his cold ones. "Gem said she had a headache and felt funny. Luckily she fell back asleep pretty quickly. Pearl and Trouper are keeping her company." He slid closer to Jason and grinned at the prod of his husband's erection through the thin sweat pants they both taken to wearing to bed since Gemma grew old enough to climb out of her crib and come to their bedroom. "I see you missed me."

"Huh. Must be that hot cabana boy I was dreaming about. Funny though, he looked like you." The low chuckle in his ear was followed by Jason nuzzling the side of his neck. "All my sexy dreams involved you. Get closer." Jason sucked at his neck and desire flooded through Ryder. All thoughts of sleep fled.

Though they'd been married almost five years, his desire for Jason remained as fresh as the first time Ryder touched him. He couldn't imagine a time when the sight of Jason wouldn't thrill him. With sure fingers borne of practice, Ryder hooked his fingers onto Jason's sweats and yanked them down, revealing his heavy cock. Ryder flipped back the covers.

"So waking up shouldn't be a total loss at this God-forsaken time of night…" Ryder bent down and took Jason deep in his mouth, his tongue flattening around the thick base of Jason's cock. The smell and taste of Jason fed his soul like the warmth of summer. He could never get enough of this man.

"Fuck yeah," Jason groaned, falling back on the pillows.

Ryder hummed, licking up and down Jason's rigid length, lightly circling the head with his tongue before flicking at the slit, already wet with Jason's pre-come. He engulfed Jason's cock fully, creating the wet suction he knew Jason craved. By the pleading sounds escaping his husband's lips and the frantic bucking of his hips, Ryder could tell Jason's climax wasn't far off.

With the wet tips of his fingers, Ryder teased at Jason's hole, sinking first one, then two fingers deep inside his ass. He curled them upwards, listening to and loving the desperate greedy sounds escaping Jason's lips. From the first, Jason had been a demonstrative lover and Ryder relished every groan and gasp. He pumped his fingers harder and faster, instinctively knowing the right places to touch to bring Jason the greatest amount of pleasure.

"Fuck, Ry." Jason convulsed underneath Ryder, exploding in his mouth, his salty essence sliding down Ryder's throat. He stiffened then shuddered to completion. Ryder drank him down then withdrew his fingers, sat up and wiped his mouth, smiling at the blissful expression plastered on Jason's face.

"Feel good, babe?"

Without opening his eyes, Jason held out his hand and Ryder took it lacing their fingers together. He curled up next to Jason, burrowing back under the covers next to him. Jason's warmth soaked through him, chasing away the nighttime chill.

"It's always good, Ry. I always feel good with you."

Jason lay still for a moment and Ryder noticed his brow furrowed as if he were troubled.

"What's wrong?"

Jason let go of Ryder's hand to pull up his sweats. "I just remembered last week, Gemma also said her head hurt. I didn't think much of it, but now she's complaining about it again, bad enough that it woke her up."

A thin trickle of dread wiggled through Ryder. "We should call the doctor in the morning." He lay on his side facing Jason, all thoughts of his own pleasure vanishing.

"Let's see how she feels when she wakes up. If she's perfectly fine, we can watch and see. I'll ask my mom too what she thinks." Jason slid his leg over Ryder, forcing their bodies close. "She raised the four of us and must've seen everything."

"You don't think anything's wrong do you?" Ryder wrapped his arms around Jason, swallowing his fear. Jason held him close, and his heart settled down to a normal rhythm. The steady, sure beat of Jason's heart thumped in his ear. It was the sound he fell asleep to every night and what he woke up to in the morning.

"Nah. She probably overdid it at the park with Jack and Emily. You know how she likes to think she can keep up with him even though he's older than her."

At that, Ryder laughed, the image of Gemma's chubby legs running after Connor and Emily's son, Jack, banishing all further worry from his mind. They had all thought Gemma would want to play with the new baby, Isabel, but she preferred to be with Jack, which annoyed the boy to no end. Hence his running away from Gemma at every chance he could.

"You're probably right." Ryder kissed Jason, their tongues sliding and tangling as they leisurely explored each other's mouths. Jason could steal his soul, the breath from his body and Ryder wouldn't care; he'd willingly give it up to him. "I love you, you know?"

Jason pulled him closer, his strong arms holding him tight. "I might have suspected. Love you, too. We'll call my mom in the morning. But Gemma's eating okay and looks good. Let's try and get some sleep."

Ryder held on tight to Jason and closed his eyes. Helen would know what to do; Jason was right. She'd seen it all and would know best. It was probably nothing at all.

About the Author

I have always been a romantic at heart. I believe that while life is tough, there is always a happy ending around the corner, My characters have to work for it, however. Like life in NYC, nothing comes easy and that includes love.

I live in New York City with my husband and two children and hopefully soon a cat of my own. My day begins with a lot of caffeine and ends with a glass (or two) of red wine. I practice law but daydream of a time when I can sit by a beach somewhere and write beautiful stories of men falling in love. Although there are bound to be a few bumps along the way, a Happily Ever After is always guaranteed.

If you enjoy sneak peeks at coming books, recipes, contests and exclusive content, join my mailing list here: bit.ly/FelicesNewsletter

I have a dedicated group of readers on Facebook where I love sharing kissing pictures, teasers, first looks at cover reveals etc. come join the fun at

Newsletter:

bit.ly/FeliceNewsletter

Amazon Author Page:

bit.ly/felicebooks

Felice's Fierce Fans:

facebook.com/groups/1449289332021166

Website:

www.felicestevens.com

Facebook:

facebook.com/felice.stevens.1

Twitter:

twitter.com/FeliceStevens1

Goodreads:

goodreads.com/author/show/8432880.Felice_Stevens

Instagram:

instagram.com/felicestevens

Other titles by Felice Stevens

Through Hell and Back Series:
A Walk Through Fire
After the Fire
Embrace the Fire

The Memories Series:
Memories of the Heart
One Step Further
The Greatest Gift

The Breakfast Club Series:
Beyond the Surface
Betting on Forever
Second to None
What Lies Between Us

Other:
Learning to Love
The Arrangement

CPSIA information can be obtained
at www.ICGtesting.com
Printed in the USA
LVHW012325040319
609507LV00017B/306/P